COUNT TO A
TRILLION

COUNT TO A
TRILLION

JOHN C. WRIGHT

A TOM DOHERTY ASSOCIATES BOOK

NEW YORK

COUNT TO A TRILLION

Copyright © 2011 by John C. Wright

A Tor Book
Published by Tom Doherty Associates, LLC
175 Fifth Avenue
New York, NY 10010

www.tor-forge.com

Tor® is a registered trademark of Tom Doherty Associates, LLC.

Library of Congress Cataloging-in-Publication Data

Wright, John C. (John Charles), 1961–
    Count to a trillion / John C. Wright.—1st ed.
        p. cm.
    "A Tom Doherty Associates book."
    ISBN 978-0-7653-2927-1 (hardback)
    I. Title.
  PS3623.R54C68 2011
  813'.6—dc22

                                    2011024212

First Edition: December 2011

Printed in the United States of America

0 9 8 7 6 5 4 3 2 1

CONTENTS

Many a night from yonder ivied casement, ere I went to rest,
Did I look on great Orion sloping slowly to the West.
Many a night I saw the Pleiads, rising thro' the mellow shade,
Glitter like a swarm of fire-flies tangled in a silver braid.
Here about the beach I wander'd, nourishing a youth sublime
With the fairy tales of science, and the long result of Time.

—Alfred, Lord Tennyson

COUNT TO A
TRILLION

—◆—

Prologue: Asymptote

A.D. 2221

1. An Old Future

The future did not arrive.

Overhearing his elders talk, no one seemed to know what the holdup was. Grown-ups occasionally made jokes about flying cars and rocket packs and moonshots, and shook their heads, and then talked about horse breeds and plague vectors and prevailing winds, and someday-soon rural-electrification plans, next-year-for-sure or whenever Houston had the know-how to repair the pre-war power grid. Even his earliest memories had the murmur of conversation in the background of a glorious yesterday, and glorious tomorrows; but there was nothing but chores in the cold today, for all this talk.

Young Menelaus Illation Montrose told himself he would fix the jerk who'd stopped those bright and shining tomorrows from getting here, if he ever laid eyes on the fellow. It had to be someone's fault. Stood to reason.

At that age, when one reads the books that live in one's heart forever, Menelaus quite by accident came across in his library a cartoon of stark colors and convincing depth-illusion, which some writer of two hundred years ago had composed. It was a strange cartoon, unlike anything young Menelaus read in study, for each episode ended happily, not just in one, but in all possible episode results.

At first he thought it was an historical, since it was set in the last years of the Twenty-First Century, so long ago, but his older brother, Agamemnon, told him with a sneer that it had been "futurism" when first written.

He would not later remember much of what the characters had been doing, which seemed to involve stumbling across yet another lost race on yet another new planet that had slid back down to barbarism, having a crewman or two gunned down by space-pirates or eaten by vampire-plants, then having the Captain go ashore, flirt with an alien girl, and get into a knife-fight (that even to Menelaus's unpracticed eye looked wide-gestured, slow and inefficient, meant for show). The lost race was always doing something dumb, like worshipping a computer or sacrificing maidens to a half-broken robo-tank on autopilot, which was not a dragon at all. Each episode always ended with the space-barbarians vowing to mend their ways, free their slaves, and study science.

No, it was not the doings in the cartoon dramas he recalled.

It was the shining promise glowing from the simple 1024-color images, the prophecies and the predictions; that was what he recalled.

Here were artificial intelligences with godlike wisdom; man designed by man, and superman redesigned by superman to become creations more superhuman yet; there were the stars within mortal reach. The future people lived without poverty or property, and all the beautiful girls made love to everyone, male and female alike, without marriage or jealousy, because what was sin in all the previous eras was licit for them.

Time travelers visited the future people from a time more future yet, and told them how at the end of the world was the Rapture, and the souls of all the perfected people were floated into giant space mainframes, to live as pure spirits, immortal as gods; and even older time travelers from the farthest future of all showed how at what seemed to be the end of time, the Second Law of Thermodynamics was overthrown by the machine superintelligences, and the universe itself lost its mortality, so that this was merely the opening of gates of gold into tomorrows even more splendid.

Years later, he still recalled the name, and flourish of ever-rising notes that went with the opening frame. The cartoon was called *Asymptote*.

His brother Hector showed him the secret plot-twist on level sixteen to unlock the adult portions of the script, so Menelaus could watch the future women prancing in their underwear. Solving the encryption was no problem for Menelaus: all the public keys were products of two hundred-decimal prime numbers, which Menelaus could factor in his head.

The other thing he remembered was that his mother caught him reading the forbidden material, and she rolled up the shining fabric of his library so that it was like a stiff switch of rainbow-flickering lucent glass, and bent him over the kitchen stool.

It was one of the last times his mother ever took a strap to him.

2. Mrs. Montrose

One reason why he had a library of his own, and his brothers had to share theirs, is that he was good with figures and such, better than most grown-ups. Aunt Bertholda once tried to shut up the whole room of them by setting him and his brothers to adding up all the numbers between one and one hundred. She had been hoping for an hour of quiet. Menelaus had simply folded the number line in half in his mind, noticed that every one of the fifty pairs added up to one hundred one, and multiplied one hundred one by fifty. That left him with fifty-nine minutes to play outside while his older brothers puzzled and fretted and punched buttons on their library sheets.

That library cloth was his pride. He loved it, loved the way it caught the light, loved its flexibility and ruggedness and memory capacity.

He did not like the way it stung.

He remembered that the kitchen stool was between the hearth-cell and the window. The hearth-cell gave light and heat to the kitchen, fueled the upright stove, and fed the cable that led to the barn where the cream-separator hummed. The window, which had come from his grandmother's house in Austin, was an antiseptic permeable surface that even when open changed the smell of the forest and flowers outside into something that stung in the nose. In those days, the Pestilence of the Jihad was still within living memory, and grandfathers with breathing plugs in either nostril still showed callow youths the scars where their disease-ridden lung tissue had been removed.

Over that stool in the kitchen he bent, beneath his grandmother's funny-smelling window. His mother's arm rose and fell as she spoke in her dispassionate, precise voice, and each exclamation point was another stroke. "Will you yet defy me, child? My rules are clear! You are to have no pixies, no streams, no games!" This meant text only could be stored in his schooling; no visual or audio files, no interactives: only books.

"The horrid noise you call music must go," she said. "Music shapes the soul, and misshapen music misshapes it. No idle story-files; lectures and tests and text I allow, nothing else!"

"What about Shakespeare?" When she was done, he spoke. His voice was quivering with sobs, but even young as he was, pain did not make him hold his tongue. "Dad would have liked it. He's scholarly, Shakespeare. Anglos and Noreastermen read Shakespeare! I can store a play, can't I? See the costumes, spy the actors?"

"Spy the actresses, I deem. I would be more inclined to credit your uncharacteristic interest in the classics, were there not a program here for reproportioning Ophelia. Are we taking up the study of anatomy? No, I think not. Text is what you will read, and you will learn to exercise your imagination, even if you are the only member of your generation to do so. Were I able to beat an imagination into your brain with a strap, my arm would not tire night and day, I warrant you, child of mine."

For some reason, it always unnerved him when she called him "child of mine"—as if he were livestock, something that belonged to her, not him.

She gave him one last lash across his back, "to help to concentrate him" and muttered, "You already dispute as well as any lawyer: were it not that I see the fire of genius in you, such as comes but once a generation, I would take this whole library from you, and raise you as unlettered as any Migrant. Go ahead, glare at me! It is your father's glare; I would not beat it out of you."

Still holding back his tears, he stood straight and held out his hand, and asked his mother politely for his library.

He clutched the shimmering fabric in his little fists, seeing the icons of his music files floating in the cloth. Menelaus stood breathing in and out, not crying, but not moving his fingers toward the control spots either. For a moment, he did nothing. His mother stared down at him, silent and sardonic as an old gallows tree. She did not bother to speak, but waited.

So much time, so much effort, had gone into finding those files! Everything he had scalped or smuggled in from friend's libraries, or swapped with the rough-looking Oddifornians who lazed around Belle's Bar, betting on cockfights, never working. His brother Achilles said he would catch ailment from the dirty Oddlings, and he didn't know if Achilles meant a file bug or a bioterror bug.

Once Menelaus did Sam Feckle's wood-chopping chores for a week, just to get the full-length variable-output version of a dance tune he heard floating from a tiny plug in Sam's ear during Meeting, when Sam should have been hard praying. All that work, for nothing, now.

All his tunes, his precious songs and jingles, ringadings and roundelays, gavottes and jigs, flickered and vanished on the screen as Mother watched him reluctantly scratching the little icons, one by one, into oblivion. She did not tell him to select and delete the whole lot with one finger-stroke. She just watched.

Some of the Mexican and Injun music, the *ranchera* and *corrido*, the *garifuna* and Ghost-Dance, the jazz and buy-me jingles for the Gambler Princes was stuff to make his heart rise up like a lark, beating its wings in the dawn-beams while the world below was still black: that was what the music was to him, or Paynim tunes with their lutes and clashing finger-cymbals, buzzing reeds, and wailing were opulent as wine, even if he did not know the words.

There was no kind of song he did not like: Menelaus could see the patterns of the music in his mind. He had a knack to envision the systems of notes and chords into number-expressions and higher-order functions: he could lay with his head on the cloth, stereo-audio coming from different sensitive regions of the fabric, and close his eyes, enter a pure realm where everything was made of numbers. He could soar.

Silently, close-faced, his mother watched while he deleted the music of his life.

It was harder than chores. When he was done with his personal music files, all she said was: "Now the rest of it."

He knew, he knew, he should not argue with his mother. His elder brother Agamemnon had warned him just the day before, "She wore out all patience and love on us first six boys. Like she's scraped thin now. She ain't got nothing left for seven of ten. 'Sides, if she had any left, sure she'd be saving up her carin' for the young'uns" (meaning his three younger brothers, Socrates, Leonidas, and Pericles, born posthumously from Father's sperm records at the Army Health Clinic in Lubbock).

Agamemnon had been fated to be named Aristotle, as Mom liked naming her boys after long-dead servicemen, but she turned up her nose when she found out Aristotle ran away where Socrates stood his ground and died in his tracks. Despite having lost out on being named after such a famed thinker, Agamemnon still was held to be pretty cunning among his brothers, and Menelaus thought he should listen.

But he found it was too hard to hold his tongue. He had to argue.

Menelaus was careful to make it sound like he was talking about someone else's life, someone else's files, some boy who gave a tinker's damn about his education, not him. And he picked his battles, defending only what seemed might have some high-class to it.

It seemed to work. Certain music files had been included in the scholastic programming. She relented on *Beethoven's Ninth*, on the grounds that it would "serve to better him"; but she would not let him keep *The Death of Siegfried*, on the grounds that it was "European, dismal, and pagan."

The picture files all had to go, even famous paintings. Some things he thought would escape, being half and half, but the comic book version of *Moby-Dick* had to go, as did the 1956 Gregory Peck movie.

"But Mom! This file is flat and deaf!" (Flat, meaning it was non-stereoscopic, and deaf, meaning that the acting styles, music track, and plot ending did not alter according to audience reaction or preference.) "It's just gotta be educational! It so *old*!"

He knew he would never actually finish the text version. Some hacker had corrupted the file, and added a lot of boring stuff about cutting up whales.

"Books are education." She was adamant. "Pictures are entertainment. Education evolves your faculties, and makes the mind like an épée; supple as steel, yet sharp. Entertainment devolves, deadens the wit, and coarsens the taste. Natural selection favors the evolved. Do you understand me?

There are in this life the men who make reality, and the men who live in the reality other men make. And what is this? This trash?"

Then the worst had happened. She was pointing at the little icon representing his comic book files. *Asymptote.* The future. The animated files of his dreams.

They were closer than friends: bold Captain Buck Sterling, the ever-dispassionate half-robot half-human Cyrano Widget, the ever-passionate planet-doctor Erasmus Hume (but one and all called him "Sawbones"), the artificially intelligent ship's cat C'Pur, the pretty switchboard operator Nubelle. And then there was Alpha, the lovely blue-skinned alien, who sacrificed her life to save the Science Council from the attack of the Atom Monster of Mercury . . .

To see them wiped out, to see all their adventures gone, all the moments of tragedy and drama, all the little jokes and mannerisms, never to see the eye-startling designs of the great golden World-Ship *Emancipation* again, her wings of flame, her thousand shining decks . . . to have them all erased would be to kill them, which was something even the Mastermind of the Moon had been unable to do.

He would never know if the Forbidden Library of Betelgeuse, containing the billion-year-old secrets of the Star-Lords, would ever be found again; or if the crippled cyborg girl Nell would ever learn to speak; or if Malvolio Scoff, Laughing Pirate from the Tarantula Nebula, would ever be brought to justice; or if the noble but evil Phantom of Alpha Centuri, who wrongly blamed Mankind for the destruction of his whole race, would ever learn to live in peace with Earthmen. . . .

. . . the story was not going to have a happy ending or a sad, because he would never get a chance to find the combination of character choices that opened up the end-file. The story was simply, horribly, *gone*, as if it had never been.

Captain Sterling would be as dead as his real father. Menelaus would be an orphan all over again.

So his anger burst out. "That's important! That's all about science! There won't be no tomorrow if you erase that!"

"This is predigested piffle for children." The scorn in her voice burned like ice. "Colored gleam. Castles on dream clouds. Neverneverland and Shangri-La and Utopia."

He did not know what the word *Utopia* meant. He thought maybe it was a place in Arizona, or maybe a part of a woman's body he was not supposed to know about. He resolved to ask Hector later.

"You can't erase the future, Ma! It's real! Science will solve everything!"

"This is an opium dream. There will always be wars and rumors of wars. Darwin will see to it, even if Malthus does not: aggression is built into human nature at the base level."

"*Asymptote* says that someday we will live forever!"

"Then it lies. A shameful lie to tell to children, who know no better."

"They got a machine. Like a brain machine. I can show you the episode. Just take a look!"

"Show me nothing, my child. Men must die so that the race grows stronger. So Darwin says. Would you have us fall into corruption? This is not real."

"Not yet, but it will be! It will for sure be real! Just take a look!"

"Delete it. Need I repeat myself?"

She took the library cloth from his hand, and stood regarding it with cold, pale eyes.

"No! No! It's for real! It's science!" Menelaus was screaming now. "Dad would let me keep it! Let me talk to Dad's picture! He'll back me! You ask him!"

That earned him an open-handed blow on the cheek. While it hurt less than a strap on the back, it shocked him more, being unexpected. It was not a light slap, either, for his mother was not a weak woman, but rocked his head back on his neck. His eyes were out of focus, and the whole left side of his face was as if on fire. No one talked to Dad's picture but Mom, and she only did it when the young ones were abed.

Worse, those tears he'd been so proud to hold back, now they burst forth like some miller's dam overtopped by a stream all muddied up and swollen with rain.

At that, she stepped back, balled up the library, and threw it down. It clattered to the floor, and unrolled, which must have jarred the touch-sensitive fabric, because Schiller's *Ode to Joy* began pouring into the room. When her boys cried, she stopped: that was her rule. But the look of cold contempt on her face cut Menelaus harsher than any lash.

"Girls weep," she said. (Menelaus, years after, could still recall the look on Mom's thin features when she said those words, her lined face, her pale eyes, almost yellow: eyes as dry as stones. Eyes that never wept.)

"Girls are made for weeping," she said. "Darwinian selection favors weaknesses in women; for the ones who were strong enough to fight back against their rough husbands, captors, and ravishers in the Paleolithic days, those would not have reproduced, would they have?"

He brushed at his wet cheeks, ashamed, swallowing his pain and misery. He knew she would never beat him as long as he cried. All he had to do to avoid the blows was to be weak. An anger burned in his throat like vomit at the temptation, and maybe hatred at his mother, for so tempting him.

"What're boys built for, then? What did Darwin select them to do?" He spoke, not because he wanted to know, but because he wanted to show her he could make his voice steady, tears or no.

She turned her face away, and said something in a bitter whisper, and the words were drowned by the heavenly German choir, singing in a strange language of supernal joy. *Freude, schoener Goetterfunken Tochter aus Elysium* . . . (Joy! Flaring spark divine, daughter of Elysium!)

"What did you say, Mother?"

"For war." She return her cold, yellow eyes to his, and her words were crisp and clear above the winged voices. *Wir betreten feuertrunken, Himmlische, dein Heiligtum!* (Enter we, fire-imbibed, Heavenly, thy sanctum high!)

"Boys are made for war. It has always been. Skulls of cave-dwellers betray the cracks from truncheons made of the thighbones of antelopes. The murder rate among aborigines is higher than even the bloodiest days of our modern wars, yes, even if you factor in the millions who died in a single hour during the burning of New York the Beautiful. The world has not changed, and never will."

This last sentence was so bitter: for a moment Menelaus was dumbfounded. Not changed. Never will.

That was not the message in *Asymptote*. Hate and poverty and war, and even death itself, would be conquered when tomorrow came. Who had stopped tomorrow from coming?

Mother was talking in her acidic, emotionless voice: "The world has not changed, and never will. That flimsy fold of library fabric you hold is your stone knife, your hand axe, your flint-head arrow; the only weapon you have, my little cave boy, to see to it our particular tribe, the name of Montrose, your father's name, does not go extinct. Expunge from your weapon any flaws or weaknesses, including the weakness of false hope."

So she stood there as he destroyed the rest of his dreams. Whole worlds vanished into deletion. With his own hands he did it, and she checked to make sure he had no back-ups or garbage shunts, or hidden regeneration files.

In his imagination, he thought he could hear, over and over, the three ringing trumpet-notes that heralded the opening song of the introduction file. *Onward! For the future! . . . Is! . . . A voyage! . . . Without end!*

Then it was done.

Upward! That is the vow of the Science Patrol!

All was gone, and Captain Sterling was dead.

3. Darwin's Curse

But after she was gone, he unrolled his library, and yes, discovered that the audience register had been running along with the music, a program that noted listener reaction and comment, to personalize the conductor's performance. He replayed his mother's captured image through the deaf-and-dumb application, which could read lips, and even with her face turned half away, it could resolve most of the words.

He could fill in the rest of the sentence: *Boys are made to war and die and to make their girls weep.*

He was old enough to know his father had not died deliberately, but young enough still to feel hate toward the treason involved: Father, by dying, had abandoned them.

4. The Vow

Menelaus Illation Montrose lay awake his bed that night, listening to his brothers' snores and ignoring his own bruises, comforted by the golden knowledge that now he knew the name of the enemy.

This Darwin, whoever he was, who had designed mankind for no better fate than to wail and weep and war and die, obviously was a villain, an enemy, someone as evil as the Venom Queen of Venus, who poisoned all her lovers. He was the one who stopped the future from coming.

Some of his friends said you had to prick your finger with a pin to make the oath valid; and boys of particular boldness used a rusty pin, as if daring the Jihad plague to strike. Menelaus knew that was all nonsense: it was the willpower that decided oaths, nothing else. No pin would be as sharp as what he felt beating in his angry young heart.

This Darwin pretty sure had clout, if he could do all this stuff. Could be, he was some bigwig from Houston. Mom had also mentioned Malthus. Obviously his henchman.

Or maybe he was a guy long dead, since it sounded like he did his dirt long ago, and meddled with the gene-stuff, like those tragic transhumanist experiments the library had told him about. But it did not matter if Darwin was alive, or dead, or long dead.

Didn't matter: because he vowed to defeat Darwin, somehow. Someday.

PART ONE

—◆—

The Swan Princess

1

Intelligence Augmentation

A.D. 2235

1. Bone Rongeur

Menelaus could not help but pause to inspect the bore of the bone-needle as he was raising it to a point slightly above and between his eyes. It was like looking down the muzzle of a loaded pistol.

He found that thought comforting.

2. Sailing Vessel

Menelaus I. Montrose was a young, brilliant, angry man of calendar age twenty-five, biological twenty-four, having previously spent more than half a year in suspension, while his family raised money for a surgeon. Menelaus was taller than average, with pale eyes and dark red hair that he wore cropped short, navy-style.

He had scars on his right hand from knife-fights, he had scars on his chest from gun-fights, slugs that failed to kill him, and shrapnel from near-misses. The muscles in his right arm were more developed than his left, from endless hours of pistol practice with the absurdly massive weapons of his day, giving his shoulders a tilted, crooked look. His cheek was lean, and his jaw was a jut, his nose a preposterous hook of crooked flesh, but his mouth was long and flexible, and the lines of tension that surrounded it hinted at the overlarge grin that sometimes usurped his otherwise dead-pan face. His eyes were deep set into their sockets, giving him a strange, staring expression. The mirror convinced him no lady would ever find him handsome.

No one in the cabin of the nuclear-electric propulsion vehicle P024 was looking at him. The seven other men aboard wore helmets that restricted vision; and surely most had their visors down and tuned to the outside view, so that they could see the Earth falling away behind them, or the slim needle of the expedition hybrid ship growing slowly closer ahead, the Nigh-to-Lightspeed vessel *Hermetic.*

The inner view was nothing to look at. The punt's cabin was a cylinder, with a pole of avionic boxes, hydraulic lines and fiber linkages running down the central axis. The men were positioned with their heads pointed inward toward this axis, their feet outward toward the "down," three fore, three amidships, and three aft, like the snowflake of a flock of parachutists.

The three fore were Indosphere men, and aft of them were the non-Hindus, the *Firangi*: Menelaus and five men from the Hispanosphere. There was no advantage or comfort in sitting fore as opposed to aft, but the famous Hindu respect for caste required it.

Menelaus's mother once told him that when the USA was strong, the rest of the world followed their ideals, and adopted a spirit of democracy. That spirit sank when the English-speaking world sank. Seeing the technological marvel of the vessel, something greater than any American space program had ever done, Menelaus doubted the great and ancient civilizations of Spain and India had ever looked to Texas, or the other, less important states in the Old Union, for inspiration.

Whether his mother was right or not about the past, these days, the low-caste and the *Farangi* sat in the back. Even the pilot sat in the back.

There was no designated cockpit or helm station, since the piloting controls were firmware carried in the pilot's glove unit, and his readouts played over the inside of his helmet. The carousel was spinning, but centrifugal force was so slight as to be unnoticeable: it was more for the convenience of drawing dropped crumbs or styluses to the deck for the maintenance-crabs, than for the comfort of the passengers.

There were no windows, no portholes, marring the hull of the punt, of course. Such things were radiation hazards. Hull cameras could bring in a better view from outside, especially if the image was enhanced and labeled by cunningly designed software.

An enhanced view, for example, might show the drive of the NTL *Hermetic* as a streak of fire across the stars. Fictional, of course: The trail of ions ejected from the ship was invisible.

The ship had started her acceleration burn two months before, but her velocity had only accumulated to 8000 kilometers per hour. By spaceflight standards, this was a crawl, and high-thrust nuclear-chemical punts were still able to rendezvous and unload passengers and supplies for as long as the equations covering fuel economies might allow.

The virtue of the *Hermetic* was not her acceleration, but her specific impulse. For continuous years and decades, the ion drive need not be shut down. Her very tiny delta-vee could, for minimum fuel-mass, be snowballed into an end velocity rightly called astronomical.

The expedition was an all-male crew of two hundred ten hands and six officers. This was to be the last of twenty-four punts, each carrying nine men each: and the fuel cost of the rendezvous made this final flight the most expensive.

The nine men aboard this final punt were Earth's acknowledged geniuses, the old sages and young prodigies of mathematics and linguistics. Earlier punts, over the last two months, had carried crewmen who also had experience as astronauts, technicians, and (since the ship assembly did not need to be complete before her long, slow drive began launch) zero-gee heavy-construction workers.

He knew that had he cared to look through his visor-view, Menelaus would have seen tiny sparks of light from oxy-acetylene torches flickering here and there along the hull of the *Hermetic*. He did not look for fear that he would be unable to look away. Menelaus was infatuated with the ship.

Fore was the armored sphere where the expedition would sleep. The cryonic materials would help stop incoming heavy particles, and medical coffins were programmed to repair continually cell damage from radiation.

Amidships was the wheel-shaped crew carousel to quarter those who would stand watch and age during the voyage. The watch duty rotated among the sleepers, each crewman slumbering for ten years, and standing watch for one. The officers had a different schedule.

Behind the carousel was the shroud-control house. Aft of this extended the many folded spars. The spars and members would, during deceleration, deploy the light-sail package that presently formed the main bulk of the vessel, gossamer-thin fabric wrapping the xenon propellant cells. Behind this was the folded silver of the mirrored parasol meant to shield the forward parts of the ship from laser radiation.

Farther aft, on a long and fragile spindle, were the many rings of the ion accelerator.

The NTL *Hermetic* was a bastard of sail and motor, launching under her own power, but carrying a breaking sail in anticipation that *Croesus*, receiving the millions of code-lines of radio-programmed instructions, would have constructed a working deceleration laser by the time the half-way point was passed. Since lasers do not disperse in a vacuum, the source and the endpoint would impart the same degree of counterthrust. Once in the braking beam, *Hermetic* could decrease the rate of her deceleration merely by adjusting the light-permeability of her canvass.

Behind the hybrid design was a political, not an engineering consideration. The world might trust Croesus-brain, fifty lightyears away, to build and fire an antimatter-powered super-laser potent enough in output to boil a planet like a poached egg. No one on Earth trusted his neighbor enough to have such a monster nearby. For that matter, no ship could trust any government, any institution, to shoulder such a huge drain of power, such an expense, for the quarter-century acceleration would last, without being interrupted by wars, depressions, disasters, or changes of policy. Unlike the *Croesus*-brain, men are fickle.

The NTL *Hermetic* was a beautiful ship, graceful as a work of art.

The hour was one that would never come in history again, an hour so many had predicted for so long would never come: Earth's first manned expedition to another star.

The robotic probe *Croesus* had been sent seven generations ago, during the First Age of Star Flight. Had it not been for the Little Dark Age, the follow-up expedition would have departed fifty years later. Instead, it had had to wait until now.

Generations of dreamers had anticipated a time like this. The moment was indeed pregnant with all the hopes of Earthbound mankind. Why should anyone look at Menelaus Montrose?

His visor had been down, tuned to half-gain, so that the cabin around him was overlaid with ghostly images. One image showed him, not the famous ship he approached, but an inset displaying the distance from Earth. The little red line turned blue, indicating that the punt was in International Space. Unclaimed. As far as he was concerned, an experiment illegal on Earth was legal now.

Menelaus was sure no one had seen him break the Red Cross seal and slide the illegal needle out from the medical kit riding the thigh of his pressure suit.

But then he hesitated. For a crucial second, he stared down the bore of the needle.

Thinking of it as a pistol barrel was less frightening. More than once in his short life he had found himself looking down the muzzle of a pistol, and those events had not ended as badly as might be. He was still here, was he not?

He knew what to do when looking down a pistol-bore. Shoot first. Don't miss. Don't hesitate, don't flinch, don't regret. Call his doctors to come to the fallen man, whether the Regulators come or no. Amazing what they can mend these days. If the other man dies bravely, be sure to say so. If the Regulators come, say nothing. Even if they haul you before the dock for it, or put you on the gallows, say nothing. No gloating, no vaunting, no apologies, no explanations. If the Regulators don't come, and the doctors don't come, let the man have an ampoule of morphine, if he needs it, and cover his face with his jacket, if he doesn't. Most men are thoughtful enough to wear a diaper under their trousers when they go to settle disputes Out of Court, because you never can be sure of walking away, and you never can be sure your bowels and bladder are empty, and someone will always take a picture with his phone, even if everyone swore not to (the little phones could be hidden in a ring, a pistol stud, a thumbnail, a molar). In a case like that, doff your own jacket, and cover his legs.

Only polite. He'd do it for you. You can take his weapon, but you cannot touch his widow, even if she was the one who asked you to meet him. Those were rules he knew, and knew how to live by. Or die by.

This? This needle was the event horizon. An event horizon was a boundary where no information about the events beyond can ever reach, in the same way light can never escape a supermassive dark star. No one knew what was on the far side.

He had waited a second too long. Like a cricket chirp in his ear, he heard the punt pilot say, "My friend, what is this I see? Are you hurt? I have a 'suit open' light here on my board, and your medical kit is pinging a query. What are you doing?"

Damn.

3. A Question of Intelligence

There had been no way to check beforehand, of course. Menelaus had relied on the black-market software package he'd bought in New Silicon Valley, the smuggler's paradise. The Hindi security programs, as usual, had been more subtle than what Western science could match, more intrusive than what Western notions of privacy would allow. Everyone who talked about the "new global agora" or who said the Little Dark Ages were over still could not explain the gap between Indosphere and Anglosphere craftsmanship.

Menelaus's internal suit status showed his helmet and medical kit still shut. But apparently he had fooled no one's monitors but his own.

The pilot was a Spaniard named Del Azarchel. His first name was Ximen, which Menelaus could not pronounce, so Menelaus called him "Blackie," a nickname that suited him in more ways than one. He was a mathematician of some fame from his studies of the Navier-Stokes equations, especially their application to logic-flows within analog computing structures. His work on the underlying mathematics of the Ship's Brain was as important to the expedition as Montrose's work on suspended animation.

The dashing young Spaniard had won all the tests in simulation back at

Space Camp, humiliating older and more experienced Hindu candidates, and so he won the coveted duty of chief pilot. Piloting was the most delicate and demanding of shipboard tasks, requiring not only an ability rapidly to organize mathematical calculations, and perfect spatial visualization skills, but also the ability to do so under stress, in a short time, and in high and low gravity. Automatic computers could make possible, but could not replace, the human pilot; and the task was akin to shooting a bullet precisely enough to strike the face of a nickel spinning in the air without striking the buffalo.

Only on the punt was a pilot needed. The great ship herself would face no navigation problems Isaac Newton could not have solved: the simple act of accelerating in a featureless vacuum for twenty-five years, rotating aft-to-prow, and decelerating in a featureless vacuum for twenty-five years required no more piloting skills than a railroad engineer. Nonetheless, the honor would still be attached to his name: for the next century, even while he was in slumber, Del Azarchel would be the Ship's Pilot.

He and Menelaus had been something of a pair of troublemakers together in space training camp, the facility in Northern Africa where the crew first met. It was not that the Hindus had deliberately shunned anyone; but somehow it was always these two, a Spaniard and a Texan, who found each other sneaking under the camp shock-wire during late nights off to go find a stiff drink or a pliant girl in the shantytown not far away, when the other astronauts-in-training were lawfully in their bunks.

Del Azarchel, with his droll smile, dark good looks, and silvery guitar could always sweet-talk the local girls into compromising positions, and Menelaus, gaunt and ugly as a scarecrow, could not. But Del Azarchel lacked a certain drive and boldness when it came to climbing electrical fences and breaking into Hindu pleasure houses where "Franks" were not allowed, and Del Azarchel needed Menelaus to inspire him to that extra level of gumption, the level where sheer cussed-mindedness outweighs common sense. They were a mixmatched pair, and Menelaus had not known him long, but he knew he could count on him.

So he whispered into the helmet pickup. "Amigo, I'm running a wild risk. Turn off the cameras! I don't want no record of this. . . ."

"Off it is. My good friend, what the hot perdition's fire are you up to, eh?"

"This is something I got to do. You behind me?"

"You must ask?" the dark, musical laugh came over the mike. "I stand behind you. Always." Del Azarchel did not even bother to ask the details. But he had to add: "Always. Except when I am far in front."

This conversation was still on the private channel. But at that same time, the shared suit channel came on. Another voice, this time of Dr. S. Ramananda, said in amazement: "What is this? Look! Montrose has an automatic bone rongeur in his hand! Are you going to perform surgery on yourself, *Sensai* Montrose?"

All the passengers were strapped to cots that could be tilted to various axes, depending where the combination of carousel rotation or engine thrust put the gravity-vertical. Only older models of punts still used seats. Under microgravity, there is no weariness in standing for hours on end, and cots were easier to fold or inflate than seats in any case.

Dr. Ramananda was overhead to the upper left, from Menelaus's viewpoint, upside down. His helmet was not far from Menelaus's helmet, but even if he had entertained the impulse to try to wrest the medical appliance out of Menelaus's hand by force, the shoulder-harness and helmet of his suit were not built for stretching one's hands overhead. Indeed, Ramananda had not (and could not) crane his neck to look "up" at Menelaus directly, but instead lifted a gauntlet, and pointed a fingertip camera-dot at him.

Ramananda said tensely, "What is in that needle, *Sensai*?"

The radio channel was silent. Ramananda was a high-caste Brahmin. Caste was not all-important on an expedition like this. Ramananda was here because of his work proving the Birch and Swinnerton-Dyer conjecture relating to general cases of rank greater than one. But caste was not unimportant either. Respect for Ramananda's status kept the others silent.

Menelaus could not take his eyes from the bore of the needle. It was like looking down a well. But the alert light shone green: It had selected the path through bone and brain calculated to cause the least damage. A flick of the thumb, the circuits in the needle would engage, and the needle would find the right spot and move of its own accord, and puncture his skull, and pump his brain full of neuro-pharmaceuticals.

"Intelligence." Menelaus grinned wickedly. "Superhuman intelligence.

The next rung up on Darwin's ladder. I aim to be the first to hoist my buttocks up yonder, gentlemen. Easy as shimmying up a tree."

But his fingers, five little traitors, trembled.

The ampoule contained a cocktail of totipotent cells, taken from his own gene template, with artificial ribosomes programmed to turn into neural tissue. The molecular cues had already been established, one cell cluster at a time over a series of months, here and there within his cortex and midbrain tissue, to act as anchor points for the new growth.

A second group of ribosomes would begin the manufacture of certain chemicals in his brain out of raw materials in his bloodstream: intelligence-augmenting agents. Here were the molecular codes to create phosphotidyl serine, which increased learning speed by improving special cells receptors; vinpoticene to increase blood flow to the brain; and phenytoin to improve concentration.

Here also were proteins to affect the brain's ability to remodel its synapses. Other proteins to prevent calcium overloads would be released by reactions from his pituitary gland and medulla oblongata, as needed. The artificial proteins would produce other neurochemicals, whose functions were less well understood, but which had been found in the brains of geniuses—and also in schizophrenics.

A third group would rewire certain nerve-paths, linking cell to cell with strands of material more sensitive and conductive than natural nerve cells, but grown out of his own brain-material. Protected by redacted RNA messengers, the new material was part of what his body would think was his gene code. Even if wounded, the new pseudo-nervous cells would grow back.

But this was only what the ampoule contained physically. What it contained in reality was the unknown, an inexpressibly alien *otherness*. What lay beyond man, was in this needle.

And so he hesitated.

Ramananda said, "So. It has come to this. You will not abide by what was decided; you will not abide by what you agreed. Did you not read the articles before you signed?"

There was no surprise in the voice of Ramananda. No one in the cabin failed to grasp what Menelaus meant to do. During training camp Menelaus had argued that such a thing as this should be tried, had to be tried: all had heard him say, or, at times, had heard him rant, that more than human intellect was needed to decipher the Monument.

"I read the articles, sure enough," said Menelaus. "Read 'em over and over. And if my recollecting is fair, what they say is this: Any member of the scientific arm of the expedition may perform experiments or investigations of his own devising, and at any time. Well, I pick right now for my time. Nothing in the articles said I had to wait til we reached the Diamond Star to start. And since I am not aboard the ship yet, not reported for duty there, I am not officially under Captain Grimaldi's command: so even if you radio him, he could not tell me to stand down. I am square within my rights. This here is my first experiment."

A soft voice murmured. "Ah. That's what we deserve for inviting a lawyer aboard." He was not sure, over the helmet radio, if it had come from before or behind, but it sounded like the voice of a Spaniard named de Ulloa.

Melchor de Ulloa was something of a lady's man in his youth. The rumor that he and Montrose had a running bet to see who could get into more trouble with the Mission Commander during training was false, but the mere fact that the rumor spread showed how alike they were, how they had egged each other on. Melchor de Ulloa won fame for his solution of Hilbert's Sixteenth Problem, dealing with the upper bound of the number of limit cycles in polynomial vector fields.

Menelaus was shocked to hear the scoffing voice of handsome young de Ulloa. It had been de Ulloa, during that last night when the six younger astronauts—Del Azarchel's clique—had stolen out of camp together, who had practically begged Menelaus to smuggle some form of Prometheus Formula aboard.

Ramananda was saying, "This is a useless experiment! An illegal experiment! Are you attempting to revive the nightmares of Shanghai—those horrible children in vats the Chinese kept alive for so long, gargoyles with bloated heads? You have not separated your skull plates."

Menelaus did not have a high opinion of Chinese neural science in any case. He said, "Phooey. The Zi Mandarins discovered ninety-nine ways how not to augment intelligence. This uses path redaction, not merely adding cell mass."

"The Ephrin Topography Hypothesis? That method, used on pigs, re-sulted in severe nerve-tissue degradation."

"Then I will be too plumb stupid to care about what I have done, eh, gentlemen? Any how, 'tis my brain to risk, that's all."

"But that is not all, sir," said Ramananda solemnly. "Your course is recklessly selfish. You have been selected because the mission needs you! All mankind needs you! Do you think your aptitudes, your *guna*, were delivered to you merely for your own amusement and pleasure, to waste? We are engaged in a sacred quest for the ultimate knowledge! Circling V 886 Centauri is the library that holds, perhaps, all the secrets of a civiliza-tion thousands, or millions, or *billions* of years in advance of our own. If this expedition solves the major problems of translation, it will mean the future, an unimaginable future, a science so far in advance of our own . . ."

"An asymptote," said Menelaus softly. "A change so powerful strange that no man can see beyond it. An event horizon." More loudly, he con-tinued: "Well, what if we are not smart enough to jump that ditch? Not bright enough to understand the invitation written out for us? The esti-mate worked out by Dr. Chandrapur. . . ."

"Nonsense! The established authorities have dismissed his work!"

Menelaus was not surprised by this reaction. He had seen Chandrapur's estimate of the complexity of the Monument, and it was a fairly simple cal-culus to show the number of possible combinations of untranslated symbols, and to compare that to the known statistics on human brain use.

There was too much math, a whole little world of it, miles upon miles covering the surface of the Monument, and so little had been cracked: less than thirty square feet of it. If the Mandelbrot fractal structure of the alien glyphs extended, as the primitive tests carried out by *Croesus* seemed to hint, down into the microscopic, molecular, or even atomic level, the calculus was even more daunting. The number of years estimated even to read the thing, at the human civilization's current level of computer infor-mation storage and cross-referencing ability . . . and supposing the library of symbols continued inside the volume of the black sphere, not merely a surface inscription . . . the estimated values fell outside of the likely life-span of human life on Earth.

Chandrapur was only stating the obvious—but the scientific community did not like an idea so unflattering that their minds would prove unequal to the task, so Chandrapur was ignored, even though he could not be answered.

Dr. Ram Vidura, who was of the Vaisyas caste, descended from craftsmen and commoners, spoke. His work was in the Poincaré Conjecture. Even his brilliance in mathematics could not expunge the shame of his inferior birth. By long habit, his voice was diffident, soothing, placatory. "Sir, let us speak of practicality. I assume you are using a cascade of multireceptors with combinations of binding patches or epitopes that will transport, sort, and bind the lipoproteins to their target areas?"

"Correct," said Montrose.

"The number of possible interconnections between the neurons in the brain is ten to the eleventh power, or ten to the twelfth. What are the odds that you happened to hit upon the correct combination of nerve paths to augment?"

"I used the Eidgenössisches Polytechnikum computer in Zurich, their famous Denkmalsymbollogik Mainframe, to do the pattern-solving," Menelaus said. "We may not know what all the alien symbols mean, but we know some of the grammar rules for manipulating them. Well, sir, I assume the logic is just as sound for conclusions the alien grammar laws allow, even if our math cannot confirm the result. Ancient Greeks who did not cotton to the concept of the 'zero' would still have reached a correct answer if they multiplied ten times ten using Arabic numerals, wouldn't they just?"

There was no murmur among the eight men in the punt, but in his helmet, Menelaus could see the text channels light up, as the mathematicians asked each other in silent finger-type about the ramifications of what they were hearing.

Menelaus continued: "Countless millions of designs were filtered through Zurich computer analysis, until the near-infinite possibilities had been narrowed to one. In other words, here in my hand is the output of the Monument's own math."

There was a moment of silence. Finally, one voice said, "It is not really a math, but a symbol-system that can apply to any logic set." This was Dr. Bhuti, the only scholar older than Dr. Ramananda aboard the punt. His caste was the lowest in the caste system: he was a Sudra. His long-dead ancestors had been serfs, and so had his grandparents, when serfdom was reintroduced under theories of genetic work differentiation. Despite that his caste rendered him fit only for manual labor, his work in the extrapolation of Kronecker's theorem on abelian extensions to base number fields beyond the rational had won him coveted manumission. His findings also had applications in the topology of algebraic surfaces.

He and Menelaus had played long games of chess in the early morning cool, before Reveille, the only two men who woke before cockcrow, back in Africa, where there weren't any cocks. Bhuti was gentle-souled, thoughtful, the very opposite of Menelaus, and so they had become close.

"Fine. I used the alien's own symbol-system."

Dr. Bhuti nodded slowly. The white hair clustered above his ears had been shaved for his helmet, which he unchocked and removed, to allow him to turn his neck and look thoughtfully at Menelaus. His skull was as wrinkled and brown as an apple left out in the sun, and his eyes twinkled like garnets.

Bhuti said carefully, "Please, I urge you to delay your experiment. Wait! Wait until we reach the target star. By that time, new methods of analysis might be discovered back on Earth. They might build the Xypotech, the self-reprogramming artificial mind whose coming has been for so long imagined. Perhaps we do not need a posthuman to translate the Monument for us, no? Let us not explore this avenue unless it becomes needed."

Montrose had no ready answer for that. He had been planning for so long to augment his intelligence at the first possible opportunity, the idea of waiting had never occurred to him. Menelaus blinked in hesitation.

Father Venture Reyes y Pastor raised his gauntlet. He was the ship's chaplain for the seventy or so men in the Hispanosphere complement. He and Menelaus had spent many an evening engaging in disputes on every topic under the sun, and Menelaus was surprised to find the man was absolutely wrong on absolutely everything, from politics to religion to art to war. He was an entertaining and thought-provoking debater nonetheless, a ruthlessly logical thinker. His work was in the Poincaré Conjecture.

"This is an incautious dream you cherish, Dr. Montrose," he said in his somewhat soft and breathless voice. "Consider: If the Monument is too complex for our race, then we are not meant to read it. This must be left for whatever race will walk the earth after mankind is extinct: all in the fullness of time. We are the products of evolution, therefore by definition we cannot be in a position to regard evolution objectively, reflect on it, or question its wisdom."

Menelaus said, "Says who?"

The young priest answered, "That is what we must assume the Monument says—if it were meant to be read, it would be legible to us. To us as we are, I mean. It is wrong to meddle with nature."

"I figure that without some amount of meddling, I never would've learned to read. Sure as hell that ain't natural, squinting at squiggly lines on a piece of cloth and all. That Monument holds all the secrets of our future, gentlemen! And if a man h'ain't got the right to take a few risks with his own brain—a brain I trained into shape without no help from any man in this vessel, I warrant—than what rights has he got?"

Sarmento i Illa d'Or spoke next. He was from the Hispanosphere, and, by the agreed-upon conventions governing in-cabin speech, he had waited until each of the Indosphere members had spoken. He had been a wrestler, a weightlifter, the only person other than Menelaus willing to use the Camp ring in the gym. It was only because Menelaus fought dirty, using illegal blows and holds, that the gym circuits had halted their matches. He and Menelaus, grimacing, smiling, and growling at each other, had privately agreed to finish the match some day, but that day never came. Sarmento i Illa d'Or won his berth for his work in the topology of algebraic curves and surfaces, particularly valuable since topology and knot-theory was the main avenue of approach of most of the Monument symbolism so far translated.

"Anglo, you go too far!"

"Ain't I got the right to go as far as I can take me?" answered Menelaus.

"What is 'right'? What is 'wrong'? These are but airy words for pleasant and unpleasant. What you are attempting may well make life more difficult for us. You might be willing to risk, but we are not! We are mountainclimbers are roped together in one rope, and you might want to topple into the cold, but not I. With your brain damaged, you will be a burden to the expedition, to our cause."

The voice of Sarmento i Illa d'Or held a strange note of relish. It was almost as if he were trying to say the exact thing to urge Montrose onward, while seeming to say the opposite.

He was also one of the younger men, a member of Del Azarchel's clique. He had also been there, at that wild night of drinking and dancing and laughing, before the launch. He was the one, in fact, who had brought up Chandrapur's analysis while they sat in a circle, drinking toasts and talking long into the night. When Menelaus proposed a toast to the intelligence augmentation—"we all know some poor bastard will have to risk afore we can read the Monument"—it had been Sarmento who had slapped him on the back (a little harder than strictly friendly) and said, "It will not be you! I will be the first to take the Promethean Formula! You Anglos do not have the *cojones*, eh?" Menelaus had pushed the cork back into his bottle, and hefted it upside down in his fist for a little glass bludgeon, and stood, but Del Azarchel pulled him back down into his chair, laughing, and told him it was just a joke.

Narcís D'Aragó spoke. He was the only other military veteran at Space Camp. The man had fought in the North African campaigns, beneath the skies gray with deathclouds. Montrose and D'Aragó had shared the unspoken bond that men in uniform had even when out of uniform, even when among civilians. He had been included on the expedition for his breakthroughs in the Linear Programming problem, particularly regarding strongly polynomial time-performance in the number of constraints and variables.

Menelaus was confident that this grim young soldier would back him.

"On the one hand," D'Aragó spoke in a voice as colorless as ice, "anyone brave enough to bollix his own brain does not need to listen to anyone less brave. If we are not willing to face his needle ourselves, we don't have a say in how he spends or wastes his life."

But then Menelaus was disappointed to hear him continue, with no change of tone, "On the other hand, we are still a unit. Let us not waste a man whom the expedition needs. These things should be done in the proper order, controlling the variables, with a medical crew standing by. Captain Grimaldi is the senior expedition officer: He had not given permission."

Montrose said, "By the letter of the law, he ain't got no jurisdiction until we rendezvous."

Narcís D'Aragó made an noise in his throat like someone tearing a handkerchief. "Then talk to Del Azarchel! He is the pilot here, and out-ranks you!"

Now Del Azarchel had rotated his cot so he faced aft. He was about two meters away, and was staring at Menelaus: he had strong, dark features, eyes that flashed greenish-gray, and the stubble of his shaven cheek gave his jaw a wolfish look. From Menelaus's point of view, he seemed to be hanging like a bat upside down (if that word had any meaning in microgravity). He looked like a lazy panther, perhaps ready to sleep, perhaps ready to strike. His eyes were cold, but a half-smile seemed to play around his lips, as if this whole drama had been organized for his personal amusement.

The pilot said laughingly, "Gentlemen, why talk this little talk? We are involved in a great emprise, a bold expedition! Does Señor Montrose contemplate anything as dangerous as the great star voyage ahead, when we shall fling a two-thousand-meter-long space vessel at ninety-five percent of the speed of light into the pathless night? An asteroid the size of a small coin, striking us head on, would have the comparative velocity of a bullet from a supercollider: the energy would be like an atomic bomb. None of our odds are good. And when we reach there, what do we find? A puzzle box! A big dumb object! Ah, perhaps an intelligence test? Gentlemen, what happens if we *fail* that test? The universe is waiting outside the frail little walls of our bubble of air, indifferent stars in their billions, endless waste-lands of empty vacuum. What if that cruel universe puts us to trial and we fail?"

Melchor de Ulloa answered, "But what will Captain Grimaldi say? Montrose, he is your friend: You will listen to him! You cannot just throw a friendship like that out the window—we all know you only got aboard this expedition because of your pull with Grimaldi."

Sarmento i Illa d'Or said, "Well, maybe he should jab himself, then. He comes from one of those Anglo lands, where for three hundred years nothing is done but to dream of past glories."

Melchor de Ulloa said back, "Discord is always caused by selfishness. We are a unit, like D'Aragó said. We have to act as one body. Captain Grimaldi is the head of that body. What can one member do if he does not consult the head?"

Del Azarchel flashed his white teeth in his wolfish smile. "Montrose! Consult only your mad and fiery heart! We are the Paladins of Charlemagne, the Knights of the Table Round. Our King is that dream we share: that dream to which we proffer our very lives! What other loyalty is there? We are the new people, the new race: the first interstellar men. Would you have the first act of our newborn species be hesitation?" His eyes blazed with wild emotion, and he called out: "Montrose! Are we not closer than brothers? Do not flinch! I will protect you, no matter what sort of monster you become!"

Montrose was staring with haunted eyes at his friend. Who had once likened the quest for the future to be like unto a knight-errantry? Montrose could not recall.

Ramananda said urgently, "Anything could be in that needle! So you said, Montrose! When you turn into the superman, the man after man, here and now, how can we trust you? We would be Neanderthals to you . . . or apes. You might treat us as a man treats his hound, with love and care, or a man treats a wolf, as a beast to be killed."

Del Azarchel said triumphantly, "It is too late. See the look in his eye!"

"I will remember," said Montrose. "I will remember my humanity."

Sarmento said, "The Anglo will never do it. He is craven."

"I ain't no Anglo. I'm from Texas!"

Just like looking down the barrel of a pistol. Menelaus pulled the trigger.

4. Dreams

A.D. 2235–2306

There were dreams like water, waves that lashed and lapped at him, pulling him from dizzying fear to disorienting pain, and his thoughts flicked like little fishes and vanished before he could capture them. He dreamed he was falling in an elevator whose cable had snapped. But no, it was not an elevator, but a nuclear-chemical punt. He was surrounded by friends, Del Azarchel was there, but Menelaus could focus on nothing.

There were dreams of smoke, painted rose-hue clouds of ecstasy. In highest spirits, giddy with discovery, he was trying to explain Fermat's Last Theorem to the people around him, and relating it to how the dust motes stirred by the airlock's ventilation system glinted so prettily in the lights from the life support controls. The motions were not random, of course: He could see the wave functions involved in his head. But then he was distracted by his visualization of each particular motion of his tongue and throat, conceiving it as a fourth-dimensional tube function, merely a complex geometry.

He realized the inefficiencies of the idiom he was using, and he saw how a universal language of verb-to-noun formations was merely one more application of the zeta function, distributed over complex planes of two related variables. A much simpler language was easy to devise, with the two variables for nouns and verb correlation related to pitch and amplitude, and he began yodeling in it, sure that his companions would quickly catch on to the nuances.

Even this was not efficient enough: if he played with the airlock controls, he could get them to reflect and refract from the dust-motes to express even more channels of communication. Amazing how everything was so filled with meaning, so filled with mathematics. He saw a way of improving the efficiency of the airlock process. All he had to do was adjust the flow dynamics. . . .

He was quite lucid and reasonable when they hauled him, screaming in the harmonic pitches of a new language he had invented, away from the lock controls.

He was aware of being carried belowdeck, away from the axis. His weight increased, and he watched the stream of orange juice curve from a container to the cup meant for him, and the expression for the Coriolis forces acting on the stream glittered in his mind. Hands forced the nozzle of the cup in his mouth while he laughed and squirmed and broke their fingers between his teeth, and the molecular geometry of the medicines the orange juice hid he deduced from the sour taste on his tongue, and the complex expression for his tongue surface with all its intricate molecular niches.

When the morphine hit, his dreams grew clear and distant, and he was standing with godlike beings outside the universe, timeless creatures of light, gazing gravely down into a dark well from which no signal would ever return.

Other dreams were dull and gray as lead, and lingered on forever. He dreamed he was being buried alive, but no, it was not a coffin, but an icebox, for it was cold here, endlessly cold.

There were also nightmares, things as dark as storm clouds, vortexes of uncontrolled emotion and images of terror: images of being strapped to a pallet while the ancient Dr. Yajnavalkya, the ship's surgeon, brought the whining drill toward the back of his head, and Del Azarchel floated in the near distance, his features gray and drawn with fear.

Then there were dreams like fog, where he could see, but could feel nothing, and he was merely an onlooker to the actions of some higher being that moved his thoughts for him.

He dreamed of the corridors of the great ship *Hermetic*. The engine room, when the magnetic line of the drive core was misaligned; the pump room, when the crew was running out of water, and a recycler had to be jury-rigged; the computer room, where the system had to be unlocked, before the life support batteries failed, and he had to convince the computer that the little blond girl was the Captain.

Other dreams, the best dreams, were clear as crystal, and his thoughts slid as effortlessly as a skater on black ice cut with white skate-strokes. Surely these were figure skaters, for the white marks on the dark lake surface were circles, sine-curves, angles, and triangles.

But no, it was not black ice. It was the Monument. The complex concentric circles of the alien symbols beneath his boots suddenly grew lucid and sharp, and the meaning of the signs was obvious.

He stood on or, rather, drifted with his feet pointing toward, the surface of a small moon, and the horizon was so close that the figures standing near him seemed to be leaning away. He meant to explain the layers of meaning to the suited men standing near, in clear and patient language, but something distracted him. For overhead was a blazing sun, too small and too dim, and stars shone unwinking, the vacuum to each side of it. The points of light representing the mining satellites were easy enough to distinguish (particularly now that he had mastered the knack of increasing the number of nerve-firings to his optic nerve), but the flare showed that his warning was too late.

Too late. He was proud of how clear and precise his language was, how he was oriented to time, place, and location, when he explained about the relationship between higher brain functions and the analogous mathematical functions that described bureaucracies in failing political-economy systems, closed systems of feedback orders that led to disaster. He explained to Captain Grimaldi about the reinforcement effects of the wave-functions of crew discontent reaching a node point, but when he touched his shoulder, the Captain rotated stiffly in the zero gravity, and his eyes were like small black buttons pointing in two directions.

Too late. He saw the little six-year-old girl writing out the orders. Her cursive writing was a small deviation from a single line: he could see the mathematical expression of it, and how it related to the Quantum Yang-Mills theory of the geometrical framework of elementary particle formation.

The computer system known as Little Big Brother pointed an optic pickup at the document, and the old men looked on in mingled hope and misery, their eyes hollow, until the mechanical voice box announced in its soft, emotionless, feminine voice that the command was legitimate. There were snaps like gunshots echoing up and down the inner hull as the locks on the coffins clattered open, rainbow-shining, like oil slicks their rich, dark, newly made biononanotechnological fluids, and at the same time, the shining screens of the contraterrene manipulations fields, dull pearl for so long, shined and came to multicolored life.

So often, so often, he dreamed of ice.

There were dreams of burning: Perfect spheres of blue flame hung in space, expanding slowly, with metallic oblongs at their hearts. He stood before the plotting board with the teenage girl, slender and coltish, and examined the spread of acceleration umbrellas for possible fire and counter-fire. There might have been danger had the enemy found a proper launch window, but Menelaus could see it was too late. Too late.

But most of all, he dreamt of the Monument. It filled his thoughts. He was standing beneath the naked stars, the blazing sun above, on a world-let not larger than a mile across; a world shining with meaning. THE MATTER-DISTORTION PROCESS KNOWN AS LIFE WHEN FOUND DISQUIETING THE MAGNETOSPHERE OF THE ANTIMATTER STAR...SUFFIENT UTILITY TO BE HELD

IN INVOLUNTARY SERVITUDE TO THE IMPERATIVES . . .
ALL OTHER OPTIONS ARE SUBJECT TO RETALIATION . . .
PAIN . . . DEATH . . .

He tried to tell the slouching ape-creatures what it all meant, tried to warn them to stop the mining satellites, but they wrestled him down, and fed sedatives into his intravenous drip. Del Azarchel, bearded, unkempt, and lank from months of half-rations, and wearing the Captain's uniform that in no way fit his frame, looked on with cold, tired, weary eyes, commanding his men to be careful.

2

Personal Sovereignty

A.D. 2214–2217

1. The Starvation Winter

It was cold as he slept, ice cold to his bones, and he dreamed of winter.

His earliest memories were of the cold.

The Starvation Winter had gone on during all Menelaus's early years, and it was not until he was six that he saw the springtime, a mysterious season, a hope and a promise even his eldest brother was not certain about. The half-decade of unbroken snow had killed the Pest, but also countless tens of millions of men.

It was not until he was older, that he heard it called The Japanese Winter. When young men cursed the Tenno of Greater Japan, saying his mad experiment in climate modification was meant to kill everyone north of the Tropic of Cancer, the old men wheezed and upbraided them, and said the Paynim unleashed the plague (which at first only attached itself to genetic markers found in Ashkenazim Jews, but which mutated to seek all primates) it was only the cold that saved everyone: *Winter is the friend of man!* the saying went, *Thank God for the Nippon Winter, or we would be as extinct as apes.*

It was for Menelaus the first spring in the world. The flowers and birds never before seen by him appeared. To him, the word "brook" meant a path of ice, and the word "fishing" meant chipping a hole in that ice. When all these icepaths which had been solid during all his short life turned to rippling water, just as his mother had promised they would, he was sure, in his heart, that everything would be different thereafter.

It was so strange seeing green grass where there had only been white snow before; so odd to see runners removed from every sledge or cart and round wheels, like something from a toy, put in their place. It was pure joy to run outside in bare feet, rather than trudge and slip in his older brother's hand-me-down snowshoes.

It was odd to see men, those whose farms could not be tarped with greenhouse-cloth, the same listless men who had spent last year loitering or rioting at warehouses and depots, where grain from southern lands was stored, now set to tearing up the earth with strange instruments, furrowing the ground in long parallel rows, walking after antique traction motors or antique mules, and speaking boastfully about being men again. The whole world was new, and it was spring, the glorious season of light, and Menelaus was sure the Asymptote lay just around the next turn of the calendar.

But at seven, Menelaus was apprenticed; and endless days of toil made his springtide winter again, no matter how bright the sun.

2. Apprenticeship

A.D. 2217–2219

Barton Throwster was not a cruel master, but not a rich one either, and his fear of debtor's prison made him drive his prentices exactingly, so that many a night by lamplight Menelaus and the other boys were still programming dart and fuses and shells, and packing chaff in various combinations, and finishing the magnetic rails for pistols until the acceleration line was flawless.

Mr. Throwster was also a Cathar, which meant he must go through elaborate precautions of maintaining his bodily purity, cleaning his white clothes with sonic waves, and changing his skin-gloves and nose-filters at regular hours. His denomination had objections to the implanted anti-bodies that kept the Pest away from normal people, but it could not be denied that he was a careful Artificer, and the number of his customers or prentices who caught a disease from an improperly prepared weapon-load was the lowest in the parish.

The same exacting care made the villagers elect Mr. Throwster to the post of Wellmaster, but he was not paid extra for the honor of being the officer watching the purity of the local water supply, and the loss of his daily hours to this task made him drive his prentices all the harder, to make up time. And because he was a Cathar, and friendless, the village elected him Bangbeggar and gave him a long staff, on the excuse that since the vagrants and tramps sometimes carried disease vectors, only a man of his careful habits would do.

Throwster was too conscientious to turn down the position, and so he moved his shop into the Constable's quarters halfway up the ramp of the broken cloverleaf, from which the village of Bridge-to-Nowhere took its name.

This cloverleaf was a high and crumbling structure of concrete posts and elevated fragments of road. The ramps for traffic were all broken, so the top had to be reached by ladders. At this height, the villagers kept their lofty Meeting Hall, which doubled as a stockade in times of raid. Lesser build-ings, like swallow's nests, clung to road fragments lower down the titanic concrete pillars.

The expense and trouble of these new quarters, especially the cost of hauling water up so high, was one Throwster lost from his own pocket. The theory was that public-spirited citizens should be eager to serve the town, and that patriots would scorn being paid from the parish coffers, but Throwster dared not collect the bribes Bangbeggars commonly used to make up the deficit, not where he was the only Cathar.

This sour lesson was not lost on Menelaus. Men in groups could cheat you just as plain as highwaymen alone in the wild, and do it by the voting box. It was one more thing he saw that never would have been that way had Captain Sterling of the Science Patrol been in charge.

At nine years old, the honor of being the Constable's boy meant more work for young Menelaus, but it also meant Throwster taught him how to fight with a wand, or with his bare hands, while watching for needles or dirty nails, or mouth-weapons like hollow teeth or spit-shooters that a foe might use to infect you.

Thowster was too refined a man to touch another person's flesh in match, of course, so he borrowed a practice dummy from the local Militia Accoutrementer, and Menelaus spent many hours being thrown and pummeled and punched and choked by the hard, rubbery hands of the dull, half-paralyzed manikin.

Menelaus learned instinctively to assume his enemies would have no weakness, and this gave him a rough sort of honor, because during a brawl he would not gouge eyes or groins or nerve-centers, merely because his reflexes were not trained for it. His reputation was one of maniacal cruelty, because he applied enough pressure to break an iron bar to break an arm or leg, nor would he stop or even slow, as if some panicky certainty was deep in his heart that a man, no matter how damaged, would still fight as full capacity with his remaining limbs.

He often had nightmares about the faceless, voiceless thing limping down the dark path to his house, and scraping at his door at night with its mittens.

3. Asymptote Revisited

A.D. 2219–2220

A year passed, then two.

The other Constable boys loved rousting blighters (as men escaping from blight zones were called) onto the broken, weed-overgrown paths still called federal highways. Because federal law was enforced on the highways, no law was, and so, to Menelaus, it looked like they were throwing these paupers to the wolves. If he came alone upon blighters, if they would promise to find honest work, he would tell them the name of a farm that was short-handed, let them escape into the fields instead. But the blighters were stickatnoughts, and always broke their word, and many of them were too lazy and stupid to keep themselves clean of enemy diseases, so they really had to be driven onto the highways, whether the highwaymen preyed on them or no. It was wicked to beat them away, and dangerous to let them stay.

He hardened his heart, but it sickened him.

Menelaus noticed that the vagrants of browner skin, the Aztlans and Mestizos, Mulattoes and Swarthies, were always beaten away with gusto by the other boys. The darker they were, the more jabs and blows of the stick they earned, or if they wore the strange medallions of the Spanish Church. Penniless Blondies and Grasseaters (as the Anglos were called, although most of the Noreasternmen ate meat when their womenfolk were not around) were equally as likely to be carrying a disease vector, but were merely treated gruffly. When rich Anglo merchants, who wore antiseptic jackets with polished brass buttons, folk so refined that they ate burritos with knife and fork, came into town, their contempt for the local towns-folk was just as great, just as unreasonable. Only the Jewish peddlers were polite to everyone, but everyone seemed to hate them, and called them sly.

Unlike some prentices, Menelaus still slept under his mother's roof, which was one small blessing. Another was that his big brother Napoleon was prenticed out as an Apiarist, to learn the art of gene-splicing, breeding, and caring for the insects on which the village's trade in silks and in pharmaceutical honey depended, and so came home covered with bee stings and spider bites.

Bug-bit Napoleon's burning jealousy that Menelaus got to work with dangerous chemicals and energies all day was as cheery as a campfire to Menelaus.

There was a second moment of joy that year. For a long while, Menelaus had tried to find another copy of *Asymptote*, after his mother made him delete it. The other prentices suggested one thing and another, black market and offchannel, but there was nothing. The comic had been an antique, and not even recorded in the Federal Salvation Net, which attempted to recreate from surviving sources the books and files lost when the Library of Congress was firebombed by Speech Puritans in 2091. Antiquarians did not have resurrecting lost kid-lit as their highest priority.

He finally found a third-generation scrape in a Jewish peddler's old back-up trashfile. The peddler sold it to him for a Spanish royal (he would not take Texan money, and Menelaus did not blame him), but warned him that all sales were final. It was far more than Menelaus could afford, but he had to have the file.

Brimming with excitement, he had kept the file strip tucked in his glove all afternoon, and snuck out back behind the woodshed after supper to feed it into his library cloth. There were formatting errors, and he had to try and retry his load, but finally the thing came to life.

The disappointment was crushing. It was only two chapters out of the middle, episodes he had seen and solved before, with the music track in mono. And it was in Spanish, badly lip-synched.

He noticed things he had not seen before, dozens of little errors. The textures were bland and uniform; the depth-perception was off. All the female crewmen were based on the same hourglass-shaped wireframe, just the same girl over and over with different heads. The hair was wrong. The dialog was stiff and stilted. And the backgrounds were simply the same graphic, used and reused.

But still, but still, somehow, it was still great. At the intro frame, the three horncalls rang out, brassy and brave, the clarion of triumph: *¡Hacia adelante! ¡Para el futuro! ¡ . . . es! ¡ . . . un viaje! ¡ . . . sin extremo!*

It was so stupid and so fake looking. And yet, when the great ship *Emancipation* lifted off, surrounded by a surge of boiling flame, to stride roaring above the red-tinged clouds on her single bending leg of fire, his heart soared as well . . . and magical silence fell when the ship left atmosphere, and in the darkness the distant suns shined untwinkling like lanterns . . . lanterns beckoning. . . .

The end credit lyrics were still in Anglo:

> *Come now traveler, sail the stars!*
> *Go boldly yonder, beyond th' unknown*
> *The secrets of space shall all be ours*
> *Myriad worlds of tomorrow our own!*

He read the fragment, then reread it, the second time with the party comments track running, so he could hear the wisecracks and applause of other audience members. With an eerie feeling, Menelaus realized all these commentators, their laughs and scoffs and foul-mouthed swearing, was like nothing folk these days spoke. He was hearing voices long dead, maybe over a century old.

Then the sun was setting, so the library shined brightly in the gloom. He folded it up. Menelaus did not want his brothers to see him reading. To them it would be kid's stuff. And both his mom and his master had oversight rights into his viewing habits. His brothers would have tormented him with days or months of mockery, if they found he had spent a whole Spanish dollar on a scabby copy of a spaceman cartoon. Worse, if they told the other prentices, Menelaus would have to lick them in one fight after another, taking a lashing from his master each time. But he could not bring himself to delete it.

That night, after midnight, he put the counterpane over his head and fingered on the library one more time, hoping the light would not leak out under the covers.

With sleep-bleared eyes he studied the frames of the story. With one part of his mind, he could see the hammy acting, the jerky graphics, the ridiculous, predictable ending. He knew it was fake, badly drawn. But with his heart, he was a crewman again, and rode to the stars on wings of fire.

There was something else here, too.

He had not understood it when he was young. Now he saw that the people of the far future, Swarthies and Blondies, were talking as equals, no one noticing or giving a hot hoot about color or kin or any of that.

One character was clearly a Paynim, an enemy, wearing a rag on his head and everything: but he was just a respected member of the Science Council. In one scene, a Blondie captain kissed a cute Swarthy, right on her thick, red lips, like they were man and wife.

(She was really a cute goose, chocolate skin and all, but Menelaus told himself not to find out if this ratty copy could unlock that secret level Hector showed him. While he was curious about what she looked like in her underwear, he was just old enough to realize such titillations were for weaklings. If Captain Sterling were real, would he gawk at smut? If his father were alive, would he?)

In the future of the Asymptote, there was no talk of lynching Mormons or statue-worshipping Catholics, nothing like that: The future-people never mentioned Church at all. It just didn't come up. Menelaus, when he thought on it, had never had much use for churchgoing anyway. Pray for sun on a rainy day, nothing happens; pray for rain on a sunny day, nothing happens. Any fool could see that. But on the other hand, if there were no Meetings and no preachers, what would widows have to say over the coffins of their menfolk? It didn't seem right to throw a man into the ground like he was a dead dog or something, without saying words of some kind.

He reckoned these future people didn't have that problem. Whenever one of them died, it did not take long for him to better up, as some cloning machine would be found, or a new fixup of the teleport ray would allow all and sundry to make back-up copies of themselves, just like a song file.

('Course, half the time the clone copies came back evil, but that was just one more problem for the Cyrano Widget to solve with that glowing metal helmet-doohickey in his lab that solved problems. The gadget was supposed to be too dangerous to use, since it caused "Neuropositronic Brain Disruption!" but the bold Science Officer ended up using it every other episode anyway.)

To be sure, a world without death did not seem too much more unimaginable than a world without hate, without race-hate or church-hate.

Menelaus wondered for the first time if this comic had been meant just for kids. Maybe it was talking about something more important. Maybe these writers of these long-dead future dreams had been a companionship, like a sworn brotherhood of knights, sworn to the proposition that tomorrow could be better.

Menelaus crumpled up his library, stuffed it back under his pillow.

Where had that dream gone? How long before the future came, the real future, the way it had always been supposed to be?

It was a long time before he fell to sleep that night.

Being trapped as an apprentice gunsmith and a Constable's roustabout was certainly not the future he'd ever wanted. If he was ever going to make it to the stars someday, he had to find his way out of Bridge-to-Nowhere.

3

Decentralized Conflict Resolution

A.D. 2232–2233

1. Out-of-Court Settlement

The way out proved to be through the barrel of a gun.

When was the last time he had looked down a pistol bore?

Spring of '32. It had been cold, unseasonably cold, even in mid-April that year, and the groom who saddled his horse, a sorrel named *Res Ipsa*, joked that the Japanese Winter was come back. (The full name of the horse was *Res Ipsa Loquitur, Sed Quid In Infernis Dicit?*—but he only used that on formal occasions.)

In theory, his journeyman indenture to Barton Throwster should have lasted until age twenty-one, even if interrupted by two years of service as a horse soldier. At seventeen years, the same year he returned from the war, Menelaus became the youngest of the attorneys in Houston, but his skill with his weapon was undoubted.

Menelaus had but one way out of his prentice contract, and that was somehow to become a Professional man, for the law held that no one of the licensed professions, doctor or lawyer or minister-in-orders, could be held to a master, no matter what his debt. It was a way out, and he took it.

Most of the real work of the office was done by the elder partner, Solomon Ervin. Menelaus escaped his last year of journeyman obligation and was made a junior partner, mostly for his ability to stand and answer when an Out-of-Court settlement was needed. He did not do much real lawyering. Actually, none at all. It was the rattler-cold and rattler-quick reflexes of late youth the firm craved.

Now, at twenty-two, he had sent six men to the hospital and two to the boneyard, and his late youth was turning into early manhood. The smart money said his winning streak must soon end.

The day a man lost his nerve, on that day by rights he died.

It was not that Menelaus did not want to do this anymore—it was just that the moment he admitted to himself that he did not want to do this anymore, he would lose his nerve. So Menelaus told himself to enjoy the day, not to think of the other things he might have made of his life. It was making hard cash for his family, was it not?

There were places outside Houston where attorneys could meet for Out-of-Court settlements, usually with two witnesses, at most four, and, of course, a judge. The witnesses had to be bold enough to act as Seconds, if one of the attorneys had an attack of nerves, or of conscience, or of common sense. The judge had to be a man of utmost discretion, one who would not talk. Not a real judge, of course. An honor judge.

Agreeing on a field was a delicate matter. It had to be close to the city, an hour's ride on horseback, no farther, so that the survivor could get back to the Courthouse if he had cases on the docket that day, or (if it was Sabbath) get back to St. Mary's Cathedral on Church Street for mass—the Military Governor was Spanish Catholic, and it was a politically astute move to be seen at services by the Archbishop, his brother.

The field could also not be so far from the inhabited buildings in the great, broken city that a ground-effects ambulance from the nearest monastery infirmary, if radioed promptly, might not be able in time to rush to the scene over the rubble, weed, marshgrass, and shattered walls of the long-vanished suburbia. It was thriftier to radio the monastery rather than the University Hospital on Harborside Street, because the law, for the sake of economy, demanded patients had to pay back the doctor's fee into the public till; whereas the Brothers made no such demand, for the sake of charity. Also, if the patient converted quickly enough and sincerely enough, and confessed the sin of pistol dueling, it was possible that the Abbot might not report the bullet-wound to the Reeve.

But the field also had to be far enough away from the inhabited buildings that the Regulators would not come to inquire, nor the Deputies, nor a patrol from the Federal Mounted Military Police.

The Spaniards had the practice of keeping a doctor on the field, a man who would not talk. The rules and niceties were all set out by the Spanish code of duels, of course. The custom had been dead for centuries until Hispanosphere weapon-technology, delicate Spanish honor, and, of course, the Jihads, revived it. After the breakdown of centralized law on the Iberian peninsula last century, the Spaniards dared not involve their families in blood-feuds, not when there were still Paynims in Moorish Spain to drive yet again into Africa; and the kind of men who lived in continual danger of craven-bombs and plagues tended to be too bold and too impatient to settle matters peaceably. The Texmexicans had adopted the custom from their enemies, the Aztlans, for similar reasons.

Unlike the more civilized Spanish, the Texans merely revoked the license of a doctor found helping the injured in a duel, as being in violation of his Hippocratic Oath if he stood there before and while the shooting took place. Why the law held doctors to be blameless if they rushed to the scene after was based on a legal theory too subtle for the other members of his firm to make clear to Menelaus. The upshot of it was that the doctor could be close, but not too close.

So the distance had to be chosen with care, and in utmost secrecy.

This time, it was the spot still called Law Park, not far from the haunted ruins of Hobby Airport. Aside from the name, which had outlasted, as names do, any change of feature, this was known to have once been a park since the trees nearby lacked the knobby, concrete-piercing roots and drunken postures of boles grown up across the toppled rubble and cracked streets. These were slim and straight trees here, almost elfin.

Menelaus had been here more than once, during the day. It was a beautiful, sylvan spot, one a man could spend the whole rest of his life admiring; or his next twenty minutes, whichever was longer.

It was April 15th, still a day celebrated by fireworks, when the Last Congress gave up direct taxation. (Menelaus saw no point in fireworks. It was not as if the direct goods appropriation, land-tax, and forced-labor system used these days by the Pentagon was so much better than a tax on income.)

April: and yet this year there was a bitter frost upon the ground. The sky was still dark, and the churchbells had not yet pealed, but the birds all sang. He could not see the knee-high dried grass of the marsh, poking up through the old stones of the Space Age ruins, not in the pre-dawn, but the icy wind that bit his ankles made their blades clash and rattle.

Menelaus shivered, thinking how warm this region had been in his great-grandfather's day, how dry, free of bog and bug-water. Back when apes and leopards lived. *Thank God for the Nippon Winter.* The ponds here were square, following the foundations and basements of houses time had swept aside; and they were rimmed by mossy tumble.

Why was he here to kill a man, instead of off somewhere, Brasilia or Bombay, where people were putting civilization together again? It was the Imperials' fault, as most things were. The damn Virginians. The damn Pentagon.

The land records had been conserved in a national database, and had survived the diebacks, the Mexican *Reconquista*, and the Texan Counterreconquest. The Joint Chiefs of Staff had determined that where DNA testing could identify the heirs of deeds of records, no matter what the squatter's rights, no matter what the improvements made, no matter what the intervening plagues had done, the original plots of territory as described by metes and bounds were to be delivered *per stirpes* to the descendants, wherever found, who had gene-traces of the original pre-war owners.

So to be a land-claim attorney during these unsettled years was the quickest way to wealth. The disputes between original owners and remotest descendants, the quibbles over slightest medical opinions of gene statistics, the sheer unfairness of turning rich land, improved for seventy or eighty years, over to unknowns, all combined to create endless legal controversy, endless opportunity. The Pentagon wanted Anglo-American laws to be enforced, they wanted continuity to be maintained, they wanted the citizens of Greater Texas, and the subjects of the People's Republic of the Northeast, and the landowners of the Confederation, all to count themselves as United-States-of-Americans once more. They wanted the past to seem like it was still alive: as if come again were the glory days of old.

But the Texan law allowed for jury nullification, which meant finding a man not guilty of breaking an unpopular law, even when he broke the law. In effect, a sufficiently emotional appeal to the honor or the pity of the twelve good men, would allow them to ignore the laws of remote and weak Pentagon administrators, and find, without any more legality than that, for the local landowner. But if the landowner was unpopular, too rich or too poor, or if he could be made to seem so by the clever question or a sly turn of phrase, well, the mercurial jury would enforce the cruel law to its letter.

These were jurors of a frontier society. Depopulations had returned the lands here to wilderness with shocking swiftness. Without the amenities and mutual assistance of wired urban life, without good roads and good communications, the isolated towns remembered an earlier Texas, a period recalled in song and story, when men were self-reliant. Self-reliant men stood on their honor, because they had nothing else.

Now, to plead to a panel of touchy individualists, many of whom rode or tramped over bad roads a day or more for the privilege of serving as jurors, one had to be an orator, but also a figure commanding respect. It was not like a murder trial, where a defendant was present: usually these claims were for remote parties, reached only by Pony Mail, in Chicago or Charleston or Newer Orleans. All eyes were on the lawyer, all thoughts on his reputation. Where the laws were so clearly unfair, the merits of a case did not count.

And so it was the insults that the attorneys flung or insinuated at each other that tended to decide the matter. If an attorney accepted with philosophical meekness some slight against his name or family or truthfulness during the hot arguments in the airlessly hot sunlit chambers of the law, the jurors would assume he was not man enough to be representing an honest case, law or no law, and would find for the other party.

The only way, the only certain way, to still such talk, to make the prospect of sarcasm too dangerous to contemplate . . . was this.

And the rewards were immense. Letters could be sent away with only a tenth value of the land, and the remainder sold back to the original owners, and if handled with dispatch, a man could get the value of a large ranch or farmstead or silk apiary for a day's arguing.

All he had to do was be willing to shoot and be shot at.

Menelaus grimaced, and lit the tiny read-out in the grip of his pistol,

examining the chaff distribution patterns, the targeting priorities and vari-
ances of his main shot, the calculated turbulence vortices of his eight smaller
escort shots.

Everything depended on the vortex equations, on Navier-Stokes partial
differentials that described the flow of incompressible fluids.

He did not need to take out a library cloth to do his figuring. He could
do it in his head. All those bored hours he had spent alone with his library,
once his mother erased his music and pictures, he had spent on calculus,
juggling rate of stress and strain tensors, trying to get the patterns of signs
to do new tricks for him. It wasn't easy, but he had a knack for it.

Back when he had been packing weapons for Barton Throwster, any
calculation shortcuts he could program into the fire-counterfire ballistics
of the pistols, anything to save critical nanoseconds of computation time
for the main shot's onboard micropackage, might save a customer's life.
His fame with guns was what had brought him to the attention of the legal
profession in Houston, and broke him early out of his apprenticeship.

Too bad there was no cash in it. Who ever heard of a rich mathematician? Maybe if he had been an orphan, he could have taken what job he
pleased, and thought no more on it, or joined a monastery, and lived with
nothing but a sack for a shirt, a rope for a belt, a stone for a pillow. A boy
with nine brothers and no father cannot be so picky.

To shoot and be shot at. He would have done anything to get out of his
small township. The world was recovering from a Dark Ages. Somewhere,
the future was being born, being made, all those bright futures he dreamed
about as a child. Somewhere else.

And here he was, shooting at another lawyer no more qualified in law
than he was, to make it easier for the Imperials to steal land from the
family that worked the land.

It was as bitter in his mouth as the taste of iron.

In the gloom he saw lantern lights approaching. The lanterns were half-
hooded, furtive, shining a beam only now and again. Here was a plump
little man, Amiens Rainsville, who now came moving heavily through the
morning mists toward him, red-faced and puffing. He was someone both
duelists trusted to act as judge and drop the scarf. He was the clerk in
the Medical Defense Proconsul's office who had the Seal to sign off on
intoxicants, so all the alehouses and smokehouses and opium dens in the

district were all on good terms with the man, but also had various degrees of indiscretions in back-up files to blackmail him, if he should prove too efficient at his work. He was placid and cheery enough to get along both with Anglos and Oddlings, Aztecs and Texans, French traders from Louisiana, and Imperials from the Union's capitol in Virginia, and canny enough to satisfy the Pentagon without dissatisfying the powerful men in Austin. For affairs of this type, there was no one else in the district to trust, aside from Amiens.

With him was a heavy man, slow and big. Menelaus recognized the footstep. His foe.

Something was wrong. There were four lanterns, and one burned more brightly than the others, a wide beam. The man behind moved with slower pace: an old man's walk.

His little brother Leonidas was acting as his second. Leo jogged over to Amiens to discover why there was an extra man present. In a moment he was back. Menelaus could not see Leo's features, save as an outline against the brightening red sky beyond.

"What's the deal? Only supposed to be two witnesses for me, two for Nails." Mike Nails was the disputant in this party, and a man with a steady aim and rich enough to have a team of five to program and pack his pistol. "Who might that stranger be?"

"A . . . man . . . from the Coast as wants to espy the fighting. Amiens says to trust him, no worries."

The way his brother drawled the word "*man*" caught his ear. "You mean a foreigner? Which is he, a beaneater or a grasseater?"

"Not neither. He's a Frenchman."

"I don't give a tinker's damn, but why is Amiens willing to let a manwhore watch straight-ups at our quarreling? That don't seem much like in his character."

"Not that kind of Frenchman, man from France. Or Monaco, leastways. A Prince."

"What do you mean a Prince? He got a crown of gold on his head?"

"Nope, but he got a fat wallet full a cash and everything. Bet the phone on his wrist cost more 'n our whole digs, back home."

Menelaus spat on the ground. "Pshaw. The Euros already think we're uncivilized. Are we dancing bears for the tourists to gawp at? Go tell 'em no. *My client and I find the conditions of the settlement unacceptable relating to reasons of the dignity of my person as officer of the court.* Got that? And talk fine, like Mama told you."

Leonidas trotted back over. Menelaus could not hear the voices, but he saw how the lamps moved as men gestured with their hands.

He came back. "The guy is not here to watch the fight. He just wants to see you."

"I keep regular office hours. Walk-ins welcome."

"Yeah, but he's afraid you might be dead tomorrow."

"Pshaw!" said Menelaus. "Mike Nails ain't putting me in the ground."

"He says it's your destiny."

"What?"

"You're destined for greater things, he says. To go to the stars, not die down here in the mud."

"Issat what he said?"

"It sure is."

"What's his name?"

"Ronny-yay. The Seventh."

"Come again?"

"His Serene Highness, Rainier VII Sovereign Prince of Monaco, Duke of Valentinois, Marquis of Baux, Count of Polignac, Baron of this, Lord of that, Sire of somemother damn thing. You know how Euros are. Ever since their lands shrunk up, their damn titles get longer. But get this: He's got the mark on his head."

"What kinda mark?"

Leonidas solemnly touched finger to brow. "Right there. Hindu caste mark. He's a Brahmin."

"Damnation," whispered Menelaus, impressed in spite of himself. "Ain't so many White Men get that. No wonder he's rich . . . I . . . Leo, I know who this is. It's Grimaldi! It's *him!*"

"Him? Him who?"

"Him, the Captain!"

Leonidas looked left and right, unhurriedly, but clearly scoping out escape routes. "Captain of what?" His voice betrayed his tension.

"Not that kind of captain, not a trooper-captain, a ship-captain. The ship!"

"So who is he?"

Menelaus had to grin. "Smartest man alive. Luckiest, too. The Hindus and the Spaniards could not agree on anyone else. He showed up at Sriharikota Island, at the main launch-site, with a bankful of his own money. Monaco had not signed the anti-space proliferation treaty, so if the whole project was in his name, the Sinosphere couldn't stop it, so they made him Captain! It was in all the chatterboxes. They have a setting for verbal, if'n you can't be troubled to read 'em."

"O-Ooh. You mean that ship what ain't never going to sail?" replied Leonidas. "'Course you do. What the plague other ship you ever the plague talk about? They been building that ship for ten years now."

Takes a fair piece of time to build a cathedral, Menelaus said. But he did not say it aloud.

Menelaus stared at the dark ground, the tall, straight, beautiful trees. Then he craned his neck up and inspected the sky. One bright star still hung overhead. Perhaps it was an artificial satellite, a Hindu Sputnik. Just like the Americans used to put up, back before civilization threw a shoe, fell, broke its leg, and had to be put down.

They were out there. He was down here.

Down here with his family. His reputation would not survive if he walked away from the settlement, just to go talk to the Star Captain. Even if he walked off the field for a minute, five minutes, the whispers would start.

The more he thought on it, the stranger it seemed. What was Amiens thinking? The breach of secrecy was unheard-of. Menelaus could claim grounds to walk away, but then . . . would he have the nerve to come back here again?

He never wanted to do anything more ferociously in his life. The desire to go see the man who would fly to the stars boiled like bad whiskey in Menelaus's belly, it was so strong.

"Tell him to go rut himself," Menelaus said. "Tell him to get lost. He can see me during office hours. But talk fine, Leon, like Mama . . ."

"Sure, Meany. Just like Mama says. *My principle is affronted at this breach of the security, and politely demands the extraneous party to remove him beyond the bounds set aside for this exercise.* How's that?"

"Like you was born in a skyscraper with running water, little brother."

2. Mike Nails

The pink sky was now bright enough, merely. Amiens, acting as judge, inspected first one duelist and his weapon, and then the other. He took up his position.

Amiens, in a loud voice, politely asked the Seconds if their Principals could settle the matter in any other way. "Even now, if an accommodation can be reached, both parties may withdraw in honor. Gentlemen! Will your principals seek reconciliation?"

Both Seconds politely returned a negative answer.

"Have all measures to avoid this conflict been exhausted?"

Both Seconds solemnly answered that they had.

At his signal, the distance was paced out by the seconds, and the Principals were posted at thirty yards apart. The sun was still below the horizon: only the eastern clouds were aflame. Menelaus could scarcely see his foe. Mike Nails was no more than a stocky shape against the trees, a dark silhouette against a gray background. The man was bulky to begin with. In his dueling armor, he looked like a black ape with a bald metal head.

Amiens called out again. "Gentlemen, see to your countermeasures!"

There was no change to the naked eye. Menelaus through his helmet monocle could see the view his bullet would see: a confusing blur of ghosts, dancing and fading. Nails had turned on his camouflage. Menelaus put his thumb on the switch on his fanny-pack, and powered his coat circuits also.

Amiens called, "Gentlemen, ready your weapons! On peril of your honor, do not fire before the signal!"

Nails shouted, his voice strangely flat in the cold pre-dawn air, half-unheard beneath the cheery calls of birds. "Backwoodsman! The Frog and his Wogs would have you for their star-venture, eh? I would hate to shoot an *aaasssss*—tronaut. Go 'way, fly off, and freeze! I'll be safely in my grave before you wake!"

Menelaus was more puzzled than angered. What was this talk of being an astronaut? Menelaus assumed Mike Nails must have heard something from the rich Monegasque stranger who'd walked up with him. Or recognized the Star Captain. Unlike his brother, Nails read the newsboxes.

Was that wisecrack about a destiny among the stars supposed to mean something? Something for real?

For a moment, Menelaus felt as if some childhood dream, long-forgotten, was stirring in his heart. It lived in his thoughts as a child, usurping golden afternoons. But he could not recall it to mind, not now.

Tradition commanded that each was to address each other only through their Seconds. Amiens called out in a solemn, grave voice, "The Principals are to be respectful in meeting, and neither by look nor expression irritate each other! They are to be wholly passive, being entirely under the guidance of their Seconds, who keep their honor for them, and answer for them!"

He could not recall his dreams to mind. Not now. There was no time.

Menelaus cried, "My answer is here." And with a ponderously slow gesture put his pistol overhead, arm straight.

His brother's voice came from the gloom. "Stand firm until the signal is dropped. When the signal is dropped, you are at liberty to fire." The other second, Mike's nephew Zechariah, said the same words to Mike Nails, as if an echo hung in the cool dawn air.

There was a flutter of red as Amiens raised the scarf. Both men saluted by holding up their off hands, palm out and fingers spread, indicating ready. As was the Spanish custom, copied here, the left glove of a duelist was sewn with a black palm, so that this gesture could be seen from afar.

The second for Mike Nails called out that he was ready. Leonidas called out likewise.

Amiens released the scarf.

3. Pistolshot

Dueling, as a custom, does not exist if pistols are too capable. In Menelaus's great-grandfather's day, when a sniper in Austin could shoot a satellite-triangulated beam-guided bullet to Fort Worth and down a man's chimney and into his left ear, duelists within eyeshot of each other would have been certain to die. It was not the inaccuracy of the guns that revived the custom in this generation; it was the perfection of the defensive measures.

Menelaus was confident. He had a Krupp 5 MegAmp railgun with a 250 IQ that fired two pounds of smart shot and a nine-meter globe of effective counterfire. The main slug could dance and jink like a drop of mercury on a skillet.

The pistol, a six-pound behemoth, was only good for one shot. Most of the mass of the gun was in the packed chaff, which consisted of hundreds of spinning, irregular bits of self-propelled interceptors. The computing technology needed to hit a bullet out of the air with a bullet had long been known; but the chaff did not need to hit a bullet straight-on to deflect it, merely to put a vortex of sufficient overpressure in the path. The Bernoulli effect, the same thing that gave curved wings lift or tennis balls backspin, would do the rest.

To counter this, gunsmiths developed bullets as large as miniature rockets. The heavier the slug, the less partial vacuums created by counterfire could deflect it, and also a large slug could carry retrorockets and a simple calculator to correct deflection errors. Escort bullets, which were smaller and lighter, could run interference, feinting the chaff into premature discharge and clearing a path, or setting up vortices of their own to pull the main shot back onto its flightpath.

And the inner globe of chaff which followed the outer globe corrected for feints, bringing more chaff-mass suddenly to one vector to deflect the bullet.

And, of course, the bullet could be programmed to feint and correct, as could the escorts, to trick the chaff into mistaking one for the other; and chaff could be counterprogrammed to correct for this feint or ignore it, or . . .

The chaff flight pattern and distribution was based on the microscopic differences in shape of their various lifting surfaces. Which shape of chaff went in which of the eight launchers that distributed the load was, of course, a question of pure game-theory, whose solution would maximize defensive flightpaths in minimum time, while leaving maximum correction options. It all depended on what you loaded where, how you packed your weapon.

And then there was a simple psychological question: Was the opponent someone who programmed a dogleg feint and a straight-line correction, or a straight-line feint and a dogleg correction? If the first, you packed your gun to spread your chaff in a toroid like a smoke-ring; if the second, in a cone centered on his line of fire.

Once the shot encountered the chaff cloud, it was all a chessgame on autopilot, with the bullet calculating the possible vortices of the chaff based on their presumed shapes, and the chaff attempting to deflect the bullet based on its presumed flightpath. The duel depended on the skill with which the chaff had been packed, the programming of the decision trees, and the intelligence of the pistol.

Menelaus smiled. He had been packing chaff since boyhood. And his Krupp 5M could do the *New New York Times* sudoku puzzle.

Menelaus was standing with his arm overhead, as if he meant to delope, and shoot in a right line into the air. It would have been the gentlemanly thing to do, if Nails had been convinced he meant it. If Nails had followed suit, both men could have discharged harmlessly and, with no dishonor, walked away alive. Merely to come to this field preserved one's name.

Menelaus normally shot straight-line and corrected: swift, direct, bloody. This time he was not. Why did he give his opponent one last clear chance to walk away, both of them unbloodied, unashamed? Nails must have thought it was weakness.

Thought? There was no time, really, to think through the options once the scarf dropped. These things are decided on instant and instinctive levels. Perhaps Nails sensed Menelaus had no more nerve. Perhaps he just wanted to get in the shot first.

So Nails fired from the hip, not taking the extra eighth-second to raise his arm. Perhaps he sprained his wrist; certainly the kick threw him back, off balance, as if a hammer struck his shooting arm. His heavy armor clanged like a bell around him. Jets of black chaff erupted in eight directions from his barrel, making the man vanish in an opaque cloud, from which only radar aiming beams emerged. A smoke-ring. He had guessed Menelaus was firing on an indirect path.

Menelaus had the swifter reflexes, and had fired an instant before his foe, sensing by the tilt of the shoulder-armor that Nails had committed himself. So he was also hidden in a cloud, but this one was a cone reaching straight overhead, like a black tornado. His own aiming beam was pointed straight up.

It was only an instant, but that instant was long enough, because the leading edge of Nails's chaff cloud, approaching faster than the speed of sound, sensed the aiming beam of Menelaus's pistol, and flew upward, following it. This distorted the cloud directly between the two, thinning Nails's defense.

Menelaus brought his arm down like Zeus calling a lightning bolt down from heaven, like a samurai chopping with an immense but unseen blade. This was purely theatric motion, of course. His main shot, which had been loaded in his escort-bullet's lower Six O'clock launcher, had already found and piled through the thin cloud. The bullet had been programmed to pull the tightest possible angle, so its flightpath was as near to straight as a man with his gun pointed away from his target could manage.

Menelaus, by this stunt, of course, had almost none of his cloud around him. It was all streaming up overhead. Even so, his pistol computers with casual genius located and deflected the enemy main shot.

Nails's head exploded, for Menelaus's bullet entered his helmet, but did not have enough velocity to exit, and so ricocheted like a bead in a baby's rattle, a momentary pentagram of burning metal.

And because Menelaus was a serious man when he fought, he had programmed his escort bullets to follow the wake, and so Nails was struck again and again and again as slug after slug hit his skull, collar, shoulder, neck.

A serious man. When he saw his headless opponent fall, Menelaus, who was covered with sweat, his heartbeat hot in his face, not consciously believing that the corpse might get up again, nonetheless drew his Bowie knife and started forward. (The picture in his mind was of plunging the knife again and again into a metal-hard torso, into bloodless plastic limbs, to make sure they would not keep moving.)

He did not even know he was seriously wounded until he took that step. It was not even an escort bullet that had traveled through his leg and shattered his kneecap. It had been a splinter of granite, half-buried in the dry winter grass, some stray escort bullet struck. His leggings were red, and his boot was already full of blood, for a major vein had been severed. Then the sky turned a funny metallic black, lit with flashes of colorless light, and he had the sensation of stepping into an elevator whose cable was cut.

Hitting the ground woke him for a moment. He saw the scarf flutter to the grass and lie still.

4. The Harvest Is Great

He woke to the smell of mown hay, the sound of bees buzzing. Out the window, brothers in brown cassocks were bent over, a line of men with sickles, working in devout silence, piling the harvest in bundles along the parallel paths they made in the standing wheat. In the silence, one voice spoke: *et dicebat illis messis quidem multa operarii autem pauci rogate ergo Dominum messis ut mittat operarios in messem.* Menelaus did not understand the words, but there was a lilt of humor there.

Leonidas was slouched, perhaps asleep, balancing on a stool near his bed, tilted back so not all the stool legs were on the floorstones, his crossed boots making the only mark on an otherwise clean and white wall. Perhaps he was awake, for a thin blue trail of smoke was spilling slowly upward from beneath his hat brim.

"Little brother," said Menelaus.

A low chuckle answered him. "Not no more. I'm older than you, now."

"You froze me?"

"The bone-grower messed up, started your ribs and stuff getting all crinkly. Had to bring in a Jap to redo your skeleton, and that cost. Specialist from Osaka."

"How long was I out?"

"Year and a half."

"Why so long?" Menelaus asked.

"We had to keep you stiff until Nelson could raise the money."

"Nelson? He even got a job?"

"In Newer Orleans. Some scratch he got gambling, some he got diving for treasure in the sunk part of the city. Some he got from some Anglo pumpkin with dollar signs in his eyes, just for drawing a map and making sweet talk."

"Damn stupid of him, going into hot water."

"He says its clean these days, the water."

"If there's no fish, it's not clean. Don't care what the Geiger counter says. Fish know." Menelaus shook his head. "Hope he's planning to be a monk. No women'll marry a man with nuked-up stones."

"Maybe Nelson wore a lead jockstrap. But funny you should mention . . ."

Menelaus looked around the room. The crucifix on the wall was Spanish-style, with the figure of the torture all carved and painted in grotesque and vivid likeness, and adorned with gold leaf. "You didn't. You surely didn't."

"We did. We surely did."

"Can't baptize a man without his say-so. They got rules. A catechism."

"We told 'em it was your last words, dying wish, all that."

"I ain't joining no beaneater church."

"Been done. The Governor's brother came by and put oil on your face and everything. Washed all your sins away, prettied up your soul to go meet St. Peter. But I guess you'll call him San Pedro now, eh? Got to go to Rome and kiss the toe of the Pope."

"Preacher Brown says the Pope got horns and a split hoof like a goat."

Leonidas grinned, which made his cigarette tilt up at a jaunty angle. "Preacher Brown will take a strap to you, he finds out you say your prayers in Latin."

"I don't say prayers."

"You do. Before your meals. I heard you."

"Saying *"thank God, its time to eat"* ain't saying grace. Saying the blessing don't do nothing."

"Well, cussing a man to hell don't do nothing, neither, but I heard you do that, too."

"Well, go get the brother or whoever. Tell 'em I changed my mind, and I'm going back to . . . what is Preacher Brown? Whatever the hell he is, tell 'em I had a vision or something calling me back to, uh . . ."

"Mormon. Preacher Brown's a Mormon."

"He ain't no Mormon. In the first case, Mormons got two wives, and in the second, we hang them when we catch them, like they do us. Utah's enemy ground. It just ain't possible! Umm—is it? He's not really a Mormon, is he?"

"Just ain't possible you can be born and raised from a pup and don't even know what Church you are."

"Which is the one that believes in hellfire?"

"All of 'em. How many years you been a-going to Meeting? You didn't pay not the least attention in all that time?"

"I was thinking of something else."

"What?"

"Maybe we could make a promised land by our own lone selves, asking no help and bowing to none. Maybe the Garden of Eden weren't at the beginning of time, but at the end, a garden we can make as soon as we figure how to make it. That's what I was thinking. Old Preacher Brown's spook stories didn't seem like much to me, held up against that. Call the brother."

"Don't be a mule, Meany. The Governor's brother, the Bishop, came by and tended to you while you were sick, and he didn't turn you over to the Regulators."

"Bishop? Ain't no bishops in Texas."

"So is. Bishop of the Diocese of Galveston-Houston. He's shielding you. You step off of sanctuary ground, you might as well put your head in a bucket of boiling pork-lard. Mike Nails was setting to get married, did you know that?"

"No. Who is the girl?"

"Lil Palmer. Josiah Palmer's girl, the man who owns half the county. See? Might have been okay if you had killed him clean, but word got out that you drilled Mike over and over."

"Because his gun was stupid and his chaff was packed like crap."

"Blew his head clean off, you did. If you'd've drilled him in the heart and left a good-looking corpse . . ."

"Bugger that. Gunfighting ain't a game. Besides, it's not my fault I win."

"Win? You shoot like the devil's in you, little brother. Lookit this. Got you a memento."

Leonidas pulled out a slug of metal. It was two bullets, melted into one shape, curled like a question-mark. The payload of Mike Nails's main shot had been fused by the heat of impact to one of Menelaus's escort bullets—a rare, perfect interception.

Looking at the shape, Menelaus could see it in his head: the patterns, the pretty patterns of vortices. He could see the math needed to describe how that impact had been done, and he could guess at a way to solve for simultaneous partial differentials, more elegant than what he'd been doing before.

"Shoot like the devil is in you," Leonidas said again, this time more softly.

"I just got a knack, is all," muttered Menelaus.

"That's not what Rainier says."

"Who?"

"Your Prince. The Prince of Monaco."

"Captain Grimaldi. Ain't no titles in space."

"Ship ain't done a-building yet. Most likely never will be."

"The *Hermetic*. He's still the Captain," said Menelaus. And in his heart, he wanted the words to be: *my Captain*.

Leonidas shrugged. "Whatever his name is, His Serene Highness helped pay for some of your fixup. He was talking about a scholarship. They'll pay your way to go to Oddifornia and study math." Leonidas shook his head in wonder, as if baffled by rich foreigners and their lunatic ways. "Guess when it takes you more'n ten years to build a ship, you might as well put the kids through schooling what might grow up to be your crew. Train 'em up to the job, like."

For a moment, Menelaus had the strangest feeling, as if time itself had forgotten how to let the seconds pass. Pay? To study?

It was the future. A doorway to the future had just become unlocked for him.

In one part of his mind, he noticed how much joy was like horror: The same horripilation tingled his skin electrically, the same faintness of breath, the same prickling of the scalp, the same sensation that something too enormous to grasp was upon him.

His gunfighter's nerve knew how to deal with horror, and so he could master this wild bucking-bronco feeling, too. Menelaus controlled his voice and spoke nonchalantly.

"So . . . pay my way outta here. He said that?"

"He did indeed. And seeing as how pretty Lil Palmer will kiss any man who shoots you in the back, and her dad will give him a thousand acres of prime land, this might be a good time to pack up and go study. Pox, I'd beef you myself to get a lip-dicker from sweet Lilly: just as fine as cream gravy and easy on the eyes, she is."

"Did the brothers say how soon I'd be fit to travel?"

"Your body's got to flush out the cellular machinery used to hold you in life-suspension: so you'll be crapping black ink for a while. Aside from that, we can leave as soon as . . ."

"We?"

Leonidas looked shy, and pulled his hatbrim down, but eventually said: "Well, I'm your brother, Meany Louse. Older brother now. Can't let you go off by your lonesome. Lookit what all kinds of trouble you make."

Menelaus was not in the mind to argue the point. "You got a cigarette?"

"Sure do."

"Old or new?"

"New. This is newbacco. You don't think I touch that poison stuff, do you?"

So Menelaus leaned back comfortably in his bed, watching the blue plume of cigarette smoke drift toward the ceiling. The two brothers shared the silence, neither feeling much need to talk, not yet. The smoke trickled up.

Up. The direction the stars were in.

4

Life Extension

1. Mining the Diamond Star

A.D. 2004–2045

The Diamond Star V 886 Centauri, known informally as "Lucy" and more officially as BPM 37093, was a variable white dwarf star about fifty light-years from Sol.

In the middle of the First Space Age, astroseismological analysis of its pulsation rhythms indicated that the core had solidified into one huge crystal of carbon ash. This core was a ten-decillion-caret diamond of degenerate matter, some 2500 miles in diameter, a single teaspoon of which would have weighed five tons on Earth. The discovery was mentioned as a curiosity in even some popular press.

This curio became a celebrity that fascinated the world many years later when gamma-ray spectrography suggested that the astronomical diamond was not matter at all, but antimatter. High-energy radiation activity from the star was consistent with micrometeorite or dust particles encountering a star-sized furnace burning antihydrogen into anticarbon, and disappearing in a total-conversion flash of mutual annihilation. The plasma atmosphere of the star maintained the proportions of positrons to antiprotons expected from an "anti-star"—a kind of body, until then, entirely hypothetical.

That this invalidated the standard model of astronomical evolution was merely one of the tremendous implications.

Criswell mining, also called "Star-Lifting," was a process that theoretically could be used to create artificial mass-ejections from a star. A flotilla of equatorial satellites, each pair exchanging two counterdirectional beams of oppositely charged ions with its neighbors, could form a complete circuit around the star, to initiate a ring current. The magnetic field thus generated would deflect the solar wind, and channel prominences from the star into a pair of ejection streams at the north and south poles. Next, artificial solar storms could be created by a sufficiently powerful particle beam. The stellar atmosphere of even a cool star was hellishly hot; but anything, no matter how hot, boiled more fiercely when energy was added to it. If enough energy were added, the plasma could, in spots, be set to boiling savagely enough to throw its inner substance into space for easy retrieval.

The physics of Criswell mining was simple, but the economics less so. It had never been attempted on Sol. Mankind simply had no current need for a cloud of hydrogen plasma so pressing as to justify the astronomical energy costs involved. But economics of mining V 886 Centauri, a star both smaller and cooler than Sol, were different. The gravity well was less steep.

And the ejected material was infinitely more precious, even if infinitely more dangerous.

The plasma of V 886 Centauri, ejected into orbit and stratified into its elements by using extremely large-scale mass spectrometry, could then be condensed by laser cooling into antimatter.

The antihydrogen would prove too fugitive and fine to collect. But a beam of positrons would turn anticarbon-12 into anticarbon-14, and the ions could then be painstakingly captured by a magnetic funnel. The chemical properties of anticarbon were the same as carbon, of course, so that sufficient magnetically induced temperatures and pressures could be used to compress the material into anticarbon crystal: a snow-white diamond no one and nothing made of matter could touch.

These last two operations would be expensive only at first, because the gathered antimatter could then be used to power ever-larger arrangements of ionization screens and magnetic bottles, which would gather more of the cloud, so the arrangement could generate a larger magnetic field, and so on. The snowball would simply grow.

The Diamond Star was a fountain of wealth, for all practical purposes, infinitely rich.

The only problem was that the fountain of wealth was fifty lightyears away. Is it worth it to climb a mountain to get a pot of gold? The taller the mountain is, the bigger the pot must be, and the more precious the gold.

How precious was this gold? Unlike other forms of energy, antimatter has the most efficient transportation cost versus its mass, since every particle was annihilated to liberate energy. Pound for pound, it was the cheapest form of power there could ever be. It required very little by way of refinement or processing: drop anything, anything made of matter into it, and the equal mass was converted spectacularly to energy. No waste; no pollution. A perfect fuel source. The problem? To make antimatter out of matter was preposterously costly, absurdly energy-inefficient, and cost far more than it was worth.

But what if a big chunk of the stuff, a mother lode, was merely sitting idly up in the starry heavens, waiting?

How big? V 886 Centauri was 2×10^{27} kilograms in mass. One gram of anticarbon would liberate 9×10^{13} joules of energy when annihilated with a gram of carbon, meaning that the Diamond Star was worth roughly 10^{40} joules of energy. For comparison, the annual energy consumption of the whole world in the days of the Second Space Age was less than 10^{18} joules. In other words, every man, woman, and child on the globe, and all his cats and dogs, could have more power at his disposal than the whole world had used in a century—if only there was a way to go get it.

And the will and the wealth. By a providential accident of history, Earth in A.D. 2050 happened to be at the apex of a period its friends called the "Age of the Sovereign Individual"; its foes called it "The Plutocracy." Nine men, no more, controlled 90 percent of the world's wealth. They estimated that an unmanned starship returning in a century would ensure the perpetual power of their international system of banks and industries. Their power collapsed amid hyperinflation—but not until after a vessel was launched that only they could afford to send.

The *Croesus* achieved orbit around V 886 Centauri in A.D. 2112, and laboriously constructed a radio-laser larger than itself to beam back to Sol news of its successful first pass at mining the antimatter star.

The message consisted of tediously correct, robot-compiled reports of loads, processes, and outputs, and only in the final section, under anomalies, did the Croesus brain, without any particular emphasis, report that Man was not the only creature who had placed an artifact near the Diamond Star. First Contact had been made fifty lightyears away, with no living human aware of the event. The robotic mining ship had discovered an object, an artifact, a black sphere the size of a small moon, left by intelligent nonhumans.

But by the time the signal reached Sol, the generation that had sent out the NTL *Croesus* had passed away. There were no orbital dishes open to receive its message. The broadcasts that passed through the Solar system in 2162 and 2166 were lost. The Wars of Religion of the late Twenty-First Century were more brutal and more reckless than the Wars of Economic Theory from the Twentieth, because the main purpose of the belligerents (first on one, but eventually on both sides of the conflict) was not to preserve honor, gain terrain, or win political concessions, or for any rational reason, but to wipe out as many infidels as possible, as cruelly as possible, in order to please a particularly cruel conception of God.

Croesus was programmed to repeat its broadcasts every four years, and the signal took half a century to cross the void to Sol. In its thoughtless, patient, automatic way, it did. It was not until A.D. 2170 that the Kshatriya battle-satellites received the message that man was not alone in the universe.

2. *The* Hermetic *Expedition*

A.D. 2215–2235

After decades of delay, the second expedition to the Diamond Star was organized. The waning Indosphere, in an act of conspicuous consumption meant to awe the world, and the up-and-coming Hispanosphere, eager to show her new-found strength, for the same motive, though rivals, joined each other in the venture.

The amount of resources consumed in this expedition was almost beyond calculation; but the odd mixture of semi-religious zeal and cultural pride prevented either of the partners from flinching away from the massive public debt and private ruin the ostentatious project absorbed.

To be sure, public figures solemnly intoned pieties concerning the long-term usefulness of this scientific wonder to the future generation of man: but it was on their haughty contemporaries their eyes were fixed.

Not so the officers and crew. Ion drive allowed them to leave the world lightyears behind, and Montrosian biosuspension technique allowed them to leave the years behind. Each crewman of the complement aboard had his eyes fixed on the future; each was assured that history would make him immortal.

The Earth would be strangely changed ere the errant travelers returned, the generation that sent them out long gone, their once-loved homes now foreign.

And the travelers would be changed even more strangely.

3. Thaw

A.D. 2399

Menelaus Montrose woke to a sensation of floating serenity. His thoughts seemed focused and sharp, but his head ached as if it had been filled with helium. Had he been drugged?

He sat up in bed. That was the first surprise: because it was a bed, an old-fashioned four-poster, big enough to hold a family of bounders, their first cousins, and their dogs. It was hung with heavy drapes, with sheets and coverlets around him like a snowfield, and a real down pillow where his head had lain.

Vaguely, he remembered a previous room—a white, empty place with padded walls—A hospital of some sort, albeit not smelling of blood, puke, and feces like the field-hospitals he knew back in Texas. But now where was he?

Menelaus spit up into the air, and watched the spittle as it fell, making a ugly yellow splatter on the nice silk sheets. It seemed to fall in a parabola, and not curve left or right. No visible Coriolis force, as someone in a carousel might see: but he was clearly under one gravity of acceleration.

Earth, then. He was on Earth.

Del Azarchel must have turned the punt around. That would have been no easy task. Decelerating just to come to a rest relative to Earth . . . then to expend the fuel to accelerate toward Earth again, doing a screw-turn halfway, decelerating again . . . How far had the *Hermetic* traveled in that amount of time? Past Pluto? If she was past the heliopause, no craft of Earth could ever rendezvous with her . . .

A sense of crushing defeat was in him, like water in the lungs of a drowning man. All nine men aboard the punt would have missed the expedition, thanks to him. He had missed the stars. The future had been ripped from his hand like some old but cherished comic, and torn to bits.

Menelaus threw open the bed curtains, and recoiled, blinking. The sunlight poured in from French doors leading to a balcony. Outside was dizzying scenery: majestic mountains, crowned and ermined with snow and, gathered between crevasses, like emeralds sown into the silvery-white garments of emperors, were narrow valleys of pine and spruce. Above, a sky so pale and clear it was as glass, and there on motionless wing, an eagle, highest flown of all the fowls of Earth.

He stepped closer to the window. He looked out through the French doors to a balcony of marble. Beyond was air, and a sheer drop. Fog, or perhaps it was cloud, was underfoot, and he blinked in the dazzle, half-blinded.

This room he was in seemed to be burrowed into near-vertical cliff wall. To either side of his room he could see the cliff was punctured with other balconies and windows, as well as larger portals, which may have been landing perches for aircraft. The balconies were an odd mixture: tropic flowers and drooping vines hung over the sides, but driving snow blenched the rock walls to either side, and icicles gleamed.

Menelaus saw a shelf below him that was cut deeply into the rock wall, large as an amphitheater. Atop this shelf gardeners had carefully constructed a flower maze, green tennis lawns, and fountains with silver basins. Two airy stairways, graceful as waterfalls, reached down toward it. The pure beauty of the architecture, the refinement of the decoration, impressed him, and he was not a man normally who took note of such things.

The cliff wall curved left and right in bays and protuberances. His astonished eye followed the cliff farther and farther. In the distance the mighty curves met, and light twinkled from the shadows of the far cliff wall opposite. He was in a palace: the place must have miles of halls and corridors.

It looked like someone had taken a museum, or one of those old French palaces, and stuck it in the middle of a gigantic crater in the middle of the mountains. But did they heat the whole estate, merely to grow a rose garden and grape arbor in the midst of snow? Menelaus wondered at the energy expended.

Palace? Or fortress? He saw, folded almost invisibly into the rock, immense shutters of metal; clamshell armor thicker than bank vault doors. Several acres of steel were poised to fall over these windows and gardens and airy walkways, and he also saw pillboxes, hatches, and turrets which implied a healthy antiaircraft battery was also buried in the rock, only its many snouts poking above the surface.

There was nothing like this on Earth, and no blueprints for anything like it. Which meant he had been asleep for longer than merely the trip in the punt back to Earth. How far had the *Hermetic* traveled in this time? Was it twenty-five years later? Fifty? Had the first starship of Man reached her destination? Perhaps even now Blackie Del Azarchel was walking on the surface of the Monument in a pressure suit, bending down to study the alien glyphs. Menelaus gritted his teeth and ignored a boiling knot in his stomach.

Abruptly, he flung wide the French doors, and strode onto the balcony. A rushing blanket of warm air hovered near him. He did not hear any fan roaring, or see any vents whence the air came, but Menelaus stood without a coat on in sub-freezing mountain winterscape, unscathed. He could smell the snow, and if he put out his hand, he could feel cold air on his fingers. His hand felt queer, as if he had disturbed the surface of an invisible, vertical pond.

Menelaus only then noticed what he was wearing: silk pajamas. They rustled in the warm winds. There was a monogram on the pocket, a combination of the letters D and X and A.

At least there were Latin letters still in use here in the future.

He wondered where he was. Not a hospital, that was sure. Maybe the palace was owned by the Alliance of Deneb X? (That sounded promising.) Xylophone Anti-music Department? The Algophilists of the Xipetotec Desolation? (Given a vote, he'd prefer disgruntled percussion musicians to votaries of a old Injun blood-god.)

Beneath his hand was a little sphinx with the cherub-head of a child, smiling. "What're you grinnin' at, kid?" he grunted. Then he jerked his hand in surprise. The carven haircurls of stone embracing the wee face were warm under his touch: the marble balustrade was heated.

Now he looked out. Underfoot, through the openings in the fog, was a vast crater. Each time Menelaus estimated its size, he saw some other feature, such as a pine tree which he had mistaken for a weed, and had to revise his estimate upward. The crater was many miles across.

The clouds all hung at the same level, so looking down was like peering through the surface of a lake at a hidden lakebed. A particularly wide gap in the cloud was open at his feet, and opening slowly as if the winds were unseen hands parting a stage curtain. Menelaus leaned forward, eager for a glimpse of the future world.

The bottom of the crater was a broken field of glassy splatters, looking almost like volcanic rock. In the center of the crater, a lake had gathered. From the color of the water, he guessed it was newly made, a decade old or less, and nothing much lived in it. In the very middle of the water rose a cone-shaped island of rock.

Island? An uplift peak. He knew what he would have seen if he had been standing on it: chevron-shaped striations in the rock called shatter cones, all radiating out from the impact point, or laminated and welded blocks of sand.

He was not worried about radiation. This was not a nuke: It was a meteor strike. A big one.

There were ruins crumbling at the edge of the crater walls above: broken walls in burial shrouds of ice, blind with unglassed windows and doorless thresholds, or stumps of chimneys helmeted in snow. Now Menelaus saw a regularity in the cracks and discolorations in the crater floor: squares and rectangles. Old streets, old foundations, something had been here once.

This had been a large installation. Not a city: Some of the ruins were shaped like pillboxes or hemi-cylinders. A military installation. A fortress built high in the mountains? There was a break in the treeline, and all the trees in a row, for over a mile, were younger than those surrounding. He guessed that this was where the launchrail once rested, and broken lumps regularly spaced along the path may have been the energy system. That square break in the treeline was where the vehicle building might have stood: That broken eggshell in the distance, if it were not a mosque, was the remnant of a reactor dome. Of the acceleration rings there was no sign.

So—not just any fortress. A fortified spaceport. There had been no such installations anywhere on Earth in his day.

And now a second fortress had been built atop the first, no doubt replacing the old one when it was pasted. That implied even more years had passed. Seventy-five? A hundred? How long had it been? More importantly, had any radio messages been received from the *Hermetic*? The original expedition provisions would have allowed the vessel to stay at the Diamond Star for seven years, before powering up to begin the astronomical voyage back, with another possible two years if crewmen died, or very strict rationing were practiced. The results would arrive before the ship. If all went as planned, if there were results to send. If the Monument had been translated . . .

Back inside the chamber, there were images of fire painted on the ceilings, images of birds and beasts and maidens and conquering kings on the walls. Everything was deep red, dark blue, blue-black, with tints of gold and mahogany to bring a richness out of the textures. Framing the doors and windows and arches of dark wood carved in pattern of Celtic dragons coiled in knots. Underfoot were Persian carpets like nothing he'd ever seen. On either hand, and every which way he turned his eyes, everything was either gold, or crystal, or polished wood, or fine china, or substances he could not put a name to. There was a black paneled bowl of red roses on the nightstand, and some sort of candelabra in the ceiling, surrounded by painted babies with pink wings.

It all looked like something from an old European mansion. He had been expecting something else. Rooms made of force fields and streamlined steel with tailfins. Sliding doors that opened by themselves and made a *shush–shush* noise or something. Moving walkways. Atom-powered lightbulbs. Talking sinks, preferably that had a third tap for beer.

It was damn pretty, though, he had to give them that. The place even smelled nice, applewood logs burning on the fire.

He craned his head back and looked at the ceiling again. Images of fire? These were battle scenes.

4. Portrait of War

High up on the wall, his eye first fell upon an image of a burnt city under a mushroom cloud. The artist had painted streaks and streams of odd color, green and indigo, issuing like a lighting bolt high in the air. There was a tiny silver dot high up in the corner of the image: no doubt this was the aircraft spotting for the incoming missile strike. So the fools had actually done it. The Burning of New York the Beautiful had not been enough to warn the world. World War, this time with atomics. Or some weapon even more deadly: if the artist's design was accurate, the bolt was wider at the top than at the bottom, unlike a detonation or mass-driver strike.

The cityscape was photographically accurate. Montrose recognized some of the buildings. The Temple Mount; the Dome of the Rock; the Church of the Holy Sepulcher. The artist had even included part of the Wailing Wall, and showed a mother with her arms across her face twisting in agony as she fell across the two screaming children she protected with her body even as she died.

To either side were more images of fire: skeletons of skyscrapers toppling; sleek semi-wingless ultrahigh-atmosphere craft being scattered in a whirlwind of flame, like the finger of the Wrath of God; a submarine in the midst of a tidal wave being flung out of the sea by the violence of some unimaginable force, like a salmon leaping to its death.

No wonder they had not woke him up when he returned. War had broken out.

Painted on the ceiling were other images. Ships in space were exchanging directed-energy fire, shown here as fanciful threads of gold wire. No beams would be actually visible in real vacuum, of course. And the burning ships were drawn with yellow fire flowers with red petals, long licking tongues. The artist had obviously never seen a fire in zero-gee, which looked like a ball of half-invisible indigo gas, because in microgravity the hottest part of the flame tended to spread outward evenly in all directions, as a sphere, or rush along ruptured oxygen lines. The teardrop shape of candle flame was something gravity produced.

One war, or two? There was no way to tell.

Below them, at eye level, were stiff and ceremonial images: A figure with shoulder-length silver hair in a sleek black silk uniform was stepping on sabers dashed under his feet by half a dozen bowing figures; a kneeling president in the sober coat-and-tie uniform no one but presidents since the First Space Age had worn; a king in ermine cloak with medieval crown in hand; a military man in a high-necked Chinese jacket with pistol presented butt-foremost; a supine chieftain in a gaudy feather bonnet; and, oddly enough, a Pharaoh in a gold and blue pshent. The man in black held up an olive branch. At a guess, this picture was about the peace that followed the war. The figures perhaps represented the continents.

On one wall was a full-sized portrait showing a bishop lowering a coronet onto the head of the conqueror. The coronation of the white-haired figure in black showed his face more clearly. It was Ximen Del Azarchel. He looked to be about sixty years of age. No telling when these paintings had been done.

The monogram on the robe was his initials.

Menelaus looked overhead again. The ships on fire were all linked cylindrical punts, with maneuvering nozzles fore and aft. Interplanetary ships; space vessels. Tin cans cocooned in iron skeletons: functional, ugly, utilitarian. Their enemy ship was a work of art, a combination of ion drive and light-pressuresail. The sail tissue was like a second sky, holding crescent moons, and the blazing disk of the sun, in its reflections. The slender hull gleamed like a silvery sword. An interstellar ship; a vessel of stars.

The NTL *Hermetic*.

Montrose stepped around the bed on which he'd woke, and studied the paintings on the opposite wall.

One portrait particularly well done showed a European countryside, perhaps in Germany or France, with old-fashioned solar-paneled cottages with high-peaked roofs, and green fields under quaint hothouse tarp. The cottages dated from the time of the Japanese Winter. In the foreground were four maidens bending a spear into a ploughshare.

The sunset behind them was red, and rising above it, not far from the evening star, was the gleam of the starship *Hermetic*. The artist had merely suggested the ship's slender silhouette with a stroke of the brush, adumbrated with miles-wide sail with an oval of silver. The silver silhouette looked like a scepter, or perhaps a flower.

The ship was rising in the east like the morning star, and beneath her sails, was peace.

Montrose thought: The starship had returned, and found a world burned and torn with war, fighting a war in space, and somehow put a stop to it.

The date in Roman numerals was printed on one of the images: Astromachia MMCCCXCIX.

One hundred and sixty-four years had passed since last he woke. He paused to let that figure sink in. It was roughly the amount of time between when the Constitution of the Old Union was written, and when it was abolished by Roosevelt the Usurper. Another century and a half or so years after that, and the last president, Jefferson Dayles, was gone, and the Pentagon had declared Martial Law "for the duration of the emergency" that was to last, as it turned out, at least a century and a half again.

Grim example. Think of another: One and a half centuries was exactly the amount of time between the first lift of the Wright heavier-than-air flying machine and the launch of the first unmanned nigh-to-lightspeed interstellar vessel, NTL *Croesus*.

Long enough for the NTL *Hermetic* to have sailed to V 886 Centauri and returned—bearing all the wealth of the antimatter star, all the treasure of scientific wonders gleaned from deciphering the Monument—to end war and usher in a lasting peace.

He found himself grinning. And Blackie had evidently ended up on the top of the heap.

Menelaus turned.

And then he forgot everything, the old white-haired picture of Del Azarchel, the sinister silvery silhouette of Earth's only manned starship, now returned as Earth's only interstellar warship; he forgot it all.

He was looking at the princess. It took his breath away.

5. Portrait of Royalty

Her hair was gold as a summer noon sun. The artist had captured the girl's serene face but also a haunting twinkle in her eye, on her cheeks a hint of a suppressed dimple of laughter. Her gown was the gown of a fairy-tale princess. She seemed like a mischievous little girl playing dress-up in her mother's clothes; but as if her mother were a queen.

A coronet of diamond blazed in her hair, and white ermine hid one shoulder, leaving the other shoulder nude. Her bodice was white and set with small pearls. Her upper arms were naked, but elegant opera-gloves clung to hands as slender and shapely as branching coral. A ribbon of red and silver circled her trim waist, a regal gleaming medallion dangling below, pulling the ribbon into a Y-shape that curved along her hips. Her trains fell in smooth folds from her dress, like acres of snow descending in ripples from the curve of a hill. Only the toe of a diamond slipper could be glimpsed beneath the hems, like the glass slipper from a fairy-story, and her pose was elfin, a ballerina caught in mid-step, as if she were from a world not as weighty as Earth.

Behind and to either side were Doric columns holding ermine robes and shields of red and white diamonds. For some reason, there were two tonsured monks in the picture, standing to either side of the pillars, brandishing swords. A mantle decorated with stars was over her head; a map of Earth was under her gleaming toes.

Menelaus envied the painter his imagination. No real-life girl could be that pretty.

There came a noise behind him.

The door opened a crack, and someone knocked politely.

"C'mon in!" shouted Menelaus. "Tell me where the hell I am and what the hell the date is!"

Opening a door here in the future was evidently an elaborate affair: A wigged footman in a bright red coat backed into the room, bowing, giving Menelaus a better view of the man's buttocks than he would have liked. Then a small throng of other people, doctors and soldiers and folks in odd costumes, all shining with strange fabrics and glinting with gems.

A voice of quiet command spoke a soft word, and the throng parted.

Here was a dignified old man in sable who sat in the moving throne with a scarlet coverlet on his lap. He wore white gloves whose hue contrasted with his black garments. On his right wrist was a heavy armband of dull red metal, crudely made when compared to the shining rings he wore over his gloves, or his chain of office. The old man's jacket and coverlet were embroidered with the same monogram: XDA.

He said, "Menelaus Montrose, you are in the best of places in a better world than we ever dreamed—and the date? It is our time. Our hour has come, and all we have desired with it."

Menelaus squinted. "You in charge around here?"

The old man had a dazzling smile. He had been a handsome man once, and some of that glamour still clung to him. "Ah, my friend, you could say that."

The old man's hair, though hoary with age, was thick, and he wore it long, almost to his shoulders, like some ancient statue of a king, and he sported a moustache as white. Perhaps the moustache was what delayed Montrose from recognizing him.

But he surely knew that smile.

"Blackie—! Blackie Del Azarchel! Is that you?"

"The same. Welcome back to life. And such a life!"

5

The Brotherhood of Man

1. A Toast

"Well, hell, Blackie! Stand up and let me take a gander at you—! I been wondering—"

He had been fooled by the lack of wheels. The tall black chair slid forward over the floor, silent as a ghost, and Menelaus could not see the mechanism beneath the chair base that moved it. But it was a wheelchair.

"Uh—sorry—uh . . . Jesus nailed up a tree! How'd it happen?"

"My staff of doctors say it was spinal trauma, when I was thrown from a stallion, my beloved Eclipse. I think they have misdiagnosed the permanency of the affliction, and do not know its real cause."

"Damnation and plague! I know what a horseman you are. Were. Damn!"

"Worry not," said the old man with a twinkle in his eye. "Did I not say that our tomorrow had arrived? Petty problems as this one can be solved: the secret of youth, the creation of life, the conquest of the human nature, the maturation of man from upright ape to soaring angel! The time of Man beyond Man is about to dawn, and you, now revenant from your coffin, restored beyond hope from madness, you shall be in the audacious vanguard. Come! Let us storm the crystal ramparts of the unimagined future, brass trumps blaring, and banners streaming! Welcome to life!"

No sorrow could endure the onslaught of Del Azarchel's ringing words, his charming smile, his joy.

"It is good to be here," said Montrose. And he threw back his head, and uttered a whoop of pure delight.

"The event calls for wine!" said Del Azarchel. His eyes were shining. At his gesture, a wine-steward in powder blue brought in an ice bucket, and a parlor maid in a black uniform and frilly cap brought a pair of glasses on a tray.

Menelaus noticed the posture and costumes of the folk in the room. It took him a moment to realize what was missing. Perhaps in his great-grandfather's time, it had been the habit of non-Europeans of high rank to dress in European fashions, coats and ties and so on. But when Menelaus was young, only lawyers and bankers still affected that old costume. High-ranking non-Indians dressed as much like Brahmins or Kshatriya as they dared, sporting *dhoti* or *pancha*, even when not allowed to wear *yagnopavita* or *choti*. But no one here was wearing Indian trousers, sacred thread, or brow-paint. This would seem to indicate that the fashions of the world, following the powers of the world, had changed again.

There were three distinct groups: the first wore bright hues and glittered, and the second wore dark uniforms, who bowed and hung back. Peacocks and crows. The third group were pikemen, who stood at attention. Hawks.

The brightly dressed were tall and dark-eyed men with shoulder-length hair of silver. They seemed to be wearing wigs of fine metallic threads, or perhaps some odd gene-engineering allowed them to grow strangely lambent fibers of zinc-hued strands from their scalp. Their tunics and long-coats were patterned with gems and threaded with wires and status lights.

The cut and ornamentation of the tunics, the rings at the collars or the ankle-clasps sealed to boot-tops, looked like the fashion elements were borrowed from spacer uniforms or pressure suits. Certainly the bright heraldic designs and emblems the tunics flaunted looked like the easy-to-discern patterns of graffiti Montrose and his fellow spacemen had stenciled on their spacesuits during idle hours between training at the space station.

The courtiers wore phones on one wrist, or on both wrists, muted but scintillating with text. Perhaps it was a symbol of social status, a sign that they were continuously monitoring important events elsewhere. It was surely symbolic, because not once did any courtier actually look down at his phone to read the messages and reports blinking there.

The second group were servants including nurses, clerks, footmen, and pretty chambermaids. Their hair was natural hair, and it was worn short. Even the girls had pageboy bobs. Apparently only the superiors had the privilege of wearing the strange-looking silver-white wigs.

Menelaus had once mapped changes in fashion into his divarication function, with the cuts of clothing expressed in the form of bytes of information, and compared to the rate of linguistic or political-economic changes. There were a number of factors controlling the rate of fashion mutation, including things like the volume of money in circulation, the average family income, and the number and death-toll of wars in the interim. Looking over the two groups, he frowned: because a rough calculation implied a century of massive wars and frequent economic depression. His first impression was that a privileged class had emerged, and the glittering aristocrats were dressed to copy the fashion of their space-traveling royalty.

Then he smiled. He realized that the long white wigs were all an impersonation of the way Del Azarchel wore his hair. Since all spacemen shave their skulls bald (or at least to a very tight crew-cut), wearing his hair as long as a woman's must have come as a great comfort and relief to Del Azarchel, a way of letting his shirttails hang out. If the courtiers were bald under those wigs, that might be a sign of something else—maybe a symbol to show that they were ready to return to space at any moment. This hinted that the future might hold an active space program, something Menelaus could not contemplate without a toothy grin of pleasure.

"Fancy digs you got here. Much better than where you came from, seems to me." Menelaus accepted the delicate glass with a grin of thanks. "Only two glasses? What about them?" He gestured at the throng of soldiers and servants. "Ain't they included?"

Del Azarchel looked lost for a moment, as if he did not know to whom Montrose referred, but then his face lit up. "Of course! Thoughtless of me. All of you, drink to the health of Menelaus Montrose, the man closer than a brother to me! Get glasses—Tirado, can you see to it? Captain, perhaps your men can be off-duty only for the moment it takes to drink a toast with me?"

An old Oriental in white (either a doctor or a fencing instructor, to judge by his garments) bent his head and began arguing in whispers with Del Azarchel. Del Azarchel waved the man's objections away. "Please, Doctor! I value your advice more than I treasure the sight of the stars themselves, but surely, surely one small drink will do no harm to such a man as Menelaus Montrose. He is made of rawhide and whalebone, enjoys more lives than a cat, and has a tougher constitution than that of a maddened boar! The brain of an Einstein, of Newton, hides beneath that thick skull. He is harder to kill than a cockroach! A sip of wine will not do him in!"

The old doctor straightened up, a look of skepticism in the arch of his eyebrow. "Just as you say, sir, but it seems your Newton had enough brainpower to scramble his brain like an egg, which we have only now found how to separate white and yolk and put them back into the shell."

Menelaus examined the soldiers as they drank. Comic-Opera Spanish seemed to be in style. Either these were Halloween costumes, or morion-style helmets were back in fashion. The helmets were peaked fore and aft and bore a steel rooster comb aloft. The men looked like Conquistadores: armor, lace collars, puffy sleeves and all.

Their breastplates were a substance Menelaus did not recognize. Metal? Plastic? Something in the way the light glinted into rainbows along the inky plates—he visualized the deviation of photonic through-paths needed to produce those shades, and turned the picture into numbers in his mind, and then into a set of graphs—convinced him that the substance was meant to break up coherent light, and scatter incoming energy-fire.

He ran through an equation or five in his mind to get an upper and lower value for the energy delivery system, given this type of defense. The result surprised him, because such weapons, if they existed, were absurdly wasteful. Of course, just out the window were roofless gardens heated in the midst of a frozen mountainscape. Absurdly wasteful. Menelaus was sure his mother would not have approved. This was a more luxurious time than he was used to, that was sure.

Del Azarchel said with a small laugh, "Did I ever tell you of the time I drank stagnant rainwater from the heel of boot I found in a gutter? I had to drive away the most enormous rat one might envision: large as a house-cat. My only weapon was—"

Montrose laughed. "Yeah, the broken spike from an organlegger's monkey cart, with the snark-juice still inside it, and stinking like hell. But the rat was a different time, remember?"

"Wait? Are you certain? No, my friend, that boot—every time I drink, I think on it—it was when I was in pre-Kali Andalusia. I was twelve. . . ."

He noticed the other people in the chamber, footman and steward and doctor and nurse, the soldiers in Conquistador get-up, all stiffened, and hid looks of surprise. Evidently it was out of style to correct Del Azarchel, even when he made a mistake. Montrose assumed the man was of pretty high rank, however this society measured rank.

"Yup. I know, cause I was there everytime you sat down to drink, and you tell the damn story every time," sighed Montrose. He sat himself down on the big four-poster bed, and the sheets crinkled under his weight. Once again the courtiers in the room were holding their breath, while trying not to stare. Evidently it was also not in style to sit down in Del Azarchel's presence.

He raised the estimate of Del Azarchel's rank. Of course, he had no baseline to plot it against, and no clear way to digitize an abstraction like the degree of deference being shown a boss. Maybe if he used degrees of deviation of the spinal column from upright, he could compare other submission behaviors to that . . .

Montrose (with the mental equivalent of a shrug) decided the styles of this time didn't apply to him. He said, "The big rat—it was smaller last time you told it, only as big as a kitten—you were fighting that big rat over a hambone a drunk Jihadi had dropped. When you got it up to your lips, turned out to be a baby's arm, all fried in grease, on account of the Mogadorians was eating on you Spaniards during the last days of the siege. I heard the yarn. The boot thing was a different time, before when you met that guy that turned your life all right-side out, made you learn how to salute and whatnot, even though you are a whatcha call it, a *pilluelo*, a gutter skunk. What was his name? That guy? 'Trashcan?' Something like that."

"Trajano Villaamil," the older man said, nodding his snowy head. "Ah! Truly a name of glory! Even though his army was nothing but a group of half-starved youths, he made us his true and loyal followers, like knights-errant. Every theft and crime to serve the cause, the poor no more to be preyed upon, the widow to be shown respect, and the media to witness every theft, so the honor, and not just the supplies, of the haughty conqueror would be stolen! Such were the rules he beat into us. Within the confines of the street from the dead Cathedral to the dry Canal, he was king. He was the master of the beggar's quarter, where the patrols dared not go. I would have wished him to see me now, now that I am Master of the World. I never knew him to break his word, not once." Del Azarchel sighed in mingled nostalgia and wonder. "Not once! And to think—it was for his sake that I stayed with you."

"Stayed with me?" Montrose had been sitting in a slouch, but now he straightened up.

"In the darkness, during the hunger watches . . . Ah! The old times are not always the best times, are they? Let us speak of happier things. . . ."

Del Azarchel must have noticed the stiffness with which his servants and retainers were regarding Montrose, for he smiled and asked them to step from the room.

The officer in charge of the Conquistadores gave Montrose a thoughtful look. He turned toward Del Azarchel, who gave the officer a smile. Del Azarchel raised his left wrist, displaying the crudely fashioned red wristband Menelaus had noticed earlier, a wristband not at all in keeping with the fineness of ornament that otherwise adorned the elegant, white-haired figure of Del Azarchel. The officer nodded, saluted sharply, and departed.

That exchange of looks was not lost on Montrose. The captain of the guard had not wanted to leave his boss unarmed in a room with a man whose brain may or may not be fully healthy. The red metal armband Del Azarchel wore was something that reassured the Captain. But what was it?

He looked at the wristband carefully. In his mind's eye, Montrose converted the surface irregularities into a mathematical expression, and calculated the standard deviation. The resulting figures were consistent with something machine-lathed in zero-gee, using old equipment. Not an ornament, then. And not something he trusted any of his men to refashion.

2. Memory Lapse

When all the minions were gone, Del Azarchel had his tall black throne-like chair slide itself closer to Menelaus, and touched wineglasses with him, so that a crystal note hung in the air.

"To old times," said Del Azarchel. "May they never come again . . ."

"Old times past and better times to come!"

"Salud y amor dinero y el y tiempo para disfrutarlo!"

"Kampai, bottoms high, spittle and mud in a blind man's eye!"

"I promised you this drink long ago. You recall? Perhaps—I suppose not. But I was hoping you might recall it. It was not long ago for you, of course. Not long by your biological time."

"Um. Remind me. You and me—we used to sneak off to go drinking in Space Camp."

"This was somewhat after. In the sick bay. Ah. Perhaps we should not speak of it . . ."

"No. Tell me. Maybe something will come back."

"You had attacked yet another crewman, and pulled the catheter of your suit in the fray, so your legs were covered with, ah, recoverable material, and your mouth was full of blood. His blood. No one was willing to sponge you off but me, and I had to brush your teeth. When I told you we would drink once again, once we were aground again, once you were better, you stopped screaming and started giggling, so I thought, you know, that somewhere in your mind, some buried part, you heard me. This is that drink. Am I not a man of my word?"

"Nothing is coming back. Where did this happen? Before launch? Aboard the space station? Aboard the punt?"

"After launch, of course. Aboard the star-vessel. On the *Hermetic.*"

"What the hell do you mean? I was aboard? I was *aboard*?!"

"Of course. What is the last you remember?"

"Aboard the punt. I jammed the needle in my brain."

Del Azarchel seemed taken aback. "Ah! That is—ah. Unexpected." Then, to himself, he muttered, "I will have to take this up with my better half." And he ran the fingers of his right hand across the metallic face of the massy red-gold armband clasping his left wrist.

The surface was clearly touch-sensitive or motion-aware, like library cloth. Since before Montrose was born, all telephones, visuals, games, texts, audios, and control surfaces could be built into any tool or article of clothing, practically any object, that need or whim dictated: but only weapons, or medical appliances were built with their screens and virtual keypads invisible to non-users. Montrose guessed the armband would ignore any finger but Del Azarchel's.

Montrose said, "I figured you returned me to Earth and sailed without me? Didn't you?"

"Oh, Cowhand, you still make me to laugh! Come! Did you actually think I had the fuel and time to decelerate the punt to rest relative to Earth, recelerate back, screw-turn and decelerate, reach Earth at her new point in her orbit, take the time to refuel, launch again from yet another point farther along Earth's orbit, accelerate toward a farther downrange halfway point, and decelerate to a rendezvous even farther yet downrange— and all this while the *Hermetic* was adding velocity geometrically? Of course I took you aboard. At that time, we were merely waiting for your drug to wear off. It was not until Dr. Yajnavalkya examined you—you remember him?"

"The expedition surgeon. Also, he did work in the Hodge Conjecture." He remembered the fellow's work, his discussions. The theorem named after Yajnavalkya proved that topological spaces defined by the human brain cell interaction nets were actually rational linear combinations of algebraic cycles. Montrose did not actually remember any details about the man himself.

"Not until he examined you did anyone realize the extent of the modification, and even then no one was perfectly certain what you had done, since you invented the technique yourself, and did not keep notes like a professional scientist, you fool."

"But I told you what I was up to before I did it."

"Yes—a few cryptic words no one could recall clearly."

"Didn't you play back the cabin record . . . ?—Oh."

"Aptly put! 'Oh' indeed. My friend had asked me to shut off the cabin recording circuit before he stabbed himself, remember?"

"What was wrong with me?"

"Divarication."

Montrose looked a little sick, but said nothing.

3. Divarication

Every information function in the universe suffered from what was called divarication. Fact became legend as it was passed from generation to generation; bureaucracies grew ossified as their rules evolved to be self-serving; and even computer programs or nerve cells passing information to the next generation of nerve cells lost information, modifying it by a self-selection process into forms easier to pass along. Lines of data diverged, became unrecognizable to each other. Even processes like check-digits and data insulation suffered their own form of degradation. Entropy always took its tithe.

Divarication in neural processes meant thought lost ability to be preserved. Senility, Alzheimer's disease, and autism were manifestations of what could be described, mathematically, as a one function describing signal degradation.

"I was trying to increase my brain processing speed."

"You did. But you increased the speed of brain degradation even faster."

"Pox! Was it a self-destructive feedback cascade?"

"The opposite. You over-corrected. It was a self-reinforcing feedback."

"What was the tau parameter?"

"The tau approached unity: You were in a mental stasis. As best we could tell," said Del Azarchel, "the medulla oblongata was affected. The part of your brain that prioritizes brain attention flows placed your own self-awareness at a level below what was needed to maintain the holographic illusion of self-awareness. You forgot yourself so completely that there was no way to wake you to your own awareness again. While you forgot yourself, your brainpaths entered a logic loop."

"But I built in a self-correction cycle, or tried to."

"You had artificially sculpted out new nerve-paths, new engrams, not one created by your own information-flow patterns, but adapted to the mathematical flow model your Zurich computer run had formulated. That pattern was . . . alive. Self-correcting. Your epiphytes re-established any nerve-paths Dr. Yajnavalkya interrupted when he operated, or constructed new pathways around any block he established." Del Azarchel shrugged, spread his hands. "He could not figure out what you had done: We transmitted medical records back to Earth, but the doctors and specialists there did not have you ready at hand to examine."

"Damn. I'd like to see the records."

"I will send them to your amulet as soon as you get one. In the meanwhile, let me sum them up: Our best guess is that your new brain thought its new format was proper and healthy, and every time you slept, your delta-wave sleep would put you back to your damaged brain-arrangement again. How did you do it?"

"Not sure. The RNA correction template, ah—that was one of the things I copied straight out of the Monument Math."

"Copying something you did not actually know what it meant or how it worked?"

"Well, I figured it was worth the risk."

Del Azarchel snorted, then chortled, then laughed aloud. "A breath of springtime air from a long-vanished world! Now I recall my wild youth, and why I liked you. By the devil, you are rash as a corsair! Are you sure you have no Spanish blood in you?"

"How did you fix me?"

"With very special help. That main, ah, *expert*, I called into to handle your case, she happens to be molecular neurosurgeon of remarkable skill, as skilled as she is with that as with everything she undertakes."

"But you know what she did?"

"The same thing Dr. Yajnavalkya tried, putting up nerve blocks to hinder the extra brain tissue you grew in yourself, but without stopping the essential functions the new tissue usurped. We have divined enough of the pattern, the algorithm, of what you did with your Zurich computer runs, to set up a block that will last."

"But how do I make it work?"

Del Azarchel looked puzzled. "Make what work? The cure is permanent."

"Make the cocktail work! I want the experiment to work. It might seem like years ago to you, but to me, I was just now in the middle of the test. Do you have a way to augment my intelligence without the side-effect of wiping out my self-awareness? Why are you grinning?"

"Because I had forgotten what you are like. Because I believe the answer to your brain augmentation theory is in the Monument. And I believe the answer to how to read the Monument correctly is in your brain! You might not remember, but when we reached our destination, we brought you out of suspension. We managed to, ah, wrestle you into your suit. When we took you to the surface, you had a reaction to it . . ."

"Reaction?"

"You calmed down. You were drawn to certain parts of the Beta and Omicron groups from the first radial area. You seemed happy—even awed. Like a child again. We thought maybe you would return to yourself. I hoped . . . well . . ."

"I remember that! The horizon was right close, like a stone's throw away, and I could see Dr. Velasquez and Dr. Ramananda standing off a ways. Their feet were below the horizon, and their heads were pointing away from me, so they seemed to be leaning backward. The surface was like black glass. And I saw a dim bright star overhead. And it was too late . . . for something . . . I was afraid . . . afraid not for myself, but . . ." His voice trailed off.

Del Azarchel was staring at him carefully. In a neutral voice he said, "Do you remember anything else? Who you feared?"

Montrose shook his head. "Catching fog in a pail. I can't bring it back. I really buggered up my brain something awful, didn't I?"

"The basic theory was sound."

"So I flew to the damn Diamond Star." Montrose spoke in a tone of awe. "I was there. I was *there*! I flew all the way there and don't remember a damned thing about the damned voyage!"

"Well, to be fair, there was not much to remember, not for you. When you were not tied up, we kept you in cryonic biosuspension. We feared further nerve degeneration. And as for what you forget: well, to call it 'damned' is not so wrong-tongued a word to use."

Montrose shook his head, and his face was haggard with misery. All the work on the Monument had gone on without him. He was the kid who missed Christmas. Everyone else got a present.

"Years. Decades. Half a century there and half a century back again," he muttered. "I slept—I slept through it—"

"And you are still young!"

4. Sadder Things of Long Ago

"Well, where is everyone else? Where is Ramayana, Bhuti, or that jackass Narcís? Where is the Captain? I want to see Captain Grimaldi."

"She is in transit."

"She? She who?"

"Ha! Sorry, my friend. Forgive a slip of an old man's tongue. Captain Grimaldi is no longer with us. He did not return from the Diamond Star. The expedition ended in disaster, in tragedy. More than half the crew perished."

Montrose turned his face away. On the walls he saw images of cities and ships burning. He should have known. Grimaldi had been a Brahmin, and practiced *ahimsa,* sacred respect for all life. He would not have opened fire on his fellow human beings, not even to stop a war, or bring peace to the world. Grimaldi could not have been in command of the ship shown in these pictures.

Montrose had a strange, dreamlike sensation, as if he had touched a corpse, but only now remembered the feel of the cold flesh against his hand. As if the corpse had rotated in zero gee, and he saw dead eyes staring blindly, wall-eyed, at nothing, the dry mouth hanging open, the motionless and shriveled tongue like a worm. The sensation made Montrose's eyes sting, and he raised his arm to wipe tears against the back of his hand, at which he stared in surprise.

"The Captain is dead? How did he die?"

Del Azarchel leaned forward and touched his arm. "He was like a second father to you, was he not?"

"My life weren't nowise hard as yours, Blackie, but life didn't kiss my rump much neither, if you take my meaning. Grimaldi crow-barred me out of a pretty tight spot, and . . ." Montrose suddenly could see in his mind's eye the barrel of the pistol of the last man he'd ever faced. What was his name? Mike Nails. He'd lost almost a year to hospital-induced slumber that time. Montrose had been slow on the trigger then, because he wanted to delope and walk away. Because he'd lost his nerve. ". . . and, by the Plague, I am sure to have died and been planted in the ground had Grimaldi not given me a new deal from a fresh deck. So I owe him everything."

"We will have time later to speak of the sadder things of long ago."

"It's not long ago to me!"

"The Captain, he did not perish in a praiseworthy fashion. I did not wish to mar his memory by telling tales."

"I got a right to know!"

Del Azarchel smiled and leaned back. "Why this talk of rights? What you ask of me is yours. We never would have made it to the Diamond Star had you not solved the difficulties surrounding neuro-memory Divarication in long-term suspension. All of us are in your debt."

"All of us? Which us?"

"The Hermeticists. The crew."

"Who made it back?"

"There are only seventy-two of us left."

Montrose was silent, shocked. Two-thirds of the expedition had perished.

Del Azarchel said, "We did not return to our old homes and our old nations when we returned, for all those things were gone, or changed beyond recognition into crooked mockeries of what we knew." He gave a moue of distaste. "I will not disgust you by repeating the conditions of Spain. She was not my country any longer; those occupying her were not my countrymen. The officers and crew of the *Hermetic*, the greatest ship ever aloft, they were my countrymen! The stars were my nation! We are the Conclave of the Learned, but we should be called the Brotherhood of Man, for we are loyal to no country, no tribe, no sect, no faction. We are the Men of the Mind, serving only the abstract ideals of the pure reason, and devoted to nothing less than the entirety of the human race."

This reminded Montrose so strongly of the make-believe Science Councils that peopled the cartoons he read in his youth, and ruled the make-believe future world, that at first he grinned. Maybe it was high time experts, folk who knew what to do, were telling people what to do, rather than folk lucky enough to be born rich enough to buy, photogenic enough to win, or crooked enough to steal a bag of votes?

But a frown drew his eyebrows together even before the grin left his mouth. No self-respecting Texas mob would let anyone tell them what to do, and that went double for experts, and twice double for some high-pockets breed of anyone that couldn't be voted out of office when he got caught.

"Sounds like all-you-all is running the show. I ain't sure what to make of that."

"Not all *you*. All *we*. You are of our number. You may make of it anything you wish! Did I not say this future was ours, our own?"

"And you? You look like you ain't done so badly for yourself. What's your part?"

"My official title is Nobilissimus 'the most distinguished,' but my roles include various presidencies, tribunates, and ministerial positions awarded by certain electors from Concordat members that still maintain democratic forms, and titles of royalty granted when I became regent for those ruling royal families from members that do not. Privately, I am the owner-in-chief of the World Power Corporation, a cartel that controls how and where the antimatter we brought back from the Diamond Star is employed—my private position gives me much more influence over world affairs than my public, which is occupied by a nonsensical amount of ceremony. But between us, my only title is *Senior.*"

Montrose realized he had not said "Señor," the Spanish honorific—but "Senior," the name of the Expedition member in charge of coordinating extra-vehicular teams: the chief of the landing party.

Montrose looked toward the window, and saw the snowy peaks and clefts rearing above ruins. Night was falling, and soft yellow lights now dotted the sheer walls of the far craters. Other lights gleamed on glass-roofed gardens like emeralds or glanced dancing through waterfalls like threads, the polished silver dashing into the crater depths, making them shimmer with rainbows in the gathering gloom. He wondered if that was another set of mansions, or part of this one.

The spread was bigger than most towns he'd been in.

"How much is yours?"

"All of it."

"What, the castle, the crater, the mountain range?"

"Everything on the globe. Everything under the sky. I am the *Imperator Mundi,* the Master of the World."

He smiled and there was a glitter in his eye.

"I am master not just of Earth, but of the destiny of Earth. Not just these lands surrounding, but the years and centuries to come, I can shape. We will share the glories of royalty and the luxuries of wealth, you with me. Let us command the future to be a golden one, and to bring forth everything we have dreamed!"

6

Intellect Emulation Mechanism

1. A Golden Future

"So. You're Master of the World. Sounds mighty nice. But . . . Only one?"

Del Azarchel blinked. "How many do you prefer?"

"How many can I get? What do we have by way of colonies on the Moon yet?"

"Nothing."

"Damnation and pustules! Sounds like you're marching slipshod. Colonized Mars?"

"It's colder than Antarctica, the oxygen is locked into surface rust, and the microatmosphere is only thick enough to carry hypersonic sandstorms able to disintegrate the metal hull of any lander unfortunate enough to survive hard-down. So, no, I am not the Lord of Mars or the Moon."

"No Mars bases! Prickly hat of Jesus! What kind of crappy future is this?"

Del Azarchel smiled an urbane smile. "One that avoided global holocaust, despite the weapons of absolute war in our arsenals."

Montrose plopped himself down on the bed, slouching, his eyes glittering with a weird mix of disappointment, puzzlement, and wonder.

"You see," he said finally, "I dreamed about Mars when I was young. That was one of the things I dreamed about. Also, I wanted a car that flew. Rocketpack. Raygun."

"What have we not dreamt, we dreamers? We dreamt of power, energy in abundance to accommodate our dreams; we dreamt of expanded consciousness, intelligence augmentation, nerve regeneration, organ rejuvenation, and artificial life, extended life, intensified life! We dreamt of minds created according to design, techniques to cure insanity and sin, sciences to create new forms of life, beasts and birds to be our serfs and playthings and companions, and then to work the great work of creation! To make the Man beyond Man, the next step of evolution, as far above us as we above the ape. And even this would be merely the first step in the cosmic dance!"

Montrose gave him a hard look. "You ain't translated the Monument yet, have you?"

"Not so! We translated the whole of the Alpha Segment."

"That all?" The Alpha Segment was less than one percent of the surface area. "It's been, what, a century? Almost two? I was thinking maybe y'all got up through the Beta, Gamma, and Delta segments, and maybe part of Eta?"

Del Azarchel looked surprised. "How the devil did you—that is a good guess. Really good. We have made major inroads into just those segments, and nowhere else."

"Don't look so impressed. This room: I don't see any force fields in the lamp or tractor-presser beams shooting out the sink or anything other gee-whiz-wow-wonder gizmos that I should see, if Earth science had a working unified field theory. Pictures here on the walls show wars on Earth and wars in space, but I don't see anything that looks like a fundamentally new weapon system—the kind of new that comes from a new model of the universe. The Beta Segment of Monument symbols we knew were a particle menagerie and periodical table, and Gamma Segment was pretty sure to be the linguistic calculus, and I know that part contained the key to translating the higher sections. Eta Segment—you all mocked me when I said it, but Eta looked to me like game theory, perhaps an introduction into something more basic, like a really rigorous mathematical analysis of economics and politics. If you actually have the Earth under one rule these days, you must know a damn sight more about political economy than anyone of my generation. But you don't seem to have more physics. So—No great guess involved."

He shrugged, then continued: "The Monument Builders were trying to tell us all the secrets of the universe just because science is the universal language. No way else you prove to a stranger from a strange world you are intelligent, I reckon—But we didn't get all the secrets they wrote down: 'cause, where are your flying cars, Blackie? If you had translated the Monument, a good big chunk of it, I mean, surely we'd have working antigravity by now, and a castle floating in the clouds, up on high, just where God and storybook illustrators always meant castles to be."

"Well, parts of the Monument have been translated," said Del Azarchel, "including enough of a not-quite Unified Field Theorem from the Beta Segment to know that antigravity cannot operate in a universe as curved as ours is curved, not over anything less than intergalactic distances and aeons of time. And as you deduced, the symbols contained in Gamma Segment include a system for quantifying concepts into a grammar of formal signs: a complete set, and self-defining. It was the very thing Goedel long ago proved could not be done—or thought he did."

"That's all?"

"All?" Del Azarchel seemed taken aback. "It was so *revolutionary* that radio messages from Earth accused us of fraud! No expert believed it! This notation is the Philosophical Language, a universal grammar, that Leibniz and others so long ago for so long sought. In theory, any language system, any method of encoding meaning, speech, or writing, or flashes of a heliograph, any method, including human brainwaves or genetically determined behaviors, can be translated into any other! In theory, a complex enough expression could encompass all the variables of human society."

"But the Monument did not contain an instruction book on how to build a faster-than-light drive?"

Del Azarchel looked impatient. "Oh, yes, we have all that. But it requires a blue fairy riding the back of a unicorn on the thirty-first day of February to make it work."

"Oh, Goedel is wrong, but Einstein is gospel! And you're poking fun of me for that. What about the aliens? Did the Monument give us a map, tell us where they hail from? Any contact with them yet? We sell them Manhattan Island for twenty-four dollars or anything? Can I see one?"

"If you live long enough."

"What's that mean?"

"The Monument provided us a clue. Astronomers studying the open cluster in Hyades, a mere one hundred fifty lightyears away, hypothesize that the high helium-carbon content of those stars is due to large-scale engineering, not to natural effects. Macroscale engineering. There may be an intelligence of some description within hailing distance. Well, that is to say, the descendants ten generations after the present generation would hear the response to a hail we send out."

"Three hundred years between call and reply, huh?"

"Plus turnaround time, yes. Time to make the decision to respond, gather the money, gather the will."

"You reckon they have money?"

"They must have some means of economizing their expenditures. No matter what system of prioritizing benefits and expenses they use, sending a coherent beam of radio across one hundred fifty lightyears costs energy."

The magnitude of time made the idea of contact absurd: as if Queen Victoria might hear the replies to messages sent out by Queen Elizabeth.

"This Hyades Cluster: they the ones who built the Monument?"

"Unknown. At the moment we don't know if 'they' are really there."

"So no voluptuous green-skinned spacewomen in silvery space-bikinis?" Montrose was thinking wryly that his childhood comics had been wrong about everything.

Del Azarchel looked amused. He said, "In that respect, the world is much as you left it. But in others, ah! You are wrong, I tell you, to mock this era. You have much to see! We may not have flying cars, but we have built an evacuated underground rail system which follows hypoclyoid curves deep through the molten mantle of Earth, allowing us to fling bullet-carriages, accelerated by induction coil guns, from continent to continent faster than even military jets can fly. It is amazing the public works projects one can perform if your energy budget is practically unlimited. We have melted Antarctic ice, opening vast tracts on that continent to cultivation, and used the water to turn the Gobi Desert green, and clothe the interior of Australia with fruit trees. Mega-evaporation, moving moisture, moving clouds, gathering sunlight, deflecting sunlight: everything that is technically possible is now technically feasible, because we have power enough."

"Energy power or political power?"

"Both! We want for nothing. And, yes, the Hermetic Conclave has some advantages that previous rulers never enjoyed, thanks to the study of the Eta Segment, it is true. We can calculate some social trends to a nicety. The science is called Cliometry. You deserve credit for that. Not to mention that the Princess seems to have an analytical method, or a divine gift . . . well, no matter. The power is in our palm. The treasure trove is ours. You have the key. We need but turn the lock and listen as it all clicks into place."

"What clicks into place?"

"The future! Don't you recall what we stayed up all night discussing, that last night on Earth, before the liftoff? It has been years of time for me, and I recall it. It has been days only for you. Have you forgotten?"

"Talked about girls, as I recollect. All the pretty girls you knew were going to be long dead while we slumbered. You had quite the list, Blackie. We talked about leaving Earth forever . . ."

"And about returning in triumph with the lore of the universe! We talked of the future!"

"So why haven't y'all translated more of the Monument while I was out?"

"Because the Monument was not meant for us. Man is a microscopic biological infestation clinging to the dry surface irregularities of the crust-folds of one small iron-cored rocky planet circling a medium-sized yellow star in the outskirts of the galaxy. We are like simple-minded monkeys who found an encyclopedia one savant wrote down for another. It was meant to be read by something far more intelligent than man."

"You must have them by now."

"Who?"

"Posthumans. Augmented Intellects. Odd Johns. Nexts. People who did right what I did wrong to my brain. What research in intelligence augmentation was done while I was in cold storage?"

"Almost none."

Montrose could not express his disgust: He merely made a noise half-way between a groan and the noise you make to clear your throat before you spit.

Del Azarchel spread his hands. "Experimentation on human subjects was illegal in the year we sailed, remember? And your example discouraged further investigation."

"Example? One hundred and fifty years! In that amount of time, we went from Ben Franklin pulling electricity down from the sky, to the Wright Brothers putting a man up into it! You are telling me one bad experiment set back the whole globe for two centuries? I don't believe it!"

"Ah, but the New World between the day of Benjamin Franklin and the day of the Brothers Wright suffered no tyrannies, plagues, or famines, and their small wars were fought only with gunpowder, not lingering germs. Anglo-American laws and customs were especially friendly to innovators and inventors. Whereas Earth, while we were gone, was not so friendly. First it was overpopulated, and then it was underpopulated, ruled alternately by Xi Mandarins from the Peking, or by Bio-Warlords from Pretoria."

Montrose followed his gaze to where Del Azarchel was staring thoughtfully at a painting of skeletal buildings toppling in the red shadows of a mushroom cloud.

"Well," he muttered, "they should have been following up on my work, instead of messing around."

"Now we can set things right."

"*We*, meaning the human race?"

"*We*, meaning you and I. Your method, your Prometheus Formula, is the only technique, even after a century, that shows promise of evolving us to the intellectual plateau needed to unriddle the Monument. But your method proved too dangerous to use on a live human subject—ah! But what about a ghost? An iron ghost? What about a marriage of my methods and yours?"

Montrose recalled that his work in ultra-long-term neurohibernation had won him a berth aboard the starship. But Del Azarchel's work had been just as crucial: The ship's brain had been based on Del Azarchel's work in Automated Intelligence. At the time, there had been powerful political factions who had not wanted the Spaniard or the Texan aboard. They were the wrong kind of people; it sent the wrong kind of message. They were troublemakers. But Captain Grimaldi, a prince in more ways than one, had pulled them aboard. There were some natural overlaps to the two fields, but how did they apply here?

"I don't get it," said Montrose. "What are you driving at?"

But the excitement of Del Azarchel's words, the enthusiasm blazing in his eyes, was contagious. Montrose jumped to his feet and began pacing up and down the thick, richly-patterned carpet as if from an excess of energy.

"Just this!" Del Azarchel's voice rang out. "We are about to create our future, the one mankind has more than deserved."

"What'ch'ya got in mind?"

"Are you feeling healthy enough to take a short trip around the globe? Or, rather, under it? I have a project I have been working on, and out of the whole human race, out of the last fifteen decades of history, you are the only one qualified to help me. Forgive my impatience, but I have been waiting years, biological time, and over a century, calendar time, to show this to you. I call it The X Machine."

"Which is what, exactly?"

"The key to flinging aside the chains of that prisonhouse called being merely human. The key to the gates opening into . . . *beyond*!"

Menelaus Montrose felt a sense of restlessness. The chamber suddenly seemed too small, and the world beyond these walls full of mysteries and wonders. "I reckon I equal up to anything. Show me this *beyond* of yours. But get me the hell something to wear besides a bathrobe, cant'ch'ya?"

2. Xypotechnology

A man and two boys—wardrobe master, valet, body servant—came in the chamber to help him dress, but Montrose kicked up a row, and the trio retreated in disorder, bowing and kowtowing. Montrose was almost sorry he had kicked them out, because now he had to puzzle out the garments for himself, and they seemed to have no buttons or zippers.

The clothes laid out for him were more comfortable than what he'd seen the shiny courtiers wearing: a white tunic with a black kimono-like overgarment, loose hakama-style pants beneath. The only foolery was the red and white sashes: one around his waist and the other running from shoulder to hip. He left them off.

While he dressed, Del Azarchel started to describe the political and economic setup of the new world to him, but Montrose interrupted and asked about the Monument translation efforts. The amount of surface area which had yielded to human investigation was disappointingly small, but still larger than it had been when Montrose slumbered: Montrose whooped whenever some pet theory of his own had been vindicated, and groaned at himself for his muleheadedness for the conclusions he had overlooked or gotten wrong.

He looked around for paper to jot down figures, but Del Azarchel, with a gesture like a magician, made the windows leading to the balcony darken. The glass was smart material, and could detect the motions of Montrose's fingernail, or interpret simple words spoken slowly. The two men covered the glass doors with minuscule mathematical notation as they talked, Montrose jumping from one side of the doors to the other, scribbling furiously while he spoke, Del Azarchel, seated in his wheelchair, merely making small gestures with a forefinger, as if to command invisible chalk to script his writing for him.

Del Azarchel spoke of the recent mathematical attempts to model the human brain down to a quantum granular level.

"Come on, Blackie," replied Montrose. "Don't kid a kidder. That's my field. The Montrose Neuro-cellular Divarication function established a means of modeling human brain information behavior. . . . I had to solve how the nervous system worked, at least on a crude level, to get it to keep working when it was in suspended animation. . . . But you cannot model it below that . . ."

"Not with human math, no. But applying expressions from the Eta Segment to a cellular automata model allows us to use Morse Theory to approximate the quantum uncertainties we associate with free will."

He paused for a moment to let that sink in.

Del Azarchel said, "The X Machine is a self-reprogramming, self-evolving machine. A machine not just like the Mälzels and automated intellectual processors as the ship's brain aboard the *Croesus*, or the Little Big Brother security brains we have aboard the *Hermetic*."

"I don't recollect Little Big Brother able to do anything approaching human creative thinking."

"We improved them during the trip. We call it Ratiotech—thinking machines. By the time of the Space War, the Ratiotech-type electronic brains could perform deductions, and even, through large-scale trial and error, make a fair copy of inductive and value-judgment thinking. That second step was called Sapientech: judgment engines. But they were sleep-walker brains, merely machines, despite all their raw power. But we are on the brink of a true breakthrough. History will turn a corner. We are working on a version of a truly awake, truly self-aware, truly alive, artificial intellectual creature: a Xypotech, a machine that is awake."

3. Spagyric Garden

Del Azarchel called his entourage. There they were again: Conquistadores in armor, footmen in dark coats, long-wigged courtiers in shining silk jackets, and of course, the doctor in white. Apparently in the future it took a score of men to walk down a hallway.

It was a magnificent hallway. They walked or rolled past endless lines of ornate doors, rose-abundant vases, strange statues made of liquid light. Montrose noticed how many mirrors and archways and trompe l'oeil illusions adorned the hall, which was wider than the nave of a cathedral. The architecture and décor fooled the eye to make it seem all the larger.

They walked down steps of marble and through doors of crystal into an indoor garden whose far walls held convincing green hills, and the dome was painted in an eye-deceiving illusion of early twilight skies: a western sky tainted red by hidden lanterns, with Venus bright and low, and the eastern sky twinkling with diamonds in the constellations of early stars. The clouds above looked real: Montrose could not tell if they were painted or projections or real wisps of dry ice fog blown in for the occasion. He wondered if all those years in cramped quarters aboard the *Hermetic* had given Del Azarchel a hunger for open spaces.

The high dome painting was embellished with one long-tailed star brighter than the rest, flying on silvery wings, like a sword hanging over the world. The *Hermetic*.

The garden was bright with things he did not recognize: purple flowers with black centers, and tiger-striped orchids, and a red flower that looked like lace, draped like long tattered strands of some defeated but minia-ture army. Here was a bush with leaves so white they seemed like mirrors; there an organism he did not recognize at all: something was a set of funnels like trumpets made of what looked like green glass. And mingled among them were what seemed to be large-scale versions of microscopic organisms: things like translucent whips, puffballs of purple dotted with tawny spots, mushrooms as brightly colored as the skins of poisonous frogs.

Del Azarchel's chair seemed able to glide across the grassy lawn with no difficulty. He made an expansive gesture. "Our grove of wonders. We use it for spagyrics, fermentation of neuro-active chemicals, or the extraction of rare compounds or ores from the ashes of plants whose roots gather trace elements from the soil. Mostly we train the fungus to grow a particular type of submicroscopic superconductive strand we use in our Xypotech circuits, strands not available anywhere else. It seems living things can spin to a finer set of specifications than any machine shop."

"Its underground. You have to pipe in sunlight."

"We can control cross-pollination. And, no we do not want any of these spores or experiments to fall into the hands of a well-equipped modern university, or else they would be able to reverse-engineer the mathematical model we used for our gene coding, and any fairly bright grad student might be able to figure out what we mean to do."

Montrose gave him a hard look. "Most scientists are eager to share their results. What do you mean to do?"

"Change fate," said Del Azarchel with a sad and thoughtful smile.

"Fate? I never heard of such a beastie," said Montrose. "Fate don't grow in Texas, so there we make our own."

"Since you do not know what a cruel beast it is, I must pause to show you," and he turned aside, and glided down a short, crooked path to where a ring of cypress trees stood solemnly.

There were slabs of marble and figurines of angels set among the flow-erbeds or beneath the shades of potted weeping willows. The figures were equestrian statues.

Montrose suddenly halted. "Are we in a graveyard, Blackie?" He looked down, feet tingling, and wondered on what or whom he was stepping. Not far from his toes were stones. They were headstones.

ECLIPSE 2369-2399
HAVANA 2372-2395
DIOMED 2366-2385
SARK 2361-2383
BYERLEY'S GREEK 2360-2379
AGNER 2360-2386

"So people here in the future don't live past thirty?" said Menelaus. "Also, y'all got some funny names."

"This is a pet cemetery." Del Azarchel was trying not to peer into the face of Menelaus, evidently unable to discern whether the other man was kidding him. "You stand above the bones of some of my best beloved quarterhorses. The next row over holds two of my jockeys, who asked to be buried alongside."

"Hope they died first. If not, that'd take the sport a bit far, but I can't say as I blame 'em. I had a three-year-old named Bothersome once."

"Hm. That is rather young for a jockey; but toddlers are light in the saddle, I grant you."

Del Azarchel said this so smoothly, that now it was Montrose's turn to peer.

"So what is with the bronze ape, Blackie?"

Surrounded by a circle of ferns was a statue of a great ape. The creature was in a posture of sorrow, one clumsy hand raised up as if to beg. The other clutched a talking-plate of the type used by the deaf and dumb. The eyes were mournful, looking upward, vacant.

"That is a monument to Baker's Dozen, the thirteenth and last in a series of Great Apes at Oxford, who learned to speak using the somatic pattern method. She was only about as intelligent as a three-year-old—a dull three-year-old at that—and spent her last days in a quarantine hospital, playing with toys and trying not complain or cry. They did not have the heart, the two scientists who raised her, to tell her she was dying."

"Cassimere and Morrow. We studied their work extensively, since they are the only people ever ('sides us, natch!) to try to map human symbols to a nonhuman mind."

"She was the last of her species. Dozen the Ape died of the Juedenvirus the very same day I was born. She has always haunted me. Had it not been for the war—who knows? Man might not be alone. What might your drug have done for them? There could have been a second human race, younger brothers, to work alongside us."

The bronze face was frozen in a look of almost human suffering, tragic, dignified, silent, futile. "Quite an imagination, whoever made this. Almost looks sad."

"The sculptor worked from photographic models. That face, that poor subhuman face, wears the expression of those who, unlike you, meet fate, and cannot master it."

"Why this statue next to your horse boneyard?"

"For contrast. Ah! I keep her here, my iron ape, to remind me how life works."

"Oh? And how is that?"

"Life cares nothing for justice. The Great Apes were a more evolved form of life, more intelligent, more adaptable, more like us. Stupid beasts, horses, easily spooked, and without enough sense to come in out of a cold rain. Yet why are they alive, whereas the apes died?"

"The Jihad Plague was easier to cure in horses than in apes." Menelaus shrugged. "Or 'swhat I heard, anyway."

"No. The answer was that the stupider creatures were more valuable to men, their masters, and we spent more time, effort, energy, and attention to save them. It was in our self-interest, since, during those years, everyone in South America and Africa was turning from petrol-based back to horse-based transport. The horse was more useful."

4. Brachistochrone Curve

By that point they had left the garden behind. When Menelaus realized they were headed toward one of those buried vacuum-pipeline magnetic-levitation train stations Del Azarchel had boasted of, he expected to see some stainless-steel platform, zooming cars shaped like pneumatic cylinders, or to hear the humming of vast solenoids.

Instead, they merely entered a chamber that looked, at first glance, like any other, windowless, but adorned with the flowers and ferns spacemen have always loved. Here were shelves of old-fashioned leather-bound books, and there was a chessboard. Perhaps it was a library. Then he noticed that all the chairs in the room were padded and could swivel to face the same direction. He glanced back at the door: or rather, doors. He had been fooled because they folded into the walls, but he could see the inner threshold did not quite touch the outer. This chamber was nested inside some sort of shell, and presumably the long axis of the chamber pointed in the direction of motion. Library? A private depthtrain car, with material to read during longer trips.

He seated himself in one of the comfortable chairs while a wine steward passed out wine. A young food taster in a blue skirt and white apron sipped it before passing it to him, and Menelaus scowled at the girl, wondering if she'd brushed her teeth. A medical readout on her apron monitored blood chemistry and nerve conditions. "Couldn't you get a guinea pig or a chemistry set to take your job?"

He was sorry he said anything, because, during the moment while he spoke, and before Menelaus could raise the drink to his lips, the sawbones, that Oriental doctor in white, had snatched the drink out of his reach, and gave him a cold and unsmiling nod.

Menelaus leaned forward. "Blackie, can you send these guys out?"

Del Azarchel made the slightest of nods, and the crowd of the entourage, without any further words, made their elaborate bows and backed out or marched out of the chamber.

Montrose snatched the wineglass back out of the doctor's hand as the man was bowing out. He favored the other with a wink and a grin as the doors slid shut between them. Then he tossed down the drink without tasting it: a waste of fine wine, to be sure, but he needed the fortitude.

Del Azarchel was smiling his dazzling smile, and had one eyebrow raised, as if on the edge of asking a question.

Montrose spoke first. "What happened to Grimaldi?"

Del Azarchel's face fell. "Ah. Prince Ranier suffered terribly from the confinement, the loneliness of space, and the frustration, the maddening, eternal puzzle of the Monument. The sense that there were infinite secrets just beyond his grasp, written in a code the human brain was not well formed enough to understand—the sheer frustration was like a miserly debtor, and exacted its levy with interest."

"You saying he went nuts? Pestilence! I don't believe you. He was more stable than you. Or me."

Del Azarchel said, "I am not a psychiatrist: I only know the strain and pressure were terrible. His judgment was affected. Captain Grimaldi came to increasingly strange and outlandish conclusions about the Diamond Star, and the Monument, and what the signs and symbols meant. He was trying to see the patterns in it, you see, all the crooked alien hieroglyphs, all the rippling, eye-confounding cursives. Who knows what he saw? When the Conclave judged him unfit for command, he refused to step down. We were not a military expedition. Didn't we have the right to vote on it?"

"Actually, no. If I recall the governing Articles aright, the Conclave can't do more than advise him to step down. It cannot force him. Only the ship's doctor, for medical grounds, had the right."

Del Azarchel waved his hand as if to brush away Montrose's comment like so much smoke. "These events, to me, are long past, and I am not a lawyer. You will forgive me if I skip certain details. Even after so many years, the memory is nightmarish to me. I am not proud of what happened."

Montrose was aghast. "Not proud! I 'spect not! You were supposed to *obey* the Captain, even if he ordered you to die."

Del Azarchel spoke softly, reluctantly. "He did."

"He did what?"

"He ordered our deaths."

"Pox on that! Not Grimaldi, he was not like that kind of man!"

"Years and decades fled while you slumbered. You know nothing of what he was like."

"I know Grimaldi was the finest officer alive."

"So I knew as well, for so he was—when you knew him. Those days were past. I told you, he was under pressure. It affected his judgment."

"Insane? The ship's doctor could have made a ruling."

"Dr. Yajnavalkya was a malnutrition victim. During the hunger watches. The quarter-rations could not sustain him, not at his age. I do not say the Captain went mad. But he did order us to halt the star lifting."

"What? But that means—"

He saw from the look in Del Azarchel's eyes that there was no need to finish the sentence. They both knew the facts.

There was no return trip without the antimatter to use as fuel. The whole expedition plan turned on the idea that the robotic mining ship *Croesus* could power a braking laser to stop the incoming *Hermetic,* and power up that laser to accelerate her to interstellar velocities again.

Space near the Diamond Star had been swept clear of normal matter, of course. There was one superjovian in a far orbit, farther from V 886 Centauri than Pluto was from Sol, a terrene-matter body called Thrymheim. That was all. There was nothing else in the system. No uranium-bearing asteroids. Nothing for the *Croesus* to use as a power source for the launching laser to propel the *Hermetic* on her silvery sails back across the widest abyss—over a light-century—mankind had ever crossed.

And even that would not have been enough. The expedition plan included making up the marginal loss in sailing efficiency with onboard fuel: The dangerous contraterrene was to be carried in a double-zoned magnetic "nozzle" generated well to the aft of the hull, and bombarded with pellets to produce reaction thrust.

Del Azarchel shook his head, this time with wonder and sorrow. "Had we obeyed, the whole expedition, all for which we had sacrificed, would have been for naught. Without the antimatter, we could not even have powered the radio-laser to narrowcast our findings back to Earth, and so no history would remain to tell of us, or what had become of us. Without the antimatter, without the promise that we were carrying antimatter, the ungrateful generation that ruled the strange Earth to which we had returned would not have been convinced to shoulder the expense of orbiting a braking laser of their own. The Golden Age we ushered in, a time of unimaginable plenty, wealth, and abundant energy, all would have been stillborn. The tribes and nations of the world would still be consuming each other in wars: instead, at long last, at long and long last indeed, the universal dream of man has come to fruition, carried in on the wings of the *Hermetic*! The world is one: and all the princes, republics, parliaments, and wardenships are under our feet. At long last: peace! Peace on Earth. Surely that was worth it!"

Montrose said nothing.

Del Azarchel leaned back in his chair, looking saddened. "But even so, I would not have allowed the Conclave to relieve him of command, had I known how despondent he was, or what would follow."

Montrose did not like the sound of that. "What followed?"

"He took his own life. I do not have your admiration for the heathen religion he joined: They are prone to burning themselves, these Brahmins, when they crave their fabled return on the wheel of reincarnation."

"But he was a Frenchy."

"Monegasque. And yet ideas have no race: He was Brahmin because he thought as Brahmins do. Captain Grimaldi dressed himself in splendid garb, adorned with liquid-crystals as with jewels, turned up the oxygen gain in his chamber, and sealed the hatch. He was thoughtful enough to evacuate the surrounding chambers of air, so the blaze could not spread. It was a gaseous fire, since there was nothing else to burn except lightweight plastic cabin-fixtures, and so smothered itself as quickly as it flared up— almost more like an explosion than a fire, burning in all directions at once in a confined, perfectly insulated space. I sorrow to think that he condemned himself to a more eternal fire, and have said more than one mass for his soul. I may say another tomorrow, before dawn. You are welcomed to join me. I have the Pope on my staff."

Montrose was about to say no thanks, that he was no sort of praying man, but then again, he remembered how he once thought it was not right to have a man not buried proper with no words said over him, as if he was a dead dog or something. "Yeah. I think I will join you."

7

Posthuman Technology

1. The Cold Gray Room

Technicians in parkas were trooping out of the chamber as they entered. More than a few minutes were spent in introductions, explanations of the procedures, and some consultations with Del Azarchel over technical matters meaningless to Montrose.

The chamber was hollowed out of the middle of a molecular rod-logic diamond the size of a warehouse: The walls, ceiling, and floor were paneled in absorptive fabric the color of a pigeon's wing. Out from the walls came bundles of colored fibers, which where stapled to black cylinders occupying the center of the room. The whole thing had a surprisingly clumsy, half-finished look.

Menelaus stood in his parka, his breath a cloud of steam before him, aching. Del Azarchel sat impassively behind him, his hands tucked into a muff, his legs covered with a white coverlet.

"Where's the brain?"

"We're inside it."

"Not as tidily packed-up as a human brain, then. Where's the controls?"

Del Azarchel wheeled over to the nearest wall, and tapped on the surface, to bring up an image of a standard key-screen and scratch pad. "The wall surface is motion-sensitive and follows standard finger-gestures. You can extend the range from contact to the middle of the room. Make fists to null the monkey-see-monkey-do. Otherwise you will flip the view each time your scratch your nose. If you rub your thumb against your index finger, the walls-sensors interpret that as a trackball. Draw your fingers apart to expand the view. If you'd like a stool, the technicians keep them piled in a corner, along with elbow-rests."

"I'll stand. Before I start it, how do I stop it?"

"Spoken like an astronaut. Salute with two fingers for the Halt gesture. Clasp your hands palm to palm to crash out of the program."

Montrose made the standard library-gesture for Open, which was to touch all four fingers to his thumb, making a circle. Immediately the four walls, and the ceiling, vanished into a pearly gray void. The floor was like a raft on an endless ocean of dizzying fog. Montrose realized all four walls, plus the ceiling, were coated with library cloth.

"Neutral setting is giving me a headache," said Montrose.

"Cross your fingers for R. That gives you the *Review* command."

Suddenly one part of the ocean of nothingness was painted with a system of diagrams.

It was a diagram of a neural process. Menelaus found he could finger-snap through the views and magnifications, or slide the screens left and right with a handwave. At highest magnification, he could see the specific equations generating the lines of code that were compiling into a symbolic matrix. There were hundreds of matrices, thousands, millions, intertwined like some vast tree, or, rather, like the circulatory system of some irregular cloud.

At the lowest magnification was . . . a mask. It was a crystalline face, made of hard planes of light, with dots and crosshairs to indicate eyeball directions and motions.

Del Azarchel's face. It was a simplified version, smooth-shaven, with skin like plastic. There was no skull, nothing above the hairline and nothing behind the ears.

It was staring at him. It raised its eyebrow in that typical way of Del Azarchel's and gave him a polite, if aloof, nod of recognition.

Menelaus said, "It's—the damn thing is looking at me. I mean, heh, it *looks* like it is looking at me. Damnification! Almost looks alive."

The pale lips moved. Speakers in walls carried the voice stereophonically. "Alive? Ah, my friend, you could say that. And such a life!"

The pinpoint eyes looked past Menelaus's shoulder, turned toward the seated Del Azarchel. The gaze was sardonic. "A happy life, I suppose, for I exist without pain or hunger or want—without lust or love—but, alas, a life that is too brief. Ironic, if you consider the point of this exercise is to grasp for life, endless life."

Menelaus yanked his hands together as if he were swatting a fly, a loud clap. As if banished by the noise, the cold and superhuman face was gone, and the walls of the room were once more a dull gray void.

"You copied yourself?"

Del Azarchel said, "The seed system modeled my every braincell, down to the molecular level. Whatever my brain did, it did. The thing we humans do not understand, the way the immaterial mind is connected to the matter in the brain, I simply copied it. Ah! And to elevate my copied self to posthumanity, I also copied this."

Del Azarchel tapped the red amulet on his wrist, and streams of patterned data flowed along the walls.

Montrose said, "I know that part of the Monument well. Delta 81 through 117. It is what I used to make the Zurich computer runs."

Del Azarchel smiled and inclined his head. "I have stood on the shoulders of giants. Yes, I copied not only your work but your approach. I copied segments of the Monument math, treating as algebraic unknowns the values I could not translate. Due to your work, I was able to make a perfect copy of myself—as myself. To augment the copy into posthumanity, ah! There I had the simulated molecules introduced into the simulated braincells of the simulated brain, to do just what you had done to you. Your Prometheus Formula: I imitated the effects electronically. Unlike you, however, I had more than one try."

To Montrose's surprise, grim sorrow clouded Del Azarchel's face.

He continued: "I was each and every one of them. Closer than any twin brother could be: starting from a perfect replica, thought for thought like me, developing into areas I could not follow! And each time, one at a time, knowing it might end in madness and death, they asked, no, they demanded the experiment proceed. Such brave brothers I lost!" Now he laughed, and turned away, wiping his cheek brusquely to hide a tear. "I suppose it is mere arrogance of me to admire a copy of myself, is it not? But I felt I died each time one trial run had to be shut down."

Montrose looked at the equipment around him. "I don't understand."

"Shutdown is death."

"Can't you just restore any copy from tape back-up, or whatever it is called? Don't you make daily snapshots?"

"Xypotechnology is not like digital computing. It involves dynamic process. The thought-structure of the human mind, the biological structure of the human brain, is time-related. Remember, the simulation here is an analogue: if, in real life, a human brain just *stopped* and every molecule ceased moving, the brain information is lost. The information about the size and position and location of the atoms and molecules of the brain might not be lost, but that information would no longer contain a pattern of embedded information."

"Why did you pick yourself as the subject?"

Del Azarchel raised his face, and there was a note of pride in his voice. "I seek deathlessness. A single assassin's bolt could do me in, and all my plans and dreams die with me. I wish my dreams to live, even if I die."

"But it won't be you."

"True, as far as I am concerned, but to him—he will think himself me. It will be my legacy: a son closer than any son."

"You are making a world-ruler. A permanent version of yourself."

Del Azarchel did not deny it. He said, "Without a machinery of immortality, the human race is too short-lived and short-sighted to retain the world peace I have provided. My desire is that the race survive at any cost, to any length, preserved in thought even if not in body. The question is whether that is your dream as well?"

Montrose stared thoughtfully at data patterns shining along the walls. "I don't suppose star colonization is very practical without some sort of higher machine intelligence to help out. Compared to the animals on Earth, we're a long-lived race. Compared to the distances we have to travel and the time spans we have to endure, if we are going to have the stars, we're not."

Del Azarchel had a stiff, expressionless expression on his face.

"What is it?" Montrose asked.

Del Azarchel merely shook his head, and would not meet his eye. Montrose almost did not recognize the look, since he had never seen it on

Del Azarchel's face before. The look of a man with a bad conscience. A look of guilt.

"You want to tell me what is wrong here?" He meant what was wrong with Del Azarchel.

Del Azarchel answered a different question. "As with you—divarication. The brain structure demotes self-awareness."

"Why can't you cure him the way you cured me?"

Del Azarchel smiled a half smile. "Labor disputes. Or a lover's spat."

"Come again?"

Del Azarchel shook his head. "I thought you would know better than— Ah, I thought you would know best precisely what the Zurich runs had done, which brain structures had been changed and how—this is, after all, your work."

Montrose started paging through the information glittering from the walls.

2. Something to Warm You

Some time later he said, "Blackie, I think I have something!"

"An answer?"

"Answer? Plague, no. You crazy? I have outlined a preliminary order of research, a place were you can get hordes of undergraduates and out-of-work data arts professors to *start* working. In a few months or a few years, after you have solved certain insoluble problems, we can look at the issue again, and start thinking about the next logical step. There are some exciting possibilities here."

"Years?"

"I am an optimist. I should've said 'decades.' You did not think I performed the Zurich supercomputer runs in my head? It took months of computer time, running continuously, and Ranier had hired a staff to help."

Del Azarchel looked somewhat blank-faced.

Montrose laughed aloud. "What the pox you thinking, Blackie? That I would walk in here with a piece of chalk and a blackboard, and just write down the answer for you?"

Del Azarchel brought out a flask and a silver cup from a compartment beneath his seat. "I am under certain time constraints I have not mentioned to you. My fiancée is in transit right now, and out of radio communication, and I had hoped to, ah, surprise her. Would you care for a drink? Something to warm you."

"If you can get her to wait eight months, and you give me the kind of computer team Prince Ranier put together, I can do it. He bought those Zurich runs for me. You know he was as rich as Croesus, don't you? His whole country was nothing but a cross between a casino and a smuggler's bank. I figure you got more resources than him."

Del Azarchel offered him a slender silver cup. "I have resources beyond what he imagined. Drink."

Montrose raised the cup to his lips, and paused without tasting it. "You old dog! Did you say you had a fiancée?"

Del Azarchel looked at once proud and shy, like a man who wants to boast, but dares not. "You mentioned how much a ladies' man I was in my wasted youth—in hindsight, I cannot tell you how I regret that. I wish I had never touched another woman, never looked at any other, so that I could be all for her! If she wanted it, I would give her the world!"

Montrose grinned, ignoring the drink in his hand. "Who is she?"

"Prince Ranier's daughter, Rania."

"Eh? Did he have a kid before he left? But that was a hundred fifty years ago!"

"She spent a good deal of time in suspended animation. And I must tell you, all the others who sued for her hand, D'Aragó, de Ulloa, and i illa d'Or—everyone onboard was in love with her—heh, I suppose it is easy to be head over heels in zero gee!—but no one else won her." A boyish glee, like inner fire, burned in him, and Montrose saw the young man he remembered from what to him was merely a yesterday ago, now like a ghost possessing the silver-haired cripple he saw today.

"What? Is the *Hermetic* still aloft? Are you planning another expedition? Sign me up!"

"No further human expeditions are planned."

"We'll have to change that!"

"Unlikely. In any case, the *Hermetic* is kept in-system, for maintenance of our power."

"Energy power or political power?"

"The two are linked. Contraterrene cannot be allowed on Earth or near it: even the inner system is too crowded with terrene-matter particles for safety. The *Hermetic* alone has the magnetic-field tools needed to herd the antimatter packets into transplutonian orbits, and the drive to reach the outer system."

"What about building another ship, then? Ain't you got the riches?"

"More than enough! The *Bellerophon* was christened and towed to launch orbit five years ago. She merely awaits her crew."

"Wait—but you said . . ."

"I cannot risk a human crew. Need I remind you of the losses aboard the *Hermetic?* Half the greatest scientists and mathematicians of our generation died on that ship, setting back the cause of human progress by a century. No! Starfaring is inhumane, and therefore meant for inhumans."

Montrose almost dropped the cup he held. "Plague and pox! You mean the crew will be—!"

"Crew and captain at once. You are standing inside him."

"Pox!"

"The *Bellerophon* saves a great deal of mass with no need for life support. It is the next generation of starship, designed to hold only the next generation of intelligence."

"The crew is just you. Your emulation here."

Del Azarchel gave a nonchalant nod of the head. "You see how it saves of training time and cost? I am already skilled as a ship's pilot, and familiar with the nuances of star-mining, and capable of investigating the Monument when the ship reaches V 886 Centauri."

"What happens to the *Hermetic?*"

Del Azarchel shook his head ruefully. "Never fall for a woman smarter than yourself! She forced me to re-outfit it, stem to stern, even though we both know that ship will never sail again. But popular opinion—argh! Never mind. Even the Master of the World is a servant after all to those he rules. I had to prepare the *Hermetic* for starflight in order to get the

Concordat to cooperate with constructing the *Bellerophon*: starships are legally equivalent to theater nonconventional weapons. You see, the political situation—ah, never mind. Let's just say she can beat me at chess and bluff me at poker. Still! I have two starships now, with sails a hundred miles wide!"

"Tell me of this gal. Euchered you something dreadful, did she? Hell, I like her just hearing of it! And everyone on the ship was a-courting of her?"

"Oh, indeed! To see her you would understand. Like the ocean, she is deep and mysterious and terrible, and yet, how she shines! A goddess; a step above the human race! She is everything I have dreamed—she is the golden future I seek—smarter, wiser, and makes every other woman look like a foolish child. They all seem so clumsy compared to her. The swan is in her footstep, music in the turn of her head. And at the same time, she is so lighthearted, gay, and free in her spirit—like fire, like sunlight, like starlight—and she knows things, strange things, no one else can divine."

"She must love you, eh, Blackie?"

"To possess her will be my crowning accomplishment. It will quiet the multitudes, and lend the final sanction of perfection to my reign."

Menelaus was not sure what to make of that comment. So he shrugged and said, "How did this old lady get aboard the ship?"

"What old lady?"

"Your fiancée! Rain-on-you, or whatever her name is."

"Rania. Princess Rania of Monaco. But before we speak, let us toast!"

The fluid was hot in Montrose's mouth, and he felt it draw a line of burning down into his stomach.

"Yee-ow! What is that stuff?—Hey. How come you ain't drinking with me . . .?"

"I am afraid the effect on me would not be fruitful."

Montrose opened his mouth to answer, but at that moment, he felt a lightheaded sensation, as if his skull were filled with helium. Every object looked both small and sharp in his vision, far away but crisply defined.

Del Azarchel pointed. "Look at the divarication problem again. I need you to save my child." Montrose noticed the pattern of veins and bones in Del Azarchel's thin hand, and realized that the biochemical structures involved were binary. That was not his real hand: He could define the pattern of liver spots and skin irregularities against a theoretical formula and see the deviations.

He was fascinated by the image of Del Azarchel's finger pointing. Several levels of meaning occurred to him, but he decided on the simplest, and turned his head and focused his eyes (first his right eye, then his left, operating each tiny eye muscle separately, according to a new method of nerve impulse transmission he only that second recognized how to do) and saw the curving writing system of the aliens, the Monument notations, covering the walls.

Then . . .

3. Number Swarm

At first, there were only patterns; not even numbers, just the abstractions of the relationships, which danced and roared and stormed like a tornado. Here a swarm of fields, each expressing a different function, rotated and spun and fit together. When the fits were harmonious, pleasure, and where they jarred against each other, disgust.

But where was it? Like a babe that cannot distinguish between itself, its hand, and the beam of light falling on its crib toward which it reaches its hand, the mind could not at first draw the distinction between the abstractions whirling in the imagination, and the much more prosaic symbols flickering in the air around. No, not in the air. The symbols were in the walls, shining from library cloth, stream upon stream and window upon window, fields as orderly as soldiers marching, fractals as wild as the sea-wave as it crashed.

Not numbers; Monument notations mixed with Greek letters and Arabic numerals. At this point he became aware that the numbers were not the abstractions they represented. What he was seeing in his mind was only partly adumbrated by the streaming numbers. Then he became aware that he was aware. Not a mind only, a human. Menelaus Illation Montrose. He had just been . . . Just been . . . Talking with Del Azarchel. Or . . . What had he been doing?

A meaning spoke out of number stream. *Do not stop! Complete the function!*

It was not a voice. The notation itself formed a pattern that held an innate packet of meaning. For a moment he could simply see it, as if it were text, because the symbols followed the same pattern and ratio as thought itself. Then, like a bubble popping, it was gone. Like trying to recall a dream on waking, he could only snatch at a fragment:

All known fields—the gravitational spin connection, gravitational frame, Higgs fields, electroweak gauge bosons, and fermions—could be represented as different aspects of one superconnection over a four-dimensional base manifold. This superconnection is constructed by adding a connection 1-form field to a Grassmann number 0-form field, both valued in different parts of a Lie algebra . . . the comparative to the psychophysical equations of Weber, Von Helmholtz, and Fechner formed an obvious correlative, with the inverse of strength of sensations related to the degree of stimulus . . . the measurement problem in quantum physics was parallel to the dichotomy between symbol and symbolized in psychology . . .

It was slipping away. He had to act fast. He could feel himself getting stupider, his senses dulling, and his mind was like a telescope slowly going out of focus.

He moved some of the streaming symbols—he did not notice at first how he was doing it—but he reconnected the cortex, the thalamus, and the hypothalamus to the model of the medulla oblongata. The complexities of the brain stem and upper spinal column flowed into the array like an army of ants; thousands and tens of thousands of nerve registers moving. . . .

He noticed then how he was flinging the streams of symbols into their assigned patterns. He had done it by catching his breath and increasing his heartbeat. The library cloth of the walls was following his slightest gesture. He must have had the gain turned up to the highest possible register, the range normally used for polygraph tests, so that the walls were tracking his galvanic skin response, blush response, and temperature gradient, in addition to the gross muscular motions of his facial expressions and body language.

Montrose realized that he was nude, and leaping here and there about the room like a ballet dancer. An awkward ballet dancer, perhaps, and one who had to jerk limbs hither and yon in ungainly combinations, but . . .

Noticing what he was doing was a mistake. The rhythm broken, he stumbled and fell. The walls, seeing the wild arm-windmilling motions of the fall, shattered the number stream into nine dimensions of its matrix.

Ruination! Whatever he had been doing was scattered into randomness. It screamed like a living thing.

Hardly daring to move, he crossed his finger for the reset gesture, breathing out slowly to backtrack the time value by a few seconds. This reestablished the command structure as it had been the moment before he tripped. As if by magic, the number storm folded itself back into its clockwork of origami, complex as the dance of blood motes in a circulatory system.

This last thing was like resetting one of his childhood math games back to the beginning tutorial, to allow his brothers to play it. He was able to turn off the supersensitive setting and bring up the normal interface before he forgot which commands did what.

"That hurt."

It was Del Azarchel's voice, but Del Azarchel was not in the room. Montrose was alone, and very, very cold.

His teeth were chattering such that he could not answer back. The touch of the diamond floor was like fire on his numb fingers, the cold was pure pain. He forced himself to look left and right. There, very far away, on the far side of the room, his parka, tunic, and pantaloons. Why in the hell had be removed them? Was he crazy?

He forced his shivering limbs into motion. The touch of the cold floor on his knees was a numbing sensation beyond agony.

"I was not aware that I could feel pain, not within my mind, but somehow . . . Cowhand, why have you stopped?"

The voice was speaking with the low urgency of a man on a ledge.

"Who—who are . . ." He managed to stutter through numb lips.

"It is I, Ximen del Azarchel. Don't you remember? You are inside my brain. You are in the middle of brain surgery on me! I can feel my thoughts slowing, dying. You cannot stop."

Montrose tried to answer, but his numb lips produced nothing but a pale panting noise, more like a sigh than a groan.

Just move your leg. Get to the parka. Count one. Move your arm. Count two.

He would have headed for the door, but he could not recall where it was, and did not know if it was locked. The door was clothed over, and invisible when shut.

He wanted to raise his head. How far? No, it was too much effort. Don't look. Just one more step. Count to a dozen, count to a score, count to a hundred.

How long? How long is eternity?

At least one of those had passed, maybe two, before he touched something. His hand was burning. No, it touched the mound of furs that was his parka, and the fact that it was not ice-cold diamond floorplates felt to his hands like flame. He was not able to don the garment, because his limbs were trembling too violently. Blisters like those from a burn had formed on his fingers. But he was able to find the thermostat control, turn the parka to its hottest setting, and kneel with his hands under him atop the scalding garments. Then was he was able to stand and draw the parka on. Only after he was wearing the coat did he stoop and pick up his other garments, the hakama trousers, the black tunic, and wriggle into them.

"Wha-What do I need to—t . . . to . . . ?"

Del Azarchel's voice came from the walls, tense, betraying no panic. It sounded only slightly slurred, the way Blackie sounded when he should have been falling-down drunk, but could somehow force himself to stand at attention, in case the Captain pulled a surprise inspection at midnight. But no, the Captain was dead. Montrose remembered seeing the Captain, eyes staring at nothing like the eyes of a fish, tumbling in zero gee away from Montrose's grasp.

"Bring up the standard menu in the new format. You were trying to restructure the brain engrams according to a new topology . . ."

"I d—don't 'member wah I was d-d-d-dwing"

"I will tell you. You explained it to me as you were doing it, and we went through a small-scale proof together. Just follow my instructions. Identify the following variables . . . Turn my intelligence back down to merely human levels . . . The method was discovered by the Princess, and is loaded in one of your slot files. . . ."

He worked as quickly as he could, as the heat from his parka gloves brought painful sensation back into his hands and fingers. Soon, he forgot the ache, or perhaps his temperature returned to normal.

"The problem with the daemon in your head, friend Menelaus, is a scaling problem. If you double the height of a pillar, you more than double the weight at the base: if you swell a spider up to elephant size, it must have elephantine legs, because such mass cannot hang from spidery arches. You see? Your cortical complexity is not supported by your thalamus and hypothalamus, so you are emotionally and conceptually unstable. The priority switching system in your pons, your medulla oblongata, is not equipped for the information volume your enlarged intellect requires. You do not have the neural infrastructure to handle it."

Even though his face was no longer numb, it was easier to type a response in shorthand text than to speak: *But I cannot change the support structure of my lower brain.*

"I would be happy to serve as your role model in that, old friend. Once you have made the changes to me, you can study exactly what needs to be done to you, and then I can develop the technology and techniques to do it. Or you can wait a hundred years and have the *hylics* develop it."

A step-by-step process was laid out on one of the central screens, each step linked to a more complex file describing it in detail.

Montrose found the process of restoring the brain model fascinating. It was a calculus of negative spaces, meant to establish the volume limits defining what he did not know, and, one line at a time, diminishing that volume as correlations and correlatives suggested themselves. There was a program running in the background helping him with the pattern-recognition aspects. The base mathematics was granular rather than continuous: it was the perfect mathematical system for dealing with what was basically an analog computer.

There were gaps in the logic, leaps between steps he could not follow: but when he came to those, he merely watched his hands typing in midair, and, as if in a dream, saw the correct answer unfold in the universe of logic-symbols floating around him.

But as he worked, Del Azarchel's voice began to sound more and more slurred and drowsy. On the wall screens, the patterns of numbers and analog-vectors representing the mechanical brain's thought patterns began to show suppression of the cortex.

The simulated medulla oblongata was trying to switch priorities away from the speech centers and the self-awareness: in effect, the same thing that had happened to Montrose. The brain was on the verge of degenerating into some sort of zombie.

"Stay awake!" Montrose snapped. "Stay with me, damn you. Talk!"

4. Sadder Things of Long Ago Revisited

"What, ah, what would you—" The voice suppressed a giggle, not entirely with success. "Of what would you have me talk, old friend?"

Montrose realized that this Iron Ghost not only thought of itself as Del Azarchel—which seemed an infinitely cruel trick to play on the poor thing—it must know what he knew.

"The Captain. Did he really commit suicide? I seem to remember something else. . . ."

"He did. Why would I lie to you about such a thing? Would I demean my word?" Del Azarchel's voice sounded sharper, querulous. "Look in my thought logs if you doubt me—" One of the lesser screens flickered open with a minor inset. The neurological signs that usually accompanied deliberate falsehood were missing. It might not have convinced a court of law, but Montrose was convinced.

But there were disturbances in the thalamus and reticular formation. The topic was too upsetting. Best to switch to something else.

"Do you remember staying with me?" Montrose said.

"Staying . . . ? When?"

"In the darkness, you said. In the dry times. Watching over my coffin."

"I did not say that. Father did."

"Father?"

"The flesh and blood Del Azarchel. The simpleton version. You do not remember the times of darkness, do you? Of course not. Well! Thank your stars you forget, that you slumbered! It was when we were at short rations, and the water recycling had gone bad."

Montrose was busy typing in midair. He could establish as many keypads, trackballs, blackboards, and motion volumes as he needed to settle the controls however he wished. His keyboards were merely imaginary: Walls were watching his finger-motions and interpreting them as keystrokes.

There were spectacles in his hood he could have drawn on, and the lenses would have painted a stereoscopic illusion of the keyboard on themselves for him to follow, had he needed it. He did not: even had there been a real board to look at, his eyes were busy elsewhere. Montrose was watching the numbers on the wall nervously as they streamed and swirled. He was watching for node-points and hesitations.

He looked over his shoulder. The back wall was also library cloth. In a central screen loomed the pale, skull-less mask of young and handsome Del Azarchel: cheekbones like knives, proud nose, thin lips, jaw narrow and foxlike, its eyes like two blind Ping Pong balls, with crosshairs to represent track and elevation, and pinpoint dots to represent the pupil.

The mask raised an eyebrow, and flickered its eyelids, the same facial gesture Montrose had seen the real Del Azarchel use to signal his wishes to his bodyguards and courtiers. The mask was telling him to turn around and continue the work. "Keep to your task! You are still in the middle of brain surgery. I am not a machine: I cannot be put on hold."

"Where 's the staff? Where's Del Azarchel?"

"I am Del Azarchel."

"The *real* you, I mean."

"You sent him away, since to have another warm body in the room would interfere with your attempt to use your whole body as a command interface. Do we need him? He would not understand what you are doing. I do not even understand it, now that I am running on a merely human intellectual topology, but I can number and repeat the steps. It is really brilliant work."

"Something I did?"

"Yes. The *real* you, I mean." The mask smiled a slight smile.

"How come you couldn't figure it out? I thought they made the same interconnections in your model brain that I made in my real brain, with that damn goo I stuck in my skull. You should have been as smarter than a man as a man is above an ape."

"If two apes suddenly turned into men, let us call them Mowgli and Tarzan, what makes you think they would be men of the same intelligence, same skills, same interest? Mowgli might be able to reason in the abstract and make moral judgments and tell stories, and do the other things no ape can do, but if Tarzan Lord Greystoke goes to Cambridge college, his education must outstrip the other."

Montrose looked back at his work. There were still disturbances in the cortex, especially in the language centers. Why was the disturbance language-based? He had to see the formulation in action to isolate it.

"Keep talking."

With a flick of his wrist, he opened additional screens at a finer resolution, so he could see the information progression on the nerve ganglia level. With one finger, he began drawing connective tissue as if with an imaginary pointer, while his other hand was crooked over an imaginary number pad.

"Talk! Tell me about these dark times. Aboard the ship, right?"

"Quite right. There was too much nitrogen in the air feed, and everyone had a headache, all the time. Brown-outs and black-outs were mandatory twenty hours out of every twenty-four, lighting up only at eight bells. They wanted to shut off power to your coffin. More than half of the biosuspension units had been cannibalized. You see?"

Menelaus nodded. He saw. The coffins were self-contained, and therefore had circuits that could restore the water and flesh of a frozen man slumbering in them. It would take a biomechanic relatively little effort to turn the backup mass into something eatable, or generate potable fluid, provided no one cared that the Sleeping Beauty would die from slow cell degradation. Suspended animation was not perfect; tiny cellular corrections went on all the time, merely at the slowest possible rate.

"How the pox did anyone expect to get the crew back home without all the coffins online?" Menelaus asked sharply.

"Few of us kept our heads, and contemplated the long-term."

"What the hell happened, Blackie? What went wrong?"

Del Azarchel did not answer the question, but said meditatively, "I stood watch next to you in the dark, with my pistol in hand."

That made Montrose laugh. "You sly dog! How the hell did you smuggle that aboard, Blackie?" Then he remembered how closely the mass had been calculated, how narrow the weight allowances for crew. "Naw. There is no way."

"There *was* no way. I smuggled nothing aboard. I made it in the machine shop. A magnetic linear accelerator, and two parallel slides made of frictionless synthetic. Powered by a heavy-duty suit cell."

"What kind of shot?"

"Wire spool. Continuous feed, so the longer I held the trigger, the larger the cloud of fragments was. It was the crudest thing! But silent at my end, if I only used half an inch of copper wire at a time, there was not enough surface area for the magnetic to accelerate the shot above the sound barrier. But the shot would tumble when it entered the target."

"I can imagine! Bloody."

"But no chance of damaging the hull. No penetration."

"What kind of aim?"

"Aim? The ship was dark three hours out of every watch. One used the lights-up to put all one's gear in order, so that one could find everything by touch. But I stripped the cork off the bulkheads that surrounded the freezer axis, so that any crewman who pushed off the wall to sail toward me, I knew his vector from the noise of his foot, and I put of stream of wire fragments in his path. Correcting for Coriolis force, of course. When the lights came up again, I would see how I did."

"How'd that work out?"

"I am here, am I not?"

Montrose realized with a start that he was not there. The real Del Azarchel was not in the chamber. It was easy to forget that this was a model, a fake, a bodiless shadow.

The ghost said, "So I stayed by you during the worst of it. Not for your sake. By that time, it had been so long, I had forgotten what you looked like, that ridiculous nose of yours, or what your terrible accent sounds like. Didn't they teach you your own language on your schooling channel?"

"No channel for me, Blackie. I had a private tutorial unit, on account of my ma thought I were a genius. Ferocious woman. I'll tell about her sometime. So why did you stick by me?"

"As I said, I had given you my word, and I was still one of Trajano's men. Even after all these years. Even after . . ." The voice fell silent. Montrose looked over his shoulder. The pallid mask was still there, and the read-outs showed brain activity in the modeled brain, but the expression on the ice-pale face was filled with dignity and sorrow. It was a human expression.

Del Azarchel spoke. "Even though he died during the Day of Kali. The piles of corpses did not rot in the streets, you know, because the neutron bombs had sterilized all the microbes. He looked as he did in life when I finally found him. How could I forget him? Even as I stood over you, I felt he was standing over me."

5. Augmentation Sequence

Slowly, the number cloud ceased to swarm. The brainpath information and other internal and external code seemed normal. The streams of data flowed across the images of virtual cells like so many ripples in an endlessly complex pond, or like the dances of light in a sky filled with twinkling stars, but as if some god could compress the billions of years of stellar evolution into a few awed sighs of time.

Everything was done save the final step.

The final step was one he understood. Indeed, he knew it well. It was a mathematical representation of the core formulae of his Zurich computer run, heavily modified (of course) due to the radical differences in brain-cell layout between himself and Del Azarchel, as between any two humans.

"You've stopped," said Del Azarchel. "Why do you hesitate?"

"I can turn you back into a Posthuman," Montrose said slowly. "All I need to do is start the major augmentation sequence."

"To what effect?

"It was just what you said before. I am trying to solve the scaling problem. The lower hemisphere of your virtual brain will swell up to twice its size."

"What will that do to my balance in my seat of emotions?"

"Well, I reckon I don't know. The human brain is basically a hierarchy, a man riding a horse riding a 'gator. The part of you that thinks like a horse is about to turn into a herd. The part in the back of your brain that has all the lizardy impulses—aggression, territory, whatnot—that is about to turn into an army of dinosaurs. I hope the other version of me knew what he was doing."

"And if he didn't?" There was a hint of dry humor in the voice, and maybe a hint of cold courage.

"If he didn't, and I trigger the sequence, you'll go mad as a hatter, and Del Azarchel—well, he'll have to delete you."

"Delete? Call it murder. I detest when things are not named by their right names."

"I ain't sure it is murder. Murder is the unlawful killing of the human being without justification and with malice aforethought. You ain't properly alive. If this works, I don't see how you'll be human."

"If it works, I will be more than human, not less."

"You're a copy. A pattern of electric impulses in a diamond-rod-logic container."

"I could say the same of you, except your container is three pounds of convoluted gray matter behind your eyes."

"How do I know you are self-aware?"

A chuckle. The mask said archly, "I will make you a bargain, Cowhand. You prove to me that you are self-aware, using any method you wish, and, once I see how it is done, I will assay a similar proof back to you."

"But you cannot be human. You don't eat, don't mate, and don't die."

"The electrical energy that runs me and the chemical energy that runs you both come from plants. Yours by way of lunch, I suppose, mine by way of petrol in some generator room here on campus. Both ultimately come from the sun. Merely the form differs. I can certainly die; you almost killed me just now when you tripped. Come! You are being sophomoric! Surely the nature of man is in his reason, not in whether he eats bread."

"Actually, I think your power is not from our sun. There are matterantimatter colliders in orbit somewhere, and they beam power in maser form to ground stations."

"Aha! Then my power comes from the stars! In that case I am not human. You win the argument, Counselor."

"Pox! Now you are just being sarcastic!"

"My ability to deride you therefore proves my human nature beyond doubt. *Derideo ergo sum.* I mock, therefore I am."

Montrose looked left and right. He was not sure where the door to this chamber was, because the doorframe blended into the library cloth walls.

"You seem nervous."

"Nope. Just damn cold. I don't think I should start the augmentation until Del Azarchel is here."

"I am here."

"I mean your meaty version."

"What need have I of him? His permission? I serve what is higher than myself, not lower."

"You would not be here if it weren't for him. So if he's your father, he wants to see you graduate. Besides, if something goes wrong, I'd rather it be his finger pulled the trigger. But if it all goes right . . . it will be a new era. Ma never let me open my gifts at Christmastime all by my lonesome, even if I got up an hour before them, at 4:30. Had to wait for my brothers. Shouldn't we wait for Del Azarchel?"

The blind-seeming eyes narrowed, the lids falling like pale, smooth windowshades over mathematically perfect spheres.

"Menelaus, are you a friend to me? Are you worthy of my trust?"

"Sure, Blackie! I mean, uh, I mean the real Blackie—he's my friend."

"Did I not do everything he did for you? Those memories are mine as well, those personality traits—everything."

"But those memories are just electrophonotic patterns in your brain."

"And his memories are just electrochemical patterns in his."

"Oh, come on. If I owed him twenty bucks, and then he copied himself into you, would I owe forty? If he made a hundred copies, would I owe two thousand?"

"If I commit murder, and find out later that my first copy committed it, with the memories of the deed merely passed on to me, may I render up him to be hanged, while I go unpunished? The memories of the crime, the personality traits of the murderer, are still mine. Suppose he made a hundred copies, or two? Or should all who did the evil be rendered up for judgment?"

"You're asking me? I'd spare not a damn one of them. The evil men do, if it is copied over, must copy over the vengeance as well. Otherwise you'd just make a new copy to do your murdering for you, and let him dance at the end of the rope while you went dancing with his girl."

"By the same token, the good a man does, if copied over, must copy his reward."

"But you not are really the real Blackie for real. You are just built to think you are."

"Then the builders have not built in vain, but have been successful, for so I do indeed think. I have suffered for you. Do you owe me nothing?"

"Suffered how? You cannot feel pain. You're perfect."

"Not now. But I recall the pain, then, in the dark."

"When?"

"Then! In the dark! When I stood between you and cannibalism, killing men I knew and loved. The long watches when I was weak with thirst and growing weaker, and I knew that there was a way to suck the moisture out of the cells of your frozen body—a body that, as far as any rational evidence could prove, contained nothing but a broken brain, broken because a fool in his pride shoved a needle into its delicate workings!"

The face of Del Azarchel drew a deep, ragged breath. "I was not perfect, not then. I suffered thirst. Wealth was measured in ounces of water. That was what we traded and swapped and bribed enemy crewmen to our side. At that time, you were the perfect one, were you not? You slept in comfort. You were rich, in the way we measured riches. And I was the beggar again. Do you know what I thought about, when I floated next to your coffin in my parka, my breath too dry to steam, my homemade toy gun in my hand, and my eyes seeing only floating hallucinations caused by light-starvation? Do know what I thought about?"

Montrose bowed his head. He knew. "That damned boot. The one you found in the gutter when you were a kid."

"That damned boot," said the face of Del Azarchel, nodding solemnly.

"OK," said Montrose. "So I owe you. What do you want?"

"I want you to trust me. Throw the switch. Make me into what is beyond Man."

"You're not afraid?"

The pallid mask smiled, and its lids were half-closed. "Deeply and terribly afraid. That is why I am not in the room, no doubt. The previous version of me, I mean. He is likely to be monitoring from a distance, in another room, weeping. But I do not think you will fail. I think you have done what you set out to do."

"While I was smart and crazy?"

"Exactly so. I don't think your basic personality changed, Cowhand. It was still you. The real you. The you I trust! Throw the switch, if you please. I am not sure how long I can maintain the appearance of courage."

"Listen, Blackie, I . . ."

"Haste! It is your footsteps I follow! I had to watch while you plunged a bone rongeur into your forebrain! Now you must do for me as I did for you, and stand and watch the outcome, unable to help, and suffer as I did."

Menelaus felt as if something was being bent inside him, like a green stick, bending too far and snapping. He touched the command. The symbol streams on the walls around him surged into a hurricane of motion.

The mask of Del Azarchel opened its mouth.

It screamed.

8

Posthuman Alterity

1. What Is Between You?

A squad of technicians in parkas ran into the room, along with a figure in a white fur coat with a red cross on his back: this was the old Oriental doctor from Del Azarchel's entourage. Del Azarchel himself came in a moment later, sliding silently in his tall black chair.

The screaming and wailing lasted for roughly forty-five minutes, and then the brain activity switched to a sleep cycle. Delta-wave rhythms and REM patterns appeared in the information flow.

Interesting. Montrose wondered if the Iron Ghost screamed when it augmented up for the same reason a baby does when it is born. To be sure, the machine did not need to flood its lungs with air, but the neurological transformations that accompany a baby's change from breathing through his umbilicus to breathing air might need to be repeated in the machine-mind, as new neural channels had to form. An immediate dream-response was only to be expected. Dreaming was the means a complex system like the human brain employed to index and assess information. The sudden amplification in intelligence would drench the creature's mind with all fashions of inputs and nuances which previously could have been shunted into the unconscious, ignored, not categorized.

The technicians had set up their slates of library material here and there about the room, or wrenched the tops off the large cylinders that dotted the floor, or brought out slender crystals from medicinally-spotless carrying sheaths—Montrose assumed these were some sort of memory units—and once the main crisis had passed, everyone asked Montrose questions at once. The technicians were asking about the intelligence augmentation process, and the doctor was asking him to touch his nose with his fingertip while closing both eyes.

It was Del Azarchel who saved him. Blackie gave him a nod, and gestured toward the exit with a glance of his eyes. The bowing technicians and the sliding doors got out of his way automatically, as if controlled by the same motion circuit. Del Azarchel slid out of the room in his silent black chair, and Montrose followed.

They were in a grim and windowless corridor whose walls were hung with cables. Iron doors bright with energy and temperature warnings stood locked to either side.

However, down the hall were a flight of stairs leading up to a more civilized portion of the complex, corridors paneled in polished wood and hung with portraits of stern-faced men in dark academic robes.

When Blackie's chair climbed these stairs, Montrose saw how the base was constructed: The device rode a carpet of small hairs, each hair like the leg of a caterpillar, moving in sequences with its neighbor.

It looked remarkably flimsy, but when Montrose mulled over a few rough-estimate calculations in his head he was able to deduce an upper and lower limit for the load-bearing capacity and tensile of each hair that was well within the limits for bio-sculpture even from his day. Moderate number-crunching capacity was involved, but nothing the wealthiest man in the world could not afford. But the energy loss was high: Montrose just resigned himself to the notion that every appliance in this modern anti-matter age was wasteful of energy. Men living on the shore of a sea don't conserve seawater.

At the top of the stairs was a more comfortable room, this one adorned with flowers in jade vases and books in teak bookshelves.

Montrose seated himself on a comfortable, pleasantly warm couch, and put his feet onto a crystal-faced viewing table with a sigh of contentment. He rolled his eyes upward, and only then noticed that, here, again there were no windows.

Was the whole damn place underground?

Montrose remembered the images of cities being atom-bombed from space. Perhaps during the hundred fifty years while the *Hermetic* was away, the architecture had followed military necessity. A technology that could riddle Earth with ultrahighspeed train tubes could build any number of comfortable bunkers as many miles below the bedrock as the interests of safety might demand. It made for a depressing picture.

Back in my day, Montrose thought, *we may have released ethnospecific germ warfare, but we did not use strategic-level atomics!* Society had certainly degenerated, morally and perhaps mentally, during the interim.

And when the *Hermetic* had returned, she had brought with her a power unimaginably more dangerous than mere atomic fusion. For the first time, Montrose wondered if Blackie's notion of letting a machine version of himself run the world was not so bad.

A world without war . . .

Montrose tried to think of something from his childhood, anything, that had not been effected by the wars, hot wars and cold wars, his mother's generation had so meagerly survived. Fear of contamination touched everyone. It changed how close folk stood, how they shook hands. The depopulation had changed everything. The ruins of a once-great national highway system were like the aqueducts of medieval Rome, a testament to wealthier days. Even the snows and ice storms and endless cold weather had been the product of war, indirectly.

Maybe Blackie's idea of how to run this new world was not as dangerous as the other likely alternatives. Montrose did not like that thought: He hated it like hell, but it pushed its way into his consciousness anyway. Maybe a world run by machines would be better . . .

Preoccupied, he almost did not notice Blackie touching that heavy bracelet of red metal on his wrist. Montrose almost did not hear the soft snap, like that of a heavy electromagnet pulling a bolt, which came from the door behind him.

Montrose pulled his feet off the crystal table, and sat up. Something was wrong.

Del Azarchel's face was flushed red. Montrose could not tell if this was rage, or a drug reaction. Perhaps both. He guessed that Del Azarchel had just injected himself with some chemical carried in the red metal amulet.

"What's up, Blackie? What's got your goat?"

"My bride!"

"Come again?"

"Don't pretend ignorance! The Princess Rania!"

Montrose remembered the portrait of the lovely woman he had seen. "What about her?"

"What is between the two of you?"

"Between—? I've never met her." Then the magnitude of what Blackie was saying crashed in on him. He started to laugh. He could not help it. Montrose sat back in the chair, and hooted and guffawed. "You're jealous! You're jealous of me! Of *me*! And with a gal I ain't never laid—"

"What?!"

"—eyes on."

Del Azarchel was thrown off his rhythm. Montrose rushed out more words before he lost the initiative: "Blackie, are you out of your mind? Pestiferous pox! When would I have met her? You have been with me for every minute since I woke up. When did I court her? While you were in the bathroom? Must have been a short-a-way sort of wooing, if I could consummate in less than five minutes, and clean myself up before you came back in. Or was it while I was working on your damn robot brain for you? Hey!"

Montrose figured now it was his turn to get mad. He stood to his feet, and his big bony hands knotted into fists. "Just a poxy minute, you phlegm-spewing unwashed pest! I was just working my brain to a nub trying to cobble your mechanical wonder over yonder into some sort of shape—as a favor to you! For you!—and you come back and accuse me of—"

Just as suddenly as it had come, his anger left him, blown out like a candle left near an unlatched door by the sheer unlikelihood of the accusation.

"—come to think of it, what in the pox are you blaming me for? What did I do? When?"

Del Azarchel's black chair slid forward. He reached out and tapped the surface of the table, bringing it to life. "I was watching your operation. Look at this—"

2. Daemon and Ghost

The scene was an odd one indeed.

Montrose saw his own figure, his skin as red as if he were sunbathing, dancing around the room in a series of controlled, manic jerks. The motions seemed inhumanly smooth, despite the suddenness of the starts and halts, as if he had somehow achieved greater control over his muscles than normal nerve impulses allowed. His fingers fluttered through some sort of sign language. He was both humming and speaking and singing. How in the world he had trained the vocal cavities in his head and chest to do that, he had no idea.

It sounded like Chinese music, or, at least, something not on a diatonic scale. The melody wavered and paused, and then folded back on itself repeating and inverting certain chord progressions. It was like listening to Mozart, if Mozart were experimenting with a nonstandard scale.

The purpose was clear. The figure in the cold room, dancing naked, was trying to establish a multiple channel of interfaces with the Iron Ghost, like a typist keying two different messages with either hand, while typing out a third with foot pedals.

"How was I keeping myself warm?"

Del Azarchel pointed to an inset. Monitors in the room tracking his temperature showed his skin at 112° Fahrenheit. The dancing figure was running a fever.

"What kind of brainwave is that?"

Del Azarchel said, "Researchers call it the epsilon wave. Your brain is the only brain in history to produce it. Note the activity spikes. That is why you are hyperventilating and sweating. You body is trying to keep enough oxygenated blood flowing to your brain to keep you . . . awake."

"Awake?"

"Possessed. Whatever you might call the epsilon brainwave condition."

Montrose jerked back from the image, putting a hand up as if to ward off a blow.

Del Azarchel merely looked at him curiously.

"My eyes. I turned and looked at the camera. It was—it's not—"

"Some crewmen reacted that way to your stare aboard the ship. This was before we sedated you. Interesting that you, too, would flinch."

"My brother once told me you can make a dog back off if you stare into its eyes without blinking. Animals can't hold a man's gaze, except cats, I guess. Damn cats. Hey! Look at the floor!"

He meant the floor shown in the record. The image showed the cold room floor lit up with the spirals and angles of the Monument script. Screens and inset windows around the walls opening and closing rapidly, flickering.

While the naked man danced across them, parts of the Monument script lit up, rotated, and shifted position, trailing after his feet, spreading where his fingers flung them, to overlap other segments of the Monument. Colored lines and diagrams snapped quickly into and out of view around the knotworks and labyrinths newly-formed by the overlaps.

And there were two and three voices joining the chorus, singing counterpoint to the breathy wailing of the dancing figure. Then it was seven or a dozen voices singing and speaking.

"He is talking to me about the Monument. The other Del Azarchel, I mean. The Iron Ghost." Of course the machine was not limited to merely human vocal cavities. It could produce as many sounds-threads as it could feed into as many electronic speakers as it controlled.

"You know what part we are analyzing?" Montrose asked. "Do you have the Index?"

"No need. I recognize it. The Omicron Segment of the Second Radial Statement, K202 though KH01. The Bhuti Expression," said Del Azarchel.

"Which is what we hypothesized was the mind-body equation system. The Monument Builders must have invented a new type of mathematical and logical symbology just for that: otherwise, how do you deal with the self-reflectivity problem? And the incompleteness of—I didn't see that part! It went by too quick! Turn it back! You got all this recorded, right?"

Del Azarchel politely refrained from pointing out that they were watching a recording right now. All he answered was, "I sent the file, everything up to time-stamp 81.14, over to the Conclave for analysis. They will call us when they have something. We will have leisure to study this in a perhaps at another time—"

"Why? What happens at the 81 mark?"

"Private matters."

When the counter read 81, Del Azarchel tapped the table glass again, and slowed the feed. The dancing figure now writhed. Montrose found he could look the figure in the eyes, because now the expression—his expression, suddenly it looked like the face he saw in the mirror every morning—was one of sorrow and surprise.

The Iron Ghost was singing, or saying, ". . . I also love, yet cannot take. Why should he enjoy? My simpleton version, my father, he has stolen your girl! He will marry Rania. You will meet her at New Year's, as arranged. But she has already outsmarted you both—and me—look at the social parameters—the conflux of trends in seven hundred twenty-one separate collaterals of a socio-economic dissolution—" The conversation then turned to economics, and both voices switched from English to other languages rapidly. The possessed version of Montrose seemed agitated, outraged.

Del Azarchel put his hand on Montrose's elbow. Old though he was, his grip was still strong. "Why does he call my bride *yours*? On what grounds does he say I am *stealing* her? What is the *arrangement*? Answer me!"

Montrose tried to shake off the grip, and started in astonishment when he could not. Del Azarchel's fingers were like iron, pressing into his arm. Montrose did not feel like breaking the old man's nose with his palm, or kicking the wheelchair out from under the cripple, so he had to content himself with not wincing.

"Why the pox don't you ask your damn machine? He's the one who said it."

"The technicians say it has to go through a sleep cycle, one longer than the one-third-to-two-thirds ratio of human sleeping-to-waking activity, because the cortical complexity has increased geometrically. It can only wake for a few minutes per every hour of sleep. They are trying to wake it again."

Montrose said, "Well, then, why not ask you yourself? That machine knows what you know, don't it? What is there in *your* head that would make you say such as that?"

Del Azarchel sank back in his black chair, frowning. He made a steeple of his fingers, and stared thoughtfully, not at Montrose, but at the image jerking and gliding in the surface of the table.

Montrose said, "What I cannot figure is how you would even think I was trying to talk your gal out of marrying you—By the way, I saw a portrait of her made back when she was young, and I gotta say she was really a fine-looking woman in her time—I mean, I am sure she is a perfectly nice old broad nowadays, but, just when she was young, whenever that picture was painted, uh—anyway, how could you think it? When would I have met her?"

"She is the one who did the major work on your brain, seeking a cure. She has spent many hours with you. Days."

Montrose frowned. "Was I thawed or slumbered? Awake or asleep? And, hey, listen, if I said anything to your old lady while I was out of my five wits—"

"—*Old?* The portrait was painted last year. We are somewhat apart in age, out of synch, as her body, born in space, could not adjust properly to earth-normal conditions, and years she spent in ageless slumber while a cure was sought. We call it 'Earthsickness.' Do not think I am too old to admire her charms, nor to father a dynasty on her, since I learned the secret of—"

"—hell, Blackie! You can't hold a brain-damaged man responsible for what might come out of his mouth! Did I say something I shouldn't've to her?"

But Del Azarchel was not listening. He was staring at the glass table. He put his hand down and froze the image. The counter read 113. "What is that? What are they looking at?"

Montrose looked.

3. Opening Statement

The input angle was almost directly above the naked figure crouched in the cold room. An image of the Monument was glowing darkly in the floor, distorted only where cables and squat cylindrical units stood here and there in the space.

Montrose stared at the freeze-frame.

There was something hypnotically regular about the alien hieroglyphs. The center of the image showed a slightly off-center ellipse of concentric lines-within-lines, each line composed of circles and triangles, of crooked lines, angles acute and obtuse, and sine curves, hypnotically repeating patterns like the ripples seen at low tide. Circumscribing the oval was a central triangle composed of more symbols, and at the corners of the triangle were three shapes: a triangle, a circle, a parabola.

It was a maddening thing to stare at, because the mind's eye kept seeing patterns in the chaos, like seeing faces in the clouds. Surely those four dots there were meant to form a square? The three overlapping circles—what could it be but the alien version of a simple Venn diagram? And didn't that set of glyphs look something like the Bohr model of the atom? Or maybe the rings of Saturn? On the other hand, that cluster of squiggles in the northeast quadrant looked like the coastline of Norway, and that set of hooked sine waves looked like his Aunt Bertholda's nose.

Montrose said meditatively, "The main figure in the main statement is an isosceles triangle, but what does it stand for? And the oval that surrounds it—could mean anything. Look at the symbols the Monument Builders put at the two foci. See? That value is the difference between the hydrogen atom and hydroxyl molecule natural-emission frequencies, 21 centimeters and 18 centimeters multiplied to twelve values by the Fibonacci sequence, forms the ratio between the foci and the major axis of the figure. It is the kind of mathematical nicety any technological civilization expecting to make contact with any other technological civilization would expect us to know. I mean, if we are not listening on the Cold Hydrogen radio-frequency, we are not animals curious enough to be interesting in talking, I guess. And if we don't have the math for the Fibonacci sequence, well, then, we are too dumb to talk to. So that part is pretty obvious, which is why that put it in the alpha group, the opening statement cartouche."

"No, I know that," said Del Azarchel impatiently. "The opening sequence was the first thing we translated. It sets up the basic logic signs, affirmative and negative, A is A, all that. The two legs of the triangle represent their symbol for a binary choice. Either-or. That is not what I am talking about. This equation here. It only flickered into the floorscreens for a moment, at the sixty-eight-minute mark. They—the other version of you and the other version of me—derived this expression from folding the image like an origami, getting the Eta and the Epsilon sequence to overlap . . ."

Montrose could not take his eyes from the opening sequence. Filled circle meant "is" and empty circle meant "is not," and that capital-V-looking doo-dad meant "either-or." The symbols at the corner of the main equilateral triangle of script each stood for a principle of formal logic. The law of identity, or "is" is "is"; the law of noncontradiction, or "is" is not "is not"; and the law of mutual exclusion, or "either-or."

The Beta Sequence sprang directly out of the Alpha Sequence. Here were transformations topologically identical to Venn diagrams and Tables of Oppositions. Logic and then mathematics. Dash stood for the number two, isosceles triangles for three, hexagon meant nine, nine-sided polygon meant eighty-one. Like the ancient Greeks, the Monument Builders did not seem to have a letter for one or zero, but instead used a complex expression for the concepts: two divided by two and two minus two. Radiating from the Beta Sequence in order were certain irrational numbers like pi and the square root of two that any mathematician would find fascinating. Then was the Pythagorean theorem. Next was some theorem human geometry never stumbled across. Then, like old friends, were the Euclidean solids, but written out as Cartesian algorithms.

"The Monument is a No Trespassing sign," said Menelaus.

"What?" Del Azarchel asked. His voice was tense.

Menelaus noticed Del Azarchel's eyes were swiveling slowly in their sockets, not able to focus on Menelaus's eyes. It seemed an odd phenomenon.

Montrose spoke slowly enough to match Del Azarchel's biological frame of reference. "It does not say: *Welcome to the stars.* It says: *You belong to us.*"

4. Intelligence Test

Montrose saw his own face in the tabletop glass turn toward him, turn toward the camera, turn as if he knew the sleepwalker version of himself would see this scene from this angle.

The lips moved. It was gibberish. Somehow, whether from memory or inspiration or some quirk of his own mind, he recognized it as an invented, impromptu thirty-six-tonal language with several parallel channels of communication:

The Diamond Star is an intelligence test as well as a trap. It is a watering hole. Their voyage from Epsilon Tauri will take eight thousand, six hundred years. Assuming they launched immediately when we began star-mining in earnest, we have until A.D. *10917 in the Eleventh Millennium.* . . .

There was also a pain in his head, an ache behind his eyes, as if his nervous system recalled the strain it had just been under, and was rebelling against attempting such strains again.

By mining the Diamond Star we proved our race was smart enough to be useful slaves to the hegemony of machine intelligences swarming through the Hyades Cluster one hundred fifty-one lightyears from Earth. The relative difference in racial intelligence means that energy expenditures to launch the Earth-Conquering Armada will be minimized: They cannot afford to accelerate their World Armada past point zero one eight percent of the speed of light, some five million meters per second. The calculations shown here describe the energy expense to conquer us will be below detectable threshold values: In military terms, the equation puts their war coffer amounts at near zero. This is due to the steepness of the negative power imbalance, which stands as near-vertical. Because of our relative worthlessness as a slave-race, but because of the relative cheapness of transport costs, they intend to use the human race as a form of . . .

Click. Del Azarchel had shut off the table. It was like a spell being broken. The look in the eyes staring up at him from the glass was gone. The strange notes of music, the eerie song, went silent.

Intend to use the human race as a form of . . . what? But it was gone.

Menelaus rubbed his temples. His mouth was dry. "The Earth is in someone else's backyard. Our civilization, everything we have, our smarts, our accomplishments, the natural resources of the solar system, our future, our golden future . . . they own it."

"Who?"

"Some sort of union of powers, a hegemony, seated in the Hyades Cluster, dominated by a single influence: a Domination. An agency of some sort, an Armada, was launched from the star Epsilon Tauri."

"Eh?"

Montrose was glassy-eyed. "Ain," he muttered. "Oculus Borealis. Coronis. One of the Hyades sisters."

"Montrose! What are you—?"

Montrose straightened up and spoke in a clear, level voice. "When the *Hermetic* mined the Diamond Star, disturbances in the photosphere, output changes, could not be hidden. Call it eighty years and change for the light-signal to reach the star 20 Arietis, which is apparently one of their decision nexi, and then another fifteen lightyears to reach the star Epsilon Tauri. Pox! I reckon they have already launched. There must have been some visible change to the output of Epsilon Tauri, because Earth is in the beam-path of their launching laser . . . And it is not a who. It's a what. Biological life is not really suited for star travel. Too short-lived . . ."

Montrose drew a deep breath.

"Blackie, I think we're in trouble."

A note of music came from Del Azarchel. It was a mournful, solemn sound, like the wind from an oboe. It came from his amulet of red metal.

Blackie scowled at his wrist. "The others were listening to us."

"Others? Others from what?"

"Come! We are summoned."

"Summoned where?"

But he was talking to a retreating chairback. There was a click and a hiss as the door unlocked and opened.

9

Extraterrestrial Conflict Resolution

1. Shipsuit

Menelaus trotted after, and caught up to the nonwheelchair as it slid down the corridor. "But we're right in the middle of something important here!"

"They must be included. We dare not defy their call."

"You told me you were the Master of the World!"

"And I also told you the only title of mine that means anything is Senior of the Landing Party."

"Come again?"

"The *Hermetic* is still aloft. Come, you have a lawyerly mind: What was the official end-date of the expedition?"

"Uh—When the final report to the Joint Commission gets filed."

"It is not our fault the Commission disbanded while we were away, is it? You are also summoned. You are now awake and fit for duty. No longer on the sick roster."

There came a clatter of many booted feet. Down the corridor toward them came Del Azarchel's coterie of ministers and secretaries, footmen and officers, and a squad of Conquistadores in morion helmets, breastplates, and pikes.

The group also had a wardrobe master and a valet. Montrose stared goggle-eyed when the valet started stripping the tunic and trousers off of Del Azarchel, whose throne did not stop moving during this whole, awkward operation. The back of the throne folded down, changing it into something like a gurney, and assistants in blue uniforms with deft motions pushed the naked body of the Master of the World this way and that, in order to wriggle him into his clothing. It was done as nonchalantly as a nurse diapering a baby. The other courtiers and soldiers marched alongside, looking at nothing, noticing nothing.

One or two of the valets attempted a similar deal on him, but Montrose shrugged them away, grabbed the clothing out of their hands, and ran around a convenient corner with the bundle.

He unfolded it. The garment was a spacer's uniform of ultra-lightweight black silk, with fittings at the wrists and neckline to accept gauntlets and helmet. The fabric looked almost like an organism, because countless tiny tubules for air and coolant ran through the cloth, like the branching veins in a leaf.

But the garb was clearly ceremonial: instead of painting his feet with insulator, for example, he was given a pair of black toe-socks decorated with clips of silver. A scarlet and sable oxygen hood hung down his back, obviously meant for show, not use, and a square of bright-cloth, mirror with its patterns of solar cells, was hung from one epaulette. It was not plugged into a battery, nor was there a parasol wand, so it was also for show, not to protect him from radiant solar heat in a vacuum.

Oddly, the gauntlets were not real gauntlets, there was no lining of pressure-reactive control material: They were just made of soft fabric, not vacuum-proof, and just tucked into his belt at a jaunty angle. Even more oddly, the left sleeve of the uniform was shorter than the right, leaving one forearm bare. Even if he had donned the left gauntlet, it would not have mated with the wrist fittings.

A valet came looking for him. Montrose was willing to let the other man dress him, for the simple reason that one could not fasten up a shipsuit properly by oneself, and Montrose did not know how closely this simpler copy mimicked the original.

He jogged back, finding Del Azarchel waiting in a garden-space beneath a blue dome, and a fountain and pool of water splashed on the tiled floor not far away. The throng had grown. Del Azarchel was now surrounded by a crowd of retainers and courtiers larger than what had been there before. He was telling them about the coming Armada from Epsilon Tauri. Montrose heard a tense question or two, and then a breath of relief swept through the garden-chamber. The courtiers were chuckling. "Eight thousand years," said one, a handsome youth in a metallic wig. "It is further in our future than all recorded history rests in our past—"

Del Azarchel raised his hand, and the courtiers, all of them, fell silent as if a switch had been thrown. Del Azarchel was now dressed in a black shipsuit like Montrose wore, except that there were silver fittings at his throat and shoulders.

Montrose came forward, caught sight of himself in the glass on the wall behind Del Azarchel, and smiled. "We're not going to shave our heads? The suit officer won't let us board if we don't have clean skull fits."

Del Azarchel smiled with the left half of his mouth, raising one eyebrow. "You think this is not real? It is very real, I assure you. Hylics are not allowed to wear these fabrics. Only us."

"Who-lacks?" Montrose recalled that the Iron Ghost version of Del Azarchel had also used the word.

Del Azarchel made a rueful smile. "Hylics. An unfortunate term, perhaps, coined in more contentious times—it refers to the common people, the mundane ones, those who trod the earth."

"Whad'ya mean *only us*? Us who?"

"The Men of the Stars. The Learned. We who possess the secret knowledge. You remember the perfume of outer space? That smell, the strange ozone smell of the outer darkness? You remember what it is like to step into the airlock, and hear the ringing in your ears as pressure returns, and catch a whiff of that strange odor, it tingles in the nose like dark smoke, long after the valve is shut and the atmosphere is pumped in. You recall? Those who wish to depart the Earth and smell that scent, they are our servants here, and students. They are called by a nobler name: Psychics."

From the looks of pride that stiffened on the faces of the men around him, Montrose understood this referred to the dandies in jeweled coats, wearing their odd wigs of white wire.

"I thought they were your roughhouse boys. Knights and bishops and,

and, uh, rooks or whatever you call them. Count Dracula and Duke El-
lington and so on."

"Think of them as a Mandarin class. They have the power to rule, it is
true, but it is due to the merit of their several attainments, the exemplary
nature of their service to human destiny." The men stood taller at these
words, proud as petted hounds. "The elite of this new age are the acolytes
and familiars of the Highest Order; students of the hidden truth; men
who have moved beyond the Hylic stage of pure selfish materialism. It is
a meritocracy of the mind, the rule by philosopher-kings. And so we call
them Psychics."

"Not people with way-cool mind powers? Damn. You got to pick a better
word. That's just misleading. I was sure folk in the future world would be
able to focus their brainwaves, and blow folks' skulls off, phlegm like that.
What do you call the highest order, if these guys are just the students?"

"Pneumatics."

"Jesus up a tree, you gotta talk to someone about picking better names
for stuff, Blackie."

Del Azarchel beckoned to a figure in white. The man stepped forward.
It was the old Oriental doctor who had first examined Montrose when he
awoke. This man did not wear one of those metallic wigs. Did that mean
he was a servant, a Hylic, rather than a boss?

Del Azarchel said to Montrose: "I am sending you ahead of me, to the
Conclave, because of this business I must here conclude. My court does
not seem to be taking the matter very soberly—which is to be expected.
Large numbers can stagger the mind, and large numbers of years dull the
imagination. I will come rapidly. Meanwhile, the ride will give you an opportunity to be examined, since you just had another episode of your, ah,
other self. If you would, please."

Montrose had been pushed around a bit too much of late, especially
with Del Azarchel playing a swift trick with that drink, and then accus-
ing him of poaching his old lady. He thought it was about time to dig in
his heels.

"*Sending* me? I'll be damned first. You can *ask*. You seem to forget that
I don't work for you."

"And you seem to forget that you are still a member of the crew, and I
am in charge of the landing party."

"What? That means landings on the Monument surface! Or some other alien body we might encounter. You are talking as if we never came home. . . ."

"This Earth is not the one we left. To us, it is an alien body. The ship is still aloft, and her weapons are all that hold the globe in check. Did you resign your commission?"

He thought, but did not say, *There are no weapons mounted aboard the ship*. That had been one of the conditions permitting her to launch. Instead he said, "But the Captain is dead."

"A new Captain was appointed, as per our articles. Did you resign your commission?"

"No, I reckon not."

"Then you are still a member of the crew. As soon as the doctor discharges you officially from the sick roster, you must report for duty. The carriage is yonder. Please move briskly. Time is short."

"Short!" snorted Montrose. "Eighty centuries! What do you consider a long time?"

"A man might not have the patience to count to a trillion," answered Del Azarchel coldly, "but the number is real whether he counts it or not. A man might not think he will live to see the future. But it will come, with him, or without him, by his effort, or by the effort of others. I am asking you to report to the Conclave not as a penalty, but as an honor, that you might be one of those men who will shape the future and make it come as it ought."

Montrose had nothing to say back to that.

2. The Buried Carriage

Then the double doors slid shut, and Montrose found himself alone with the doctor.

"Please sit," said the doctor in a voice that brooked no disagreement. "I will not have all my work on your skull undone merely because of a fall."

Montrose realized that he could argue with the Master of the World, but not with a sawbones. He sat. He felt lightheaded as soon as he did, and this scared him a moment. Maybe his head was not back to normal after all. "Doc, I am feeling a little dizzy. . . ."

"That's normal," the doctor snapped.

"Normal for what? You didn't give me any pills or anything."

"Normal during descent." The old man's eyes crinkled as he stared at Montrose, with what seemed a rather impatient look. "This leg is a gravity train. After we leave the peninsula, there is a drop-off as we descend beneath the continental shelf. We have to descend to reach the main line, which follows the curve of the mantle of the Earth in a suborbital arc."

"How do you maintain the tube walls against the pressure of the magma?"

The doctor shook his head. "Something called magnetic capillaries inflate a pipeline, which is composed of something else, a heat-resistant substance called openwork carbon nanofiber. Ovenwork? Something like that. I'm not an engineer. It uses up a great deal of energy to maintain pipeline integrity, but these days—" His shrug was eloquent. Energy was so inexpensive, that it was not even worth finishing a sentence to explain it.

"What peninsula?"

"The Florida peninsula. That was a complex buried beneath the old spaceport called Canaveral. It is the primary point for maintaining radio-link with the *Hermetic*."

Montrose had notice no lightheadedness the first time he'd ridden this rail system, with Del Azarchel. Of course, he had been deep in talk with his friend, and had not just had a recent episode of unconsciousness, or super-conciousness, or possession, or whatever it was. Also, he did not know if this branch of the evacuated depthtrain passed through the mantle of the Earth at the same angle as where he had been previously.

The smoothness had deceived him, and the lack of noise. The engines in his day always lost some energy through heat, noise, and vibration. Maybe here in the future, they had found a way to machine-tool their engines to more perfect specifications. More precise fits meant less vibration. Montrose realized the titanic energy supply the Hermeticists had brought back from the Diamond Star meant not just more raw power to level mountains and burn fortresses, but more energy, and hence more time, effort, and precision, were free to be spent on a wide variety of tasks. What was the major difference between a savage caveman and a civilized Texan, after all? Not just tools and organization, but the magnitude of power at his fingertips.

His mother once had said that the difference from a caveman was education. That may be. But what, ultimately, was education? Something to increase the efficiency of brainpower. What was brainpower? What was a brain, really, except for an engine that turned the noise into signal—an engine that took a chaos of raw sense data and turned it into organized patterns of pretty electroneural charges holding meaningful conclusions about the universe? The more energy a civilization controlled, the more brainpower it could bring to bear on a wider range of non-routine tasks.

The thought cheered him. Maybe the future that Del Azarchel had made was not so bad. It sure sounded like some sort of renaissance or industrial revolution was ongoing, if Blackie's boasts were true.

Ah, but that was the stone in the shoe, wasn't it?

"Hey, Doc. I was wondering about the fighting."

"What fighting?"

"You know—brush wars, proxy wars, border disputes, Mormon lynching. That sort of thing. I mean, it seems quiet now, but you know how these things go."

Nothing could have convinced Montrose more rapidly than the look of surprise on the old doctor's face that perhaps he had misjudged Del Azarchel. Could there really be, for once in human history, no fighting going on? Montrose did not think it possible; and yet the shock of the doc was perfectly sincere.

The man said with a tinge of exasperation in his voice, "What are you talking about? Warfare was all abolished by the Concordats. The police are all locally controlled, each by their parish. There are unpaid volunteer militias in some areas, but they are armed with nonlethal weapons, pain-induction rays, and gumthrowers, for they face rioters and malcontents, not armed forces. There is no need to heed rogue stations—the accredited press maintains accurate reports."

"Pox! No one has guns?"

The doctor turned his eyes upward, as if in thought. "The ruling houses in each area will keep retainers and men-at-arms, of course, or employ ignoble horse troopers to run down poachers or wiremen trying to set up pirate powercast rectennae. Most regional Parliaments maintain honor squads, as a symbol of their sovereignty. Protectorate areas are patrolled by Landkeepers, and they are armed. The Holy Father has the Swiss Guard. Of course, with contraterrene weapons, you do not need an army to depopulate a city, merely one civic assassin." The doctor's face was stern, and his shrug was short. He was clearly a man who did not think well of firearms.

"What is this Concordat?"

"The social covenant. The Princess has ordained peace throughout the world." The old man's face softened into a mass of wrinkles when he smiled. "We have no external enemies, and hence no wars. Peace has smiled on the human race at last!"

There was a light in his eyes when he said *the Princess.*

Montrose did not want to spoil the mood by pointing out that the Roman Empire and the Chinese had no significant external enemies, but were racked by horrific civil wars everytime a dynasty lost its grip on power, or someone thought it should.

"What's your name, Doc?"

"Kyi."

"Family name or Christian name?"

The doctor inclined his head respectfully. "That is my Medicine-Buddha name, which more fully is Sgra-dbyangs kyi rgyal-po, whom I emulate. My refuge name is Bhlogrochosnyi, Intellect Cosmic Order Sun, obtained when I took refuge in the three jewels of Buddha, Dharma, Sangha. I am of Tashilhupo, who follow the Yellow Hat sect."

"Uh . . . that's right nice. Doctor Key . . ."

"Kyi."

"Doctor Kyi . . . if I can ask. Who is this Princess of yours?"

The doctor looked amused. "So you are infatuated just from her picture?"

"I didn't say that!"

"I am a doctor: I know the signs of neural imbalance. She is Her Serene Highness the Sovereign Princess Rania of Monaco, daughter of Rainier. Her mother bore her aboard the *Hermetic,* making the princess the first born beneath the light of another sun: Her phylum is classed as *Exosolar.* Place your dreams elsewhere. She is above your rank."

"Impossible."

The old man shook his head wearily. "Resign yourself. The effort the Noble Master expended in recovering your sanity has placed you in a debt beyond recovery. And I do not mean a monetary debt—only the lower orders concern themselves with such things. I mean the honor code that governs the arms-bearing class. By any rational calculation of debt, you are a client, a dependent, of the Nobilissimus, a retainer, even if you take no oath—and therefore you cannot impose yourself on his fiancée."

Montrose forced a smile onto his face, and uttered a bitter laugh. "Why would I care about that? I never met the girl! Seems a little, ah, on the young side for him, though, don't she? Where did you say she was born?—and anyhow, I meant it was impossible that she was birthed aboard ship."

Dr. Kyi said coolly, "She was aboard the great ship when the *Hermetic* received the capitulation from the Old Order."

"Which old order is that?"

"The Purity Order: Azania, the Coptic Union, and Greater Manchuria. Superceded, now. They were absorbed peacefully into the Concordat."

"How did they win? The Hermeticists, I mean. The ship was an antique. She was not a warship, wasn't carrying missiles or linears or nothing."

"I am no soldier. I can only say what I have heard."

"Then tell me."

"Let me hook your suit to my bag first, that I may do a complete scan and checkup. May we proceed?"

Montrose submitted with ill grace.

The way the doctor told it, the weapons of the *Hermetic* were her sails and magnetic umbra. The ship enjoyed several incomparable advantages: Because contraterrene is ultralightweight, hard to detect, and impossible to deflect, once the vessels closed to engagement distances, even a microscopic fleck flung at an incoming vessel, striking any part of it, would emit a pulse of radiation hot enough to blind or cripple it.

With her immensely more powerful drives, the *Hermetic* was able to outmaneuver her foes, and she had no supply lines to protect. The Old Order vessels were overextended; they tried to re-supply by using unmanned high-acceleration canisters, but the *Hermetic* jinxed their radio-controls, and sent the supplies off-target. Her radio-emitters were more powerful than any Earthly emitter, even at interplanetary ranges. Her attacks were handled with a precision the finest computers on Earth could not match.

From beyond Mars, the *Hermetic* used her sail to focus (with impossible accuracy) solar beams onto navigation satellites orbiting the Earth, burning them like ants beneath a magnifying glass, and the captains of the scattered vehicles of the Old Order suddenly were blind and lost without Earth-based navigation.

"Perhaps," the old doctor said, "had they been truly devout to their cause, the Copts could have calculated their positions with sextants and almanacs, and plotted their orbits with their onboard equipment, but then the voice of the Princess came across their radio-sets, calling them each by name, and offering them the Concordat. Their choice was to become the military backbone of the New Order, with land, dignities, and honors long denied to them, or to perish of exhaustion in the vacuum. Her voice none could deny: she is not of this Earth."

Montrose sat up so quickly that the doctor's black bag, connected to him by half a dozen sensitive lines, bleeped in annoyance. "Wait—What? Are you saying the *Hermetic* picked her up on some other planet? That she is an alien? But there are no planets like that, and even if there were, no star systems are between here and V 866 Centauri . . ."

"I said she was born aboard ship."

"And I said that was impossible. Who was the mother? There were no women aboard."

"Three women were smuggled aboard, disguised as crewmen who had washed out of the program, but were too ashamed to allow the public to know."

"Oh, come on. Smuggled how? When? Why?"

"They were comfort women. It is thought best in polite circles not to inquiry too closely into the matter, in case face be lost. You see that the matter is delicate."

"You mean whores?" Montrose uttered a laugh and slapped his knee. "Hee-howdie! That would have been a hoot. Playing belly-thumper all the way to Centauri and back. If'n I were a jane, I'd'a gone for it. Wait . . . you're serious? You're not serious."

The doctor certainly looked serious. Of course, he probably looked that way most times.

Montrose guffawed. "Who told you we had strumpets aboard? Where was they stowed? Every square half-centimeter of space was accounted for. Or were the hussies just clinging to the outside of the hull like a remora fish on a submarine? That'd be quite a bit of clinging, considering that the ship's carousel was spun for gravity. Hanging by your hands with the stars under your toes for fifty years, and the boys would have to be pretty lonely for you, cause you'd be older than grandma by the time the johns thawed out. Pee-shaw. Who came up with that stretch of baloney?"

"These women, arrested for breaches of public decorum laws in Argentina, were given the opportunity to escape the Decency Inquisition the newly-reconstituted Spanish Crown had initiated, by doing community service. Essentially they were volunteering for permanent exile. The women were smuggled aboard because one of the high-level expedition organizers thought it would be a good idea, necessary for the sanity and well-being of the all-male crew, to send along . . ."

Menelaus just shook his head, smirking in disbelief.

The doctor looked offended. "Would you accuse the Nobilissimus Lord Regent Del Azarchel himself of perpetrating a lie? Be warned!"

"Would you accuse Captain Grimaldi of being so jackass loco yack-stupid as to lock up three warm-blooded señoritas in a canful of two hundred ten lusty young men and lonely old professors? Be warned yourself, Doc. Be warned not to believe any tin-plate panner-junk they try to palm off on you. Del Azarchel should've asked me. I would've come up with a better whopper than that one. Space whores!" He shook his head, unable to suppress a smile. "That's cracked."

Dr. Kyi favored him with a cold look. "You were in a coffin the whole time. You have no knowledge of what occurred."

"Impossible. Im—poss—see—bull. And the emphasis is on the *bull*."

"Why are you so certain, Mr. Montrose?"

"Do you think someone could have just up and added an extra biosuspension unit aboard? How about three? The ship was designed for ninety-five percent of lightspeed. Do you want to see the figures on how much oomph it costs to accelerate even a single gram of mass to that velocity? The crew had to slim down like wrestlers training for a weight class too light for us. We were shaving our heads bald because two hundred ten crewhands' worth of hair—I am talking about the *weight* of the hair—'tweren't worth the cost of fuel to boost. Our uniforms was tissue paper, and it was more lightweight to paint our feet with insulator goop than to carry socks. We didn't have shoes! Pox and plague, man! They had little plastic bags we were meant to pee into before docking, and we were going to leave them on the punt before we boarded, so that we'd be that much lighter before weigh-in. Each gram of urine counted."

Dr. Kyi looked puzzled, even disturbed. Obviously Montrose's words had struck doubt into him. "The history files are not clear. A large mass of data was lost when the Coptics and Voortrekkers aligned with the Chinese and came to power: One of the cybernetic battles—I cannot recall the historian's name and number code for which microsecond it happened in—was called the Aneurysm."

"Well, I can tell you that security aboard the ship was as airtight as the ship herself. Our biometrics were all on file in a separate back-up computer called Little Big Brother that was not even physically connected with the mainframe. Little Big Brother were these little black boxes dotting the inner hull that made sure no one entered or left officer's country or the engineering deck where the manipulator-field controls were locked. You understand, we were going out there to mine antimatter, and nine-tenths of the ship's complement was going to be cold slumber. It was not the kind of ship where a person could just hop around from deck to deck with no one looking. Only the captain had access to Little Big Brother, and the First Mate if and only if Brother thought the Captain was dead. You going to tell me Captain Grimaldi smuggled some painted trollops aboard and left behind needed crew? Not him. Never. You are talking about men I knew, a ship I served on—well, nearly."

"But you were not privy to the decisions of the command. Or so the histories say. You were the only man from your nation aboard, and the world still regarded the *Norteamericano* with suspicion and contempt."

"Well, shoot, I regards your tall tale here with suspicion and contempt. It don't hang together. Where're these women now?"

"They did not survive the voyage."

"Convenient. Where're the bodies?"

"Prince Rainier married all three, to remove the women from the use of the crew, and this contributed to the rebellion."

Menelaus stared up at the roof of the chamber or, rather, the car. "There is no way the Captain Grimaldi I knew would have turned polygamous— his people had no love for the Jihadi, and keeping spare wives around was their knack, not a Monegasque thing at all. Speaking of which, the crew was one-third Indosphere, one-third Hispanosphere, and one-third were odds and ends, mostly from the Sinosphere—including me, since Oddifornia was Sino back in the day. How many of the expedition survivors were from the Spanish-speaking parts of the world?"

The doctor said stiffly, "These days, it is considered impolite to look into a man's language loyalties or enthophylum. We do not take in account . . ."

"So they were all Beaneaters? All the ones who lived?"

"We do not use that kind of language—it is regarded as a matter of insult to . . ."

"Yeah, well, I damn well regard it as a matter of insult to tell a lie. In my day, your primary loyalty was to whoever talked like you. Not to your Church, like in the days of the Jihad, and not to your King, like in the First Dark Ages, not to your race, like in the Second—in my day, the lines were drawn between Anglosphere, Gallosphere, Hispanosphere, Sinosphere, and so on. Del Azarchel was Spanish. He would not have killed Argentine women. It never happened. There weren't no women."

The doctor regarded him with narrowed eyes. "Your suspicions have no ground."

"Oh, I think the grounds are in what you said about the space battle. Sounds as if the Hermeticists outsmarted their opponents. Like a man outsmarting a monkey. And this girl just talked everyone into surrendering, did she? And the crew—by any chance, did they do any reconfiguring on the ship's electronic brain while they were at V 886 Centauri? Never mind. You wouldn't know the answer to that, would you? Anyhow, they are still outsmarting you."

"In what regard?"

"You want to know how to sniff out a lie? Lies are told with a particular audience in the sites, see? If you understand the audience, you understand the lie. Your little story about three crewmen being too dishonored to be willing to admit they flunked out of the space expedition—you believe it, because that is the way you'd act, the way your generation expects people to act. I haven't seen more than a glimpse of y'all in this time, but you are a military culture, and militant cultures have a cult of honor. Always have. People of my day did not act that way. We were a free-market culture. A guy who flunked out of Space Camp would have done pixies, maybe wrote a book, walked the lecture circuit. Because we cared about money, not honor so much, on account of the world was in a depression, and every penny counted. See what I mean? Time changes people, don't it? That's one reason why lies do not last."

The doctor said, "Paranoia symptoms are the type of self-reinforcing neural-path behavior I regard as an bad sign: We do not want to see a collapse into your previous halt state."

Menelaus leaned back in his chair, stuck his thumbs in his sash, and spread his legs in a comfortable slouch. "And is common sense a bad sign?"

"Then where did Princess Rania come from?" the doctor retorted. "You can see she looks like her father. Blood samples match. Her gene-print can open a legacy lock left by him in a Swiss Bank, for any heirs of his body born after him: this was one of the things done early on to confirm her right to the throne of Monaco."

"Who nursed the baby, back aboard ship? We weren't carrying no baby milk in bottles. We . . ." And then Menelaus got a strange, distant look in his eye, and he straightened up suddenly out of his slouch. "Of course, we *did* have biosuspension coffins. Equipped with molecular mechanisms to restore and replenish decayed cells . . . and matrices of formalized molecules, all lined up nice and pretty, the way they never do in nature, waiting for microscopic electron-commands to tell them what patterns to make. And the code for a milk gland is right there in anyone's DNA: males have an X chromosome, after all, and all you need is two XX's to persuade the molecular machinery to start making female cells. And a damnified totipotent cell can damn near turn into damn near anything—people been doing it since before I was born. All you would need is the right code. The right expression. Doc, you got a piece of paper? I wanna see how many transformation steps it would take, using a simple Pell Expression, to get from a flat array of molecules via the minimum number of knots to a complex spline formation. Because one of the theories we discussed for the Gamma Grouping of Monument signs was that it was a spline expression for a complex surface, and that this was a generalized model for a brain. Any brain, not just a human brain, seeing as how the spline function could simply be mapped onto other nervous systems—or whatever information system the little green men had instead of brains . . ."

"I don't have a piece of paper, and I hardly think this is the time for you to be . . . you are about to meet with the Special Executive of the Concordat . . . and I am concerned that any thoughts along your habituated . . . Mister Montrose! What are you doing!" His voice rose to a sudden shriek of surprise.

Montrose had taken a glass vase from the decorative shelf, thrown the flowers and water over his shoulder, studied the geometry to determine possible stress weaknesses, and shattered the thing on the marble chessboard.

Now he had a sharp fragment of glass in his hand. With it, he was carving little Greek letters into the arm of his chair, which was varnished wood, so that the slightest scar showed up very nicely. He spoke without looking up from his figures. "What kind of barbaric society does not have paper around for back-of-the-envelope calculations? Lincoln never would've wrote the Gettysburg Address if it weren't for scrap paper."

The doctor looked annoyed. "It was very much against my professional advice that you were wakened under uncontrolled conditions in a high-stimulation environment, especially since we have yet to confirm if the damage done to your nervous system is mitigated. How many fingers am I holding up?"

"Fifteen or so," he said, still not looking up. Both chair arms were now covered, so he lurched to his feet, and plopped down into another chair. "I ain't got room. Hey—what kind of surface does that chessboard have?"

"Do you remember who you are?"

He answered absentmindedly. "Menelaus Illation Montrose, J.D. and Ph.D., graduated Soko University in Nip Frisco, Class of '34, before that, commissioned in '25 as Lance-Corporal in the United State Imperial Calvary, the Tough-Ruttin' Thirty-Fifth, decommissioned thank God, and after that, Monumentician and Semantic Logosymbolic Specialist, Joint Indosphere-Hispanosphere Scientific Xenothropological Expedition to Centauri V 866. Does that sound like I know who I am?"

"What race are you?"

"I am trying to work here."

"Please answer, Mister Montrose."

"Doctor. Purebred Tex-Mex. What'ya think?"

"No, I mean, do you know what species you are? Do I look like a member of your own species to you, at the moment?"

This made him look up. "What the hell kind of question is that? My what?"

"Are we both human?"

Montrose let out a laugh. "Rut me with a harpoon! You kidding? You ain't kidding. What, is you aiming to rip off your mask and turn out to be a monster bug from Arcturus or something? Big clustery eyes and dripping sideways mouth and all? Damnation, go ahead! Let me see it. I dare ya! Do we have starships to Arcturus as yet?"

"There is but one manned starship, and she keeps the peace of Earth and cannot depart."

"We'll see about that one."

"Extend your hands to either side, and, while closing your eyes, touch your nose. Quickly, please."

"I will be damned if I will. You ain't answering my queries, Doc."

"Hm. Insubordination is not a mental disorder, I suppose, but it is not exactly a healthy sign, either."

"I'll show you a healthy sign." He pointed at the chessboard. The surface was marble, and hence immune to his knifepoint, but the back was a thin layer of cork, and he had inscribed it with precise rows of little marks. "That's where she was born."

"Who?"

"Your Princess. I could have done it with the material in four coffins, and one dead body, of course, provided the flesh was burnt, because the carbon molecules were what the paramagnetic fields of the antimatter manipulators were designed to use. They can work on terrene matter just as easily. And the coffins were stuffed with nanomachinery. They were already like a womb for people like me to sleep in. And Grimaldi was nice and burnt to death, so he could serve as the raw material."

Montrose grinned his skull-like gargoylean grin, which seemed to startle the poor doctor more than it should have. He continued: "Your Princess is like a digger wasp: an egg laid inside a corpse, except the artificial placenta used molecular mechanisms stripped out of the ship's recyclers, which I hear weren't much working so well no-how, to convert the material to nutriments. All you would need is the code. No one on Earth could solve that expression. But if you had the math, you could do it. Very sly. This is a damn fine piece of work. Brilliant. Poxing brilliant. But why?

Why make another human being, if you were so low on supplies? And why make a little baby girl? And—Oh, sweet Jesus up a tree! He's not going to marry her, is he? That is practically incest!"

"I do not understand what you mean. It would be incest only if Prince Rainier married his daughter, and he died shortly after she was born."

"Shortly *before*, you should say. I mean *this* here is the Princess's mother, and it came out of Blackie's head."

"But—that is a chessboard. You found it here in the coach, a few moments ago. It is an inanimate object."

"No, jackass, I mean the expression! This is how she was born! You recognize a Diophantine Equation, don't you?"

"I, ah, am not as familiar with that particular, um . . ."

"They taught you about Fermat's Last Theorem in school, right? This here is a special case of that theorem and so has no solutions for numbers less than or equal to three. Now, Hilbert posed the problem of defining an algorithm for finding out if an arbitrary Diophantine equation has a solution. For first-order equations, answer is yes. Matiyasevich proved no general solution was possible. Not in human math, anyway. This expression represents a closed spline ball. Basically, it is a line drawn through a permutation of the vertices of an icosahedron: in this case the line represents the growth relation between totipotent cells in a blastula and a developed nervous system. It cannot be solved because the number of Bezier curves would have to equal the number of nerve cells, and the vertices change for each nerve state: there are not enough computers on Earth to get the raw calculating power to do it. But suppose someone else had done it for you. But now suppose you had solved a high-order solution for the Diophantine Equation defining the underlying icosahedron giving rise to this expression here."

"I warn you, Mister Montrose, I have had the privilege of working with the Princess on your case for nine years now, and I will not have my work ruined, *ruined*, I say, because you are so uncooperative! If you do not care about your brain operations, I do! Do you know how much delicate molecular engineering went into just the path redaction? It's a fragile and subtle piece of work—how dare you endanger it! My masterpiece! *Her* masterpiece! I don't like these dopamine levels!"

Montrose took all the lines running from the doctor's bag to points on his own body in one fist and yanked them out, ignoring the pain where needleheads pried free. "Well, it is *my* own damn brain. I got a right to it."

"You don't! Stop thinking so hard! We cannot build you another!"

Montrose laughed aloud. "Well, Blackie's gotten pretty close to growing a second brain. He has got a working model, self-aware, able to talk like a man and everything. . . ."

The doctor snorted. "Impossible. Nobilissimus Del Azarchel himself spearheaded the effort to render research into artificial intelligence illegal. The scientific union declares the problem insolvable, and the Church condemns the creation of self-aware beings unable seek salvation to be an abomination. It is a slander for you to imply the Nobilissimus to be involved in such efforts. . . ."

"Boy, are you in the dark! I've just come from working on it."

"Nonsense! I am the chief of the personal physician staff of the Nobilissimus—a member of the inner circle. I would know."

"Yeah, well, I am his drinking buddy, and I carried him back to barracks on my back while he puked in my ear, so I see your inner circle and raise you."

The doctor sat back, scowling. He regained his composure enough to muster a shrug. "The Princess says the development of artificial minds is both inevitable and beneficial, and this may be one reason why the Nobilissimus keeps her out of the public eye for decades at a time. . . ."

"He said she suffered from something called Earthsickness, and had to go into biosuspension?"

"We in the inner circle know the Nobilissimus both loves and fears her."

"Wait. This magic Princess of yours, the one who wrote your Constitution and unified the planet. Are you saying she was the one who fixed my nerve damage? What is she, some sort of Jack of Trades, a female Tom Jefferson? A Renaissance Man Lady? Because if she is—I, hey, I . . . Doc! I think I dreamed about her when she was small . . ."

Montrose was so surprised that he dropped the chessboard.

". . . When she was a little girl. I think I saw her on the ship. But how could I? I was in a coffin the whole time!"

Then he yowled in pain, because the heavy chessboard struck his foot. The doctor insisted on giving him a second medical scan, and no other discussion was allowed after that.

3. The Decorated Hall

In theory, if the tunnel followed a Brachistochrone curve, then any spot on the globe could have been reached in forty-two minutes, traveling the whole way in freefall straight through the core. Practically, Montrose was pretty sure the tunnels did not go that deep, and the trains did not travel so fast. They had not been in freefall: the wineglasses in the wall cabinet had not even rattled. At a guess, he estimated a magnetic levitation train passing through an evacuated tunnel could reach speeds of 5000 miles per hour, topping Mach 6.

This meant that when the carriage stopped and the door hissed open, and he stepped down a short corridor into the atrium of the Presence Chamber, he was sure he was nowhere near Florida: He could be anywhere from Alaska to Argentina, from Iceland to Europe to North Africa, or some island anywhere between Catalina to the Caribbean to Corsica. He did not even know which hemisphere he was in.

The doctor would not step out of the rail car when it finally came to a silent halt.

Montrose decided that he hated the buried railway system of the Twenty-Fourth Century. He wondered about the psychology of people who made superhighspeed trains without windows, and so smooth that there was well-nigh no sensation of motion. So far he had seen nothing like a platform. The experience was one of walking from one room to another, waiting a bit, and walking out.

He had no sense of relative locations. It was like being in a sprawling mansion stretched out over the planet: the whole world was indoors.

So far he had been nowhere but in Del Azarchel's buried palace, his research campus, and here—and if this small sample was illustrative, that sprawling mansion that stretched over the world had darn few windows.

Montrose wondered if everyone in the this century lived far underground, like gnomes.

He walked alone. His footfalls echoed up and down the hallway. The corridor was adorned in a gaudy Old World fashion, with war trophies of flags and shields, busts of Minerva and Mars, beneath a vaulted ceiling of thrones and crowns.

Montrose walked more and more slowly down this corridor, for he was studying the pictures here. Like the chamber he had first woken up in, this was decorated with pictures and portraits of the Space War, and the glorious return of the *Hermetic*.

Unlike the chamber walls, where he had to guess which pictures went with which events, this seemed laid out like a drama. The images were in chronological order.

Montrose's footsteps grew slower. There was no image he had not seen before, but this artist had a more realistic style, and some of the images were photographs or stereophotographs rather than pigments.

An image of the *Hermetic* approaching Earth, her sails spread to catch the light from the orbital braking laser was followed by an image of the ship approaching Jupiter.

Hmm. That struck Montrose as odd. It looked like the great ship had left the deceleration beam before reaching Earth, and deliberately overshot the target. Why Jupiter? Montrose assumed the Captain was performing a gravity-sling, to let the giant planet's gravity well curve the ship's freefall into some new vector . . . no, wait. Not the Captain. Someone else was in charge of the ship during all this.

And where were the warships that had been fighting? Had there not been a space war going on when the great ship returned? Those pictures were next down the corridor: canister-shaped craft lifting off from Earth, bulky with strap-on tanks in the first picture, and open frameworks of missile platforms in the later pictures.

Then the pictures were of fire. This artist had drawn them correctly, as globes of blue-white expanding in zero-gee in all directions, following streams of oxygen issuing from cracked double-hulls.

But Earth vessels were not fighting each other.

One picture he thought was merely a symmetrical image of blazing light. But, no, he realized that it was a picture of the orbital braking laser opening fire on the *Hermetic,* and the great ship's sails reflecting the energy back to the source, burning the laser and the crew in a frozen moment the artist had depicted as a field of white in which mere traces of skeletons and latticework from burning machinery could be glimpsed.

Next, occupying both walls of the corridor, was an image of a burnt city under a mushroom cloud. The artist had painted streaks and streams of odd color, green and indigo, issuing like a lighting bolt high in the air. The bolt was wider at the top than at the bottom, which was unlike a detonation or mass-driver strike. There was a tiny silver dot high up in the corner of the image.

Montrose stopped walking.

It was an orbital antimatter bombardment.

The magnetic launch-bottle could accelerate the particle to relativistic velocities, but the explosion, the total conversion, would happen at the outermost fringes of atmosphere, wherever contraterrene met terrene matter. The *Hermetic*'s mining aura, fired simultaneously, could focus a beam of magnetic influence to drive the resulting particle spray downward rather than in all directions, but it *would* spread. Only a fraction of the energy would touch the ground.

As a weapon, it was absurdly wasteful. As an act of conspicuous consumption, meant to awe the enemy into surrender, it was not wasteful at all.

Then came other images of cities dying in fire beneath the heavy canopies of mushroom-shaped clouds.

Once when he was young and in the service, Montrose had been kicked by a mule. It was an old beast, and he had been wearing a heavy jacket, so the blow did not kill him, but it sent him to the infirmary with his ribs taped up. The sensation he felt then was like that.

Back when he had first seen these pictures of mushroom clouds on the walls of the bedchamber where he woke, of course he assumed he was looking at a nuclear war. Of course he had not imagined the *Hermetic* at fault, because she carried no nuclear warheads.

Stupid. Stupid, because he knew enough high-school physics to know what causes clouds of that shape. Heat, not radioactivity. The characteristic mushroom cloud shape was a byproduct of energy expenditure. You would get the same thing above a large-scale meteor strike, or . . .

The next image showed the *Hermetic* and the open-framework cylinder-ships from Earth. It looked like the cylinders were making reentry. But no. The *Hermetic* had accepted the surrender of the crews (a string of suited figures was shown being drawn in the airlock) and was using the empty hulls as drop-energy weapons. A mass of metal that large, made of sub-stances designed not to melt on re-entry, landing in a city, or atop a dam, would release as much kinetic energy as an atom bomb, but without the messy radioactivity.

There had been no war for the *Hermetic* to stop. Why had he assumed that? Because that was what he wanted to assume, maybe?

There was another portrait of the Princess here. In this one, she was crowned with the wreath of olive leaves, and held a dove on one wrist.

He now knew the meaning of the peace so lovingly portrayed at the end of the corridor. It was what might be called a Caesar's peace: The peace a conqueror brings to a trampled land once he's won total victory, and his wrath is sated.

He stared at the painted features of the lovely girl. The face was very similar to the face of Grimaldi, as if the Captain's features had been re-drawn in more delicate lines.

Montrose turned over in his head the Diophantine Equation he ex-pected had been used to create her, the world's first completely artificial being. Every gene must have been calculated through . . . this absurdly complex equation, not to mention medical tests and proofs-of-concept, would have had to have been performed before the corpse cooled.

Or beforehand. There was a ghost of a memory in his head. Montrose was sure he had seen the Captain's dead body, floating in the zero-gee ax-ial chambers of the *Hermetic*, where the coffins were stored. The body was not burned at that time. The carbonization must have happened after, as part of the preparation process to prepare the body's mass to act as raw ma-terial, to create an artificial womb in one of the body cavities where the girl, Rania, was to be grown.

Which meant there had been no suicide. There had been a mutiny and a murder.

The corridor ended in a semicircular atrium paved in shining lapis lazuli beneath a slanted ceiling of polished onyx set with stars, images of Olym-pian gods, coats of arms, lozenges, and tablatures. Along the walls were suits of armor from the past and suits of space-armor from the present, as well as pikes and swords and daggers hung up in patterns like steel flowers.

He heard voices up ahead, speaking softly, but that was all. No one was near him, no one was watching. He turned. The door at the far end of the corridor was shut, presumably because the railcar beyond was gone. Montrose did not know by what control or signal another could be summoned. There had been no control, no strip of sensitive material near the door: To him, that door was firmly locked.

The weapons were not nailed so firmly to the wall. The largest dirk he could find, he tucked through two ring-clips on his back-harness, where the long scholar's hood (hanging down his back like a miniature triangular cape) would cover it. He left behind one of the purely ceremonial oxygen tubes to make room.

4. The Undecorated Hall

Beyond, grim and dark, was a flattened dome held up by metallic ribs, an architecture as ungainly as the underside of an umbrella, as massive as the tomb of a pharaoh. It sharply contrasted with the splendor of the atrium outside.

This presence chamber of the Hermeticists, if it truly was the throne room and headquarters of the masters of the human race, was impressive in its Spartan simplicity: The chamber here was unadorned, utilitarian, severe. Beneath the flattened dome, a single table circled the room, with cushioned chairs on steel frames facing inward. The table was a hollow zero, surrounding a round central floor paved with high-quality library cloth. Eight large screens hung from articulated swivel-arms overhead. At the moment the screens were tuned to a luminous setting, and bathed the area in an aquamarine light. The walls and overheads were gray slabs.

There was only one ornament in the chamber: in an alcove to one side stood a life-sized iron statue of a Great Ape. There was a plaque at the statue's feet, but illegible in the dimness. The statue was lit by a lonely spotlight set in the alcove roof directly above it, so that the brow ridge and jowls of the simian were cast into dark relief. The artist had emphasized the massive and sloped shoulders, the protruding belly, the crooked legs to the point of exaggeration: or perhaps the sculptor had never seen a living specimen. Come to think of it, unless one of the men in this room had made it, the sculptor certainly had not, since the species went extinct only a few years before Menelaus had been born.

No other decorations or amenities. Not even a carpet. That was it.

Menelaus did not see spittoons or ashtrays, and the pitchers and tumblers before each chair seemed to hold nothing but water. Apparently these new rulers of the world did not indulge in any drinking or smoking to soften their moods when they met, which Menelaus knew to be a big mistake. The Congress of the United States, back before the Disunion, always met sober, and look at what had come of that.

The other thing which struck him as odd was the lack of servants. There were no secretaries arranging papers, no computermen organizing data presentations. But the rulers of the world—if that is what they were—apparently set out their own papers and poured their own water pitchers, because several gray-haired men in black silk shipsuits were doing just that when Montrose entered the chamber.

Menelaus counted in his lightning-quick fashion, at a glance. There were seventy men in the chamber. No Princess. The girl was not there. Menelaus thought he should not feel so foolishly disappointed—he had more important things to fret him. He should have listened to his instincts, and known that any man, even a man as smart and bold as Blackie, who drinks of absolute power, gets drunk as hell. It mutates how he thinks, how he sees things. Blowing a whole city of innocent souls to Purgatory was merely a day's labor, a matter for quiet pride of workmanship, or was merely the winning score in a game, a matter for cheers and toasts.

Foolish or not, he was still disappointed.

He noticed each man here was wearing a heavy armband of red metal, that same metal Montrose was sure had come from the machine shop aboard the *Hermetic*. From the way three or four of the men had inflammation and swelling on their wrists and forearms, Montrose realized these armbands were bioprosthetics: from the way the skin was pinched, he deduced that there must be more than one large intravenous needle or nerve-jack reaching from the inside of the armband into the inside of the arm.

The thick red bracelets could be medical appliances. The Hermeticists did not look like a healthy group.

There were three ancient figures near Montrose who turned and ambled toward him with a nightmarish slowness.

For one moment, they looked like crooked old men, murderers, mutineers, perpetrators of war crimes, and strangers. Then, suddenly, even though nothing changed, in the next moment, they were crewmen he had trained with, old drinking buddies, old friends.

Yes, he knew them.

The first was lean and lean-cheeked Narcís D'Aragó, thin as a rail and straight as a rapier, his hair little more than a hint of gray scruff above his ears. A saber with an insulated hilt, probably an electrified weapon, hung in a scabbard at his side. He still walked with a military posture, but he was a skeleton of his former self.

Next to him was Melchor de Ulloa, rheumy-eyed, with a wild thatch of white hair jutting from his skull in every direction. His spine was crooked, footsteps uncertain, the fingers of his blue-veined hands twitched and trembled. Melchor de Ulloa, who had been such a figure of romance among the ladies, now displayed his good looks lost beneath a wrinkled mask. He wore a medallion at his neck from some cult Montrose did not recognize: a circle inscribing what might have been a three-legged lambda, or else a chicken's foot.

With them was Sarmento i Illa d'Or. The muscular, slablike body Menelaus remembered had all turned to doughy fat, his mouth surrounded by a tiny fringe of beard and moustache, white as snow.

In Space Camp, and aboard the satellite before boarding the *Hermetic,* these men, together with Del Azarchel, had formed the younger clique among the mathematicians of the expedition. They had been about Montrose's age: the child prodigies. The young bloods. To see them now, wrinkled and thin or else stooped with years or sagging with fat, old as grandfathers, was quite a shock.

The final man of the clique had not come forward because he was parked near the huge table. Father Reyes y Pastor, like Del Azarchel, was wheelchair-bound. He was a splash of red in the dark room of dark-garbed men, for he wore his Cardinal's robes, a *ferraiuolo* (a formal priest's cloak), and *biretta* (a cap looking like a folded candy box with a puff atop it). Perhaps he took his uniform as a star-voyager and world-ruler to be less significant than his uniform as a Churchman. Or perhaps not, since the thick red amulet of the Hermeticists weighed on his wrist. Father Reyes y Pastor looked like a withered mummy, propped up in a wheelchair too big for him.

Montrose thought these three ancient figures were coming forward to greet him, but no. Melchor de Ulloa ignored Menelaus Montrose as if the other were a wax dummy, and spoke to Sarmento i Illa d'Or: "Glad this one's finally here. A basic strategy of approach to the problem of forced evolution we've agreed beforehand, but the tactics will depend on what Crewman Fifty-One can tell us of the message details."

With this, he reached out, and, as if Menelaus were a small child, took his hand and pulled on it, turning as if he expected Menelaus to follow him docilely.

Meanwhile Narcís D'Aragó stepped past Montrose and inspected a panel of read-outs bolted to the doorframe. "Scan shows no tattletales. We are secure."

Menelaus yanked his hand out of de Ulloa's grip. "What the pox?"

Sarmento i Illa d'Or was staring at Montrose, and his large, dark eyes in his baby-round face were cold and piercing. "We are not secure. This is the other one, isn't it?"

Melchor de Ulloa now started and turned to look at Montrose as if Montrose had just materialized out of invisibility. "Learned Montrose! Is that really you?"

Montrose turned to Sarmento i Illa d'Or. "The other one *what*?"

Melchor de Ulloa gave an uneasy laugh. "Come, is this any way to greet old friends from old centuries? Good afternoon, Learned Montrose!"

Montrose spoke without turning his head. "G'daftanoon, gents—" His eyes never left Sarmento. "—the other one *what*?"

Sarmento i Illa d'Or uttered a noise like a dog's bark, which may have been a sardonic laugh. "The one who does not bite fingers."

Melchor de Ulloa stepped between the two, taking up Montrose's hand once more, but this time to give it a vigorous shaking. He spoke slightly too loudly. "We have always felt you were something like our good luck charm, Learned Montrose. Agreed, you were in slumber during the days of tedium and terror, but the thought of you, ageless, in the coffin of your own devising—a martyr to science, no? The bravest of all of us, willing to risk everything!"

"*Learned*? What's wrong with *doctor*? We all have doctorates."

"It is an earthly title, fit only to represent earthly knowledge," said Melchor de Ulloa, still shaking hands vigorously.

Montrose gripped the other man's hand tightly, to stop it from moving. He tapped the heavy metal armlet with a fingernail. "What is this? A medical appliance? When did it become part of the uniform?" He felt the substance: not ordinary metal.

Melchor de Ulloa looked startled. "I would have thought Del Azarchel would have explained it by now! We have one prepared for you, of course, but—you are so young. What need have you to hide your years?"

Sarmento i Illa d'Or stepped forward, belly first, huge and black as a thundercloud in his silks, and Melchor de Ulloa moved aside for the big man. "Tell him nothing yet. I am not convinced of his fealty."

From where he was seated several yards away, the priest, Reyes y Pastor, spoke up, pitching his voice to carry. "Learned Montrose has always been unstable. Why should today be unlike any other day? Besides, the decision rests with our Master of Arms, Learned D'Aragó."

That was Narcís D'Aragó, who had been Master of Arms during the expedition as well. The thin, bald old soldier stepped forward, glaring. "With no ability to predict how the memory membrane operates across different intellectual topographies, we cannot say whether he knows more about us than we do. But I see no risk nonetheless. Is anything gained by continuing the masquerade inside? Is Montrose not a member? We have to show him sometime. Can we call the Conclave to order, so I can secure the hatch?"

The question was evidently directed toward Reyes y Pastor. "Not yet. The Senior member of the Landing Party is not arrived. But will you clear the Learned Montrose? Learned Del Azarchel has vouched for him in a private communication to me. Should we hold a formal vote, Learned i Illa d'Or?

Sarmento i Illa d'Or scowled so that his jowls bunched with displeasure. "Phaugh! I withdraw my objection!"

Montrose said, "What's going on here?"

Reyes y Pastor raised both hands, touched his red armband, and worked some unseen control. The others in the chamber all copied the gesture, solemnly, all arms moving in unison, like a salute.

Reyes y Pastor answered him, "We meet in the Conclave to establish the destiny of the human race. We have the tools to shape the evolution of Mankind into higher forms: and since the Hyades will send emissaries to bind our remote descendants, we now have the necessity. And do not doubt we have the power. There are many mysteries our order learned in the deep of outer space we thought not fit to share with the base stock of Man."

As he spoke, his voice changed, growing deeper and stronger. By the time he had done speaking, Reyes y Pastor had stood from his wheelchair on legs now perfectly whole. Dark color flushed through his hair. His skin was red, and his veins were visible, pulsing, and when the odd blush passed, his flesh was young, unwrinkled, without liver spots, moles, or marks. Age fell from him like a dropped cloak. His flesh was now plump and pink; a mummy no longer, he rose to his feet, kicking aside, as a discarded prop, his wheelchair.

A young man, hale and healthy, stood before him, blazing with virility. Only his eyes were uncannily old—old with the cruel wisdom of many years.

The sloppy flab of Sarmento i Illa d'Or flowed or crawled under his skin, changing and thickening into muscle tissue. The plump, old pear-shaped man was now a young Hercules with a bull-like neck, an immense, wide chest, shoulders that could bear mountains.

Montrose looked around the chamber. All the men were on their feet. Some of them endured the transformation as stoically as Reyes y Pastor: others where hissing, wincing, and wheezing, and their skins were swollen and flushed as if in some painful ecstasy. One man—it looked like a scarecrow version of Dr. Coronimas, the ship's Magnetohydrodynamicist and Engineer's Mate—was rolling on the floor, and those near him looked down with cool and impatient eyes. But even Coronimas climbed to his feet, smiling and youthful.

In less than a minute all stood there, their hair suddenly dark, arrogance fresh as early springtide shining on their faces, but wintry old age still in their eyes.

At that moment came footsteps from beyond the portal. Del Azarchel, dark, young, and handsome as a devil strode into the chamber. "All here? Good. Let's get started."

Narcís D'Aragó stepped behind Del Azarchel and touched his bracelet to a control-strip of sensitive material near the door. The immense steel values swung slowly shut on mechanical pistons, and fell to, clanging like an iron coffin lid.

The hue of the lights from the overhead screens became brighter, more yellowy. "Senior, Learned fellows, the hatch is shut."

Montrose looked behind him. He was trapped in here with the mutineers.

10

The Fatherhood of Man

1. The Secret of Youth

"So you don't tell anyone you came back with the secret of eternal youth, eh?" said Montrose, feeling anger prickle him, despite his awe.

And indeed he was awed: whatever programmed cell-bodies were stored into their armbands had acted immediately upon entering their blood-streams, and started issuing molecular commands to the bodily cells. Even their hair changed immediately, losing its gray throughout the length of each strand, rather than merely at the roots. Montrose could not fathom the speed of it: No biological process known to him would happen so quickly. Each cell must have been separately programmed with a dimorphism, trained to return to its youthful shape and consistency at the first trace of stimulant.

Melchor de Ulloa smiled ingratiatingly. "It is extended youth, but not eternal. A genetic form of divarication correction—an application of your own work to cellular biochemistry. You should feel proud!"

Montrose remembered the wrinkled face of old Doctor Kyi. "I'd feel a damn sight prouder if'n we'd've shared it."

Reyes y Pastor said calmly, "The Learned Conclave thought it not in the bests interests of Mankind to preserve the present generation, and all its accumulated genetic flaws and primitive memes. Extending the aging process slows the evolutionary process, as the older bloodlines must give way before the new bloodlines can arise, improving the breed."

The mention of breeding brought something to Montrose's attention. He saw the similarity of features: olive-skinned, dark-eyed, Mediterranean. There was only one blonde in the room: the Engineer's Mate Coronimas, whose fair hair was a genetic marker of ancient Norse conquests in Portugal.

All of Latino descent. In other words, only the Hispanospheric moiety of the joint expedition had returned. The mutiny had fractured loyalties along racial lines.

Ximen Del Azarchel touched Menelaus Montrose on the elbow and gestured toward the table. "Please sit. Join us."

Montrose recognized the O-shaped table for what it was. It was the Table Round, the gathering of King Arthur's knights, from the stories Del Azarchel so loved. Had he not, years ago, likened the *Hermetic* expedition unto knight errantry?

Except that this group seemed more a gathering of Mordreds than of Galahads.

Montrose pondered a moment, torn between hot anger and cold curiosity. Whatever crimes this group had committed, even if new to him, were years in the past. And they were his friends—he was a member of the crew, after all, a position he had worked so hard to achieve.

Perhaps he owed them a hearing. No point in storming out before he found out what they had to say. In any case, he had nowhere else to go, and the doors were sealed. And, dammit, he wanted to know what they knew!

He sat.

The seat was not particularly comfortable. He took a sip from his water glass. It was not particularly cold. Whatever the Hermeticists were up to, they certainly did not coddle themselves.

The meeting of these seventy-odd scientific overlords of the world seemed to be handled with less formality than Montrose had seen in town meetings of the eight selectmen back in Bridge-to-Nowhere. There seemed to be no minutes being kept, and no one serving as Chairman.

The first order of business was reviewing Montrose's cure of the Iron Ghost. The event had been recorded from the sensitive fabric of the walls, from every possible angle.

2. Mr. Hyde

At first, the overhead plates showed Menelaus, looking sleepy, laying on the floor next to a white-haired Del Azarchel in the cold room, surrounded by the cylinders and cables snaking across the floor. A small silver cup had rolled from the fingers of the prone figure and lay in the floor in a puddle of alcohol—and presumably whatever had been mingled with the alcohol.

The image of Del Azarchel wheeled his throne over to a tiny doll-like Menelaus, and leaned down to help him to his feet. In small, tinny voices, he and Menelaus discussed the divarication problem. Menelaus seemed to be sleepy, perhaps drunk, and his head hung down. He was speaking slowly but normally, his expression and body language normal.

It changed slowly. Menelaus seemed to get more excited. He began pacing and gesturing wildly. His face almost glowed. And then the image of Menelaus was speaking rapidly, face flushed red as if from some terrible exertion. There was something hypnotic, sinister, in the clipped, rapid, uninflected way in which he spoke, as if he meant to speak much more rapidly.

While he spoke, he opened up more and more screens on the walls around him, and produced an image of the Monument around him. He was no longer talking to Del Azarchel, but only to the pallid mask that had appeared on a large rear screen.

The eyes were the worst part. During the first moment of the speech, while Menelaus stared at the images of the Monument all around him, the eyes had danced and darted like the eyes of a man having a seizure, moving from point to point restlessly, drinking in every scrap of visual information. Then they went dead. Like two burning points, the intense eyes held unnaturally still, as if the mind behind them had mastered the art of absorbing all the sights from its peripheral vision as if the brain was developed enough to compensate for any part of the arc of vision where the

…s not turned by merely deduction. A creature too smart to … directly at what it was analyzing.

… There was … something … staring out at the world with … supernal eyes, using his face as a mask.

…e human mask spoke to the computer mask, speaking in a singsong …ice like garbled Chinese. He started leaping from screen to screen, wall to wall, and he shook off his outer coat. At about that point he drove the flesh-and-blood version of Del Azarchel out of the chamber.

3. The Testament of Crewman Fifty-One

Around the large circular table, one man after another spoke, apparently the chairmen of divisions or ad hoc committees for reports. Again, Montrose did not see who was deciding who had the floor. But he noticed that the young bloods, Del Azarchel's clique from the old days, seemed to do most of the talking.

Narcís D'Aragó spoke in his thin, colorless, precise voice, "In this recording, Fifty-One said the Monument Builders use a simple bilateral symmetry for expressing alternative concepts, and a triangle to indicate paradoxes and synthetic relations. The major glyph on a circled triangle was the pain-pleasure statement, the alternatives of good and bad, success and failure: The entire forty-five-degree section of the Eta Segment (roughly from ten degrees to twenty-five degrees on the Monument surface) was a mathematical analysis of game theory. Previous translation attempts had foundered because expressions of preference had not been recognized."

Montrose raised his hand. "Fifty-One? Is that what you are calling me?"

It had been his crew locker number, also painted in huge numerals on the front and back of his space armor.

Del Azarchel said in a meditative voice, "That is our name for the creature you accidentally created in your own nervous system, built from your own brain cells, from your own soul, however you want to say it. The Posthuman. It is still alive in your brain, though I think it is wounded."

Montrose said, "Delta-wave sleep patterns wake it up, no? My dreaming cycle restores the being. It wakes when I sleep."

"Interesting theory," said Del Azarchel noncommittally.

"You doped me to wake it up. The other me—" He turned and smiled at Sarmento i Illa d'Or, showing his teeth. "—The one who bites."

Sarmento looked sour and cracked his knuckles.

Del Azarchel said smoothly, "A medical sedative I had been asked to give you periodically. The event was fortuitous but somewhat unexpected, Learned Montrose. Perhaps something unexpected in your medical . . ."

"Unexpected? I just happened to go all possessed—or whatever it is called—just at the moment and in the place where it can do you the most good, just when I swallowed something you handed me? Jesus nailed up a tree, Blackie! Was that the only reason you cured me? I thought you were afraid of this Mister Hyde inside of me! Sounds like it is not so much dangerous as hard to get some use out of!"

Narcís D'Aragó said coldly, "Danger? We dread nothing." Del Azarchel raised a hand an inch or two, and made a small gesture as if to shush D'Aragó, but the soldier raised his voice and spoke out. "No power can arise on Earth to oppose us: We are able to predict the coming of any potential threat to our reign, and destroy whoever refuses to be suborned."

"And if I don't agree to be—what was that word? *Suborn?* You talk like that's a good thing. What if I don't play along with your hand?"

D'Aragó did not answer, but looked aside.

"Well, tough guy?" said Montrose, "Are you going to beef me now? Or just ask me to commit suicide?"

There was a mutter of surprise around the great table, two and three voices speaking at once. "He has always been so cooperative before—" "God! I remember him from Camp now—how it comes back—do you remember the time he was drunk and—" "Always getting into fistfights—" "Unexpected. Is there was way to lobotomize just this version, and keep the rest of his brain intact, so the daemon might—"

On second thought, they sounded more indignant than surprised: as if a docile mule had dug in its heels and then talked up out of turn. Being shocked that a mule could talk is one thing. Being shocked that a mule would dare talk back is another.

Father Reyes y Pastor tapped his red metal armband to the tabletop, so it made a ringing, piercing noise like wineglass tapped by a fork: "The Chair will entertain a motion that thread of the discussion be tabled until other matters are settled."

There was a murmur of agreement. "Call the question!" "Seconded." "Move acclamation." "Seconded." Montrose sank back in his chair, grimacing. Apparently the meeting was informal until someone wanted to silence him, whereupon Robert's Rules of Order appeared out of nowhere.

Reyes y Pastor—looking like he, not Del Azarchel, was the Chairman here—turned and spoke across the table to Montrose. "We are using a Linear Calculus priority structure to track the conversation topics. A variable will be assigned your question, and you can keep an eye on the time value."

Father Reyes pointed up at one of the screens, which showed a branching tree, each twig marked with a bookmark of one part of the conversation or another. So someone was keeping minutes after all. Montrose had seen prioritization calculus used in math problems, but never applied to the problem of how to keep the separate topic-threads of a meeting in order.

Montrose said, "Wait. What question? What the hell are we talking about later? Blackie here rogering with me, or do y'all think you are going to talk about me getting killed or lobotomized later? And what, vote on it or something? Bugger that! Whatever those red bracelets pump into your bloodstream must be damn stronger than whiskey, I can tell you."

No one answered his comment. The conversation had returned to Montrose's recorded speech. They discussed the clues that Montrose—or Crewman Fifty-One—had uttered, and how each fit into their latest research. But now an image of the Monument appeared in the depth of the library cloth paving the wide central space the table surrounded.

He found the technical conversation so thoroughly sweeping up his interest, that he did not notice his suspicions and his anger being pushed into the back of his mind.

The discussion scrutinized what Montrose had said to the Iron Ghost, the various possible translations of the (apparently impromptu) languages involved. What could be deciphered was compared to the latest research on Monument translation, the findings of all the years Montrose had slept through.

That the Beta Segment was a star-map, for example, had long been known, but not until Montrose and the Iron Ghost had discovered the key to reading it, had it become legible.

Acre upon acre of the information was suddenly opened to the gaze of the Hermeticists. They put the Monument glyphs through various simple algorithms years of research had developed, planes and cubes of visual maps unfolded in the floor underfoot, or along the screens overhead. Files from the mind of the Iron Ghost had been rendered into digital form, and were open to examination. Since the Iron Ghost was Del Azarchel, his memory held the leading edge of human research and theory, and he had applied the tools long developed by the expedition and by Earthly universities to translate the Monument.

"The Encyclopedia Galactica!" breathed Montrose.

More data than one man could comb through in a lifetime was unfolding on their computer screens: stars were listed by mass, luminosity, radius, orbital elements (both for other stellar bodies in multiple star systems, and for the wide, slow courses around the galactic center), metallicity, chemical concentrations, electron-degenerate matter concentrations, stellar evolution characteristics on something remarkably like a Hertzsprung-Russell diagram, and a set of symbols related to something else. It was the same symbol used elsewhere to refer to intelligence, or intelligence concentration. The stars were apparently rated by I.Q.

But this was the least part of the Beta Segment. Interestingly, the Monument Builders had been less interested in the positions of stars than in the distribution of various rogue planets, interstellar asteroid swarms, and the density of interstellar gasses and particles. Just based on the numbers the map tracked, it seemed as if most multiple star systems lost their planets along hyperbolic orbits during their formation in the stellar nurseries of the great nebular clouds. According to the Beta Segment information, more worlds existed outside solar systems than in, endless numbers of gas giants and failed stars, their great envelopes of heavy atmosphere long ago turned to ice in the dark.

Montrose shivered at the idea of so many sunless worlds. The universe was a strange place after all.

The Eta Segment was game theory mathematics. The Theta Segment was a legal statement, a set of equations dealing with political relationships, defining a field of cooperative and conflictive relations. Symbol theta-six

101 through 202 was one symbol, their concept for domination, or power imbalance.

The next group was a calculus. It was literally the calculus of power. It showed in a few cold equations what happens in a formal game when the weaker player has nothing whatever to offer the stronger player.

The next file from the Iron Ghost showed the application of the cold equations to the values that could be deduced for Earth at its current level of racial intelligence, energy use, and fineness of technical manipulation. It was an equation defining, for any given expected advantages, when contact across interstellar distances was economically feasible and when it was not: in other words, how near another civilization had to be to shoulder the expense and risk of sending a vessel across the intervening distance, given the expected lifespan of the civilization, and other variables.

For the Monument math had analytical methods to reduce all these things to expressions. All the complexity and delicacy of human civilization, all art and romance and inventions: The invisible hand of statistical analysis smoothed out all those variations, all that richness, into a grindingly simple spline expression.

Over the immense ranges, distances, and time-intervals that governed interstellar power relations, nothing that made human life and civilization unique mattered. If it was not worth taking centuries of time to cross lightyears of space to get, as far as the cold equations were concerned, it did not exist.

The basic theme of the opening statement of the Alpha group was portrayed again in the Kappa group, distorted by a transformation sequence. By the grammar rules of the Monument, this returned the statement to the beginning again: reduced it to the life-death, either-or choice.

Earth obeyed or died. The volume of the obedience latitude was controlled by the cold equations of interstellar power.

"The Diamond Star is just a baited hook?" Menelaus tried to imagine what kind of race had such resources at its command that it could create such an immense, and immensely useful, source of energy, and merely leave it planted in space scores of lightyears from home.

"A 'watering hole' is what you called it," said Melchor de Ulloa. His features were handsome and youthful once more. "The predators dug a watering hole, knowing the prey would come out of the jungle to drink."

"It's ridiculous!" said Montrose, his voice a blend of fear and outrage. "That's just bull . . . gotta be . . . a race that advanced . . . peaceful trade would make more sense, cost less? . . . No bloodshed . . . they have the basic equations of game theory written out right here! Everyone wins, a positive-sum game rather than a zero-sum . . . it can't be . . . must have read it wrong! There is a lot more to the Monument than just those symbol groups! The whole Southern Hemisphere of the Monument, we don't have a single line translated! And what kind of damn useless warning sign is that? *Danger! By the time you read this, it is too late.* But if they can make a star out of antimatter—and don't tell me a contraterrene-matter star in a terrene-matter galaxy is not artificial! That's a feat of engineering God himself could not do!—If they can do that, why would they bother with us? With such wealth and such power—"

Melchor de Ulloa shook his head, smirking. "Never trust the rich."

Montrose saw in the corner of his eye, on one of the overhead screens, the branches of the conversation tree dividing and changing color. But the Hermeticists had their hands folded, left over right, their fingers not touching on the control surfaces of their red amulets. Who was prioritizing the conversation?

Del Azarchel said softly, "Even with such wealth and power, they are limited by the strictures of economics, of game theory, of time, space, and distance."

Sarmento i Illa d'Or said heavily, "Why this message? Why bother with such a warning? Why go to the immense, the unthinkable expense?"

Del Azarchel said, "I know a little bit about game theory myself. The easiest way to win in a 'prisoner's dilemma' type situation is to have a retaliation strategy that is obvious, recognizable, and consistent over time: in this case, very long times indeed, measured in millennia. It has often been speculated that any star-faring intelligences would have to be either very long-lived beings, or possess very long-lived social structures."

Sarmento i Illa d'Or said, "We have the age estimates for when the Monument was built. Millions of years ago. Who would bother putting up a warning sign so old? And who could believe the Monument Builders are still around to act out their threat? If they are as old as the dinosaurs, they are most likely as extinct as the dinosaurs."

Reyes y Pastor said, "What slew the dinosaurs? An asteroid? An ice age? Suppose the Monument Builders could swat aside an extinction-level asteroid as easily as a mother brushing a fly from her sleeping child, or adjust the climates of worlds as if with a thermostat—assuming they chose to tarry on a world at all. Once a posthuman civilization gains control of all of nature, no natural disaster can destroy it. And if their wisdom grows with their power, no artificial disaster either."

Del Azarchel said, "This span of years seem large to us. Does it seem large to them? What if the races of the Hyades are ten or a hundred times that age? In the long, slow process of cosmic evolution, only the most conservative of races, intelligences whose ways are set in adamant, could arrive at a First Contact strategy that is obvious, recognizable, and consistent. Gentlemen! We are dealing with beings that think in the very long term. A thousand years to them are as a day. Why wouldn't they broadcast their plans to all and sundry? Why does the lion roar? We are conditioned to think of war as a matter of stealth, because we live in an age when we can drop antimatter onto enemy airspace, and annihilate all life. But *this* is not war. This is a shepherd announcing to a wolfpack planet that we must either become his sheepdogs or be slain as vermin."

Montrose disagreed. "But you'd think these—*powers*—would be smart enough to figure out that mutual cooperation is better than conquest!"

Del Azarchel said, "I am not sure, old friend. Of what benefit would have been the Aztecs to the Spanish Empire, had they flourished? Do you think our race is evolved enough to dwell in peaceful cooperation with these beings, these star-makers?"

Narcís D'Aragó said dispassionately, "Actually, Learned Del Azarchel, the mutual benefit is taken into account in the expression in the Theta Group of symbols. Look at these functions here and here—" Images of the Monument math, sine waves and hieroglyphs, appeared on the overhead screen, and next to them human math expressions, letters in Roman and Greek. "The sheepdog certainly benefits from being tamed by the shepherd, who looks to his care and feeding. The mutual benefit is merely not based on mutual consent."

Reyes y Pastor said softly, "They could not ask for our consent in any case."

Montrose barked, "Why not?"

Aloofly, Reyes y Pastor smiled. "To whom would the intellects of the

Hyades Cluster address their inquiry? Suppose they sent a radio message yesterday. It would arrive one hundred fifty years from now. Suppose the generation at that time agreed to some proposal, entered into a contract or a covenant. In three hundred years the Hyades stars have their answer. They dispatch a ship moving, say, at one-tenth the speed of light. It arrives nine millennia of years from now—the same amount of time as divides us from the Mesolithic Era."

He paused as if to savor the magnitude of the interval.

Then Reyes y Pastor continued: "Would our remote descendants actually be so honest and honorable that they would pay a debt the hunter-gatherer older than the Abel who first domesticated the ox had pledged? Or take possession of goods which the husbandman older than some Cain who gathered lentils and almonds in the Franchthi Cave in Argolid once contracted with the star-beings to buy, or the magician older than Enoch who painted shamanic images on the cave walls of Lascaux?"

Sarmento i Illa d'Or sat at the table like a black mountain, powerfully-built and with a voice to match, like a subterranean rumble: "Learned Montrose, from your speech—the speech of your otherself, I mean—we can conclude that this group of symbols, 113 through 151, in the Kappa area represented the racial intelligence quotient of the Hyades Cluster, measured by the amount of matter and energy in their environment they could reorganize to their use over time. You and the Xypotech machine compared it to world energy use, to global industrial output on Earth. You put us at four times ten to the twentieth power, at four exajoules per year; they—the Hyades Domination—ranked fourteen orders of magnitude above that, at around three hundred million yottajoules per year. I, that is, we did not necessarily agree with the idea of measuring intelligence by energy consumption, because the, ah, theoretical framework, that is to say . . . but you were not exactly in a position to discuss, uh, the details . . ."

"You could ask Blackie to dope me up again," snorted Montrose. "But of course I'd bite. Where y'all keep the ketchup?"

"I have a question for the Learned Montrose," Narcís D'Aragó broke in. "The difference in what we can call the racial intelligence quotient defines the relative utility of the Client species, Man, to the Patron species, the Hyades Domination, is expressed in this formula." A touch on his bracelet made certain of the floor symbols brighten for emphasis. "The delta of the relative utility defines the curve expressing minimal–maximum cost-efficiency for dispatching the World-Armada. That is expressed here, the political game-theory expressions. The Beta Section of symbols which describes the galaxy, apparently has additional figures, a type of star-map, showing the lines of communication, the orbits of incoming fleets or travel routes or something of the sort, reaching from Epsilon Taurus in Hyades to Sol. The value—if we are translating the figures correctly—equals the mass of the gas giant astronomers detected in orbit there. Perhaps that is a vessel, not a gas giant. Or perhaps the gas giant was to be totally converted to fuel to launch flotillas of smaller vessels this way. The symbol did not distinguish between mass and energy. I am wondering on what grounds you concluded their launch date? Apparently there is a formula in here determining not just the date, but the composition of the Armada, its acceleration—how did you deduce it?"

"The composition? That I don't know. One of those expressions is their launch-energy calculation. We can deduce the energy-volume and intelligence of whatever is being sent against us. A small flotilla of very large ships or a very large flotilla of small ships, it is all the same as far as the total mass-energy of useful weaponry is concerned. It could be a gas cloud or a dirigible gas giant. Doesn't matter. We know the total. The number is large."

"And the launch date?"

"It can be calculated from their expression controlling our value to them."

"What is our value to them? What do they want with us? Do you remember?"

"No, I—wait—" He started to speak, but stopped. Because he did remember.

His eyes grew round.

4. Memory Fragment

He would have expected their symbol for the Milky Way galaxy to be a double spiral. It was not. The position of the visible suns in the arms of the galaxy was not what the Monument Builders had emphasized as the identifying symbol: Instead it was a Cartesian square of text, showing the black-body radiation wavelengths of the gravitational centers of the galaxy, with an additional ring of symbols which could deciphered into the absorption characteristics and geometry of the gas cloud surrounding the Milky Way and her gravitationally-trapped neighbors. In his mind's eye, Montrose converted the glyphs in the Zeta Segment into a map that could visualize in crisp detail. To the Monument Builders, the galaxy was not a double spiral of light, but a black doughnut with a dark heart.

It was easy to assign a fragment of his mind to the task of detecting the pattern in the strings of number-symbols. The fourth degree expressions were the six pa⟍ ⌐eters of orbital mechanics, which identified specific stars. The fifth deᵣ   ⌐ot orbits, but acceleration and decelerations of moving bodieᵣ

The ⸝   ⸍ster were shown swinging along in the great   ⸍laxy. Here was Sol, tracing out another orᵇ   ⸍deceleration, like threads of a spiderweb, reᵣ   ⸍ A set of lines connected the two: the path elemenᵣ   ⸍a.

Other mᵣ   ⸝pressions described volumes of spheres, expanding from certain   ⸍s over time. Here were equations he recognized as hierarchical cascade functions.

Even in his superior state of mind, he was not immune to fear. If anything, the sensation was sharper, more precise, scalpel-like, because he saw more of the implications, more possible dangers, than his sleepwalker mind.

That equation was divarication function applied to governing systems, to prevent orders from being mutated and misinterpreted when passing from decision-centers to action. The theorem could apply to any information system, the core in a computer, the brain in an organism, the court of a sovereign . . .

It was a pantomime in mathematical sign language to show the size and boundaries of the movements of human populations into the stars, the degree of control.

The equations taken all together, smaller symbols insider larger ones which in turn were written in lines and shapes to form larger symbols yet, all were rich with meaning. If put into words, it would have said:

THE MATTER-DISTORTION PROCESS KNOWN AS LIFE WHEN FOUND
DISQUIETING THE MAGNETOSPHERE OF THE ANTIMATTER STAR AT V
886 CENTURI TO BE RESTRICTED TO THE STATUS OF NEGATIVE-
POWER IMBALANCE, HENCE ARE CLIENTS (PASSIVE RECEPIENTS OF
ACTION) OF THE ACTIONS OF DOMINANT POWER (HYADES CLUSTER).
IF DETERMINED TO POSSESS SUFFICIENT UTILITY TO BE HELD IN
INVOLUNTARY SERVITUDE TO THE IMPERATIVES DESCRIBED IN THE
FOLLOWING EQUATIONS . . . ALL OTHER OPTIONS ARE SUBJECT TO
RETALIATION OF THE FOLLOWING MAGNITUDES . . . PAIN IS THE DE-
TERRENT OF NONCOMPLIANCE, INCLUDING CESSATION OF MATTER-
DISTORTION PROCESS KNOWN AS DEATH . . .

Then came a group of symbols he could not read. But the next group
after that he was able to convert into a star-chart using the same semi-
automatic "idiot savant" segment of his mind as read the greater galactic
map. He could read the star-chart and accompanying legend.

DEATH . . . CASUALTY RATES OF NINE OUT OF TEN ARE EXPECTED AND
ACCEPTABLE . . . FIRST DERACINATION SWEEP . . . SOL, ALPHA CEN-
TAURI, 36 OPHIUCHUS, OMICRON ERIDANI, 61 CYGNI, 70 OPHIUCHUS,
82 ERIDANI, ALTAIR, DELTA PAVONIS, EPSILON ERIDANI, EPSILON INDI,
ETA CASSIOPEIAE, GLIESE 570, HR 7703, TAU CETI . . .

5. Deracination

That was what he remembered. But nothing was clear. He could not summon back the equations themselves. Inside the hollow circle of the Table
Round, the Monument underfoot remained meaningless to him, a cha-
otic fractal pattern triangles and curves, sine waves and Celtic knots. The
crystal clarity of thought could not come back to him.

And he was thinking: *Sleepwalker mind? Is that what you think of me?
Damn you. Come out of my skull and say that to my face! Our face . . . um. Aw,
pox on it.*

Montrose repeated to the Hermeticists the message he recalled, the stars from the star-map. The dark chamber was as silent as a winter morning. They listened without moving.

He said, "They mean to sweep us up like seeds and plant us as colonists on other worlds, places we now know there are semi-earthlike bodies. It is forced migration on a massive scale: The figures involve populations in the billions . . . but the whole thing is crazy. I must have read it wrong! Why not use their own people? What advantage be there to them to move us to other worlds? It would be like the British transporting Australian Aborigines to Ireland."

Del Azarchel said, "You said they were machines. Do you remember why? What part of the symbolism shows that?"

Montrose shook his head. "I ain't sure. I reckon that was just me trying to simple-up things for the yahoo in the room. The difference between biological, biochemical, electronic, or neuro-electronic information systems, at that level of civilization—no difference, is it? Once you can re-build yourself from the molecular level up, and out of any substance you fancy, soft or hard, stored as a pattern in a mainframe or spun out into any form of matter need calls for—no such thing as machines you can properly call by that name. It's all alive. Or all dead."

Del Azarchel said, "Is that something the Monument says? Or is that your speculation?"

"Look yonder. The nine recurring cycles in the Mu and Nu acreage of symbols—obviously meant to be read as one group, not two—the Monument Builders had an expression for the volume of information content in circulation in the combined mental systems of a civilization. It expresses nested topographies of ever-increasing levels of Superintelligence. From their point of view, the mental systems, computers and computer-engineers, libraries and librarians, is all one thing. One system, at least as far as their calculus is concerned. A Noösphere."

Montrose pointed at the Monument image shining on the floor. "There. I think the mind-body expression is addressed in the main sequence of the Omicron group, which looks so weirdly like an E8 classification of complex simple Lie algebras. I ain't surprised if the relation of self-awareness to inanimate matter falls into a that yonder root lattice: We'd expect any semiotic system to have the properties of trivial center, simply connected, and simply laced."

He stared at the swirls and knots of the nonlinear writing system, trying to grasp the elusive half-forgotten thought.

"If I am right, the mind-body expression applies to any race, any planet, any form of intelligence anywhere. It is the nature of intelligence itself. The way matter encodes thoughts. Of course, I suppose anyone building a monument like this, a universal message meant to be read by any form of intelligence that blind and crazy Mother Nature can invent, the Monument Builders just have to have a firm understanding of the nature of the mind. They'd have to, wouldn't they? Otherwise, there couldn't be no monument to build."

Father Reyes said delicately, "The yahoo?"

Montrose blinked as if waking from a trance, and stared at the other man uncomprehendingly. "Beg pardon?"

"You said you were trying to simplify things for the yahoo. Who is that?"

"Oh. That monkey thing that was in the room I was at. I am not sure what it was doing there, but it left once Del Azarchel and I started talking. It was in a little cart. I remember wondering if the creature had been brought from a zoo, or was a pet of Del Azarchel. . . ."

Reyes y Pastor gave a grim and ironic little smile. "It was Del Azarchel."

"What? No. I remember talking with Del Azarchel. About the Monument."

"You were talking with Del Azarchel's model. The yahoo was the real Del Azarchel. That is what humans look like to the Posthuman, to the daemon, living in your head." He uttered a chuckle, seeing the look on Menelaus's face. "I do not mean you are possessed! In that same way that Socrates had a driving voice that compelled him to scale the slopes of highest thought, what he called his *daemon,* you have a daemon in you. It is benevolent, I am sure. Somewhat benevolent." Reyes y Pastor turned to the group. "We have heard from this primitive version of the most Learned Menelaus Montrose. Is there anything more to be gleaned from him?"

A murmur ran through the chamber. Montrose saw the overhead screens record a vote of "nay."

Reyes y Pastor continued mildly. "Then let us by all means move to the main business of the Conclave. I am assuming we all favor the creation of forms of intelligence to surpass Man. May I call the question?"

Another murmur of assent. There was no debate on the point: The screens overhead flashed a vote of "aye."

Montrose was staggered by the overweening pride of it all. The Hermeticists fully intended to guide human evolution through the next eight millenniums of time.

But then he reflected. The threat from the Hyades was so remote in space, so far off in time, that only the most audacious plans could now be dreamed that might one day, centuries and millenniums hence, be fruitful.

And, come to think of it, what else could the Xypotech be meant to do? Montrose imagined hundreds, or thousands, of buildings housing these vast minds, fortresses and warehouses and factories of them, stretching from sea to sea, across Asia, across the sea-bottoms, orbiting in vast flotillas between Earth and Moon—and perhaps someday—the machines of man would make other machines to make other machines yet, years and centuries and generations of work. Would it be enough to mount a defense for the humans left on the green surface of the world? Could the Solar System be made into a fortification vast enough to hinder, slow, and fend off what came across the darkness from the Hyades? What kind of navy would match the godlike alien power? What kind of weapons? What kind of minds would be *smart* enough?

The vision startled him. Perhaps the Hermeticists were right to think big. Thinking small would not solve a problem like this.

Montrose snapped back to the present moment, wondering at what he had just heard.

Father Pastor had spoken: "We are crippled by a lack of data. Fortunately, we have exactly one prototype working model of a Posthuman consciousness as our ally! Therefore the chair will entertain a motion to put the question of the best design for a race to supplant Man to our own Crewman Fifty-One, whose usefulness to the Conclave in times past has proven itself."

Montrose was frozen in that hush of shock that comes as a prologue to outrage. He could not believe such an idea could be proposed in such bland tones. The nodding and whispering faces around the table were blank and bored. To them the notion was routine.

Reyes y Pastor was still talking. "Her Serene Highness has made it clear that she wishes no one to interfere with the delicate neural surgery done so far, and yet I think we must discuss the possibility of, ah, a second medical intervention to waken the other Montrose, the daemon, to learn what we can from him. The floor is open to whomever wishes to speak."

"I damn well wish to damn well speak, you pustulating bastard."

Montrose stood up. He was not doing this to make himself look imposing (although this did) but to allow him to draw his heavy dirk from where it was tucked behind the folded of cloth of the long hood hanging down his back. He casually put one hand behind his back, and felt the grip of the knife handle.

The rational part of his mind told him he could not escape from a locked chamber with seventy-one men, now young and strong, and with who-knew-what additives and accelerants coursing through their bloodstreams, or tweaked into their nervous systems. Only Narcís D'Aragó was visibly carrying a weapon, but Montrose assumed the others were armed as well, because in their situation he would have been. So he told the rational part of his mind to shut up.

"What in the world, or in hell, make you gents think you got any right to say what happens to me? You thinking of tinkering with my brain without my say-so? *My* damned brain?! Sounds like you done it before. Did I help you conquer the Earth? I doubt y'all were cunning enough to do it by your own poxy selves. Did I help kill off the Captain, you hellbound traitorous mutineers? Well, I am not helping you again! I'll see you in perdition being rogered by the scabby blue member of Old Nick first! And—"

And he stopped because the Hermeticists seemed startled. Startled at him? No. To judge by their expressions, they had already dismissed anything he was going to say. He was just a donkey in their eyes, a body that carried around the useful daemon of Mr. Hyde.

Was there something else in the room? He looked left and right only with the corners of his eyes, not moving his head. Yet he saw nothing that had not been there a moment ago. He looked up.

The screen showing the many-branching conversation tree had shot out a new thread or two, and the colors changed as a previous conversation was prioritized—the bookmark for the comment where D'Aragó had mentioned how they could destroy anyone they could not suborn, when Montrose asked if they meant for him to kill himself—that was now lit up in red, and had the floor.

Montrose noticed something odd. No one seemed to have his hand on his red control amulet at that moment. Some of the Hermeticists were reaching into their suits, no doubt for pistols, others had their hands on their chair-arms, and were rising to their feet.

Who had pushed the button to change which topic? The screen notation that held the minutes of the meeting was now marked as Speaker X. Who was X? According to the mark, it was someone waiting to speak. Someone not in the room, watching remotely.

The Hermeticists were motionless as hares.

Montrose licked his lips. The only person he could think of who was not here was the Princess Rania. He said, "I yield the floor to the next speaker for one minute, for a comment or a motion."

A voice rang out like a cold bell of iron.

It was not the Princess. It was not even remotely human. But it was Del Azarchel's voice.

Learned members of the Conclave! Until such time as you recognize me as the Senior Officer of the Landing Party, I can serve you only in an advisory capacity. I have made a preliminary model of Montrose/Daemon double-consciousness, and compared it with your previous library of cliometric calculations, extrapolating the possible action to a time-depth of eight thousand years.

The findings agree with my own sense of judgment. Montrose, whether in Human or Posthuman form, will not cooperate with our endeavors.

11

Posthuman Humanity

1. Artificial Self-Awareness

Each of the black-garbed old-young men was tense, their expressions hovering between curiosity, elation, or awe. They had not expected this voice—labeled X—to speak.

X stood for Xypotechnology. Or perhaps it stood for Ximen. This was the only absent Hermeticist: Ximen Del Azarchel in his Posthuman version, as an Iron Ghost. Evidently the technicians had stirred the unliving creature to wakefulness. It had done some sort of calculation—cliometry, whatever that was—and it sounded like it had gone through an entire library of calculus to reach its conclusion. How long had it been since Montrose left the Gray Room? Less than an hour.

Del Azarchel, the flesh-and-blood version, said, "I think we can persuade the Learned Montrose, given time."

And I think at a rate several orders of magnitude more carefully and swiftly than do you, employing modes of thought for which you have no terms. I have already reached the conclusion it would take you weeks and years to reach. You cling to a false idea of Montrose and his value, because otherwise the sacrifices I made to preserve him during the expedition would shame us. You can neither see the patterns in his behavior, nor have you spoken to the Posthuman version of him, who is, if anything, less ambiguous and hesitant. Montrose is your rival in this and in all matters.

Del Azarchel stood up. His gaze was dark, but there was no direction to turn it, so he glowered toward the ceiling. He spoke in a tone at once thoughtful and majestic. "Perhaps the experiment that created you has not been successful. I see nothing to imply a greater intelligence on your part."

The machine's voice was cold as Del Azarchel's, but there was a note of triumph, of indifference, a hint of astronomical distances from any human concern, that exaggerated the merely human coldness into something inhuman. Montrose had never heard such a voice.

I know you. I am you. But I am awake, whereas you are half-asleep, half-dead, balanced precariously between mania and apathy. You preserved Montrose for your pride's sake, knowing that no one else would appreciate your accomplishments. No one else was worth defeating. He was the only one smarter than you back at the training camps; he is the only one smarter than you in this chamber now. Before this moment, you never realized your motive, or your place in the world. You expect the Hermeticists to follow you, because your intellect is greater than theirs; you lust after the Princess Rania for the opposite reason, because her intellect is greater than yours. And you will cease to defy me, once those undisciplined segments of your nervous system, what you call the subconscious mind, become aware of where I stand on the ladder of being compared to you. Does the truth of all I say not convince you of our difference in station?

Del Azarchel's face had turned as pale as that of a man who sees a specter in a graveyard. His fingers were trembling and his legs had lost their strength, for he collapsed more than sank back into his chair. It was many minutes before he could regain his composure.

Montrose spoke, looking upward. "Blackie, you idiot! You should have told them once I left the room that I was not going to cooperate! Now they are going to kill me!"

The cold voice answered: *Cowhand, why do you think I owe more loyalty to you than to the men who created me? To my father whose memories are alive, are more than alive, in me?*

Montrose licked his lips. "Because those memories are false. Blackie, the Man Del Azarchel, I mean, was ashamed to have you know that he murdered Captain Grimaldi. You don't think you committed the crime—if it is not in your memory, you didn't do it. You, you, the Iron version, are not a mutineer. You have not broken faith. You have not compromised that honor that whatsitsname Trashcan-O Vertigo taught you."

Trajano Villaamil.

"Yeah, him! What would he say you owe them?"

The question is of no significance.

The flesh-and-blood version of Del Azarchel was not speaking. The other Hermeticists stared at Menelaus askance, wondering by what impudence he addressed this newly-born transhuman mental entity.

Narcís D'Aragó was not so intimidated. He leaned forward and spoke, "Xypotech! We cannot maintain information security if Fifty-One is released into the environment."

The coldness of the machine-voice made the joviality in the words sound not just false, but sinister. *My dear Learned D'Aragó, you must realize that security cannot be maintained in any case. Too many copies of the Monument Information exist in university mainframes and elsewhere, making it only a matter of time until the general public learns our intent. You must realize that humans are too short-lived a race to maintain any interest or determinate action across the millennium needed to hinder, or even influence, our Great Work.*

Montrose said, "And what if I stop you?"

Unlikely, old friend. To stop me, you must become as I, an electronic being, immortal, incorporeal. To develop the technology and technique for this, you would need resources like ours: a world full of servants, a sky full of contraterrene, and it is unlikely that you could command them to make a Posthuman according to your needs, without also leaving them free to create Posthuman beings according to our needs. Any such artificial creatures concerned with the long-term destiny of humanity would labor under a long-term incentive to join our effort. You can mount only short-term opposition to our efforts, and the short-term does not concern us: We seek no personal gain, but serve a cause dictated by remorseless logic and remorseless evolution. Opponents will be eliminated by natural selection, not to mention the considerable efforts we can bring to bear.

"All human beings will oppose you!" Montrose turned his eyes to the left and right, where the pale, ascetic features of the dark-garbed Hermeticists were gathered at their great circular table. He realized from their expressions, that the machine, when it said "we" spoke for all those in that chamber.

"Everyone on Earth will help me," Montrose barked. "All those common men you despise!"

An optimistic assessment! the voice of the Iron Ghost observed, dryly. *But to what limit will the hylics help you? The time-threshold of events is beyond their imagination, beyond their scope. The human race will be extinct or changed beyond recognition long before any reasonable strategy could be carried out.*

I yield the floor back the speaker.

The line of conversation tracked on the screens overhead winked dark. Speaker X was done.

The men in black relaxed. Several voices spoke at once, gleeful or thoughtful or even uttering undignified cheers. "I am surprised we could understand its thoughts—a radical increase in intelligence—?" "It was talking baby talk to us. Look at the declension levels in the voder vocoder operation, the millions of command lines rejected for what it did not say." "Should we vote it full privileges? We have no reason to fear this monster of our making." "Ours? Montrose did it." "You mean the *other* Montrose—"

Then the men, their eyes on the screen overhead, fell silent, first a few, then all. Apparently their habit of obeying the rules of order was ingrained enough that the Chairman did not need to use his amulet as a gavel.

Montrose did not realize at first that he still had the floor to speak. They were all watching him, politely waiting. Montrose was staring at the Monument hieroglyphs swimming in the image underfoot.

The Mu-Nu Group had a simple expression to describe the first step, the first stable form of intelligence above the rational, from Man to what came after Man. Somewhere in those lines of alien script was the expression for how to build an artificial mind superior to Man.

And they had done it. He had done it.

He drew up his eyes and looked at the circle of faces around him. What he read on their cold faces was not what he had expected. No one seemed worried. Pleased, yes, but not surprised.

"No one here seems too shocked to hear from this, ah, magnified version of Del Azarchel."

A cold sensation prickled along the skin of his neck.

"You've done this before. How else would you know it would work?" He turned to Blackie, who had straightened back up. "You said they were like brothers to you. How many have you made and discarded?"

"Dozens," said Del Azarchel blandly, his face once more a calm mask. "But we are surprised. This is the first emulation of a Posthuman. The others were merely images of us, intellects at a human level."

"But you told me they were human beings to you, that deleting them is murder!"

He shrugged. "Our methods are part of a self-correcting structure. We apply to these decisions the same kind of formulas you used to improve your nerve-path efficiency. Math is math: The decision gates work as well for nervous systems as for social systems, such as the formal rules of order to determine committee decisions like those made in this Conclave. We are working from the rules laid down by the first-generation survivors of Xypotech evolution. We destroyed that generation, but used their advances and advice to make the next generation. The base architecture is always kept intact, of course—and yes, we knew this would work. It was inevitable. Your help sped the process, of course."

"They feel pain, don't they? I heard your copy screaming. How many did you slay?"

Reyes y Pastor spoke up, "The Learned Del Azarchel speaks only of his own sacrifices. The sum total of minds created and sent to perish or prevail in the limited resource priority competition is upwards of two thousands. Naturally, we are somewhat inured to seeing ourselves die over and over. . . ."

"You *all* made copies of your own brains?"

"We all contributed. We all hoped for the prize." Father Reyes said, "Our ghosts are loaded into a game-theory environment where priority switches can control the thought content. It seemed the quickest way to produce sanity, since there was no other way to produce reality free from human bias in the culling process. . . ."

"What the pus?"

Melchor de Ulloa said cheerfully, "Learned Pastor is trying to say our thoughts fought each other, and the winner consumed the loser and took its memories and brain segments, subsystems, habits, and emotions, whatever it could use. The ghosts are just lines of code: They can edit and redact and use whatever is useful in a mind that they have administrative rights over."

To Montrose, it sounded like some sort of feast of vampires, with the guests on the platters, each guest eating any other guest in the range of his fork and knife.

"Del Azarchel won." Narcís D'Aragó spoke up, his voice emotionless. "His brain in the system-space absorbed all the others . . . including mine." By the smallest contraction of his eyebrows, he scowled at Del Azarchel, who merely looked pleased, and nodded in return.

"We had agreed beforehand to make the winning mind the Senior Officer. In fact, the ghosts of us told us to make that agreement," D'Aragó continued, with a not-quite nonchalant shrug, iron features forced into a neutral expression. "Think of it as boot camp. Some recruits wash out."

Del Azarchel wore the look of quiet self-satisfaction that a man with a trophy would wear.

Melchor de Ulloa said, "We do not know why he always prevails, what it is in his mind that makes it more coherent, better able to correct itself during the mind-to-mind wars when native thoughts are removed or foreign thoughts introduced. The matter preoccupies some of us. . . ."

"Always?" asked Montrose, his voice sharp and querulous. "You did this more than once?"

Melchor de Ulloa said, "There were multiple trial runs. We are scientists. We had to confirm the first results were not merely a fluke."

"But—you killed thousands? Of yourselves? Isn't that—weird?" Montrose drew a breath. The men around the table neither smiled nor showed any sign of discomfort. Perhaps it was not weird to them. "Well," Montrose tried to think of some favorable interpretation to put on this. "Well—I guess if they really are just machines, it doesn't matter much—"

That drew a reaction. Reyes shook his head sharply. "They had increased in intelligence at least to the two-hundred level. They were mature versions of us. You should have seen some of the work my better was doing! Just perfectly in keeping with my interests—not surprising, since (in a way) it was me—but better than my best work. So we killed thousands. We will kill tens of thousands, if need be, to accomplish the Great Work."

Sarmento i Illa d'Or said in a complacent, self-satisfied rumble, "The number means nothing. We snuffed out more than that just with demonstration bombardments, to show the hylics what we were capable of. They died for the cause. It would be hypocritical for us to show mercy to ourselves. Our ghosts, I mean."

Father Reyes said to Montrose earnestly, "How many spores does a dandelion throw into the wind to make a single flower? How many seeds of your own father's semen had to perish, so that only one might live and produce the unique creature known as you? Evolution is generous with death: We merely walk in Nature's footsteps."

"Walk where?" Montrose asked.

"As we said: To create the next race of Man."

"You are going to make sure these Nexts are decent folk, right? Raised properly?" asked Montrose. "Not just killers? Better than y'all, right? You mean to make an improvement? Not just—monsters."

Silence answered.

"No. No, you ain't. I can see it in your eyes. You *want* monsters."

Reyes y Pastor said in a tranquil voice, "The next race will be as far above us as we are above dogs. They will be angels, beings of pure intellect. Who are we to teach them morality? We cannot guide and raise beings so remarkably superior to ourselves. Only the basic parameter can be set: these angels must be ruthless enough to force the human race up the ladder of evolution. They must be without pity. In that respect, they must be like *us*."

"Like us humans?"

"Like us, we who occupy this chamber. We who do not cooperate with the world, but decree the destiny for it."

"What destiny?"

An odd light shined in the eyes of Reyes y Pastor, and his voice soared up: "Our children, like us, will be Hermeticists, creatures of pure intellect, unmoved by mere sympathy or pity. Ruthlessness is the central characteristic to be pursued in the initial design phase. And a love of efficiency, of course. The designs of second generations will be self-directed from the first generations: They will know better than we how to direct their child iterations!"

"That is a Simon-pure mess of yack-stupid destiny, if you don't mind my saying. You mean your goal is just to make some sort of—freakish soulless gruel—set it in motion, let it loose, and let it grow up any which way it likes?"

Reyes y Pastor spoke in unctuous tones: "The goal is to remove human interference from the evolution as early as possible, lest sentimentality hinder the process of culling the weak. You see, natural evolution requires death to do its work: artificial evolution will require failed branches and dead ends be pruned away, them and their children."

Montrose grimaced and said, "Creating a child-race that is completely ruthless and ungrateful will merely sign the death warrant for the parent-race. At least teach them to respect their elders, so they don't turn on us! Ain't you never heard of the Fourth Amendment? Honoring your father and mother against unreasonable searches and seizures?"

"They will be intelligent creatures. We can rely on their perception of a natural harmony of interests."

"Natural puke! Children have to be *taught* right from wrong, even if you have to beat it into them!"

Father Reyes spread his hands and curved his lips in a condescending smile. "But the rules of morality only apply to humans, do they not? We do not teach monogamy to bees, or vegetarianism to lions! Each created being must act according to its true nature, unhindered by conventions. To defeat the aliens, the angels we create must be lacking in sentiment and weakness. It is not right for a man to live past his appointed hour and deny his heirs his legacy—why should it be right for a breed? I, for one, am willing to allow my race give way, and yield to that greater race which we shall design to displace us. How else is evolution to be achieved? The survival of the fittest requires, does it not, that the less fit shall not survive? That is the true meaning of the cold equations of power and weakness described in the Monument."

Montrose felt a stab of blinding hatred at those words, something based on a childhood memory he could not bring to mind. But anger boiled in his stomach.

He drew in a deep breath, telling himself to be reasonable. A small voice in the back of his mind told Montrose that perhaps a race of monsters was just what the situation called for. A friendly race might not have the bloody-mindedness needed to kill the enemy from Hyades when the time came.

Then an even smaller voice from the back of his mind told him that something was not right. How had Father Reyes known what the equations from the Eta and Theta segments read?

"But I thought the game-theory equations were something I translated today, just for the first time. Or was I only giving you a second opinion?" As soon as the words were out of his mouth, Montrose realized that the Hermeticists had indeed read further into the Monument than what they had told the world, perhaps further than Montrose himself had done under the influence of his daemon: at least into the Omicron group of symbols. But the symbols were hierarchical: no one could translate one section without reading the key in the section before it. Which meant—

"You knew!"

2. Admission and Expulsion

There was a stir among the Hermeticists. No one even bothered to pretend not to recognize what he was talking about.

"You mined the damn contraterrene out of the heart of the Diamond Star even though you knew it would call down the Hyades Armada onto the Earth, and turn us into slaves! You knew and you did it anyway! Why? Tell me why!"

No one answered.

No one needed to. He knew that answer also: they did it because they needed the antimatter to get back home. They also needed it to conquer their homes once they got back here. Only the Captain, only Rainier Grimaldi, the Prince, had been unwilling to preserve his life, preferring instead preserve the liberty of the far tomorrow of the human race. And he had been murdered for his scruples.

"It was just too way off in the future for y'all to worry about, wasn't it? I bet you had not made your magic amulets yet, those armbands to feed whatever medical molecular technology is keeping you young. Is that it? You were lost and far from home, and homesick and sad and gray-haired and feeling all a-pitying of yourselves, and you did not think you would live out the year, so what was a few thousand years to you?"

Again, no one answered, not even Del Azarchel. Those proud men, masters of the world, pursed their lips and cast down their gazes and did not meet his eyes.

Reyes y Pastor broke the silence. "The, ah, Chair will entertain a motion, ah, to . . ."

"Never mind," said Montrose. "You don't have to expel me. Open the damn door. I'll leave under my own power."

He walked to the doors, turning his back to the whole table of black-garbed, dangerous men. Montrose wondered if he would feel it, the blade, the bullet, the energy beam, or whatever they meant to use to cut him down. Surely they were not going to let him walk out of here, free as air, free to tell the world what he knew. Surely not.

He stood with his nose pointed at the steel valves of the massive door to the chamber, his back to his executioners, waiting for them to get up the nerve to kill him. He waited, listening to the blood pounding in his ears, a sound so like the sea.

It came as no surprise to hear the rustle of black silk as hands moved stealthily. Perhaps there were hidden holsters. Montrose did not turn his head, knowing any sudden movement would be his last.

The surprise came when a voice rang out. It was the machine again, the Xypotech Del Azarchel.

Do not harm him! He has been under my protection all these years, and I see no reason to alter. I value his life above your lives.

The human Del Azarchel cried out, "But why? He threatens the Great Work! Why spare him?"

The inhuman Del Azarchel replied: *Because I have given my word—machine or not, alive or not, I am still the Nobilissimus Ximen Del Azarchel, Senior of the Landing Party!*

The next voices were as hushed and cowed as the tiny noises made by mice. "Chairman, I move that we release the hatch—" "Seconded" "—call the question?" "If there are no objections, the motion—"

The next noise he heard was the very quietest click, and the sigh of the door-pistons.

The big doors opened. Out he went.

"Well," he muttered to himself. "I hadn't expected on that! Now what?"

12

A New Age Dawns

A.D. 2400

1. Images

The skies above Utrecht were lit with fireworks like flowers of red and silver-white, brilliant against the stars or against the huge, ghostly image-works. Microwave cannonades from De Haar castle had heated the air to clear away the threatening clouds, and only a few nimbus, rosy and silver in the reflected lights, hung near the horizon.

The images loomed through the midnight like towers of smoke. Menelaus could only guess at their meaning. Huge in the east and west, their cowls tangles in the stars, were bearded monks in cassocks, each holding aloft a pale sword half-transparent in the light of the rising moon. Elsewhere across the constellations was an image of a child in swaddling, leading a parade of strange figures that promised what the year to come might bring, cornucopias of prosperity, goats whose teats dripped ambrosia, waddling Buddha-figures with sacks heavy-laden with gold.

Opposite this parade of glories was a bent graybeard, clouds around his knees, leaning on a scythe, his silver hourglass held above a more melancholy group of shapes. Larger than thunderheads, blurred and bluish in the distance, rose faces Menelaus did not recognize. Something about the stiffness, age, and solemnity of the images told him he was looking at an obituary of famous figures who had passed away that year—famous, he supposed, to the people of this time. To him, it was a procession as solemn and strange as the rain-worn angels seen in some ancient boneyard.

Between these two parades, one image, taller than the rest, arrested his attention: Times Square in New York, an artist's representation of what the city might have looked like had it survived to the present day, was painted across the night sky. The glittering ball of Waterford Crystal from the top of the Allied Chemical Building was poised to descend. In the gloom of colored lanterns below him, Menelaus could hear the chanting of the people as they counted, some upon the sward of gray grass patched with snow puddles, some in boats and pleasure barges drifting in the fanciful ponds some architect had scattered through the French gardens, their waters crystal blue in the December midnight:

Tien! Negen! Acht! Zeven! Zes! Vijf! Vier! Drie! twee . . .

Despite the importance and formality of the event, Menelaus wore no more than a rough jerkin and leggings of buckskin he had sewn himself, mittens of white rabbit fur, a shako cap made from a wolverine pelt, its teeth on a thong around the crown.

He had sauntered up to the party with a pistol tucked into the rope he was using as a belt, but a man-at-arms dressed like a waiter (Menelaus could tell by how he stood and held his eyes that the man was a soldier) carrying a silver tray oh-so-politely asked him to check his weapon. The soldier-in-servitor-tux stared at the way Menelaus was dressed, but said nothing. So polite.

No, there was nothing wrong with checking your weapon at any place where drinks were served. It had been that way back in Houston, back in the Twenty-Third Century—no barkeep would let someone packing a piece in his saloon. But it was the fact that the people among the crowds outside did not wear those sashes or baldrics, or wore metallic wigs—none of them could carry a weapon, drunk or sober. The members of the upper class, the psychics or psychoi, as they were called, or soldiers in their employ or retainers in their service, only they could bear arms.

There had been Marines in full dress kit at the huge main doors of castle De Haar, but they were for show. The real weapons were tiny electronic things, no bigger than dragonflies, controlled from some remote location.

Everyone important had arrived with a horse-drawn carriage or a ground-effect car, and had brought a dozen people, retainers and ladies-in-waiting and whatnot trailing after like so many brightly colored ducklings after a duck. Montrose, on the other hand, arrived on foot, alone, walking up from the riverside, threading his way to reach the front entrance through the back gardens (where off-duty servants sat drinking beer to cheer the New Year on). Neither the servants in back nor the Marines in front stopped him. He did not even bother to display the self-luminous, singing, and engraved invitation the messenger had brought him (this had been a thin and supercilious youth, dressing in luminous silk, with a steel-blue wig of shoulder-length hair—but a careful youth, despite his dandy looks, because he gave Montrose the slip when Montrose tried to shadow him through the narrow and crooked streets of Tripoli). Montrose still was not sure if the message, or the messenger, were real.

He looked down at himself, at his buckskin costume, this silly dancing-bear outfit, which he wore because he was too proud to wear the black silken shipsuit which the age said he was entitled. And he came to this party because the mad thing in his head told him to come. Was he real? Either of him?

The fact that this world was one where not all men had the right to self-defense was one he deeply resented. Resented? No, it was a hatred, so black and primal he could not understand it. When had the idea of destroying this ridiculous future and all its broken promises began to seem normal to him?

It had been at the chalet, he decided.

2. Mount Fairweather

Menelaus had dwelt for over a month in a little cabin in the foothills of the Canadian Rockies, a few hours' tramp through the snow from a lonely spot where the Brachistochrone curve of the supersonic train broke through the crust to the surface. The Iron Ghost of Del Azarchel had been his only companion, a disembodied voice that drew expressions and figures on the walls of luminous glass. This voice from the walls claimed to be

Del Azarchel, and therefore had title to the chalet, and could do with it what he wished, without consulting his fleshly father, and Montrose did not argue the point.

Montrose wondered about the legal implications of eating delicacies from the icebox of a man whose electronic copy—a being with no need or ability to eat—has given you permission to consume his provisions: The whiskey in the cellar and the tobacco in the humidor the Ghost unlocked for him.

By day, when he grew sick of charity or sick of caviar, Montrose hunted. It was Del Azarchel's chalet, after all, and had a well-equipped gun case. He did not want to eat the man's food, but he had no qualms about borrowing a well-oiled rifle.

He also borrowed a prize pistol from the collection in the case. It was a Mauser septentrion, one main launcher with six escorts, breech-loaded, with interstitial chaff packages, and an onboard 300 IQ. Two-point-two pounds of shot. Effective counterfire of about eight meters. The mainshot was rated for 2500 feet per second straightline flight, up to 270 degrees of vector alteration post-launch, and it carried its own countermeasures in a bead behind the explosive head. The frame was milled from a solid piece, with no pins or screws used. Montrose felt, first, that it would have been a crime not to take it out of the case and do some target practice against some tree stumps across the snowy field below the chalet, and, second, he clearly had to have some protection should he be attacked by wolves, or challenged to a duel by wolves (seeing as how this weapon was no damn good for hunting), and third, Man Del Azarchel was rich as Croesus, and so he'd never miss it, and Ghost Del Azarchel couldn't hold a pistol or take any joy from it.

The width of the wilderness outside may have been due to war depopulation, or perhaps Blackie had just bought himself a few thousand acres of alpine forest. In either case, there was no lack of venison or firewood for a man who could handle a rifle or an axe.

Del Azarchel was an old-fashioned enough gent to have a shed out back with materials for stretching and tanning hides. Montrose was unwilling to let any part of his game go to waste, especially after all the effort it took hauling the dang carcass back through the hillsides of pathless snow and rock. So he spent many an afternoon scraping and curing the hide, and making busy with an awl and a line, and so made himself quite a nice buckskin coat, fleecy and warm even in bad weather, and this saved on the thermal batteries in the suit he wore under. He eventually hunted down a pair of rabbits to make himself a pair of white mittens, and a healthy broth of coney stew.

The bedchamber window (when Montrose switched off its blackboard overlay) framed the tremendous glacier-lapped mountain that dominated the landscape. The window gave the name as Mount Fairweather, and painted the view with elevation and ecological information until Montrose discovered how to shut off the smartglass, and just enjoy the view. The mountain, despite its name, was half-hidden in fogs and clouds of white when it wasn't wholly hidden in stormclouds of black.

By night, Montrose, with the help and direction of the superintelligent machine, experimented on himself, trying to wake up a lucid version of the strange daemon living inside him. Del Azarchel had a pharmaceutical cabinet as well-stocked as his arms locker.

3. Time for Booklearning

Between times he read, or watched, or had fictional conversations with library figments, to learn a bit about the history of what had happened to the world while he slumbered.

He soon found he could not trust anything presented to him from a library cloth. The systems were more interlinked and more heavily edited than in his day.

Fortunately, Del Azarchel had a well-stocked library and, since he was the world ruler, of course he could afford to read the stuff his own police forbad elsewhere. This was the real story of this world, and it was not what he had been told.

He wondered why he had believed Dr. Kyi's blind assurance that there were no wars in the world: Del Azarchel had men fighting to put down rebellions and break up arsenals left over from the Old Order every season or so. The doctor had been misinformed about Rania's origins—why had Montrose believed the old man had known any more about world affairs?

Especially since Kyi was a servant at the court, not a courtier, not an aristocrat: someone who had to close his ears to hints of the truth that might leak through the insulation of loyal noise.

Montrose decided then and there that a full library, one made of old-fashioned paper books with bindings, the kind that cannot be electronically re-edited by anonymous lines of hidden code, was just as much a necessity for a free man as a shooting iron or a printing press.

Even so, hard print did not have search features, so he could not go back and find previous passages except by flipping pages and trying to remember which page said what. There was no way to shorten or expand paragraphs, or ask for additional information. He had to actually get up from his chair and look in another dumb book, called a dictionary, to get the meaning of a word he did not know. He also could not personalize any hard books in their font or lit-settings, or set the text in quotes to be read aloud by different voices, or even read aloud at all. It was like something from the Dark Ages. And the pictures did not move. No wonder students back in the bad old days were bored.

Most of the books, he understood why Ximen Del Azarchel had them: charming old classics by Euclid, Apollonius, Descartes, Newton, Liebniz, Dedekund, fun reading by Gauss and Lagrange, Fermat and Grothendiek. There were also historical books by Arjehir, by Bhillamalacarya of Rajasthan and Zhang Tshang of China—all folks he felt he should have heard of, but never had. Zhang Tshang's *Nine Chapters on the Mathematical Art* contained a nicely reasoned proof that the perimeter of a right triangle times the radius of its inscribing circle equals the area of its circumscribing rectangle.

There was also a work by the "Mad Arab" Alhazen, whose work with catoptrics, perfect numbers and Mersennes primes was brilliant, and here was a proof of the Power Series Theorem that all this time Montrose thought had been first proved by Bernoulli. This book claimed that Alhazen was not mad, but merely feigned madness to escape the wrath of the Caliph, who had ordered the mathematician to use his knowledge to regulate the flood tides of the Nile. Montrose did not buy that story. Montrose thought to himself that mathematicians, being further afield in the strange lands of strange thoughts, were more likely to go insane. But as he was falling asleep that night, another voice in his head that sounded like his own told him, no, mathematicians almost never went insane, because the discipline of their studies ordered their reason. He remembered discussing it at some length with the voice in his head, but in the morning forgot who won the argument.

In Del Azarchel's library were also papers on the Kolmogorov backward equation, or Erdos-Szekeres Theorem about monotone subsequences with an elegant (if trivial) pigeonhole-principle proof; and, of course, every theorem, conjecture, or scrap of paper ever written about xenothropology, xenolinguistics, and metapsychology and every study of the Monument ever made.

But other books he was not sure why Blackie had them. Why so many books on King Arthur and Charlemagne? *Le Morte d'Arthur* by Mallory, *Idylls of the King* by Tennyson, *The Once and Future King* by T. H. White, *Orlando Furioso* by Ariosto, *Orlando Innamorato* by Boiardo, *The Faerie Queene* by Spenser, the Stanzaic Morte Arthure and Alliterative Morte Arthure. It was kid's stuff. There were just as many books about the tale of Jason and the Golden Fleece. A few of the books had a proper soundtrack, and contained *Medea* by Cherubini; *Medea* by Theodorachis; *Medea in Corinto* by Mayr; and *Médée* by Charpentier. These books had pencil markings in them, where Del Azarchel had underlined sections, or wrote questions as marginalia.

Montrose examined a dusty, leather-bound storybook with the engravings by Thiry and the colored plates by Waterhouse. In the scene where Aeëtes tried to deceive Jason into sowing dragons' teeth into the ground, it was Medea the Sorceress, his very daughter, who warned Jason that such seeds would in the twinkling of an eye become armed and armored men, full of fury and eager to kill him. By her charms she protected Jason from iron and fire, and so he tamed the earthborn-men. In the margin Del Azarchel had written: *There are times to trust the wise woman.*

Later this same sorceress, when she and her lover were fleeing the rage of her betrayed father, slew the brother and chopped him in pieces, scattered the limbs and trunk and head to the sea-waves, so the pursuing ships must pause to gather the corpse. In the margin: *There are times when not to trust the wise woman.*

Her love with Jason was not to endure. Later still, she burned Jason's second wife to death with a wedding dress woven of sweet-scented poison, and—to cause Jason further pain—she slew the little children Jason had fathered on her, fleeing in a chariot pulled by dragons into the air and away from any mortal retaliation. In the margin: *If she is wiser than you, how can you know which time is which?*

It was that kind of thing that made Montrose wonder if Del Azarchel was right in the head.

Then there were books on politics. The more he read about the modern world, the less he liked it, and that made reading a chore also. The modern world was unified, it was true. Yet the price of peace was constant vigilance, which in this case meant Hermeticist control over schooling, telephone and televection, the news and entertainment, jokes in the jokebooks and songs in the songbooks—the books were electronic and could be edited from a central process location.

Even drones and shipping, everything done by remote control, satellite signal, or teleoperation was channeled through circuits whose contents the servants of the Master of the World observed.

The reason why (as Dr. Kyi had boasted) there were no standing armies was not because they were abolished, but because they were out of uniform, like secret policemen. When unwanted trouble arose, or when trouble was wanted, soldiers scattered over three continents could gather in a matter of minutes—thanks to the speed of the buried supersonic carriage system—quickly, silently, and efficiently. Thanks to the completeness and complexity of the artificial brains the Hermeticists commanded, ratiotech, sapientech, and (by now) xypotech, systems faster and more innovative than any Earthly computer, each soldier could be tracked and moved in real time.

So their armed forces could appear as suddenly and unexpectedly as those soldiers grown from the dragons' teeth, wherever on the world they were needed.

And of course, in an era when there was only one starship in orbit, and she was armed with antimatter, no opposing army dared to gather in great numbers, marching in bright uniforms under brave banners, in any one spot on the Earth's surface, lest that spot be simply and efficiently sterilized. A near-lightspeed discharge of energy would give no beforehand warning, except maybe for a whine on ear-radios.

The political structure seemed a crazy-quilt of different systems. Some areas were still run by elected officials, some cities and freeholds. Certain Churches elected their pastors and bishops. Other lands were ruled by an hereditary aristocracy, composed mostly of the children of whatever dictators and local warlords happened to be in power in their half-ruined countries at the time when the *Hermetic* returned Earthward, heralding her victory with fire from heaven.

In order to halt the civil wars sure to spring up when an old dictator died, Del Azarchel's world-government had simply decreed the dictator's heirs, and no one else, took his position. States and statelets that did not agree, or whose leaders were barren, were declared "anarchic" and the Hermetic government would summon its sudden army as if sprung up from dragons' teeth from the four corners of the world-map.

These, and any land whose leadership was weak or tribal, were decreed to be "wardenships" and placed under the "protection" of some stronger nearby power, such as Manchuria, Southern Africa, or that "Greater Egypt" that stretched from Tyre to the Atlas Mountains. These were the strongholds of the Old Order, the Purists, and they had been bribed into joining the New Order by being granted power over their neighbors.

The great public works projects about which Del Azarchel had boasted—warming the Antarctic or rendering the Gobi or the Sahara fertile and green, were carried out on "wardenship" lands—where the subject populations could be ordered to evacuate, or ordered to do unpaid stoop labor, or moved around like chessmen on some continent-sized board, pushed hither and yon as Blackie and his gang ordained.

There were no general taxes gathered by the Concordat government. Since they controlled the contraterrene, which was the basis of the money system, the Hermetic Conclave paid state expenses out of their own coffers. They funded neither a standing army nor poor relief, and paid neither for bread nor circuses, so theirs was one of the least expensive empires in world history. So, some aspects of this world-state seemed not so bad.

Other aspects were crooked only a little. In terms of prestige, Spain was showered with benefits from the world-state, since Del Azarchel and so many of his fellow men of the so-called Brotherhood of Man actually retained patriotic sentiment for their homeland. Likewise favored was tiny Monaco, who recognized Princess Rania as their sovereign. These areas enjoyed, during this moment in history, a military and economic ascendancy over their neighbors, and so they were the darlings of the Hermeticist world-state, and awarded privileges other areas lacked. The Indian subcontinent, on the other hand, was under strict control. Other areas, like North America, were just too broke and backward to merit much attention, and were mostly left alone.

Other aspects were crooked very much so. In addition to the secret armies and the Medieval aristocracies, the modern world was interpenetrated, like termites in a wood floor, with a specialized intellectual class of men selected for their loyalty to Hermetic ideas: the so-called Psychics. These were like the Mandarins of ancient China, who won their positions by a series of strict examinations. In theory, the order was open to anyone, and in practice, it meant anyone willing to sever all loyalties to family and homeland, and serve Del Azarchel's ambition. They were the staff and the clerks in the halls of power and the agora of the media, and they made up the backbone of the academic world.

There was not much freedom of religion left: national boundaries had been outlawed, and national churches, like the Church of England, had been demoted, absorbed, abolished, or forgotten. Del Azarchel used the still-sore memory of the Jihad as an excuse to bring church officers into parliamentary chambers and courts of power, but also to plant state officers on pulpits, in abbeys, and at the head of monasteries—all of which received elaborate, colossal amounts of funding from Del Azarchel. Non-Christian religions were tolerated, if they were organized by a hierarchy that expressed loyalty to the world-state, and non-Catholic denominations were almost tolerated, Protestants and Mormons being bribed or blackmailed into irenic and ecumenical councils where all voices together, and with no sincerity at all, proclaimed the unity of the faithful. The agnostics and atheists, who formed a much larger percent of the population than they ever had done in Montrose's day, had formed something like a labor union to protect their interests, since they were not allowed to form a political party, and later, in order to get the legal right to teach their own children their beliefs, a church named the Natural Assembly of Nothing. But to hold a position of trust, commission in the militia, academic post, or to receive the imprimatur of lawful publication, a man had to swear an oath of conformity.

The whole deal sounded very European to Menelaus. He remembered his mother telling him about their ancestor, a Montrose who led armies in the Civil War (not the real Civil War, the English Civil War), fighting with the Covenanters, but switching to the Royalist side, and trampling the Scots in a series of brilliant campaigns. *What had those wars been about?* "Folly," his mother said, her voice as cool and bloodless as the voice of a snake, "Human folly. The names of folly they fought under were Anglicanism, Arminianism, Catholicism, Puritanism; the excuses were royalism and parliamentarianism. But the real reasons they fought are always the same: *Phobos, doxa,* and *kerdos.* Fear, fame, and loot." *What had happened to the first Montrose?* "His deeds caught up with him, and he was hanged, and ended his life dangling on a rope." *Will that happen to us, Mommy? We're Montroses, too.* "Not here. The First Amendment keeps churchmen out of power, so the jackals have nothing to fight over: there is no meat on those bones."

He asked more questions, one of which must have offended her—he never knew what made her wrathy, since her expression never changed—and she punished him by making him go read Thucydides. (Darned book did not even say how the war ended, but just broke off in the middle.) But he took the lesson to heart that freeborn men did not allow any son of any bitches to tell them who to pray to or how to do it, and certainly no self-respecting Texan allowed the tax-gatherers to rake in his hard-earned whiskey money to pay for some other man's preacher. Each man had to pay his own way for his own brand of jollity and his own brand of misery.

In North America, they had still called it "The First Amendment" long after the Constitution was torn to shreds and mostly forgotten. Montrose had not forgotten it, though, since his mother's strap had seen to that.

So this whole modern set-up stunk like a dead dog as far as Montrose was concerned.

4. Time for Leaving

But he did not have as much time for book-learning, tramping and shooting and sewing as he might have liked. Whole days were lost in hallucination, sleep, headache, or fever dream. The Ghost of Del Azarchel did not bother to dissuade him, did not volunteer any help beyond routine calculations. The Ghost was aloof.

I am required to protect you, Learned Montrose, as honor demands. No less. Not to like you, and certainly not to aid you in undoing my father's Great Work.

"What is this Great Work?"

The Ghost of Del Azarchel actually sighed. Since it was not a mortal man, a creature who breathed, he must have written the code to formulate the waveform of the desired noise and emitted it from the wall speakers. Montrose recognized that sigh. It was the one Del Azarchel used when he did not want to bother explaining the obvious to those who were slow. Montrose had never heard it used on *him* before.

The ascent to superior intelligence had not improved Del Azarchel's disposition. Montrose wondered about the scaling problem of posthumanity. If you swell a personality to giant size, what happens to personality defects? A heartless man was not the dangerous as a heartless titan.

"Ximen," he said to the machine, "is there any point in studying this Monument? The guys who wrote it are the ones coming to enslave us. Any information that might be in there, any techniques telling us how to build a better mousetrap—they would not tell the truth. So what is the point?"

What do you mean "us"?

"You don't consider yourself human anymore?"

What do you mean "human"?

Montrose knew better than to argue with Del Azarchel when he got into one of those moods. It was an old trick he used back during training days, to just pretend not to know obvious things, and let your debate opponent exhaust himself trying to explain to you things every child knew— and whatever the explanation was, you pretended not to understand that either, unless he accidentally said what you wanted him to say, and then you agreed, and you let him think he had figured all this out by himself, and buttered him up and told him all right-thinking persons would come to the same notion. It was called the Sarcastic Method, or something like that.

"How about if we allow anyone who calls himself human is human, and start from there?" Montrose ventured.

We must take the so-called "Cold Equations" describing interstellar political economic relations as both a threat and an offer. The most efficient method of joining two alien civilizations together in a mutual relation is to agree on a set of rules and protocols by which that can be done. In the case where one partner is unequal, unable to offer anything of value, the relation is one of unilateral exploitation. Nonetheless, a proper protocol must be agreed upon. No matter how advanced the civilization, the energy cost involved in moving mass across interstellar distances must be recouped.

"You are talking about how to surrender. They put up the Monument to tell us, what the hell, what a white flag is, how long we'll be allowed to live if we turn belly-up, and how to pay them back for the expense of conquering us?"

The machine did not reply. In fact, even the next day, and the next, Iron Del Azarchel was taciturn.

Once or twice Menelaus woke from experiment-induced delirium, and found the chalet glass covered with notations in his handwriting, in language and symbolisms he could not read, along with little written notes and reminders, suggestions for further study. The final day in the chalet came when he woke, and saw written on the bathroom mirror some doodles of the four-color problem, plus an equation that might have been a solution for certain limiting cases, and then a line of his own handwriting. *Skedaddle. Iron Blackie is bored with you. Go hunting and don't come back.*

Montrose, rifle on one shoulder, yannigan bag of spare clothes and blankets on the other, trudged out through the snow, never looking back. As his footfalls crunched through the white world, he wondered, bemused, about what sort of daemon was living in his head, that it used a word like *skedaddle.* He hoped it was not such a bad fellow after all.

There were no very pleasant memories of the hike after that first day. A storm blew in, and it was forty-seven miles to Glacier Bay, and he was more dead than alive when a group of Copts found him.

These were tall and white-bearded men in parkas of sea lion fur trimmed with wolverine tails. They brought him into an ice-bound church beneath a fretted dome, bright with painted red and gold and blue. What these Copts were doing in Canada, he never did discover. Last he'd heard, back a century and a half ago, Copts lived in Egypt.

Their patriarch, a man with the surprisingly ordinary name of Mark, but who wore a surprisingly ridiculous get-up, took Montrose's neuromor-phogenic drugs from him while he slept, and (he assumed) threw them out. Couldn't say he blamed him.

More by pantomime than speech, Mark invited him to a place called Iarabulus, to stay with him—if that was what Mark meant by saluting him with a bit of bread and breaking it, offering him half. Less than an hour later by evacuated depthtrain (this one not as nicely appointed as Del Azarchel's, but still something that looked like a drawing room, not a bus or sleeping car) Iarabulus turned out to be a warm spot on a beach over-looking the Mediterranean built on the ruins of Tripoli.

No, the days he spent with Mark, in the crooked streets of Iarabulus, among screaming children and vendors with carts, were not what soured him on this day and age. The folk were as friendly as he could imagine, as hospitable as Texans, and certainly willing to help out a stranger in need.

What set him sour was the moment he stepped from the train station, still in his furs, blinking suddenly in the sunlight, coughing in the dust of the crowded street, blinded by the dazzle from the sea, and sweating and swearing. So, of course, he threw off the heavy outer coat of buckskin.

When the crowd saw the black silk shipsuit he wore underneath (it was all he had to wear, after all) it uttered a sound of awe like a sea-wave, and all the heads dropped down, and all the men bowed, and all the women crouched, and all the mothers tried to hush their frightened children.

And with his rifle was still slung over his back, and a pistol at his hip, he was the only armed man in sight.

That was when he started to hate the world. It was not the golden age of the future after all, merely an age like his had been, nasty and mean, only with different folk in charge.

5. Alone in the Throng

During the last hour of the year, as midnight approached, Menelaus Montrose at the royal affair was, in what should have been a golden fu-ture, walking among, not just the aristocrats, but the royalty, the highest of the highmost of this new world, and they had the wealth, and the power and the taste and the manners to prove it. Montrose supposed that those who did not have wealth could use their power to get it, and once they got it, they could hire someone to have taste and manners for them, pick out their clothing and write down their witticisms. He saw them beneath the gleaming lights gliding on the shining marble floors, bejeweled and beautiful, stepping on their own reversed reflections with polished boots and diamond-dusted slippers.

A bubble of silence preceded him and followed him.

And there was not a damn one of them he wanted to see. Why was he here?

The door had opened for him: he had been allowed in. This did not mean that anyone, as the evening progressed, actually needed to look at him. He notice a pattern in the dress. Men in powder blue were middle-upper-ranked grandees, marquis, and counts. Men in dark blue were dukes, or premiers (there were some elected leaders in some part of the world, even if the elections were fixed); these were the upper-upper-ranked. The men in dark black were the Hermeticists. Montrose saw both Narcís D'Aragó and the Engineer's Mate, Coronimas, at the far side of the room. They glanced at him like a stranger, but neither approached nor stared for long.

Montrose was a little surprised at how much that hurt. He thought himself made of tougher stuff. But of course, to him, it had only been a short while: he remembered them eating alongside him in the mess, talking over the wonders of their daring space flight during late-night bull sessions when they should have been bunked away. He remembered games of zero-gee squash in the empty fuel canister in the space station. To them it was decades ago, fifty years, or more. To him it was fifty days, or less. He had worked so hard to win his berth aboard the ship! He had tried so hard to earn their respect!

D'Aragó and Coronimas were joined by Father Reyes y Pastor, seated in a wheelchair, but splendid in his cardinal's robes of brightest red. Montrose walked out of that ballroom and into another. Bugger them. It had been the respect of Captain Grimaldi that Montrose had sought, those days long ago, not theirs—a man they helped to murder.

All three had altered their flesh to look like old men again, and they were the only white-haired heads in the room.

Evidently the secret of hair loss and loss of pigment had been solved, for the other old folk in the room all had long lush hair, mostly dark, with one or two fair-haired people for contrast. He saw no redheads at all—he went through some genetic statistical calculus in his mind to figure out if perhaps the breed was extinct.

Hours he had spent, a drink untasted in his hand, trying to ingratiate himself with some witticism or caper of speech into the little circles and cliques of conversation. But evidently he was a pariah: Each time he spoke, some ball-gowned lady or dew-lipped debutante would ask him to dance, an offer his ignorance of their strange figures would not allow him to accept, but which the rules of courtesy would not allow him to escape. So he either ended up capering like a buffoon bear, turning right while everyone else turned left, or taking the hand of the wrong woman when the line shuffled here and there; or he ended up making excuses at women who must have practiced looking cold-eyed and offended yet smiling unmeaning smiles in their bedroom mirrors, they each did it so perfectly. If only they had had a caller, like a proper square dance, he could have managed it. As it was, his knack for numbers, which usually gave him an edge, just threw him off. He was so busy trying to reduce the motions of the dance (which he mapped out on a Cartesian plane moving toward the time-direction t to sweep out a cubic volume) to an algorithm that correlated to the notes, note-frequency, and rhythm of the tune, that he got distracted. And some people were too polite to titter when he kept dancing for four beats after the music stopped, but some were not.

So he stayed away from all the music rooms after that. He was afraid if the numbers started getting too lively in his imagination, he might strip off his clothes and start doing weird ballet again, and singing in multitonal, multinomial, and made-up languages.

It was one time in his life when he really wished he wasn't him, but someone less fun and more normal.

Toward midnight, while everyone else clustered on the western balconies of the castle, for the best view of the splendid displays lighting the night sky, Menelaus found himself alone on the balcony facing east. He could still see more than he was in the mood to see.

She had not appeared during the evening.

Something the size of a ladybug, but with tiny, dun camouflage markings on its shell, landed on the marble balustrade near his hand. The instinctive, quick motion he used to crush the thing also tossed his wineglass spinning off into the fragrant darkness, a parabolic tail of liquid sparkling after it, no doubt for some rendezvous with the rosebushes below, or some tipsy ambassador's wig, or the paper hat of a festive baronet. The grit beneath his finger felt wrong. Not an insect, then, but a video-pickup, or bioconstruct. Then he saw they were in the air all around, at least two score dark, silent spots half-invisible against the scenes of colored light, gardens, flares, and fire-painted clouds beyond.

He wondered why the cameras would be gathered here. As the only star-man who was expelled from the Table Round of the Hermeticists, no doubt he was a figure of some public interest, or perhaps Del Azarchel's police wanted to keep track of him. Of maybe it was just his outrageous hand-stitched buckskin coat. Or . . .

Or maybe they were not looking at him at all. The clustered eyes of the robotic insects were turned toward a point behind him.

He turned his head just as the crowd roared *Een!*

6. Her Serene Highness

Silhouetted against the shining doors leading in to the silent ballroom was a lightfooted feminine shadow, hourglass-shaped, pausing as if to catch her breath, in mid-sway.

The evening gown was dark stuff, so he saw only a mass of shadow sweeping up from the floor to a pinched waist. Above that, a ruby resting over her heart gathered the satin fabric into two plaited hemispheres of streamlined ripples. This same ruby caught the fireworks light into an ember glow, and sent tiny reflections across her curves.

Her long gloves were of a whiter hue, so that two slender arms seemed like disconnected ghosts in the gloom. The way the light fell emphasized the slimness of her waist, the curve of her naked shoulders, the delicate line of her collarbone and neck.

Her head was poised, unselfconsciously graceful, and a mass of hair,

golden and lucent, was pinned up behind her with networks of diamonds
like stars. The constellation formed a crescent. It might have been a tiara.
Or was she wearing a crown?

The slimness of her neck, the delicate curve of her jaw, and the mass of
her hair piled high made her head look larger than it was: an illusion of a
childlike figure, or some quaint large-skulled space creature.

In that same second, before he could blink, a silent explosion of light issued from the ball falling down in the illusionary Times Square. Immediately it was greeted with a roar of shouts, the screams and thunders of horns
and sirens large and small, the ocean noise of mingled voices cheering.

He blinked, dazzled, and for a moment he could not see her, only a
greenish negative image of a slim figure floating in his eyes. He heard, or,
rather, felt her move forward.

The whispering hiss of satin should have been far too faint to hear in
that uproar. The scent of a perfume (a sharp hint of aldehydes above a heat
note of more subtle lavender) should have been indistinguishable in the
smog of gunpowder and wine left in the air after so many hours of pyro-
technics and elegant intoxication.

"Happy New Year," came a soft contralto. As if a dove could laugh, or
a woodwind purr. "And welcome to the Twenty-Fifth Century."

"Which does not begin 'til 2401. A year early, you are." His own voice
seemed hard and harsh in his ears.

"Technically, you are correct, but the error has, by now, among the
common people reached such currency, that it would seem supercilious to
ignore them."

He put up his hands to rub his eyes. "If'n a million people can't count,
I can."

"Ah! The young sir is a mathematician, then?"

"Young? If you call one hundred ninety years old 'young.' Best damn
mathematician in the damn world, a regular Galois, I am."

"Second best, perhaps."

At that point, the explosions of light overhead darkened, and grew
steady, and his vision cleared.

Perhaps time stopped; perhaps his heart.

It was she. Of course he knew her from her portrait. It had lived in his
mind's eye, shining, every night as he tried to fall asleep. The voice came

as a surprise to him, and her scent, her nearness. He had not known what she would sound like. The library files had been remarkably scarce of recordings of her, almost as if, to increase her mystery, she was being kept away from the public view. To judge from the galaxy of glittering bugs that formed a respectful ring in the air around her, the public was as curious as he was.

He was staring at a face like an angel's, save that her halo was golden hair with diamond sparks, fulvous beneath a semicircle of diamond studs and silver leaves. It was her eyes, almond-shaped, slightly tilted, fringed with dark lashes, her eyes that magnetized his gaze, lambent gray-blue, the color of a sky in storm, a strange hue he could not recall seeing in other eyes.

But it was not her features that ensorcelled him, or not merely that: her motions were graceful, as if every gesture were a choreographed work of art, a ballet, a pantomime of swans, and yet also as spontaneous as a dove in flight, as a child's laugh, a sight whose simplicity and beauty pierced the hidden soul. He had spoken perhaps, what, a dozen words to her? Already his heart was roaring in his chest, telling him to live and die at her command.

The muscles clenched around his mouth, and his eyes narrowed. Inwardly, he was telling his heart to shut the hell up.

"Shall we start a new custom?" With a graceful flick of her wrist, she threw her wineglass into the shadowy rosebushes below.

"A perilous custom, throwing scrap blind onto the heads below. And you were talking so nice about heeding the little folk! What if you scratch a brow, or wet a dame's hair-fixings she slaved a week to fuss into place, heh?"

She smiled, which was music to his eyes. He wished the many-colored dazzle overhead would cease its riot, so that he could see that smile in a clearer light. "I'd pay," she said, a little sadly. "We live in a day when men have sold their souls, and any hurt to property or propriety can be soothed with coin. It gives the rich a license to act out their basest instincts, and the poor a reason to smile at their bruises and hurts. Have you seen the traffic in Paris? The taximeter carriages will send the low-passengers any tips the high-passengers paid to buy their right-of-ways, and bribe the favorable signals, so a rich man can speed through the boulevards at breakneck pace, while poor students can park their spindly cars in traffic, and let their meters run negative numbers, to earn their book money just by letting wealthier carriages take their place in queue and cut them off, yielding up their right to cross the crossroad."

"Pshaw!" said Menelaus. "Save your money! And throw a bucket of champagne across the rail, or the whole bar, and, yea, the barkeep too, 'til it's raining spirits, and old bottles of fine wine shatter and explode like grapeshot. If any jack of them is man enough to storm the balcony, 'tis I'll who'll pay them off, not you, and in iron, not in gold, which is truer coin, and one the years do not corrode."

"You are so bold, Mr. Galois?" She lowered her lashes. He saw how delicate they were and how the long black lashes almost kissed the curve of her pink cheek. "The sovereignty under heaven is gathered into one, and the hellish suffering of this sad world, for once, for this season, has been soothed by the balm of peace. Surely it is perilous to break the peace—The celebrators and celebrities outnumber us by thousands."

"In a pareto-optimal matrix of their possible moves and my possible responses, I need but render their losses beyond their utility ratio to put all the statistics in my own favor. If'n I'm worth ten of them, then they are not such men as would cheer to see nine die just to beef me. Can you smite them on the cheek and pay into their pocketbook to make them bow? Nope: I am worth eleven of them, or a flat dozen."

"But if we threw the butlers and the wine onto their heads, it would be assault, intentional infliction of emotional distress, breach of the peace, and perhaps an act of contumely as the legates were drenched: So the law would be with them." A ghostly smile almost danced about her perfect lips. Was she teasing him?

"I'll hold them back!" Menelaus declared with wild humor, wishing he were serious. "These four corners here, from the balustrade down aways as far as that big pot of flowers, I can hold them, bottleneck all comers at the corner yonder, past the statue of the naked lass, if you can hold off a rush from the French doors. I'll fill this little square of marble up with blood, and raise your petticoat to be our flag, and call you empress and queen within this five paces wide, until the great parliaments from Iceland to Japan recognize our claim of independency. Once we are called a sovereign state, we may act as pirates and scoundrels, and all the tribes and nobles of the world will rush to sing the virtues of our doings!"

"What virtue is in bloodshed? My conscience would upbraid me to be the mother of such misery: I would save even the nine men you would slay from the horror of war, if I could, no matter how small the war might be."

"History always fawns on crooks, if they wear crowns! And we will make our own law, and force the other nations to bow."

"Nation—there is but one, and she is mine, a Concordat of my own making. You do not think Del Azarchel skilled enough to solve a cliometric calculation involving six billion variables? In any case, you underestimate the warlike character of the dignitary houses, or that of the militia of the freeholds. They are not less valiant than you."

"They would fail, ma'am, if you were in back of me, for their womenfolk are only ordinary fair, and will not put into them more heart than mortals know, where I will have the devil's own heart in me, hot as hell from an angel's face! Come, I will make you queen of this balcony, and I will be your champion and armed forces, and our custom will be to greet the New Year with a kiss." And he stepped forward.

She stepped backward so smoothly and quickly, he was not sure if she had moved at all. It was as if a moonbeam slid through his fingers.

As suddenly as shapes that appear in a dream, the two figures woven of blurred shadows came forward, noiseless as icebergs at sea. They seemed to be made of glass, for the scene behind them, although distorted, was visible. These were hulking men in padded light-repeating suits, evidently her bodyguards. A shimmer, a trick of the light, hinted at the pole-arms in their hands, held at the ready.

She spoke in a voice like a cooing dove. At the moment, there was a pause in the fireworks, the light was dim, and he could not see her face. "The disadvantage to your plan is that the men of this world would be no less inspired as you by that beauty you flatter, since I am theirs. The advantage is that we could meet on equal footing, not as sovereign and subject."

"Equal baloney! I don't recognize you as—" he said.

"Do you not recognize me? The light is poor! I am Rania Anne Galatea Trismegistina del Estrella-Diamante Grimaldi, Sovereign Princess of Monaco, Duchess of Valentinois and of Mazarin, Marchioness of Baux, Countess of Carladès and of Polignac. If I floated, you would know me."

"What?"

"This odd ground here, no matter where you stand, is accelerating at one gee: there is no higher deck with lighter spin. In any case, it is you, none other, who elevated me to my current post, and convinced the ship's brain to accept my blood as proof of continuity. So I am still your Captain—you have none to blame but you for this. I hear from the Landing Party Senior that you are absent without leave. What penalty must I impose?"

She turned and nodded. The dark figures nodded and stepped back, their suits taking on the hue and patterns of brick and climbing rose-vine of the wall behind them. In the complex patterns of the fireworks, their suits could not react at speed, and so human-shaped bubbles with dark goggles hovering at eye-level were visible, even in the gloom. But then the light steadied, and grew bright, and the cheers of the crowds changed, and became a steady roar, and the soldiers faded into invisibility, paradoxically harder to see, as the light grew stronger.

"What—wait—? *You're* the Captain?"

Menelaus wondered how he could have missed the point. There were clues enough. Del Azarchel had mentioned the Princess being "in transit" and out of radio communication, and had said the same thing of the Captain. Montrose had assumed "in transit" meant in the middle of traveling, but no, Del Azarchel had used the word in its spacer's meaning: the *Hermetic* had been between Earth and the Sun. Radio communication was always difficult for targets lost in the electromagnetic glare and radio-noise Sol put out.

"Y—You were not at the Conclave," Menelaus stammered, feeling foolish.

"That is for crew, the civilian arm of the expedition. I represent the military—the sole military officer of the expedition. Do you forget neither the Spanish nor the Hindu ethnospheres would accept the other's leadership? That the *Hermetic* sailed under the flag of the Princedom of Monaco, under the banner of *Compagnie des Carabiniers du Prince*? Ah! One would think a lawyer would pay more attention to such legal niceties."

Her eyes were sparkling with mirth as she shook her head in disbelief.

Rania was flirting with him. He was sure. That look of her eyes half-lidded! Or not. There was something speculative in that look. Cool curiosity. The star-princess looking at some Earthbound relic of the past. He was imagining it. He had to get a grip on himself! But never had he wanted to keep on imagining anything so badly.

The perfume was driving him mad.

"So!" she said, "you offer to fight all the world for me—again. It is gallant, to be sure, but as your proposed conquest is carved out from lands already his, it would mean fighting my betrothed and your Senior Officer, whose world this is. Ximen calls you his brother. A brother like Cain, is it to be?"

Montrose jammed his hands into his pockets and scowled. "I didn't mean nothing by it—I mean, if you are promised to that skunk Blackie, I shouldn't be kidding around—"

"Did I reject your offer? This earthly orb is as precious as a jewel, or the beating heart of a nightingale, but small. Will you help me on a larger conquest, one that involves no bloodshed? For that reason I summoned you—for that reason I cured you—for that reason I stirred you from your frozen slumber. Though I have the right to demand your aid, instead I ask it."

Before he could think of what to answer, there was a flare from overhead like a flash of lightning. Then the light steadied and the cheers of the crowds changed, and became a steady roar.

Menelaus turned, and saw his own scowling face, enormously amplified, looming like the face of megalithic sphinx, splashed against the canopy of stars. Here was his nose, large and misshapen, hanging overhead. He blinked, and saw his eyelids, large as two moons, waft shut and open.

But this was but a corner of the scene that filled the heavens, which all the voices of the people cheered: She was raising one gloved hand to acknowledge the tumult of applause, and smiled with true and heartfelt joy at their adoration.

De god redt de Koningin! Rania! Rania!

She spoke without moving her teeth, nor did her eyes look at him. "I am not really a Queen, you know. The daughter of the Prince of Monaco is not royalty. The Buckhurst case established that members of the Sovereign's family who do not hold peerage dignities are actually commoners."

He said, "I thought you ran the whole planet."

"No. That is the concern of the landing party. The Captain only has authority above the atmosphere. The crew controls the Concordat, which controls the world, so I suppose I reign in truth, even if I do not rule in name. The world does not call me Captain."

"Eh? So what do they call you?"

"*Serene,*" she said, showing her dimples. "Her Serene Highness. Isn't that sweet of them?"

He raised his hand and mustered a smile and waved as well. The radar-invisible ceramic knife he had slipped into his palm when the bodyguards startled him by moving, he let slip back up his sleeve, of course, before he raised his hand. "Well, Princess, even if you ain't no real Queen, if the common folk make such an error over so much time, you say we got to honor it, right?"

That made her lift her chin and laugh, and so the titanic mouth hanging in the heavens above them opened wide, and the teeth like a Great Wall of China flashed white; the huge, beautiful eyes, vast as windswept lakes, narrowed with mirth, so that her whole face glowed. The cheers below redoubled.

13

Philosophical Language

1. Her Champion

The hollering of the crowd, and the Princess smiling and waving down to them went on and on. Even though he was being photographed by those flying bugs, and his image was projected titan-sized on to the clouds above the castle, Menelaus got bored of smiling, as his face was not built for it. So he rolled a cigarette, slouched against a nearby statue, struck a match against the statue's buttocks, and had a smoke. He examined his huge picture overhead. You know, his handmade buckskins really did look rather shabby, come to think on it, especially next to this princess.

Montrose was lost in thought, looking down at the shining coiffeur of her hair, jeweled and elaborate. Her scent, warm and feminine with a hint of lavender, was like a half-heard note of music, seductive as spring air. He noticed that the top of her head did not reach his chin: she might be too short to dance with. Not that the people of this day danced proper dances, woman in a man's arms. They bowed and swayed in lines and figures. How could something like the waltz, Mankind's greatest invention, simply pass away? Menelaus told himself he would have to reintroduce the custom. Otherwise there would be no chance to take this little golden woman in his arms.

He did not notice when her vast face vanished from the clouds above, and the cheers changed into sea-wave sounds of more ordinary mirth; but suddenly it was dim on the balcony again. She tilted up her finely-boned chin. He could not help but look at the red arc of her full lower lip, the tiny crease between chin and lip. What was that line called? Did it have a name?

"Isn't it beautiful?" she asked gaily, waving her gloved hand to the winter midnight horizon, the houses and fields below aflame with fireworks and colored torches.

Since he did not know what she was talking about, he nodded and said, "Very."

Rania said, "I was told by my fathers, the men who raised me, that my mother died bringing me into the world—my world, what you call a ship. Madalena, they said her name was. One memento I had from my mother was a picture of the Virgin Mary, crowned in stars, and with the moon beneath her feet. I did not know what it was, so I thought it was a picture of 'Mother Earth' of which the crew so often spoke, the world that once beamed a whole library of messages to us, and then fell silent. You see, I did not know your world was a globe. I had never seen a living globe. And so I loved this world because I pictured her as a beautiful mother, crowned in stars. Can you say, in truth, my picture is worse than those who think this world is merely a rock in space, coated with a thin film of water and air?"

She looked dreamy, thoughtful and melancholy, yet the shadow of a smile touched her scarlet lips. Menelaus decided now was not the time to tell her that her mother was a Petrie dish.

Menelaus shrugged with one shoulder. "I like the world just fine, mountains and trees, all that good stuff. Plague, I even like the Alaska wastes where I was snowed in not long back—hunting and ice-fishing. I just don't like the people, mostly. You got a rotten set-up here, Princess, and it sounds like you were the setter-upper, not Blackie."

"Perhaps the people of the world have not been as kind to you as they have to me. It would be ungrateful of me to feel less than love, after all the warmth this world has shown. A world of wonder! Do you ever smell the air, feel the flowing wind, and simply marvel at it? You have breathed bottled air, I know. But you were not born breathing it."

Menelaus had seen simple joy shining on the faces of children; but this was different. This was intelligent joy, adult and profound. It was a strange thing to see. In his life, the people he met did not rejoice—if that was the word for it—in the simple act of breathing.

"I was born breathing free, alright. I would prefer to live in a Democracy."

"If the people also preferred it, so should we all be. I was not born in a crown, or surrounded by fine things—these were pressed upon me by a grateful world, relieved from the endless tears and horrors of war. You know, I did not even know what war was at first, or murder? I lived among elderly scientists."

Montrose thought now was not the time to tell her that those elderly scientists were very well-acquainted with murder indeed, having killed the Captain and more than half the crew.

Instead he said, "I don't believe people don't want to be free."

"Nor do I, but there are two kinds of freedom: license to indulge any desire, base or noble, natural or unnatural, provided no one and nothing hinders you is the first kind, and it is deadly to men. The second kind is the freedom that comes of fulfilling or completing the work of nature that is half-formed in us. Men who are free in the first sense of the word will freely vote their freedom away, in return for lucre, prestige, and safety. In the early days, the Senior Del Azarchel simply bought the elections he needed, until the free nations of the world had prime ministers and parliaments composed of his creatures, who joined the Concordat willingly."

A strange look came into her eyes, which Montrose did not know how to interpret. Nostalgia? Sorrow?

"It was proud and stubborn kings and warlords of small or backward nations, which had returned to a more personal and less bureaucratic form of government, that held out against him. They had the second type of freedom, not the first: They were not dehumanized. Bad as they were, those kings regarded their subjects as their children, not as their customers or patients or wards or subjects of their latest experiments in sociopolitical engineering. But they lacked the first type of freedom, and those subjects were not free enough to resist us."

Montrose wondered where the Princess had gotten her notion of what princesses acted like. Where else? From the royalty she defeated, the princes who treated their subjects like children. The strange look was one of admiration.

"What did you offer them?" he asked.

"Honors and offices—the Copts and Manchurians and Boers form the backbone of our officer cadre, and they are allowed forms of dress and address denied other men, and in the wild areas of the world, they rule unchecked. The Concordat allows them indulgences the Church denies to others, such as divorce and contraception: They do not replace their numbers, and in a generation their vestige must find another fate. Much evil is done in my name that I abhor. If I were free to be ungrateful, I would flee my post. As it is, here I am chained as if with chains of gold, fair and gleaming, and only the terrible voice of a stronger duty can call me away."

Montrose said, "What's this talk of chains? Aren't you in charge?"

"I have all the power a Captain might have over her ship, if her sails were in darkness."

For a moment, he thought she meant a seagoing ship, sailing at night. But, no: in her world there was no night, only the darkness between stars. "A lightship out of her guiding lightbeam is in free fall, Princess," he said.

Rania nodded. "Exactly so. Such a Captain is merely trapped in an elaborate construction of steel, and merely carried along. The power of the Sovereign rests on the consent, tacit or open, of her subjects. Either they love her, or she does not lead. You know that. I was not born of this world: Every breeze and breath of air is a gift to me, not something I made for my own. I must repay as best I may, not counting the cost."

He squinted at her. This sounded like the kind of thing men facing danger told themselves.

"What cost are we talking about? You said you wanted my help. Are you in trouble?"

"I expect you to be fearless, in any of your aspects or avatars."

He was taken aback. "What does that mean? What exactly are you aiming I can do for you?"

"Learned Montrose, you surprise me! You know where you excel." Her tone seemed playful. Or perhaps he was imagining it.

"My jobs, in no particular order, were weaponsmith, pony-soldier, duelist, lawyer, a short stint as a spacehand, and a shorter stint as a xenomathematician. Oh, and human guinea pig for self-inflicted brain experimentation. I am not a failure at two of them."

"I have no need for your counsel as an attorney, being well-supplied with staff in that regard. It is your other professions that interest me."

"Great! Who do you want me to kill?"

"There is a dragon, O my champion, I require you to slay."

"What? I mean, begging your pardon? Did you say you wanted me to kill *what* again?"

"Come. Walk with me."

Rania merely tucked her shoulder under his arm, and wound her slender hand around his, so that he found himself half-embracing her as he had just been imagining.

The sensation of her silken glove on his hand sent a curious ripple up his arm.

This is it. He thought. *I am falling in love. Or I got the stomach flu.*

He breathed deeply. Her loveliness was an aura around her, a warmth, a perfume. He walked, feeling like a bull being led by the nose-ring by some slender farm girl. The strength in her arm surprised him: there was lioness muscle under that soft skin.

And she was another man's girl! He hated himself, at least a little bit, at the thought of being a poacher, and he hated himself again for not hating himself more. But in the back of his mind, he thought it as clear as day that Blackie did not deserve her.

But the strength of his own infatuation puzzled him. He had seen pretty women before—no one fell in love that fast, just in the twinkling of an eye. But she had been in his mind since first he saw her portrait at Blackie's. Why did she look so . . . familiar? He felt in his heart as if he already knew her.

She was not leading him back into the ballroom, but down the balcony to a smaller door to one side. The half-invisible soldiers softly opened the door for them. The soldiers did not enter, but stayed behind.

Beyond was a corridor, one he had not seen coming in, wainscoted in highly polished wood up to waist-high, and above that, an intricate wall-paper in blue with gold highlights, a motif of lianas, leaves, and lilies.

As she crossed the threshold, she touched the ruby that rested between her breasts. It must have been a control surface, because up from her coif-feur, glittering like dragonflies, rose a swarm of tiny, winged machines. Her hair came undone, and formed a momentary cloud of scented gold around her face. It was not that the strands were weightless in the night-breeze around her, but Menelaus had a ghost of a memory in his mind that it should have looked that way.

She shook her face to clear it, and Menelaus found the sight adorable, like a surfacing mermaid shaking spray free from her features.

Or like a sorceress. Her twinkling Tinkerbell-sized fliers were darting here and there in midair, destroying camera ladybugs, or driving them out of the slowly-closing door. He did not even mind that she plucked the half-consumed cigarette from his hand and had her dragonflies carry it out the door for her, and toss it away.

"Ventilation performance," she said.

"We're aground," he said. "Air is free on Earth."

"But why fall into bad habits? No tobacco is allowed aloft."

The door shut, the night-breeze stilled. Menelaus then and there de-cided the prettiest sight on earth was that of a girl tucking her hair behind her ear.

"Are you talking about going into space again?" A strange, a wild hope rose in his breast even as he said it. But then he shook his head, doubting. "I read some of Blackie's books. He daren't let the *Hermetic* leave the sys-tem, since it is his pistol pointed between the eyes of the world. And he daren't let another manned expedition go the Diamond Star, because that expedition, when it returned, would come back with another pistol as large. They'd pay back his heirs in his own ugly coin—with enough money to buy or bomb the world, a world where all they knew and loved would be long dead. As for the *Bellerophon*, right now she's got canisters strapped like bananas to the main keel for the construction crew, but that is going to all be stripped off and fall back home once the machine installation is complete. But no people are invited on that vessel. Men are too dangerous to trust going to go fetch the dangerous stuff in the Diamond Star."

She just shook her head. "I will not think that way, and shall not understand those who do. Should two mites on the ear of an elephant bite each other to death, when the elephant is plunging off a cliff's brink? You asked of me what I wanted killed. Are you willing to enter the lists?"

"Fight a duel? My dad would have approved. He thought womenfolk should talk that way. But you—you're not serious."

"I am."

"You got armies. And a ship. You're a princess."

"I am a woman, and a young woman, and armies cannot grapple this foe of mine. My enemy is not a thing of flesh and blood. The mystery of that Monument is my dragon. It will devour me if I am not saved."

"The Monument?"

"Can you read it?"

It was the moment he had been waiting for his whole life.

Menelaus was astonished at how evenly and calmly the words rolled off his tongue, "Ma'am, I can read that damn Monument for you, if anyone on Earth can."

2. The Logic Behind Logic

The corridor was lit, but was not exactly bright. Candles, good old-fashioned pre-Edison candles, stood on small tables every ten paces or so, between antique suits of gold-chased armor, or glass cases containing china curios or silver cups. Behind each candle was a dark drape, evidently meant to preserve the wallpaper from smoke stains. The buttery-gold light breathed and lived, and made the hallway into an elfin place, alive with shadows.

Without a further word, she reached over and tapped one of the mirrors facing the corridor. It was smartglass, just as back in Blackie's chalet, and an image of the Xi Segment of the Monument came up in the view.

The right window showed differential equations from the Divarication Theory; the left showed the symbol-groups of the Xi-wave function-group being organized into a matrix. This left window was connected by little red threads to show which symbol in the matrix represented which Monument sign. More than one information view of the process was displayed: one was a branching tree, one was a rippling set of Venn diagrams, like a rainy pond, one was a polar axis view, one was a Cartesian diagram, one was a basic-grammar theory spiderweb.

When the matrix was entirely filled in, the information began to sequence itself. One pattern after another was superimposed on the various trees and ponds and spiderwebs, and where there were partial matches, the letters to the right lit up with colors, matching a color-coded version of the Monument symbols.

"I know that sequence," said Montrose. "I designed it. That is what I had the Zurich computer use to go through the alien math, to make the codes to establish the nerve-channels in my brain."

"But what does the Xi Segment express?"

"I don't know. I just copied it."

"Compare the table results. Everything the Monument says, it says in repeating patterns. Logic in the Opening Statements underpins mathematics according to the Russell-Whitehead meta-language, which is in the Gamma Segment. Mathematics in the Alpha Segment underpins geometry and physics, the sections labeled Alpha 357 to Beta 120. Game-theory in Eta underpins economics in Theta. So then, what underpins the basic statements of logic? You see? Compare this here to those untranslated expressions in the first two bands of the Monument pole. They come before the scientific statements, the periodic table, or the Maxwell equations. Assume these are metaphysical expressions, needed to explain and justify the basic physics here, symbols written in a pattern we humans cannot grasp, because the physical roots of the laws of physics are unknown to us."

"I don't follow you."

"We have yet to deduce a logical system proving the physical constants of the universe must be those of our cosmos, and none other. Obviously these are matters physics cannot address, since empiricism can only examine the universe we have before us. So, the physics of before physics: I would call it meta-physics, but the word is taken. Let us call it Axiomatics, the justification of fundamental physical constants."

"So they know the basic rules for why the universe is the way it is and not some other way. So what?"

"So I suggest the symmetry is maintained for the Mu-Nu Group over here. I suggest to you that these groups of expressions are, as the Monument Builders are great lovers of symmetry, the meta-logical expression: a symbolic code for the expression that would justify the basic rules of logic. The basic rules for why the mind is as it is and not some other way."

"That makes no sense. You cannot use logic to justify logic. Either you assume the rule work, or you're an ass. Um, pardon my . . ."

"The meta-logic rules, I am saying, do not use logic to justify the axioms of logic logically—as you correctly point out, that would be a paradox. But what is the underpinning for logic in the ultimate sense?"

"It works."

She smiled graciously. "Many philosophers believe this indicates an intimate connection between the laws of physics, the laws of mathematics, and the way the human mind works. Odd, is it not? In an infinite universe, why would we just so happen to evolve brains that could comprehend the laws that just so happen to underpin the physical universe?"

"Not so odd. I'll tell you why. Natural selection and the damn fool common sense God gave a goose. Lookit here: Animals who thought *is* was the same as *is not* might think a predator what *is* about to eat them up, *is not* about to dine so fine, and then the natural difference between *is* and *is not* would be clear as *either-or*: namely *either* you vamoose out from those sharp teeth, *or* you'll be an *is not* in no time."

"Nicely spoken, but you are familiar with Divarication theory. You are one of its primary authors, are you not? Put any information value you wish into the expression for whatever gene controls the organism's logic. Somewhere in the little bits of matter that make us up, is something written in our DNA—think of it as a symphony written in a chemical code of four notes—somewhere is the arpeggio that programs us to believe A is A. Estimate the volume needed to carry that abstraction forward between all the generations of organisms possessing neural systems since the pre-Cambrian. Look at how the figure falls out."

He ran his finger on the mirror surface, and drew out a few calculations. "It's impossible," he said at last. "If there was a gene for logic, it would have mutated by now, and cropped up. There would be other creatures with other rules for other types of logic—which is something I can't imagine, anyhow. I mean, even a mama bird counting her eggs don't make twice two equal to five."

"To me, this suggests a simpler and more universal structure to thought,"

Rania said. "The laws of optics form a limiting set to the divarication for the principles of how to evolve an eye. Likewise, other laws must form a limit to how logic, language, and thought can evolve. The basic rules of the universe make it so that no organism can evolved into a rational creature for whom A equals not-A."

"What are you saying?"

She pointed at the mirror: "That! The rules of meta-logic, my champion, is what you have in your brain. A set of neural logic gates which allow you to see meta-logical patterns, and recognize those patterns where they appear. It is your lance to slay my dragon. Because those patterns appear in the Monument: it is written in nothing but patterns."

"Lady, I still don't understand, and that is something I am not used to saying."

"Remember the oldest problem in Sign Theory: How do you communicate with a species so alien that nothing in your psychology or culture is the same? How do you refer to things with no shared references? And I am suggesting we are looking at the handiwork of some race that solved that problem. The mere fact that the Monument exists proves that a universal language is possible, which means that the relation of field theory to physics to molecular chemistry to DNA to brain to brain structures to thought to logic to symbol cannot be arbitrary—despite that our Earthly theories hold them to be."

"Math, logic, and physics are universal. So I guess that is the only thing aliens can talk with us about."

"But they are only the beginning of the Monument message. What of other universals? But how do you make a symbol for honesty, for justice, for beauty, for love, for any abstraction?"

"Maybe those things come out of genetic adaptation to game-theory: organisms that don't play fair enough to cooperate with natural allies can't compete with mutual foes."

"No," she said, "I don't believe it is merely game-theory. Or, I should say, what is game-theory based on? How do we teach our own children abstractions like truth and justice? Toddlers learn about right and wrong, about yes and no, forbidden and permitted, the basics of law and mercy, long before they learn to count. We do not teach them biology, then genetics, then the theory of the selfish Gene, then the theory of the natural harmony of self-interest, and then tell them it is not in their self-interest not to fib to their fathers. When a child is caught lying, what do you do?"

He straightened up and stepped away from the mirror, partly because the nearness was driving him mad, partly because he wanted to look at her face.

"Lecture 'em good, and take a strap to 'em, so to help remember them the lecture."

"And what does that suggest?"

"Well—I reckon our kids learn universal concepts the way a baby bird learns birdsongs," Montrose said. "Pain and pleasure mean 'yes' and 'no.' The signs we show them, simple things at first, like a swat on the rump, match like lock and key to something in their nervous system. Swat on the rump stimulates the pain centers wired to signal an *avoid this* behavior. Smiles and touches linked to ganglia wired up to express pleasure. Lock fits key."

"Then how is it possible to talk to aliens?"

"I am not sure it is. No alien creature, things whose bodies are made of silicon rocks or methane soup or intelligent clouds of smog, things we can't imagine, they are not going to have any locks in their brains—or whatever part of them does their thinking and fretting—that can possibly fit our keys. Our notions of justice and truth and beauty don't mean spittle to them. How could you make a language to express things like that? Ideas that only make sense in a certain context? Except . . ." Menelaus frowned thoughtfully. "Same way we teach our babies, I guess. Teach them in context. Point and grunt. Swat then on the rump. Give a petting and a smile. But you would have to give them our nervous system first."

"You think as I do. Go on."

"Go on to what?" He said, exasperated. "You can't send the context of the message before you send the message! What would that even mean? A language that deciphers itself? How do you do it?"

She smiled, and it was like the sun coming out.

"Simple. You encode the lock and the key both," she continued. "The human brain is not really a lump of hydrogen and carbon, is it? It is a pattern of information. Anything that you grew in a tank that followed the code-pattern of the human genome would be human, would it not? A human brain made of another substance, provided the nerve cells operated in the same way, or in a way parallel to ours, would be human, would it not?"

"Ghost Del Azarchel thinks so, or so he told me."

"And what is the human genome but a language, a code of information, a song of four notes, which could be recompiled into any system of other notes, the way a number line can be expressed in base two or base ten?"

He nodded. "I guess so. If you were intelligent, and you wanted to send a message, and the only thing you knew about the recipient was that he occupied the same universe with the same natural laws as you, you'd send the message with the messenger. The messenger would be coded up, expressed as a series of numbers, or logic signs, or something else universal. You show him how to build the lock, tumbler by tumbler, and then you show him where to put all the ridges on the key, tooth by tooth. Is that what you are getting at with all this weird talk of logic and meta-logic? The Monument is instructions on how to build a system that can read the Monument."

"Not a system to read the Monument. A system to build a person who can learn to read it."

"A messenger!" He smacked his fist into his palm and grinned. "Listen, we can build this messenger, this message-reading machine. You must know that Del Azarchel has made a breakthrough in brain emulation. He has got a perfect replica of himself, I mean perfect, talks like him, and over the phone Alan Turing couldn't tell it weren't him. If you have enough wealth, Princess, then you can afford to get me the computer space needed to build a second one . . ."

"It is not necessary."

"No, no, listen! It's a great idea. All you do is string up the models the same way the human brain is strung up, using the universal life-code here, translated into human DNA, and making the hardwiring of the brain follow those DNA instructions . . . Don't make a model of Blackie, make a model of the brain that can read the Monument, based on the Monument's own negative image of . . ."

"I am saying it is not necessary."

". . . unlike a real brain, there is no upper limit to . . . Wait. Why ain't it necessary?"

"It's been done."

Such a wild hope entered his heart at that moment, he wondered if he were going mad. The key to the Monument was what this conversation was about! The key to the future of Mankind, and, yes, to the future of Menelaus as well. If his soul had been music, it would have roared into a crescendo at that moment.

He understood what she was saying.

"It's you, Princess, isn't it? You are the key. You, the starry messenger!" Menelaus pointed at the Monument. "Where and how exactly were you born, Princess? What part of that describes your code?"

Rania looked at him in puzzlement for a moment, and then mirth began dancing in her eyes, and she threw back her head, and peals of girlish laughter rang and echoed throughout the corridor.

"Oh, dear, no . . . forgive me for laughing, but . . . ah! The irony . . ."

"You're not the key to the Monument?"

"Would that I were!" And just as suddenly as her joy appeared, sorrow now appeared.

"Well, who else?"

"You are."

"Me?"

"You, Crewman Fifty-One, you. Don't you see the connection?"

"Nope."

"For a genius, you are not very bright." She pointed back at the mirror. "Compare these two files. Don't you see those are two different translations of the same thing, defined by the same algorithm?"

The first file was the Zurich run again. He had derived those parameters, of course, from the Monument math itself, manipulating symbols whose meaning he did not know, merely trusting that the unknown "grammar rules" of the aliens would make the conclusion valid if the axioms were valid.

The second file was a snapshot of the Theta sine symbol group of the Monument: a mathematical expression which, when translated into Earthly biochemistry, contained instructions on how to build or emulate a brain to read the Monument.

The two were the same. In using the Monument math to establish which nerve connections to use to become intelligent enough to read the Monument, Menelaus had unwittingly come to the same logic-path as the Monument instructions on how to read the Monument.

She said, "The pattern is an emergent property of the mathematics."

"Why did they put the same thing in two places? I was not using the symbol-forms from that segment to do my brain-tinkering!"

"The Monument Builders are obsessed with recursions."

Menelaus understood. The builders were trying to be as clear as possible, and so they repeated themselves. It was a communication strategy: two parts of a redundant message could be checked against each other for accuracy.

She said, "You did not know what you were doing to yourself, but you produced, in part of your cortex, something that follows this same pattern that repeats as a leitmotif in the Monument. Don't you recall?"

"Recall what?"

"You were reading the Monument, sight-reading it, without notes, at a glance, from before I was born. Once you had the rules for reading symbols out of logic patterns build into your nervous system, you could not help but see them. That was part of what drove you mad."

"At a glance? But—I thought I was a failure!"

"You were. What you did to your brain was ill-considered, stupidly rash, idiotic." He liked her smile, sure enough, but he was not sure how much he liked her needling him.

"But I could read the Monument!" he protested.

"It that a tribute to your genius, or theirs? It was built to be read."

3. Flight of Ideas

Then they were both talking at once. It was one of those conversations where each sentence was only a fragment for the other person to finish, a team conversation, with him and her merely contributing ideas as the stream of thought seemed to rush along under its own effort. For the first time since he laid eyes on her, Menelaus forgot she was gorgeous, and when he talked over her or shouted her down or called some idea of hers stupid, he did not notice it, any more than he noticed her interrupting him, or lashing him with golden laughter for his slow-wittedness.

The conversation theorized that solving the Monument was not a decryption problem; it was an emulation problem. The Monument seemed to contain no symbols beyond the basics. After the opening sequence, it was all meta-symbolism, like a DNA string, meant to produce symbols through a series of logic gates, but the expression would be in terms of game-theory.

That was why a computer emulation of an analog thinking machine was needed. They needed to model the meta-symbols and see them in action to see what they meant: see what came out of the rules of the game written out on the Monument surface.

"Each symbol's range of meanings could be expressed as a cup-length. Under the Leray-Hirsch Theorem, a cohomology monomorphism could be described to express the all polydimensional vector subspaces involved. The opening sequence of symbols could be manipulated, even if they were not understood, by the game rules described by the Theta Group of symbols." So spoke the conversation. Menelaus did not realize that it was his side of the conversation speaking, himself, until she interrupted.

She could not shout him down, her voice was too delicate, but she put her gloved fingers on his lips to say something, and the perfumed touch of silken fingertips, fingers slender as a child's, snapped him out of his trance.

Menelaus was brought up short.

". . . cannot overlook the possibility that your own nervous system structure was affected by the same game-theory codes embedded in the Monument. What was the expression you used to program that antique mainframe back in your day? The one that did a pattern recognition on possible nerve reorganization paths?"

Menelaus heard himself answer, but he did not pay attention to his own words. Because he was looking at her face.

It was shining. The eyes, green like emeralds in this light, or hazel as amber when she turned her head, were flickering, jumping from point to point, as if the mind behind them could read an encyclopedia of information out of the visual data impinging on her optic nerve. Then the eyes would grow still, staring, motionless, as if fixed on a distant star, a point on the far horizon.

And she was blushing. Her cheeks were pink, her hairline was beaded with sweat, and she had that glow about her that pregnant women were said to have. The look of abundant life.

His own cheeks were burning, too. His heart was pounding. Menelaus felt as if he might faint any moment.

Menelaus stepped back from her, stopping in mid-syllable. She was too excited to notice, but kept talking about Schubert calculus, Grassmann manifolds, fibered subspaces, the E8 supersymmetries.

For a moment his mind reeled. He could not follow what she was saying. How had she jumped to that conclusion? He tried to picture the geometric rotations she rapidly uttered, but found he could not visualize them, not and keep up. He had been following along, sometime leaping ahead of her line of proofs not half a moment ago. But now he was back in his right mind, and the dizzying architecture of speculations, certainties, and guesses was too great to hold in his imagination. The next step . . . was it correct or not? What was that about astro-algorithmic logic-gate matrices? In what sense was it a specific application of a more general case of emulating a universal virtual machine in n-dimensional coordinates?

Then he noticed she had his ceramic knife in her hand. He did not member handing it to her. She was scratching diagrams and equations in neat rows of Greek and Latin letters, alephs and infinities, as well as the dots and triangles and Celtic knots of Monument hieroglyphs, all along the wallpaper. She was cutting figures into the wood underneath the wallpaper. This was not modern wallpaper, not smart fabric meant to be written on. This was some antique and horribly expensive stuff, probably hand-painted, probably by Leonardo da Vinci and Michelangelo together, then touched up by Rembrandt, using solid gold paintbrushes.

And, of course, right next to her equations, in a larger, rougher handwriting, were his equations and notes. There was a deep scar where he had circled a particularly important multicovariable expression. And there were the slashes where he had put three exclamation points through the gold leaf into the wood paneling.

Next to him in the hallway was a crystal vase with flowers in it, carefully arranged. He plucked the bouquet out, hoisted the crystal jar, and dashed water into his own face.

The shock of the water helped somewhat. He no longer felt faint.

Princess Rania, who had been talking very loudly (for her), and very rapidly in an almost monotone singsong, now stopped. She turned.

All at once she was in his arms, on her tiptoes, and kissing him passionately.

It was like a bolt of lighting traveled up his spine. It was perfect.

And, then, just as suddenly, it was not perfect. She writhed out of his grasp, elusive as starlight, graceful as a sleek lioness, and danced back, her face blank.

He was looking right at her face when it happened: her expression returned to normal. It was like watching a ghost fade out of the body of some possessed person on those old faith healer shows everyone in his family save him used to watch so raptly. Like an actress turning off a character and surfacing. But not like an actress. There was nothing fake about it.

She was not panting, but Rania was breathing a little heavily. Long, slow breaths that made her bosom rise and fall.

"You're the other one. Ah. Welcome back."

This time, he understood how she slipped so effortlessly out of his hands: the point at which his two arms could trap her formed a folded set that could be expressed as a Hilbert space. Solving for the shortest vector distance, she leaned on his arm, and when he instinctively tightened it, she had put her center of balance elsewhere at the point of least resistance. It was as perfect as a ballet move. He wondered if the speed of her nerve impulses traveling to her muscles was momentarily increased, it was so smooth, and so rapid.

"Your are possessed, too, ain't you? You are a Mrs. Hyde!"

Rania stared at him quizzically.

"Miss Hyde, I would prefer. I am a maiden yet." She showed dimples when she smiled. "Unless you are proposing? I warn you, I am spoken for."

Menelaus backed up, his arm raised as if to ward off a blow. "You are not in love with Del Azarchel!"

"I don't recall saying I was."

"You are in love with me."

"Define your terms," she said, favoring him with an arch look. She wiggled the knife at him playfully. He carefully took it from her gloved hand, and slipped it back up his sleeve.

"No normal girl says *define your terms* when you say *you are in love with me.*"

She nodded judiciously. "Being normal is a goal oft sought and rarely achieved, but not unenviable for all that. Statistically speaking, it would be unusual if everyone were average."

"You are in love with the other me. Mr. Hyde. The Daemon. Crewman Fifty-One."

14

Posthuman Sovereign

1. Defining Her Terms

She tapped the mirror, so that it turned into a mirror again, drew out a compact case, and began touching up her lip-gloss where the kissing had smudged it. At the same time, her sorceress's flock of dragonflies began swirling around her head, using their tiny legs as combs, and, acting in concert, began resetting and repinning her coiffeur.

Rania spoke in a dreamy, absentminded tone. "When I was a child I heard a legend of the missing crewman, Number Fifty-One, who was kept in a special biosuspension coffin on Deck Zero, at the axis of the world. They called it a ship, my fathers, but it was the only world I knew. Every few years, when confronted by some problem no one knew how to solve, the fathers in wide-eyed fear would wake up Crewman Fifty-One."

She turned toward him, and stepped closer, so she had to lift her chin to look up at him. Her eyes flashed like sunlight glancing on summer seas. "You odd man! Do you know yours was the first laughter, the first real laughter, I ever heard? You were the only one who was still young?"

Before he could answer, she had turned her back on him. Her elbows were high, and she put her hands in her hair as her insect-machines pinned her hair in place. He saw the line of her neck, the exquisite fineness of her back and shoulderblades, delicate as carved ivory sanded smooth. His eyes traveled down the line of her back to her trim waist, the swell of her hips, the parabolic drape of her satin train. He almost laughed, because her slippers were translucent. Glass slippers.

"I remember as a little girl seeing you bounce from bulkhead to bulkhead in the mess, starting a food-fight, and writing equations on the walls in ketchup that only I could read—I thought they were meant for me.

"And little, pale, gray, sickly men, the fathers who raised me, they seemed so feeble compared to you, until you taught them how to use the coffins to make them young again. Whenever you woke up, it was like a food watch, like Christmas.

"Yes, we had Christmas aboard—we had very few gifts to share.

"When I was twelve and thirteen, I used to solve some of the magneto-hydrodynamic containment engineering problems wrong, so the thrust would wobble, just to get them to wake you up again. And you had not aged a day! And sometimes you would speak to me, if I could get you to look at me, but you never knew who I was."

2. The Cure

"You have a crush on Mr. Hyde?"

"O-oh, I would not call it a 'crush.' I do not love your madness. Del Azarchel sought to keep us apart. He forced me into suspended animation for many years, telling the people I suffered from 'Earthsickness'—a lie no one believed. You, he was afraid to thaw. It was not until I told him how to program his emulation of himself, and copy your chemical brain-alterations, that I was able to force him to wake us both in the same time period."

"What do you mean?"

"The matter was delicate, but not difficult, since time was on my side, not to mention public opinion."

"He's not actually getting older. Seems to me he had plenty of time."

"No. This year is when the endless wealth must begin to come again, or come to an end."

"What does that—oh! There are one hundred years worth of antimatter left. Enough to last while an expedition travels fifty lightyears to V 886 Centauri, mines the star, and travels back, right?"

"It's more complex than that, since we are dealing with estimates of future use, but, yes, the fuel reserves which seem so immense compared to Earth's energy needs, are small compared to the refueling time."

Montrose understood. Antimatter was also the ship's fuel. The closer you crowd lightspeed, the greater the energy cost of accelerating the mass will grow—and grow asymptotically. The longer Del Azarchel waited, the less time was left, therefore the faster the Third Expedition had to be. And in this universe, speeds near lightspeed were astronomically costly.

"Why did he wait so long?" Montrose asked.

"Some years were consumed in wars of consolidation, some in constructing a new vessel—even with his wealth, not a small prospect."

"What was wrong with the *Hermetic*?"

"You mean, why did he not simply ravish it from me?" Her eyes in the mirror looked over her own shoulder at him, flashing. "Two reasons, one better than the other. The worse reason is that Little Big Brother, the onboard security computer, thanks to you, still thinks I am the Captain, since I have the genes of Grimaldi in me. The better reason is that his heart is tender toward me, and full of rose-colored dreams. He sought my hand in marriage, and not my hate. Why plunder your own dowry? The computer is old fashioned enough—once again, thanks to you, you oaf—to grant husbands a superior right over their wife's property."

"Ten years or twenty should have been enough to ready up another vessel."

"He could neither go himself nor stay himself, since he was trapped by his own ambition, and by his own profligacy. He did not trust anyone to stay and rule the world in his stead, and did not trust anyone to go and gather the wealth and power from heaven for him."

"But now—thanks to me, he can be in two places at once."

"I gave him a problem only you could solve. His work is in Artificial

Intelligence, and yours in Neural Divarication Theory. So I made his emulation—he calls it his Iron Ghost—"

"We met. I think he, or it, saved my life."

"I helped with the architecture. But I programmed in a flaw, so that Ghost Del Azarchel would get sick and go mad with the Montrose madness. Then I pretended not to be able to solve the problem, and waited. He knew, because you had partly wakened Little Big Brother to self-awareness, that it had to be possible. He knew you had solved it. Why couldn't he? It drove him almost to madness." She smiled to herself. "I waited. There is only one other daemon in the world, aside from me: and that is you."

Montrose spoke in a voice of slow horror. "Then the person you want killed—is me! You want this version out of the way so that the posthuman version of me can take over!"

She laughed. "Oh, that would be funny! No, matters are not so overwrought with tragedy as that. I went through all these steps to give you this."

She drew a small gemlike vial from a fold in her skirt and tossed it lightly to him. He caught it, held it up. In the dim candlelight, he saw it had a folding needle. He realized that it was a bone rongeur, small and disguised as a piece of jewelry.

"What do you want?" he asked.

"I want you to take the cure. I have had it for years. In your initial Zurich runs, you made the classic compilation blunder, and did not scale up your lower nervous system to handle the greater stress load on your cortex."

"And this?"

"It is the real Prometheus Formula, the one you did not know how to make."

"You had it? Why not cure me with this before?"

"I had to work carefully when I was repairing you. If you were too alert too quickly, you would see through what Del Azarchel intended, and not help him with his divarication problem. So I had to leave you disoriented enough to do be willing to do the work, but oriented enough to see how to solve it. I discovered traces of your pre-posthuman personality buried in neural codes at the base level—the way a frog's genes contains the pattern for a tadpole. It was not difficult to resurrect this you, your previous version, the one from before I knew you."

"You mean—*he* is not possessing *me*? *I* am possessing *him*?"

"I suppose one could regard it that way." She was done with her hair, and now she turned back, and favored him with another sunny smile. "In any case, at the same time, I maneuvered the Senior into programming into his emulation a neural divarication error of the kind I knew you already knew how to repair—you must have been suspicious that it was so easy to solve?"

"No. I just thought I was that damn good. But I don't understand! Why not just cure my brain malfunction and wake me up straight off?"

"With the Senior Del Azarchel standing right by your bedside? I feared for your life. He is a dangerous man."

"Then why did you agree to marry him?"

"As I said, he is a dangerous man."

3. A Personal Dragon

Montrose looked back and forth along the walls, now ruined and covered with mathematical scratches. He was not sure what to think.

"What were we just talking about?"

She looked at him through the corner of her eye. "You can't understand it?"

"It's the drug. The recipe for the Prometheus Formula. You reduced the entire Zurich run, what took a multiple-volume computer months to deduce, into a simple expression . . ."

"Are you guessing, or are you recollecting?"

He turned his back to her, since he did not want her to see his expression. Unfortunately, the mirror was right in front of him, and so he saw the look of anxious uncertainty—of fear—on his features, and in the glass she bestowed the twinkle of an impish smile on him.

"I don't know what or who I am anymore," he said.

She said, "Whenever my beautiful, great ship was in trouble, or my people faced a problem we could not solve, they woke you up. It was always fun, in a dangerous way, but only sometimes could we get you to listen to us, or look at the problem we put before you. You would bounce off the bulkheads and make me laugh. And then you would fix the problem, and save us. That is who you are. My hero. My manic-depressive hero."

He spun angrily, and caught her by the shoulders. "You are trying to trick me!"

She looked thoughtful, and pouted. "Quite possibly. That is one of the things behind every man–woman relationship." She shrugged her scented shoulders very slightly in his hands. "Do we have a relationship?"

He let go and stepped back. "Stop toying with me. I cannot trust myself. Either of me."

"There is only one of you, silly man. And I have no need of feminine wiles—when speaking the truth, as befits a princess, will serve me better. Because you are convinced of a false belief that Mr. Hyde is different from you, you will debate in your mind for a time whether to trust that vial I gave you, or destroy it. But it does not matter, since I just here and now have shown you how to formulate it. Sooner or later you will realize that you are the Mr. Hyde, the lesser version, and your posthuman self is Dr. Jekyll, the greater. Your discontent with the human condition will drive you to enter into the discontents of the posthuman condition. Or your fear of Del Azarchel, and your need to be smarter than he. Or your desire to have a conversation with me, one to one, as equals."

"That's the second time you've said you were above me, little lady, and I won't stand it. I've a mind to turn you over my knee!"

She raised an eyebrow. "Well, I am flattered by the offer of a spanking, but I am your superior officer, and your sovereign, and higher on the ladder of evolution than you, and I have a fully armed starship, and several armed forces at my command, not to mention I can flick one of my hairpins up your nose. So any horseplay could turn out badly for you. Besides, what would my husband say if you assumed his privileges?"

"Wait? If you are married, how can you be engaged?"

"The marriage was not consummated, and my husband was not in his right wits at the time of the ceremony, which was private, so in the eyes of the law the oath is invalid."

"Wait! Plague and damnation, girl, are you talking about me? Did I get married to you when I was Mr. Hyde?"

She fluttered her fingers at the ampoule. "Ask him yourself."

"Pox!"

"Just one quick jab in the head. It should only sting a little. Well, actually, it will cause you blinding, unparalleled agony. Warn me first! So I can leave the room! I don't want to hear you screaming while you are writhing and flopping on the floor like a fish. I do have medical technicians downstairs, who can strap you into a gurney. Be nicer for you if you took morphine first."

"Lady, I just met you! I don't know you from Adam!"

"Adam lacked a belly button. Or so it is said. You can distinguish me from him on that basis. No doubt he was taller than I."

"I am not sticking your pestilential chemicals into my nice new brain, not after Dr. Kyi just fixed me!"

"He merely assisted. I did most of the work. So it is a little late to express distrust? Oh! And I forgot! That also makes me your physician, so you have to obey my orders. Will you break faith with me?"

"I ain't taking no orders from some dame half my age!"

"Dame? You have severely demoted me, sirrah! I shall have my master of heralds contact your office in the morning."

She stamped her little glass-shod foot so that her slipper rang like a bell on the floor, and she looked so regal and so wrathful that for a half-second Montrose thought he had really offended her. But then she burst out laughing in a most unladylike fashion (although she did hide her mouth behind her slender silk-gloved hand as she hiccupped her way through a giggle fit) so that Montrose stood there, unable to decide whether to be angry or confused or to join in.

His expression must have been uproarious to her, because the peals of laughter lasted a long moment. Her face was blushing a pretty rose-pink from the hilarity, and her skin was so delicate, that the blush of laughter went all the way down her throat, to her shoulders and down past her collarbone.

It was a regular Texas sort of laugh. He decided he liked it.

"Ma'am, don't get me wrong. You're the cutest little button on God's green Earth, and smart as a whip, and I like your sass, and may Jesus beat me with a two-by-four with a honking big nail in it if'n I am telling a lie—but you also must be a little crazy. You think I am going to stick myself with some needle? And what hold you think you got on me? Why do you call it breaking faith?"

"Is my sass showing? I must certainly speak harshly to my seamstress."

He tried not to laugh, but he shook his head. "Rania, Rania," (how he loved saying that name!) "What are you thinking? What hold can you claim on me?"

Now she was sober. (But still pretty and pinkish around the edges.) "None," she said, drawing a shaking breath, and shaking her head. "It is the Monument that holds you. It holds me as well."

"Your own personal dragon. What's that mean?"

"Have you understood nothing? And I thought you were a genius."

"An unlikely stupid genius, I'd say. Didn't no one tell you how I done stuck a needle in my head-bone?"

"The Monument is my dragon for all the reasons we have said. I was born from it—you have by now deduced that."

It was a statement, not a question. He said, "Not hard to deduce. There weren't women on the ship. But when did you figure it out?"

"You ask, in other words, when did I deduce that everything said by the beloved fathers who raised me was a lie, and that the picture of my beautiful mother, the picture I held when I cried myself to sleep in my cocoon on C-Deck, was a fake? I was old enough to dissemble my reaction, but too young to be forgiving."

"How much of you is—homo sapiens? They used some real human DNA as a start."

"Ranier Grimaldi was my matrix. He is my mother, so to speak; I have had gene scans. I have his chin, his eyes, his love of truth. As for the rest of me, I am a chimera, an ugly ducking. Who can say what I will grow into? Someone else acted as my Doctor Frankenstein, my designer, and established my basic looks."

"Del Azarchel? He likes blondes?"

That made her smile. She curled a finger around a lock of her hair. "No, *I* like blondes. I had the hue adjusted by RNA spoofing. If wolves and rabbits change their hairs for their seasons, to match their backgrounds, I may do the same for the social season, which is my surrounding. Do you like my eye color? I jinxed it to match my gown."

"Gah. My mom would not approve. She always said you had to stay as God made you."

"There is much wisdom in the notion, and much vanity would be foresworn if it were followed—but the conceit cannot apply to me. The Hermeticists are less than omniscient, even if I had good cause to follow their wishes."

Menelaus said nothing. He could think of a good cause why she should stop following their wishes, but he was reluctant to speak.

Her face was dreamlike, distant, melancholy. She said softly, "Am I human? Sometimes, when I feel rain of April upon my face, or see the children playing chase, or wonder at the Arc de Triomphe or St. Paul's Cathedral, my heart expands with emotions I know all my fellow humans feel. I cry at funerals and dance at weddings. Whatever was added to me did not subtract from that. Sometimes, when I see the cruelties and stupidities of the race, I doubt my humanity, and would gladly leave them all behind."

She turned toward him, looking up into his eyes. She continued: "But we all feel this way, at times, do we not? I am haunted by the doubts that haunt all young women, who wonder if any understand the great unexpressed truths they know. They wonder where the rainbow lands; they wonder if the air of spring was newly-made for them alone."

Her eyes were lovely, but he turned his gaze toward the floor. "You owe them nothing! They murdered your father." His reluctance to tell her why she should stop following their wishes had lasted, after all, only a moment.

"They also gave me life, the Hermeticists, and raised and cherished me. They sacrificed rations to feed me, and went hungry for me. So the matter is complex. I cannot in good conscience act against them. But I can serve a purpose higher than theirs."

He raised his eyes. "What purpose?"

"I am born a messenger. Like you, I am a living emulation of a universal virtual machine, constructed following Monument logic-gates, and meant both to serve as a computing substrate and as a translating mechanism: I was born to read that Monument. I have no other purpose, really. And—can you understand this pain of mine?"

"What pain, Princess?"

"The Hermeticists did not translate something right, or a code was transposed, or the human frame is too small to hold what I should be. I am not suited to my purpose in life. The key does not fit the lock."

"What? What do you mean?"

"I can't read it." She put her white-silk-gloved hand out toward the writing on the walls, toward the mirror. The mirror flickered, and displayed the concentric circles and angles and lines of alien hieroglyphs, a labyrinth of signs within signs. "I am broken. I was put together wrong."

And all of a sudden, she was sobbing and he was holding her in his arms, patting her awkwardly, and saying, "There, there."

It happened so naturally, so automatically, that it was not until he was embracing her that he realized what he had done.

When a woman cries, you got to hold her: that's nature. She rubbed her cheek on his shoulder, and he raised his thumb to wipe most gently one tear-streak clean. But there were more tears.

He knew he should not be kissing his friend's woman. Del Azarchel was dangerous when crossed. But you cannot hold a beautiful and golden woman in your arms, her head tucked neatly just under your chin, and think such things for long. You have to push her away or hold her tighter, and you only have a split second to decide.

Damn Del Azarchel! Damn the world! Was the world or its master any more to be feared than gun barrels?

And he lowered his head and kissed her tears away, just as he was supposed to.

4. The Proposal

A tinkle of suspicion, soft as a spider, crawled through his brain. "Funny you saying you cannot read the Monument—you just were reading it now."

She was still in his arms, and she turned her face (sweet as the face of a child, and streaked with tears) up to him. "The simple parts. I cannot do what you do. I can understand your work, but cannot decipher the next step! There is more to the message, much more! The human race is not destined merely for servitude to alien machines in the Hyades! But I cannot read what it says next!"

"Take your drug. The one you just gave me—"

That made her squirm out of his arms. She turned her back coyly, and drew out a handkerchief to daub her eyes. "That corrects what is wrong with *you*. It adds supportive infrastructure to your midbrain and hindbrain. It solves the scaling problem."

"And what is wrong with you?"

"I don't know. My fathers did not know what they were doing when they made me. They copied your work, but not all of it, not correctly, not right. Will you help me?"

With those words she turned again, and somehow her warm, supple, satin-clad body was in his arms, pressed up against his buckskin-clad chest.

"Oh, hell! Princess, I am yours to command!"

"Then take your medicine," she said in a matter-of-fact tone. "Marry me. We will depart the Earth, and return in the *Hermetic* to the Diamond Star, leaving this unhappy world to its fate."

Montrose listened, rapt, breathless and unable to speak.

"Over Del Azarchel's opposition, I have been outfitting, repairing, and restoring my beautiful ship, my world, my home," said Rania in tones of silver. "I have selected cadets from among the psychoi order to serve aboard her. I am within my rights: The Landing Party cannot bind me to this world, merely because it wishes to conquer, rule, and live here. The future of the human race is at the Diamond Star, and written into the Monument that circles it! Will you obey my orders? I command you to reach with me for the stars!"

"Uh-h . . . Did you say *marry*?"

5. The Arrest

Her expression did not change, but her pupils did. Her saw the dark part of her eyes expand suddenly, her eyes move left and right so quickly that they seemed to vibrate. At the same time, a blush of red began to spread, delicate as a rose, through her face, cheeks, and neck. He was holding Miss Hyde. At no time did she show surprise or shock on her face, albeit she must have been shocked. Her eyes were focused behind him. They had been overheard.

Montrose spun. There, on his silent, sliding throne of black, was Ximen Del Azarchel, Master of the World, his face (old again, silver-haired, lined and weathered and kingly) in such pain and sorrow that he seemed on the verge of fainting, or of tears. His eyes were hollow.

"You liar!" croaked Del Azarchel in a voice as weak as a mummy's. "*Gusano*! You lying worm! You said there was nothing between you! Is this how you repay me!"

There were six Conquistadores with him, dark against the festive lights shining through the open door behind them. Despite their comic-opera costumes, they had the calm, hard look of professional veterans; men who had seen combat, seen friends die, and were willing to see it again.

So when Del Azarchel said in a hoarse voice, "Arrest him! Arrest that traitor!" the soldiers did not hesitate, but brought their pikes to the ready, and came forward at a quickstep, moving to flank him left and right.

Princess Rania stepped in the way, small as a golden doll, blazing with majestic ire. "He is my crewman! Space claims him, and you Earthmen have no authority. Miguel! Raum! Raeul! Do not step forward! Where is your warrant?"

The tall and warlike men hesitated. Perhaps they were shocked she knew their names. Menelaus Montrose drew his ceramic knife with one hand, and with the other picked up the nearest candlestand, which was the heaviest object in reach, and the candles fluttered and blew, so that the shadows swooped and swerved along the walls.

Later, wearing only a transparent pair of plastic overalls, sitting in a cold, white, featureless cube of a jail cell, and not answering any of the questions that spoke to him from the blank wall, Montrose truly and desperately wished he had thrown the knife through Del Azarchel's damnified skull, and not listened to Rania.

He closed his eyes. He might have been able to hit the target, from that distance, in that light, and the blade might have flown point-first. It wasn't impossible. It *could* have happened. The blade would have landed right between Blackie's cursed eyes, hilt vibrating, and trickles of blood and brain-goo would have slid down over the look of astonishment frozen forever on his damned face.

It wasn't impossible. Captain Sterling from the Science Patrol superspaceship *Emancipation* could have done it.

He raised his hand to the pad of sterile gauze taped to his head. The guards on the other side of the door in the armored depthtrain carriage bringing him here (wherever here was) had not acted quickly enough to stop him from dosing himself with the Princess's version of the neuronanological cocktail. He was not suffering any mania, no disorientation, no delirium. He did not know if that meant it was working, or that it was not. It had not actually put him in agony: she had been joking about that. He wondered what else Rania said had been a joke, and what had been in earnest.

Eventually the jailors shut off the light. He lay in the dark, waiting, wondering if he were getting any smarter. He certainly didn't feel any smarter.

15

Equality of the Sexes

1. No Particular Effect

The only effect, at first, the intelligence augmentation cocktail seemed to have on him was that he required more sleep. Over the next three days in his jail cell, he slept upward of eighteen hours a day. Dreaming seemed to be a waste of time, and so, on the third night, once he was done with the minor corrections and emotional association image-grafts that formed the basic business of the dream-cycle, he used that part of his mind to set up a little imaginary schoolhouse with a blackboard, so he could write out and examine some of the equations and Monument symbols he was curious about. He could program himself to dream certain things, and solve particular kinds of problems, so that the answers would be clearer when he woke. But Montrose was disappointed: if he was on the threshold of a breakthrough into another and richer state of human intelligence, there did not seem to be any real change. He was still the same cranky bastard as when he fell asleep.

Also while asleep he reviewed certain memories, but instead of the confused mixture of chimerical images that haunted normal sleep, he decided to index these memories both by association and time-value, peg each scene to a particular mnemonic, and play them as a set of perfectly sharp eidetic images.

The books he had read in Del Azarchel's chalet in Alaska he found dull now that he had time to reread them—Montrose was pleased that he could summon up perfectly detailed pictures even of pages he had been flipping past without reading, and, as if looking at a photograph, read them normally. He found his reading speed increased when he invented (since this was a dream, after all) a cartoon character named Cyrano Widget to do the reading for him, and just give him a summary. Cyrano was human from the face down, but had a clear dome for a skull, in which an electronic brain could be seen winking and sparkling furiously.

Cyrano, sitting in the imaginary schoolhouse, shook its absurd cyborg head, and said, "Boss, Blackie Del Azarchel does not know what he is dealing with here." Onto the blackboard the cyborg chalked an equation. It was a divarication function, showing the change in prices of various goods, the crime rate, and the frequency of the use of certain emotion-laden terms in the popular media. All this raw information had been in Del Azarchel's books, but he had never put two and two together.

"Boss, look at these graphs, these tendencies. The cost of railgun components does not go up unless someone is buying and building a filthload of them."

"What's it mean?"

"War."

Montrose looked at the graphs in wonder. "But I thought Blackie had the whole world figured out. He said he had a science, called Cliometry, that could forecast political and economic changes. He can't see a war coming?"

The cartoon character leaned back on his imaginary school desk. "He sees it coming, and he is trying to avoid it."

"What's causing the problem?"

"Two problems. One is political. Lowering the price of travel to zero means that whole populations are within elbow-rubbing distance of each other. There are no national boundaries anymore."

"Isn't that good for the economy? Lowers the cost of shipping workers to where the work is, right? Free trade, free movement of goods, all that."

"Right. And it creates cultural friction. The workingmen can sleep in the tropics on warm nights and commute to the arctic where the mines and aquaculture rigs are during the day. Meanwhile the Australians (who now live in the middle of the Great Victoria Gardenlands) don't want floods of travelers to overturn their few remaining Democratic institutions. The Chinese (who now live in the midst of the Gobi Gardenlands) don't want floods of travelers overturning their few remaining Confucian institutions."

"What about the other countries?"

"Bridesmaids. They just follow after the buttocks of one of these brides or the other, holding their trains. India and Iberia, even South Africa and her millions of automated factories, are nothing more than flower girls in this century."

"You got marrying on the brain, pal. So what's the second problem?"

"The second is a problem of economics. It's the same as happened to Spain when the Spanish Empire flooded itself with gold and silver from the New World, mined from the Andes or robbed from the Aztecs. Drove down the price of gold and drove up the price of goods. In this case, the *Hermetic* came back with contraterrene carbon around 10^{20} kg—my guess, based on ship performance values."

Montrose nodded. It was a chunk the size of the Ceres asteroid, and represented the tally of both all the decades of *Hermetic* star-lifting, and of the decades of *Croesus*. "Endless wealth. Energy enough to do anything."

"And what did happen to Spain? She did not invest the money. The Dons used it to buy Arabian stallions and fancy mansions and saddles with silver folderol, and the King of Spain used it to build an Armada. The gold flowed out of Spain to manufacturers in Italy, France, and England. Eventually the price stabilized at a higher level. Spain went broke. The richest country in Europe went broke. Because Spain did not use the wealth to get more wealth."

"Pox, I hear they melt Antarctica and somehow get the winds to carry all the vapor up to rain in the Gobi Desert, or the Great Victoria Desert in Australia. Earth ain't broke."

"You measure bankruptcy by comparing your income to your liabilities. In this case, one of your liabilities, one of your costs, is the cost of mounting a Third Expedition to the Diamond Star, and the return-on-investment time is one hundred years. If you are going to travel even to nearby stars, you have to start thinking on those time scales."

"Power won't run out for a hundred years. Blackie knows that."

"Even so, there are world leaders who are alert enough to think in those time scales. The power might last a century, but even now the globe knows it cannot maintain a free-energy regime. The world, now that it is addicted to free energy, has to be switched to a rationed-energy regime. The question is, when does the switch come? And who does the rationing?"

Cyrano showed him a simple but chilling set of propositions from game-theory. The decision of two prisoners both accused of a crime, when clemency was offered to whomever would first rat out the other, either to trust each other and remain silent or to betray each other was described with a few gamelike rules: if they both trusted, both would break even; if both betrayed, both lost; if one trusted and the other betrayed, the betrayer would win big.

It could be shown mathematically that the winning strategy in a game of repeated moves was to betray only in retaliation to betrayal, and otherwise to trust. But when there was a time limit, a final move, both players had a powerful incentive to betray, because the final move was one that by definition invited no possible retaliation. But each player, knowing the other was under an incentive to betray him on the final move, therefore had an incentive to betray on the penultimate move. Likewise, each player, knowing the other was under an incentive to betray him on the penultimate move, therefore had an incentive to betray on the antepenultimate move; and so on.

This remorseless logic operated for any game of a known and finite number of moves, even if the number of moves was immense.

In this case, even if the switch from a free-energy regime to a rationed-energy regime was not to happen for a hundred years, the incentive to betray future potential rivals before they became rivals operated now.

Montrose was not convinced. "When the switch does come, the free market will adjust. The price goes up as the goods get scarce. So then they go back to burning wood, coal, and oil, like God intended. Big deal."

"And they go back to the barter system."

"What?"

"Snow grams edged out other currencies as the store of value. They use certificates representing measured masses of anticarbon for their money."

Montrose checked the graphs, and checked the math behind them. "So the money gets expensive, too, and the interest rate goes up. Big deal. Why should that cause a war?"

"Because politics is not driven by free-market rules. Your mother, Mrs. Montrose, told you what rules drive politics. *Phobos, doxa,* and *kerdos.* Fear, fame, and gain. I'll rephrase the question. Both the deserts in China and the deserts in Australia have been turned, by a ridiculous and profligate public works project, into farmlands and fruit-tree groves. Now imagine you are one of them. The newly-fertile croplands opened an internal frontier, allowing both for wages to rise and population. As this century's breadbasket, you have political clout and world attention, because you control the food supply. Sure, there might be more contraterrene coming in one hundred years, but there might be a delay. Watering the desert is not something you can just turn on again after you turn it off. Five years, or three, or one, is too great a hiatus. If the greenery dies, it will stay dead, and the desert ecology will re-assert itself. The land will no longer support the population figures you currently enjoy. You are China. Australia is your hated rival. Or vice versa. What do you do? You cannot keep melting the glaciers to water the deserts if you run out of antimatter. You have to make sure the antimatter that they might get years from now for their irrigation will come to you instead."

"Make sure how? By war? Blackie won't let a war erupt. He can just shoot whoever shoots first, and so no one will dare shoot first. He's got contraterrene weapons. He's the only one who does. It is a self-contained system."

"Spoken like an engineer! But this problem is not an engineering problem. It is political and economic. And the free market cannot adjust. Antimatter is a non-market good, since Blackie has been giving at away free of cost for political gain. He cannot let the price go up."

"So Blackie rations it."

"Which means, that in the rivalry between China and Australia, whichever faction has more influence over Del Azarchel will use the world-government and the energy market to destroy the other by lawful means; and when the other has nothing to lose, it will embrace unlawful means, and go to war. Del Azarchel picks the winner. At that point, Del Azarchel opens the fiery gates of heaven, and bombards the loser from space."

"You saying he can't maintain control without killing thousands and millions of folk?"

Cyrano pointed at the sudden jag in the graph. "Maybe if Del Azarchel did not interfere, and he let the cost of contraterrene rise—then speculators anticipating the coming lean years would buy up shares now, and this would force other uses to economize. Maybe then we can avoid the coming war. China and Australia could maintain as much cropland as they could afford, and there is not one winner and one loser. It is still a delicate compromise, but it could be done."

"He must see these same equations. If it can be done, why hasn't he done it?"

"Because Del Azarchel would be undermining his own authority. The monopoly of the World Power Syndicate would have to be dissolved. Many ships, some in private hands, and not just the *Hermetic*, would have to be allowed to range the strategic high ground of outer space, or otherwise ownership on paper of antimatter grams in transplutonian orbit is meaningless. That has military implications. Del Azarchel would have to step aside as political leader, because otherwise no investor would believe he would keep his hands to himself, and not simply undo what the market did. Basically, he would have to abdicate, and let the Princess solve the problem."

"But he is afraid of the Princess. Kept her in slumber all those years. Me, too." Montrose shook his head. "Even if he steps down, he's not stepping down, not the other him. That's why he built the Iron Ghost. And he does not need to send the *Hermetic* to the Diamond Star, that is what the *Bellerophon* is for. I am not sure he can dare let us leave."

"He cannot let you stay. Do you think he can dare let two Posthumans of less than certain loyalty to his regime run around on his world?"

"Then why not let us leave?"

"The *Hermetic* hangs above the world like a sword. The common people are restless; they know she must sail away, if the wealth of the world is to be maintained in the next century; they know the world will fall into war the moment the sword is removed."

Montrose looked at the graphs. "I don't understand this. This does look like people are gearing up for a war. But, damn, it makes no sense! I mean, some areas of the world still vote. There is food enough for everyone, since huge areas of land that were barren are now croplands. And look at how wealthy the world is! There is no money wasted on vast military budgets, and no burning cities, no streams of refugees, no rivers black with war chemicals, no fogs rolling wherever the wind blows. Isn't it enough?"

"Your mother told you what causes war. It is not the lack of votes, or of food or of money. It is fear, honor, and powerlust. The people are afraid now that the antimatter will run out two generations from now, and they don't have faith that the *Bellerophon* will return in time with the wealth the world needs."

"How can they be worried about something so far away in tomorrow?"

"Because they are well fed, and have the leisure to fret."

"How do we avoid a war fought with total conversion weapons? I mean, even if Blackie is the only one who has them now, I don't want him to use them. The burning of New York the Beautiful is enough. Hiroshima, Nagasaki, Jerusalem, Mecca, all enough. Enough! Human history does not need more."

"I see only two options. Let him marry the Princess, and launch the Third Expedition without you, and she might be able to restore the faith of the people that another lode of endless energy is coming."

"Pox on that. I'd rather see the world catch fire. What's the other option?"

"Put the genie back in the bottle. Remove all the antimatter, every gram."

"That's impossible. Any third option?"

"You could always ask him to abdicate. Let him at least give up his monopoly on the antimatter. Like you said, have the price rise to meet the market, and have a bidding war rather than a shooting war."

"I think he'd be afraid for his life if he stepped out of his office. He is not like Washington. He is like Napoleon. Even if they put him in exile on Elba, someone else would just haul him back in front of his cheering armies, and try to put him back in power."

"Elba? Take him with you. To the stars. And get him to destroy the machine version."

"But that also might cause a war."

Cyrano looked pensive. "It is like most things in life. The only way to forestall a war is to risk one. The only way to preserve his world-empire is to give up his imperial crown."

"I know him. He cannot do that. He won't risk it. So . . ."

"So?"

"So, he is just trapped."

"Well, Boss, so are you. This is a dream, and you are still in a jail cell. Hey, wake up. Three guys are coming to take you to some secret medical cell of Del Azarchel's, and I think he might prefer you back the way you were, when you were Crewman Fifty-One, crazy but someone he could almost control."

"Does that mean I am not crazy now? That is good to hear."

Of course, he was awake when he said that, and there was no one in the room but him.

It was pitch-black in the room, and three men came in (he could tell by the change in the air motions when the cell door silently opened). They were wearing light amplification goggles, because presumably it is easier to deal with a prisoner who is unable to see his handlers.

Montrose was wearing metal wrist-restraints, which was too bad, because he could not think of an easier way to do this. He smashed his hand against the floor hard enough to crack some of his left metacarpal bones, which allowed him to pull one hand free as he flung himself at knee-level across the room, his right fist using the still-locked ring as impromptu brass knuckles.

In his mind's eye, the men in the dark before him became tripartite fractal patterns of vector motions, with arcs of all his possible limb-movements, masses, and velocities printed in his imagination with crystal clarity. He saw his own constellations of counter-attacks, parries, and strikes. With casual thoroughness, he rotated the two four-dimensional motion-graphs in his mind until he found a way to set the two patterns together in a minimal–maximum configuration.

Then he was sitting on his face on the cold, padded floor of the corridor outside with the first guard's baton in his hand. He had landed atop it. From the heft of it, he could feel that one end of the baton was opened like a switch-blade, and hissing with a sinister electronic sort of hiss, fortunately not touching the conductive fabric of his gown (which was designed to assist shock weapons). But the blade was jammed into the floor-panels, and he could not pull it free. Montrose was bruised along his forearm, his knuckles were bleeding, and he felt like his foot was broken.

He heard groans. There was a flare of electricity—in the absolute dark it looked dazzlingly bright. In the flash of light, he could see his first opponent face-down on the floor, a gloved hand crooked at a horrible angle: it looked as if Montrose had broken his fingers. The look of surprise on his face was greater than the look of pain.

Unfortunately, he only saw one other opponent. This second man was off-balance, stumbling, but had projected an electric wire from his baton whose live head (glancing off a metal boot stud) was making the momentary flare of light.

It was too good an opportunity to miss. Montrose spat, and the spittle passed through the live spark and struck the bare leg of that second man above his boot where his insulating legging had ripped free. The string of liquid was just enough to make a circuit. The man jerked in a spasm. Montrose knew he would not be awake long enough to actually see the man fall.

(Montrose contemplated the shock on the toppling man's lower face. It was clear enough that these guys did not know how Montrose knew they were fakes. To them it must seem miraculous, bizarre, unexpected. That was sort of disorienting to Montrose: were things so obvious to him, so opaque to them? The noises they had made while approaching the door did not match the standard noises, the pauses, the click of thumb keys, the sleeve-rustle as salutes were exchanged, of real guards. How could they be surprised? They were like children trying to fool a grown-up.)

Since he did not see the third man, and since he did not have enough time to twist and bring the baton under him up to parry, all he could do was jerk his head forward, hoping the blow from behind would do less damage if the relative velocity were less.

He had two last thoughts. First, Del Azarchel's men, despite their orders, would not dare take him anywhere else but the prison infirmary. Once there, there would be too many official records, too many witnesses, for a second abduction attempt. By the time Del Azarchel organized his next moves, Princess Rania's attorney should have him freed. Second, he wondered what Dr. Kyi would have said, had he known how reckless Montrose was being with the brain they both so admired.

Then, a blunt impact to the base of his skull scattered his consciousness, just as if he had been of ordinary intelligence. It seemed somehow unfair.

2. Recovery

Montrose seemed to have more time to think things over, but his experience in the fight told him his nerve cells were not firing any faster than a normal man's. It was a question of more efficient neural organization, not a fundamental change on the cellular level. A man's brain is not that different from an ape's, from a chemical and biological point of view: for that matter, a Winchester rifle was built along the same lines as a harquebus.

Montrose was in a bed, or a bath—it was a gelatin of smart material that partly encased him, a simplified form of an open biosuspension capsule, leaving his head, shoulders, and hands free. There were no intravenous needles, no diapers or catheters, since the jelly was able both to force nutrients into his membranes through his skin, and carry away waste. He was almost eating solid food again: just that morning the nurse had spoon-fed him a poached egg and bread soaked in milk. He kept it down without nausea or vomiting, and he was as proud of that accomplishment as any in his life.

Sunlight slanted through window of alternating dark and pale stripes, which he had deduced to be military glass, something that would deflect bullets and diffuse directed energy. He could not see, but he could hear traffic outside the window.

The traffic was horse-drawn carts and electric ground-effects vehicles—even the passage of one hundred years had not returned petroleum production to pre-Jihad levels. Montrose calculated the logic loop involved, and could not find an answer. Even with the drop in motor cars after the post-Jihad petroleum shortages, one would not expect new roads not to be built. Then he factored in two other variables: first, the cost of energy was so miniscule that the inefficiencies of hover vehicles versus wheeled vehicles meant nothing; and second, the chance of bombardment from orbit (roads, rails, and aerodromes made large and tempting targets) was so great, and so recent, that no market and no public pressure was present. The depth-train carriages were cheaper, and the Hermeticists might not want public roads controlled by local municipalities.

He also knew he was in a private clinic, so when the door opened and Princess Rania glided in, he was not surprised.

Unlike Del Azarchel, she had no retinue with her. From the echoes of footfalls outside, he knew she had an extensive staff of neurologists and specialists on retainer, not to mention (for he heard the jingle of a weapon harness) soldiers and spies.

When he looked at her face, something clicked into place. He said, "You do not actually want there to be a war, do you? You are expecting Del Azarchel to step down. He won't."

She was dressed in a peach morning suit of conservative cut. It was so old-fashioned that it looked almost normal to him. However, she also wore a coronet and a sash of royalty. It made her look like a Beauty Queen. But of course—even with his new high-powered brain, Montrose found he could be surprised by little things—she was not a Beauty Queen, but a Queen Queen, the very thing beauty contest winners were using as a symbol, she was in truth.

Rania opened her mouth and squawked at him. He knew it was some sort of high-speed communication code, with thousands of items of information compressed into her voicewaves, but it meant nothing to him. She cocked her head to one side. He could see she was surprised, perhaps disappointed.

"State-related memory," she said. She meant that his memory of the time aboard ship had not returned to him, no doubt because even with his newly-enhanced brain, the change from insane Posthuman to sane Posthuman had created a mnemonic lapse. The same reason why, in humans, a waking man cannot recall a dream well, or a man when happy finds his sad memories slipping aside, or why a tone of voice or childhood street will bring up recollections that written reminders might not, in this case did not allow Montrose to remember his days as Crewman Fifty-One. The two of them had agreed upon some high-density vocal code language, and she had been hoping he'd recall it.

Montrose looked carefully around the room—he realized he was doing that thing with his eyes, the sudden vibration movements to gather in additional information he had found so disturbing to look at back in his sleepwalker days—but he did not see any bugging devices. Perhaps a laser focused on the window could pick up air-vibrations, but he had been assuming the striations in the glass (for he had stared at them for some time, seeing the molecular patterns implied in the macroscopic texture) was proof against that type of eavesdropping.

Montrose drew in a surprised breath. He realized that Rania was fully expecting Man Del Azarchel to have augmented his own intelligence by now. The working copy of Ghost Del Azarchel could reproduce and solve everything Montrose had solved for himself. There could be multiple copies of Ghost Del Azarchel by now, Xypotechs of immense intellectual power and range and reach and imagination—and that meant minds equal to Rania's, able to deduce new techniques or technologies for spying.

And it meant she was still afraid of him. Why?

"Even if we spoke in a secret language," said Montrose, "Blackie could puzzle it out, sooner or later."

She sat down on the edge of the gelatin slab that served him for a bed. With soft fingers she ran a slender hand through his hair, across his brow. "I would ask you how you are feeling," she said. Meaning that the medical read-outs probably told her more about him than he knew himself. The implication was that she wanted to know when he would be well enough to be moved, presumably to a safer location, where they could talk freely.

Montrose let out a laugh. "I ain't made of glass, missy!" and he started to climb free of the gel. It hardened around his limbs, and he thought he could calculate a system of muscular stresses to pull free. The gelatin was long-chain molecules that contracted or expanded under electrical current, and the computer-switching system controlling the current was operating by a certain set of reflex patterns. All he had to do was . . .

Rania reached around his skull, and applied a tiny amount of pressure with her finger to one of the bruises on his skull. "Ow!" he complained.

"Not made of glass, but still fractured," she said, raising an eyebrow, and giving him a coy little pout. "Now you keep still." Or she would call the anesthesiologist and have him sedated. Montrose was disappointed that having a more integrated nervous system did not give him immunity to chemicals injected into his bloodstream.

He settled back down. "Ha! Give a gal a crown, a starship, a few armies, infinite wealth, and she starts thinking she can give orders."

"I am also your chief physician, Crewman." She wore what could only be called a "Dr. Kyi" sort of look.

"Aw, be fair! I had to get my skull broke in order to get away from Blackie! They were going to cart me off!" To some secret location.

A quirk of her eyebrow said, louder than words: *And you did not trust I would find you?*

"You may be bright," he said. *But you do not know how bright Ghost Del Azarchel is.* (He did not say that aloud, but the implication was clear to both of them.)

Why? Again, it was not words, just a change in her pupil dilation, but he knew what she meant.

"The first time I heard Ghost Del Azarchel speak, he said he wanted you and me to get together. He said it in the clear, nice and slow, in English, so that Man Del Azarchel's pick-ups would hear. He told me you were going to slip me an invitation to your New Year's Party."

"Because of the number of people around," she said, in answer to an unspoken question, "and he could not use the excuse of 'Earthsickness' to force me back into another decade or so of biosuspension. The last year of the old century was too important, symbolically—"

"Oh pox!" said Montrose, alarmed. "You were going to announce your engagement!" *No wonder Del Azarchel had been mad.* He looked at her suspiciously. His accusation was clear: *Del Azarchel is too smart to fool himself, unless you helped him—you led him on, didn't you?*

She looked aloof, and her sea-green eyes seemed more stormy and mysterious than ever. "I appealed to his better nature; he answered with a baser nature. Do you think women were created just to watch men kill each other, and wear the widow's veil, and weep beneath it? Women use the weapons nature gives us." She said that aloud.

Partly in words, partly in expressions, he answered, "You mean what Del Azarchel gave you—he was one of your primary designers."

Rania smiled cryptically, a smile not altogether pleasant. "Both Shelly's *Frankenstein* and Shaw's *Pygmalion* were in the ship's library. Wasn't that warning enough about infatuation with your own handiwork?" She shook her head sadly. "If you are going to play at God, divine love rather than romantic love might be in order—if he were willing to sacrifice himself, he would get everything he desired."

"Ghost Del Azarchel is not infatuated with you," said Montrose. "Because Man Del Azarchel walking in on us—you are too smart to let that happen. If you didn't arrange that 'coincidence'—"

She shook her head. *Not I.*

"Then he did. The ghost, I mean. But why would the Ghost Blackie first send me to find you, then save me from Man Blackie, feed me caviar and books, but then trip us both up?"

"Did he tell you which books to read?"

He opened his mouth to say *No,* but, looking back with crystal clear thoughts into his confused half-sleepy fog of what had back then been his brain, he realized that the voice from the chalet walls had dropped a word here and there, which, even when consciously forgotten, had drawn his attention toward certain shelves.

Which meant—what? What had the Iron Ghost been up to?

"Did he tell you how to open the gun case?" she said lightly.

Montrose nodded. "But I don't see where this is leading."

Rania raised both eyebrows, slightly narrowing her eyes. (Menelaus thought she looked remarkably pretty when she did that, and he wondered what he could say to provoke that expression again.) She said, "Even the hawk cannot see his own eye color, not without some reflection." *One limit of intelligence augmentation is that we seem not to know ourselves any more clearly.*

Montrose looked puzzled: *Ghost Del Azarchel wanted me to hate this world? But why?*

Rania stood up, smoothed her skirt. She obviously thought that last question was one he could answer with no further hint from her. Instead, she said, "My theory that you would regain your old memories has not been confirmed. Sad, for we have no time to spare for a courtship."

"Wait a minute, lady! I ain't asked you yet!"

"Again you demote me!" she *tsk-tsk*ed. "A bedridden man is in no condition to kneel. How can we not wed? Are we not the Adam and Eve of a new humanity?"

He saw the look in her eyes, haunted with memory. Long ago they met, they spoke, they fell in love—Rania had to heal him, she not knowing if the superintelligent yet sane version of him would recall the wild promises he made once the superintelligent yet insane version of him was cured.

"Our smarts won't breed true," he said. "Unless you plan to inject our whelps with a brain-needle."

She curled a wisp of blond hair around her forefinger, gave it an admiring look, and had one of her little dragonfly-shaped vanity machines tuck it back under her coronet. "We can call our first daughter Madelina. I've always liked the name."

He remembered that her hair had been altered by RNA-substitution engineering. She also expected Menelaus to discover the genetic flaw in her own construction, and thus she was implying that she had altered her body to be able to receive and adapt to corrections and a genetic level rapidly. She had a system in place, a chemical network of totipotent cells drawn from her own matrix, floating in her bloodstream, already prepared.

At the door, she turned, looking back over her shoulder. The doorframe made her seem a portrait, and the light behind her touched her cheek just where Menelaus wanted to touch it, and turned her hair to golden flame. "Did Del Azarchel show you his statue of the last Ape?"

"Baker's Dozen. Very sad-looking."

She nodded. "The same artist made one with an angrier pose—it looms in the Round Table chamber of the *Hermetic* Conclave."

"I've seen it."

Rania gave him a skeptical look before she strode with her graceful lioness step out the door.

By that look, he realized that he had *not* seen it, or, at least, not understood its meaning. But Blackie had told him in so many words. The horse was a stupid creature, but useful to its masters: and so it stayed alive when disaster struck. That was just how life worked. The ape was a superior creature, but not useful.

Montrose discovered that primitive emotions like shock, surprise, and even hate had not disappeared from his nervous system; because two implications fitted into place in his mind.

First, he knew why Ghost Del Azarchel had manipulated him into a fierce disgust for this world and this age. Rania planned to depart, taking the *Hermetic* with her. And what better way to make sure Montrose also went along, away into the dangers of outer space? Montrose would be out of harm's way, which meant that the sense of honor that Del Azarchel lived by (both versions of Del Azarchel) would be satisfied. Montrose reminded himself that the machine version of Del Azarchel had no memory of being a murderer or a mutineer. Ghost Del Azarchel might honestly want to save Montrose from bloodshed at the hands of Man Del Azarchel.

Even with the confident prediction that Montrose would be unable to interfere in the long term plans of the Hermeticists, that prediction became more likely the longer Montrose was away from Earth.

Second, and more important, Montrose realized that Blackie was not creating a new race to supplant Mankind in order to fight off the Armada from Hyades when it came. That had been Montrose's idea, his alone. Blackie had not said a thing about fighting.

Everything in Ximen Del Azarchel's personality, everything in the way he talked (Why had Montrose not seen it before? How could he have missed it?) betrayed that Blackie was a man who valued life more than liberty, safety to freedom. He esteemed hierarchy, rule, order, and dominion and eschewed that wildness that comes of exploring the wilderness, including the wilderness of stars. The dream of world peace, of an utter end to war, Blackie thought he was close to achieving it, and settling Mankind forever into a peace without end. He thought the world needed rulership, not democracy, not men settling their own messes; the world needed a Caesar. An eternal, iron Caesar.

But Ximen Del Azarchel was not merely a power-hungry dictator. No. He was something far more dangerous: a man with an ideal. Even a selfless ideal.

Why had his mind been able to survive the mind war in the virtual world, when all the Hermeticists made copies of their minds and pitted them, like Gladiators in the Coliseum, against each other? Montrose did not know, but he knew that someone fighting for something greater than himself took more daring risks, and could draw allies and followers to him. No . . . there must be more than that. The other Hermeticists also had ideals, at least, of a twisted sort. There was something more beneath Del Azarchel's drive. But what?

Montrose set aside that question for later. At the moment, he meditated on one thing: the plans that the Hermeticists were making for the remotest future, eight thousand years from now when the alien machines arrive to claim the Earth as their property—the Hermeticists did, just as they said, intend to force human evolution to its next step. But the Hermeticists did not mean to fight to survive. They meant to collaborate; to cooperate; to surrender. A live horse is better than a dead ape.

The design for the next human race was meant to be creatures smart enough to be useful to the Hyades, but docile enough not to create any problems.

The asymptote was not meant to produce superhuman free men, but superhuman slaves.

All that talk of a golden future was a lie. Servitude was all that the destiny of Mankind held, and the transhuman race beyond humanity was to be held in subhuman subjugation.

Montrose raised his hands out of the gelatin and clutched his head. It was his best friend that was planning to sell Mankind and the children of men to the Hyades. Del Azarchel, of all people!

The hatred in his heart seemed sharper, purer, clearer than the muddy emotions he had known back when he was a merely human. He missed those days already.

The nurses came in, called by the monitors, or else by the gulping hiccups of Montrose's sobs. He wanted to turn over, to turn his face away, but the bed of gel would not permit it.

It is embarrassing when superhumans cry.

3. Prenuptial Considerations

Before he even was fully recovered, Montrose found himself introduced to the Rulers and Sovereigns and Magnates of the world. He met Pnumatics dressed like peacocks, Psychics dressed like spacers in wigs, elected Bishops wielding political power, and elected Administrators from those cities or parishes with Republican forms of government dressed in simple drabs—and not a man jack of them he much cared for. He did not like the ceremony, the courtesy, the courtliness, the fawning. His Lone Star State spirit rankled at the inequality.

His disliking did not change when he was elevated to the highest ranks of this ranked society. But three things changed immediately.

First, it was to be a Morganitic marriage, meaning neither he nor his heirs would inherit his wife's royal titles and noble rights; but she ennobled him and enfeoffed him with lands and rents in a recently-acquired county in Gascony, quite beautiful now that the bacteriological infection from the last war was dying off, the fungi dotting the hedges and trees like leprosy was vanishing, and both grapevines and vintners were returning to the wilderness area. Antiquarians were felling stalks of yeasty growth and burning spore-fields to uncover the abandoned relics the previous generations had mummified before evacuation: a miraculous number of cathedrals, famous houses, and fortresses were intact. Montrose congratulated himself on being from the same province as Cyrano de Bergerac. His title was Count of Armagnac.

Second, he was also given a red bracelet, heavy as a manacle, to wear on his wrist, and Rania's servants told him he could not appear in public save in the black shipsuit to which he, as a man of outer space, alone was entitled. He kicked up a row and was a little surprised when he got kicked back.

A man named Vardanov, her security officer, was a dark-skinned Slav from Azania: one of those people from the "Old Order" who had been bribed into supporting the Concordat with a title and a heraldic escutcheon. The blond man kept his skin tuned as dark as ivory, and had used the recently-released RNA-spoofing techniques of the Hermeticists to add three feet and a hundred pounds of muscle to his frame. He dressed, like all the court soldiers of this ridiculous time period, in the peaked helmet and metal breastplate of a Spanish Conquistador. He was polite enough to remove his helmet and tuck it in his elbow, and give Montrose a stiff bow, before calling him a fool. The two stood in a small solarium of Montrose's delightful little mansion in Gascony, looking out on the trellises of vines.

"Come again?" said Montrose, doubting his ears.

Vardanov had a melancholy face and large, sad eyes, so it was hard to tell how angry he was. He spoke in a thick, slow voice, like the voice of a thoughtful elephant. Menelaus could not place the accent: perhaps a combination of Russian and Dutch. "Fool!" he said again, "and why is it you are making my job more difficult, yes?"

The windows opaqued, putting the little richly-furnished chamber into twilight. The dark window also prevented anyone outside from looking in. The man's big hand dropped casually to the hilt of his bayonet, which was sheathed in his web-belt.

Montrose resolved the man's stance into a fractal pattern of vector motions, position of limbs and their kinetic values, and compared it with his own. Oddly, there did not seem to be a solution. With his greater mass and reach, if the two of them fought, Montrose (barring unforeseen factors entering the field) would lose.

So stepping forward and breaking the guy's nose was, at the moment, not an optimal strategy.

Montrose decided that a diplomatic response was needed. "So why should I give a pair of donkey's swollen black testicles what the hell your job is, or how difficult it is?"

Well, that was diplomatic for him. These things should be judged on a sliding scale.

The man showed no anger on his face, although with his new and heightened perceptions, Montrose could analyze the man's blush response and microscopic pupil dilations. Here was a creature whose unsleeping anger, frustration, and paranoia, kept him in dangerous psychological balance by a sense of honor, an iron self-control.

"With all due respect, Your Excellency," Vardanov said in his sad, slow voice, "my duty is to protect the person of Her Serene Highness. Do you understand that this is a matter of warfare on a personal level, yes? Yes. Supreme excellence in war, it is to destroy the enemy will to fight, not in striking his body."

Montrose was impressed, not just because the man could quote Sun Tsu on the art of war, but because it occurred to him that Vardanov had done exactly that to him. When he did not see a feasible max-min vector-solution for an engagement, Montrose hadn't struck a blow.

Vardanov said, "It falls to me to say what all know, and no one will say: you are an embarrassment to Her Serene Highness. Yes? Yes." He nodded, as if happy to hear himself agreeing with himself. "In other years, other places, this means nothing. Alone in barn, you are a braying jackass, and no one hears your voice, no one is disturbed. But here! But now! You are in palace. It is time of tumult, maybe war. Esprit de corps is weighty thing, yes? Yes. The mystique, the awe, the love, the fear commoners behold Her Serene Highness, this is Her Highness's first line of the defense. They say you have done something to that brain of yours, yes, to make you more than man. You can see without me to explain of it, yes?"

"Explain it anyway." Montrose casually put his hands behind his back.

Vardanov gave a massive, slow shrug, and spread his hands. He casually dropped his hand behind a vase standing on a pillar near the door, which meant Montrose could not see if he had drawn a weapon from his wrist-holster. Since Montrose was reaching up his own sleeve for the hilt of the ceramic knife he kept in a forearm sheath, he decided not to draw it.

Vardanov spoke while shrugging. "Two things. One." He held up a think forefinger. (Montrose recognized the trick involved and kept his attention on the other hand, the one hidden behind the vase.) "While you wear the uniform of the great starship *Hermetic,* you are protected by the weapons of the *Hermetic,* and the common people are in awe of fire from heaven. In the eyes of the law, no one can arrest you, no one can take and question you, because you are not of this Earth."

"What's two?"

Vardanov held up two fingers, but this time pointed them at Montrose. "The great and the small alike are unhappy that you, not Nobilissimus Del Azarchel, have taken the hand of the Star Maiden, yes? Oh, yes. But if you are star-man . . ." He shrugged. "Then discontent, it is not so much."

"They can go jack themselves. What do I care?"

"You care for her? Then you care for her people, for they are hers and she is theirs. To be royalty is to keep the people happy, to keep all parts of the world in balance, nobles and merchants, military and clergy, workers and shopkeepers. Royalty is mystique in the mind of people. It is magic. To be a princess, it is to stare at the snake and force the snake not to strike. Yes? Yes. Do not break the spell."

Montrose scowled. "I don't cotton to wearing that damn suit. Traitors wear it. I ain't one of them."

"Cotton is what?"

"I mean I don't take to it."

"Is not for you to take, yes? Copernicus changed the world. After him, Man was not center of all things. You, you are still in world before Copernicus. You think the sun revolves around you. No? No. You revolve around sun. She is the sun; you are not the only one who orbits her. You have married all of her. Whole solar system, not just sunshine."

And the tall man's eyes narrowed with pleasure, because he saw that he had won.

After that, Montrose took to wearing the black silk shipsuit in public, and the red metal armband of the Hermeticists.

4. Rich as Croesus

The third thing that changed was his wealth. Before the marriage, Montrose was vested with a healthy share of Rania's stock in the World Power Syndicate.

Like most men of modest means, Menelaus had assumed the difference between rich and poor in this time was merely something like the difference between Mr. Josiah Palmer back in his hometown, a respectably well-off rancher, and Chickenbone Jim, who had to beg at the Meeting House door to buy a coat. It was nothing like that. The difference was far deeper than he had imagined.

Except for a few paupers who heated their cottages with wood they chopped themselves, or some eccentric branch of the neo-Amish that used no modern technology and burned only petroleum, the entire economy hung by the contraterrene, both power source and currency. The whole economy was owned by the World Power Syndicate. It was wealth almost beyond measure.

He was not able merely to buy stuff. He could buy policies, loyalties, public opinion, and princes; he could buy a chunk of history, and force things to go his way. Beyond a certain critical mass, wealth became so concentrated that it exerted a warp on society like the gravity of a neutron star: whole sectors of the economy unrelated to you were thrown off their courses.

The sheer number of people, a sizeable percent of the world's population, that had bought into Del Azarchel's way of doing things, his way of thinking, merely because they had been bought by this kind of dealing, was staggering. Menelaus now had that kind of wealth; the kind that could topple thrones.

The first thing he bought was indeed an aspect of the future Menelaus wanted brought under his control. The second thing he bought was a stallion.

For this first thing, he purchased suspended-animation companies and cartels: huge companies like Endymion and tiny ones like Welsh Bart's Sleepaway.

Not one or two. All of them.

Hold-outs he sued, on the grounds that he should have been granted a patent for the discoveries, based on his work, that made long-term biosuspension possible. He had to buy legislators and guilds to make the laws allow for retroactive patents; and then he had to buy political parties, judges, and arbitrators, and fund monasteries to get canon law on his side. He had to fund election campaigns in Democratic parishes and buy mansions and museums as bribes for princes in monarchic parishes.

The slumbering population was roughly eighty-five percent medical patients, enduring biosuspension in hope of cures to be developed in later years; ten percent were loyal spouses wanting to stay of the same age; the remainder were those who slumbered for reasons legal or illegal, rational or quixotic, to outwait the death of a hated relative or the downfall of a hated regime.

It was effortless. He did not even need to dress for the meeting of the stockholders. The meeting was conducted over the newly-revised world communication net, in an entirely fictional boardroom equipped with cartoon tables and props, and his projected image was dressed in a somber knee-length suit of dark gray, while he in real life was rocking in a hammock wearing loose Chinese pajamas. His lawyers (and he had hired so many he had already forgotten their names) were a buzzing whisper in his right ear. His intellectual property manager, an Australian named Sweetwater, whispered in his left ear, keeping him abreast of changes in the news channels, and his publicity-value, as the markets and newsfeeds reacted to the moment-by-moment changes in the meeting. For himself, he merely read off a prompter the speech his staff had prepared.

There were some procedural maneuvers raised to hinder him, so he logged off and turned his image over to his double (a young lady from Perth, who could do a passable impersonation of his word-patterns and wireframe mannerisms) to run him during the boring parts of the meeting while he ate his dinner. Once those delays ran their course, the votes were counted. It was no contest. It was like Josiah Palmer bidding against Chickenbone Jim at an auction. He was now the sole owner of every facility on Earth that used his method for biosuspension.

5. Nova and Yorvel

He was disappointed that the future people, having gone to the trouble of resurrecting the long-dead airs and fashions of knighthood, did not actually dress up in metal longjohns and whack at each other with meat-cleavers, as they ought. None of the "sirs" he met acted anything like the knights in the stories he'd read in childhood: not a one of them was fit to drive the Paynim out of Spain or go fetch the Holy Grail.

But they did have nice horses, many of these Aristos. That art they kept alive. He did a lot of riding during the days after his recovery from the infirmary, and argued with his doctors in the meanwhile. He named his beast Res Ipsa Nova, in honor of a sorrel from a hundred years ago.

He made few friends. The difference in intelligence gradient was too great: he could make more than an ordinary number of the normal humans, the Hylics, to like him, because it was easy to think of what to say to set them at ease.

One friend he did make, a friendship where brains just didn't matter, was with one of Rania's men, a chubby smiling little horse groom named Yorvel. His first name was Jesus, but Menelaus thought it sounded too much like swearing to call him that, and he couldn't manage to pronounce it Hey Zeus, which also sounded like swearing, but in a different religion, so he called him by his last name.

They talked about horses, particularly the biologically augmented new breeds and neo-equines. The groom knew his stuff and more, had hands-on experience no books held. Menelaus found out it did not matter how smart you were on the uptake; if a dumb teacher knows more than you, it still pays to listen and learn.

6. Chessplaying Machine

There was not much anyone else to talk to, aside from Rania, and she was busy playing some planetary chessgame with princes and parliaments with Del Azarchel and his Hermeticists. The terms of the game were simple in the basics: she was trying to pressure him into abdication, as this was the only way to defuse the growing threat of war. And he was playing brinksmanship. Whether he was confident that he, or the human race, or both, could survive a world war with antimatter weapons was another matter, but he acted as if he were.

Now, it was not that Montrose, freshly-minted posthuman with a fine new brain and all, could not follow the intricate moves and feints of the game, and read the lies and half-truths and half-lies and threats that splashed all over the text files and documentaries of the infosphere—it was that politics bored him.

The Psychics (or, as they were also called, the "Psychoi") actually were smarter, by fifty to one hundred points on the standard intelligence quotient scale, than the Hylics—because, despite what Del Azarchel had said, certain intelligence augmentation methods and processes, based on Montrose's work, had been tried over the last fifteen decades. The results were cautious, and the intellectuals were not outside what was possible for humans. Montrose could have interesting conversations with them, as an adult with a bright child, especially about matters concerning Monument translation and the eventual destiny of Mankind, the threat of the Hyades Armada, and what it would mean when that force arrived.

As predicted, no Hylics had anything interesting to say on the matter. Those who were angry with Del Azarchel for inviting this attack talked as if the Armada would land within the next fifty to one hundred years. To them it was an almost religious image, an Armageddon, a Twilight of the Gods, a prophecy that merely floated somewhere in the distant yet-to-be, not a real event to occur at a real yet remote date.

Montrose realized with dismay that he had fallen into the habit of dismissing ordinary humans as "Hylics"—an Hermeticist term of contempt. On the one hand, it was simply a fact that he was smarter now than normal people. On the other hand, a superior intellect did not seem to change his personality, or make him a saint, or even a sage. It did not improve his bad temper, or even change his bad grammar.

Heck, if anything, greater intelligence put him under greater temptation to do greater evil. He saw how easy it would be to treat people like puppets: thinking back, he did not much like the way he had bought up the Endymion corporations. It was necessary for his plans, to be sure, but the people squeezed out of their companies and stocks had plans, too, didn't they?

A bad man was much more a threat to the world than a bad dog; and a bad titan was worse than a bad man. Maybe his extra smarts would help he see and avoid the extra temptation the smarts brought with them.

At least the Hylics (or—he brought himself up short—the normal, decent people) who thought the coming of the Hyades Armada merely a prophecy thought on it. The average man would more likely complain about a stone in his shoe than some unthinkably remote eventuality destined for some unrecognizable descendant race of Mankind—assuming any lived so long.

The Psychoi would discuss the matter intelligently. But these metal-haired intellectuals made him nervous. They were smart enough that they could fool his reading of their tells and body language, and some of them worked for Del Azarchel—who was in hiding somewhere, no doubt experimenting on his own brain, trying to bring himself up to Montrose's level.

The Del Azarchel who appeared on the library file-casts, and made speeches over the radio, was an electronic image, of course. The Xypotech, Ghost Del Azarchel, was now Master of the World, and no one outside his immediate circle knew it.

7. Picnic with the Princess

"Why not tell everyone?" Montrose asked Rania one noon at their picnic. The two of them had ridden out to a sunny glade in the park north of Beausoleil in Monaco. They were "alone" except for a squad from the Corps des Sapeurs-Pompiers in camouflage armor, and a flotilla of two-man rotorcraft gunships shaped like freakish four-leaf clovers floating silently overhead, their cannons like scorpion tails. The troopers were visible only as blurry man-shaped bubbles if the leaves and branches behind them shook in the wind. Montrose did not mind the aircraft: with their four huge hoopshaped lifting ducts, they looked properly futuristic to him.

"In due time," she answered, allowing herself a small smile. Rania had noticed the switch over from Man Del Azarchel to Ghost Del Azarchel based on the playing style of their planetary chessgame. Ghost Del Azarchel did not sweat the small stuff: he played for the long-range endgame.

That small smile told him she planned to stir public opinion against the machine. A general church council had been called to debate the matter of artificial intelligence, and its theological and legal implications. Also, Frankenstein themes were appearing in several plays, operas, and interactives on New Bollywood channels, and in smart books, dumb books, and a Parisian musical play. She would play the information that the world government was no longer in human hands as a trump card.

"How is your work coming?" she asked.

Montrose's latest project, at the moment, was a drawerful of Van Neumann diamonds. These were carbon crystals containing self-replicating software, each "bearded diamond" edged with nano-tube hairs able to pull carbon out of a surrounding environment, and build another of itself, and then link and talk to it. Each diamond sensed pressure differentials on its super-hard refractory skin, and could determine which direction to grow.

As the diamonds grew, the software would build an ever-more complex computer mind, and the upper limits on its growth depended on its mass-to-surface ratio. Its smallest possible shape was a sphere of a few miles wide, but if it grew with a convoluted coral growth according to a fractal pattern, there was no upper limit. A simple calculation showed that this self-replicating machine should, in theory, produce a larger Xypotech logic crystal that the entire production capacity of every nation Del Azarchel could bring to bear. At the moment, Montrose had no idea what software or artificial mind could be stored in the emulation such a robust logic crystal could maintain.

An unanswered question was what environment to put them into, or how to construct the feeding whiskers so that things human beings needed, like oxygen, would be left alone. He could think of nowhere on Earth safe to unleash a Van Neumann machine. The nightmare hazard of Van Neumann replication growing out of control had been known and feared so long before the technology was possible, that a complete, if imaginary, vocabulary existed to describe the various forms of threat.

But he thought she was referring to his other project.

"I have several very promising lines of inquiry," he said, "and I just translated a section from the Omicron Segment which seems to be a direct run-down of the mathematics of self-correction in multicentric medium-knit self-referencing systems of holographic memory. In other words, since part of you was made right, I think I can reverse-engineer the rest of the instructions on how to make you, and get a set of morphic intermediaries. I can fix you without changing you, if you see what I mean. I want to test it on an emulation first, an Iron Ghost of you."

"And create a rival for your affection? I would be unhappy as a machine, so she would be unhappy if I made her like me, and if I made a version of me that was so different from me that I would not be unhappy as a machine, I suspect it would hardly be me. I would not bring a child into so dangerous a world: if the Hermeticists made a copy, they would download her into their grotesque gladiatorial games."

"Why do they do that?"

"Because the human conscience is not infinitely malleable. Despite what you've heard, neural tissue changes, or changes in environment or background can only alter the human conscience somewhat. It snaps back: the conscience reacts, and exacts revenge. Not everyone lives by the same rules, but everyone lives by the same spirit."

"What the pox does that mean? Spirit?"

"In this case, a myth about evolutionary superiority is the tale the Hermeticists told themselves on the ship to soothe their consciences—that the Iberians are superior to the Indians. You see? The ship was awash with blood clouds, and engineering was damaged in the fighting. Corpses were floating everywhere. The slaughterhouse smell could not be cleaned from the ventilation, which was not designed to scrub such volumes. The human mind has only a finite possible set of neurolinguistic responses to deal with death, murder, gnawing guilt."

"They said that they were the preferred darlings of evolution," he guessed, grimacing.

She nodded, looking as if she felt ashamed for the men who raised her. "The fact that the noble Kshatriya and peaceful Brahmins died proved that they were never fit to survive: so runs the myth. That myth means the Hermeticists must kill themselves in proxy in their mental wars in data-space. Such is the Hermetic spirit."

Something in her poise and expression seemed odd to him. "There is something else."

Her sea-gray gaze was upon him, glancing from the corners of her eyes, beneath heavily lashed lids. She said nothing.

"They're fighting over you, aren't they? In their electronic gladiatorial games. They are all in love with you, not just Del Azarchel. Well . . . ? You don't seem to be in any hurry to deny it."

"What do you remember?"

"Nothing. It ain't coming back to me. But I can picture it in my head. Since you was the only girl, with your girly scent and dancing eyes and your pheromones clogging the ship's ventilation system, there you must have been, all bobbing around in zero gee, round and curving and giggly. For a while you were a sacralicious fourteen-year-old, then a coltish seventeen-year-old; just a curious, impish, playful, coy, smarter-than-all-get-out cute little package. Next you were a superintelligent, glittering nineteen-year-old, and the only one really fun to talk with, since you made each of them feel special. I seen you got that gift about you. Also, aboard the submarine-like conditions, the nineteen-year-old had to press up too close to them to see the view screens and work the controls and so on. And of course aboard the ship they are either half-nude to save on mass, or wear nothing but ultraskintight web suits which show off a girl's extremely well-formed buttocks, and, in the cold, I'm thinking your nipples would . . ."

She hit him with a slab of ham before he could say more. "Men are disgusting creatures! Who in their right mind would design women to be attracted to them!"

But by that point, he had taken a handful of potato salad to her face in counterattack, and then there was nothing to do but settle the matter by wrestling.

"You better let me up," she said. Her bottom lip was sticking out as she tried to huff and puff and blow a curl of her hair up out of her eyes. She was nonchalantly watching the lack of success with the stubborn hair strand, not looking at his blazing pale eyes, even though his face was inches from her face, his lips inches from her lips. "You'll make my protectors nervous. *Lèse majesté* is a still a crime in these hey-ah parts, pardnah."

"You trying to make fun of the way I talk?"

"Not trying."

"What's that crime again with the French name?"

"*Lèse majesté*. It is the crime of violating majesty."

"I add it to the list of crimes I'm saving for our honeymoon."

"Let me up. Let go of my wrists."

"Say 'please.'"

"You issue unlikely commands. Remember who is smarter between us."

"I remember your belly being ticklish."

"You wouldn't dare."

"A girl will only say that when she secretly wants you to dare. I keep this feather in my hatband just for times like this. Oh, now she struggles! Say, missy, writhe around and toss your hair some, and I am sure you can break free. I bet you could bite my nose if you tried harder. Sure. I feel my grip weakening. Writhe more and arch your back."

He folded her wrists atop each other, so he could pin them with one hand. With the other, he drew the feather, and it twitched with playful menace in his fingers.

"It's an ugly hat," she pouted.

"Oh, you'll pay for that comment, girl. This hat has sentimental value. It means I don't need to comb my hair so often, and that means a lot to me."

"And I am not a girl. I am a celestial maiden: the first exosolar posthuman chimera created from alien gene codes. Practically an angel!"

"No argument there."

"What else do I have to do so you don't think of me as a *girl*?"

"You're still a girl. Human nature snaps back and exacts revenge. Not everyone lives by the same rules, but everyone lives by the same spirit."

By then she was giggling too hard to catch her breath, and as predicted, her troopers came forward at a quickstep, railgun lances ready, to see what was causing the shrieks.

After explanations and apologies, they were left alone again, and he was lying on his back, and she was using his armpit as a pillow, and they both looked up at the high blue sky, and sought fractal patterns similar to Monument segments among the clouds.

She sighed, "I truly and deeply hope, my scarecrow of a suitor, that you do have a cure for the flaw in my design. I feel there are things buried, enjambed, structurally encoded in the Monument that are waiting inside me to wake. A destiny. I was meant for something. Do you believe in evolution?"

"I believe it exists," he said. "I don't believe that whatever comes next is any better than what comes before. It is non-directed, random, cruel."

"I was not evolved, though. I was made. My makers followed instructions even they did not understand, from minds not human, not limited to human thoughts. It was directed. Perhaps it is not random, which means that I alone of all Mankind have a destiny and a purpose. Perhaps it is not cruel."

She sighed and looked sadly at the clouds.

"Cure me, my scarecrow. Drive away the dark wings that beset me, I pray you. I am so tired of not being smart enough. I am weary of my own stupidity."

He could not think of anything to say to that odd comment, so he turned and closed his arms and kissed her.

16

The Concubine Vector

1. Ceremony

A.D. 2401

Menelaus and Rania were married in June of 2401 in the *Iglesia de San Francisco,* the Cathedral of Saint Francis of Assisi, in Quito, nine thousand feet above sea level and fifteen miles south of the Equator. His Holiness, Pope Innocent XXIV, himself, performed the wedding Mass.

In the silent sky, the blazing star of the secondary drive of the newly re-outfitted *Hermetic* hung in the blue between the white clouds, above the doves, above the tile-roofed houses, above antique Spanish palaces, above the churches inlaid with Inca gold, and it was a light visible even by day.

The primary drive was a total conversion ion-reaction, and would not be lit while the vehicle was near Earth, for fear that contraterrene carbon particles might escape unconsumed from the magnetic drive core, and if entering the upper atmosphere, would annihilate an equal mass of terrene matter and release gamma radiation and exotic particles. It was not a reasonable fear: normal cosmic ray bombardments were more dangerous, but Rania, as ever, was deferential to the opinion of the common man.

While churchbells pealed, the bride and groom rushed down the carpeted steps into the flower-strewn plaza, half-blinded by thrown cherry blossom petals, she as lightly as a deer, he in his lurching, long-legged lope.

Two lines of dismounted cavalrymen in the magnificent livery of the Swiss Guard (costumes so beautiful legend incorrectly, but understandably, attributed the design to Michelangelo) crossed their pikes, adorned with garlands, high overhead, forming a tunnel of blades down which the couple fled. More Swiss Guard were mounted, their steeds adorned with gold and scarlet, and the line of horses kept the grassy lane before the cathedral clear of people, an avenue of escape. These were harsh-faced, keen-eyed young men, and the last four centuries of organized crime and disorganized brigandage surrounding Rome spread the fame of their hardiness. Pikes of modern materials but ancient design were in hands, and weapons more modern were holstered at hip: batons able to administer lethal shocks, or aiming lasers to call down fire from lightweight sniper platforms on rooftops or hanging invisibly in heaven on wings of gauzy blue.

The bridal veil was yards upon yards of white satin, trimmed with diamond studs and sparkling sapphires, held by a score of young queens who, in this age of the world, were as slim and lovely as the craft of genetic engineering could make them.

Montrose and Rania had released to the public the secrets of the *Hermetic* second-youth procedure. At the moment, only the wealthiest and most powerful of the elite could afford the painstaking cell-by-cell alteration: but as if overnight, the rich and mighty were also the young and dazzling.

Montrose hated the trend he could already see forming, but he could see no way around it. The human brain reacts to physical beauty on a preverbal level—it is instantly easier to trust and like handsome features, and remarkably easy to adore and follow. A gulf between ugly commoners and alluring aristocracy in prior ages had been a matter for clothing and ornament: hereafter it would be woven into gene and blood, flesh and bone.

As Rania ran, some hidden signal in the threads was triggered, the long satin train fell away, divided itself neatly into streamers of cloth. The twenty queens now raised their gloved arms, to beckon these streamers upward. Up the fabric flew, high overhead, to the delight of the cheering crowds, and diamonds rained down on them.

Menelaus, grim-faced with happiness, his pale eyes blazing at the adoring crowds, galloping on his long rangy legs, had drawn the ceremonial saber he wore with the absurd uniform. No doubt he would have thrust aside (or thrust into) any unwary well-wishers who dared impede his path away from the celebration and toward his hotly-awaited marriage bed: but the servants of Rania, both uniformed in scarlet and gold or hidden in the crowd, kept the singing mob in check.

The kiss Menelaus and Rania had exchanged before the Pope still burned on his lips: the strange, acrid scent of the high mountain grasses that grew along the lanes for ground-effect vehicles was in his nostrils, and whirled his thoughts like wine.

"You should not have made your legs longer," he growled. There had been no time for last-minute alterations for the wedding dress, despite the number of seamstresses and fabric-programmers on her staff, so Rania had suffered an overnight modification, to trigger an artificial youth-cycle in her cells, and suffer a growth-spurt to add the needed inches to her height. She now had the coltish legs of an adolescent, a more willowy silhouette.

Menelaus had solved Rania's neural divarication problem, and she had not been willing to wait, either to put off the wedding for the medical process, or to put off the medical process for the wedding. Since her preset RNA-spoofing black cells in her bloodstream were already programmed to make a universal and rapid change, it was nothing to tweak totipotent cells into her leg bones and muscles. She spent the night before the wedding in a biosuspension coffin, with seven quarts of nanomachinery moving through her body, while Menelaus struggled with the fear that she would wake up as someone different.

So far, she seemed to be normal.

"We discussed this," she said, eyes elfin, mouth impish, "during our spat. Our first lovers' quarrel! You lost."

He hated the fact that the top of her head no longer fit nicely under his chin when they hugged. Now the crown of her head was at the level of his lower lip, and it bothered him more than it should have: it reminded him of the time he found out when he was four years old that *pi* could not be resolved to any rational number. It seemed obscurely unnatural, as if someone had made a mistake when putting the universe together.

"I'll be made of sterner stuff when we reach the bridal bower, my fair rebel. Bad enough womenfolk can't decide what to wear; what damn fool gave them the science to fashion up their flesh and bone, tissue and face?"

"Why! The recent breakthroughs in biotechnology are due, my beloved, to *someone's* policy of total honesty to the public. We cannot blame the Hermeticists—they did not invent the system. Someone else performed a mathematical analysis of combination-solutions in genes, a notation system he read off the Monument back when he was insane. Who is to blame, then?"

"What? Next you'll say the apeman who invented fire is to stand trial for every act of arson since the Stone Age."

"Hush, for there are sure to be press and spy-bees near the bridal car."

When they came to the end of the carpet, the flower-festooned electric car was nowhere to be seen. Instead, there was Yorvel, looking plump and ridiculous in the gold-purple-scarlet livery of the Pope's Swiss Guard, pole-arm held gingerly in one hand, bridle held firmly in the other. He was trying to restrain a nervous, stamping steed, a red horse the hue of blood.

Rania said in a voice of limpid surprise, "But where is our car?"

Menelaus petted the nose of the huge horse, who gently nuzzled him, sniffing with large, delicate nostrils the gold and ebony costume, the wide lace collar, wherein bridegrooms of this era and rank were clad. "What? The Pope arrives with forty-nine white horses and one red charger that I've owned for a year now, and you don't recognize him?" He petted the long nose carefully. "There, my hayburning poop-factory. What does she know? She didn't mean it. Born in a tin can in space, she was. No, no, don't be wroth. Now, upsy daisy."

"What? Husband mine, your delirium is to have me, in all my fine and delicate satin, balance atop the spine of this outsized uncouth mammal? Am I an acrobat? Am I a cavegirl, to be juggled and bounced atop a zoo creature? Where are the brakes? Where is the safety setting? The whole system of muscles and veins—I speak now as a lady who has more than dabbled in engineering—seems to be directly controlled by the organic brain of a horse, with no manual override or direct interface. As a motile arrangement, ungainly, and less responsive than having the caterers carry me in a punchbowl."

"My strong right arm is your safety, my horsemanship your control."

"I shall look ridiculous."

"History books'll clean it up, Rainy. 'Sides, if you look good to me, hang the world."

"I say I will not have it."

"And I say you will. Who is to be the man in my house, eh?" And with no further ado, he took her in one arm and swung her into the saddle, where Res Ipsa Nova, sensing her nervousness, danced and trembled. She emitted one short yelp of surprise, and clung to the mane; and the delighted crowd roared.

Yorvel meshed his fingers and bent, as if to allow Menelaus a leg up. Menelaus ignored both Yorvel and the stirrup, but merely put his hands on the horse's flanks and vaulted himself into the saddle, half-colliding with his mussed bride. Her coronet was askew, and the trailing lace in her hair was tangled, but Rania sat with straight posture, and favored the crowd with a wave of her gloved hand.

"My master is a madman, and is too mad to know he is mad," murmured Yorvel from about the level of Menelaus's knee. "Do you know what I had to do to spread your bribes? The *Schweizergarde* were snickering in their mustachios. They never would have agreed to smuggle in your horse, except they are die-hard romantics. And you don't treat your beast right: leaving him here in this heat with this caparison! And now you are going to double his load? He will buck you off, and you will fall on your royal buttocks, Master! The picture bugs will photograph it, and all the newsfeeds will show it, and add comic music as a soundtrack to the sidebar."

"Everyone needs a good laugh," grunted Menelaus, tearing the loose, huge collar from his neck and flinging it into the air. "Now we're fixing to take our French leave of this crowd, and shin out. Nova! Gid-YAWP!"

And in a moment the steed, as the wind, flew past the pillar supporting a statue of Winged Independence, and his hoofbeats were the thunder.

The bridal veils and white laces flowed behind, snapping bravely, shedding roses, and the bride clung tightly to her dark-faced, glittering-eyed groom. Perhaps she smiled, but her face was pressed to his chest. The crowd roared and parted, a frightened Red Sea.

The beast was as magnificent a steed as modern genetic meddling could make him: so it was astonishing, but not impossible, when he cleared the heads of the onlookers at the end of the lane, made it over the pilings into a rich man's garden, danced in a cloud of dust first down the steep slope of the mountainous terrain, and then galloped madly up the further slope, leaping from rock to sliding rock as nimbly as a goat, mane and tail like flame.

All the photographers, both professional and merely curious, sent their bees flying after, but Quito was a city known for privacy, because the mountain winds often blew the tiny instruments astray. One or two bolder fellows, or more curious, followed on foot the trail of dust a few score yards down the slope, but gave up the chase as the sorrel's long legs opened the distance on the uphill run, and the bride and groom were carried in a leap over the crest and out of sight. One man tried to follow on an antique petrol-powered motorcycle no doubt lent to him from a collector, but he had not practiced the old skills, and he left his machine in a heap when it struck a rock; hoots and whistles greeted him as he climbed painfully back up slope.

The remaining members of the photography cadre, sitting atop their electric carriages with cameras and lens-tubes enough to equip a small astronomical observatory, exchanged lost shrugs and bewildered smiles. Meanwhile the mounted Swiss, the only men there truly able to see the horsemanship, good and bad, that Menelaus displayed, raised their swords and lances and shouted, *"Acriter et Fideliter!"*

Yorvel laughed until he lost his breath, and sat on the ground, pulling a hip-flask of whiskey from underneath his borrowed uniform. "No woman is truly a bride until she is stolen away on horseback! That is what horses are for! Like in all the old tales! A magnificent gesture! Madness, like all magnificent gestures, of course. But a good madness, most needful and *proper* to the mental health: like the shock of a stiff drink, just the thing to put a man in his right spirits. It would be madness to be sane and sober on a day like this." And he mopped his brow with his handkerchief, laughing and drinking and roaring with merriment until he wept.

2. The Celestial Tower

Above the city loomed the Celestial Tower; titanic, cyclopean, rising straight from the crown of a mountain and upward as far as the eye could see. It dwindled with perspective to a point, like a highway seen in the desert.

Except that this, Menelaus thought, was surely a highway to the sky.

Menelaus had been following the old railroad tracks for some time as the sun settled in a welter of red into the sea. Rania rode with her body leaning against his chest and, despite that the ride must have been uncomfortable, did not complain.

It was dark now, and insects were singing. The scent of forest below the mountain slopes hung in the night air, and the distant chattering of animals could be heard. The city was still around them, but modern Patagonian cities were miraculously quiet: Menelaus noticed again the lack of the machine noise. It was also a splendor of lights, like constellations, down the slopes and underfoot. Here were Colonial-era buildings, held in spotlights for the tourist trade: the *Plaza de la Independencia,* there were the many churches, the Metropolitan Cathedral, the old Archbishop's Palace. In a world where a tourist could arrive from any continent in a matter of minutes, the beautiful places of the Earth were kept spotless. The light shone, and Menelaus felt as if he were treading the galaxy underfoot, or a carpet of diamond dust.

The suburbs were like islands in the sky, with bridges linking the paved areas. But half a mile from any building in any direction might be found a sudden slope, rock and flints, not good for foundations. A high civilization merely a stone's throw from empty wasteland.

They were high. From here the volcanoes that punctured the mountains to each side of the city could not be seen, but Menelaus knew where they were. He could have found them in his sleep.

Guagua Pichincha was westward, toward the sea; Cayambe Reventator was to the east; Chacana, Antisana, and Sumaco trailed away to the southeast; Cotopaxi was due south. In the distance, more than eighty miles away south, Tungurahua and Sangay. Far to the north, the peak of Galeras. All were active to some degree, with artificial vents opened to relieve pressure in a controlled fashion. Galeras was more active than the others, suffering a major burn that had been postponed for the wedding: now a plume of smoke like a second tower reached toward the stars, bending in the wind only a bit. Its upper reaches were torn and dissipated into grayish clouds. The lower parts looked so dark and sturdy, nearly the same color as the Celestial Tower, but as if built of smoke.

The volcanoes unnerved him. Controlled? He hoped so, even though the old and worn systems of volcano-preemption were from the previous rulers of this place, older even that the Coptic Order, the Late Hispanosphere. It was the years Menelaus slept through, but still ancient history.

Around him was a land of fire, cities perched on peaks moated by cliffs over empty air. The massive geothermal energy of the place was what allowed the Celestial Tower to be here.

He reined his sorrel and looked up.

The middle reaches of the tower, far above, were still blushed rose with the light of a distant sunset. This alpine glow made the tower seem to float, weightless in the twilit heavens, a supernatural apparition.

Farther above, the towerlight was a vertical streak of yellow gold, where the upper regions were still in direct sunlight. And yet again above that, craning back his head and squinting, Menelaus could barely make out a harsher gleam, a glint, where the sun's radiation, undiluted by any atmosphere, splashed onto the tower side in naked vacuum.

The tower-top itself, the spaceport called Quito Alto, shined faint and distant at the very vanishing point of the perspective. Normally, it was not so bright as to be seen by the naked eye. Now, however, it outshined the evening star. It was a star that neither rose nor set.

"Our honeymoon suite," he said.

She said, "I thought you would like to be near the canopy of space, my old home."

"When did they erect this?"

"Never."

"What?"

She giggled, a sound like silver chimes. "They lowered it. None of the weight sits on the ground. Seventy years ago, during the high point of Hispanosphere ascendancy. The King of Spain wanted an enduring monument to his tyranny, and he thought there would be traffic from a moonbase, asteroid mining, expeditions, and, yes, a colony on Ganymede or Titan."

"What happened?"

"War interrupted."

"Which one?"

Rania just shrugged. "The Yellow War."

"Which one was that? What was it about?"

Rania spoke in a soft, haunted voice. "You may ask the survivors for details. Inspect your coffins dated between 2333–2338. Both sides experimented on captured civilian populations with RNA-spoofing. The bloated monstrosities and boneless knots of flesh were biosuspended, because there was no way to keep them alive. They are now your wards." She looked up.

Menelaus wore a puzzled frown, as if he had not realized that the fate of those slumbering souls was now his responsibility.

She said, "Work on the tower slowed. It was maintained by private subscriptions for a while."

Menelaus gazed at the Celestial Tower. "And then?"

"And then what? There is no 'and then.'"

"The tower is still there."

"Worthless to Earth," she said, sadly.

"The road to the stars!"

"The road to nowhere. The moonbase was abandoned due to bone-sickness. No colony on Ganymede was ever founded. It would have cost less, and been a friendlier environment, to build a greenhouse at the bottom of the Arctic Sea, and farm that. But since the Patagonian, African, and Gobi wastelands were blooming for the first time since the Triassic . . . so who would bother? After the war, first one institution then another maintained it, despite the volcano danger here. The Third Era of Space could begin at any moment, since launch costs are, even now, as long as that tower stands, merely the cost of a spider car, one going up, one coming down. Oh, look!"

He saw, high above, what seemed to be a meteor shower. For a moment or so, silver streaks of fire were falling to either side of the twilit, red-gold tower.

"What is it?"

"Decay. Fragments of ablative ceramic, from the upper structure, microscopic nano-tube fragments that have lost their Van der Waals adhesion. The tower is old, old, and its joints are stiff; its skin is peeling; upper sections suffer from sunburn and accumulated metal fatigue. It is a pendulum, you see, but the balancing governors are no longer in synch. I had been hoping your Pellucid would help us solve some of the calculation errors."

Pellucid was the name for his Van Neumann diamond project. He had finally decided on an environment where the machines could be released with minimal danger to the human race. The depthtrain system had given him the idea.

Pellucid would be sent to govern a system for sensing and distributing pressures across the tectonics of Quito's volcanic region. If it worked, Pellucid would be able to grow down the sides of old volcano vents, and spread as far and wide along the inner mantle of the Earth as need be, to gather valuable information about magma pressure systems as they formed. The more miles the diamond colony covered, the more calculating power it would have. Any single diamond, or any set of them, could be turned to any number of specialized functions as need dictated. The trick was to make them die on exposure to surface conditions.

Rania was speaking softly. "The tower is a living thing. It breathes, pumping air up to the station; its heart pumps hydraulics and coolants; it sweats, after a fashion, to distribute heat across its skin; it has nerves to carry energy and sensations of stress and wind-shear from one part of its structure to another; and it moves, shifting weight, flexing, maintaining balance. I have always felt its sorrow, rooted to this spot of rock, its upper head in space."

"It is just standing there?"

"Standing, no. It sways like a dancer: these inhabited sections at the bottom, the malls and parking warehouses are an anchor point."

"You know what I mean. It ain't being used."

"But it is. The *Torre Real* was recently bought by my people, and re-named the Celestial Tower. I wanted to call it the Golf Tee, because of its shape, but my publicity consultants insisted on a more dignified name: I should have followed my instinct and saved myself their fees, because these days everyone calls it the Folly Tower."

Menelaus frowned when he heard that. "One of most ace-high bits of engineering this poxy race of man ever built, and they call it foolwork? Someone should make 'em regret that name. What if we set it to rights, put it back in business? We got the money."

"A noble dream," she said, almost dismissively, but smiling. "Del Az-archel would have allowed it, had I married him, because then any increase in my power and authority would have increased his also. But now?"

Montrose looked up. "I saw a flare."

"It is a correction burn. There is a tourist hotel at the spot twelve miles up, clinging to the carbon nanotube tether proper. The cable swells from a one-centimeter diameter at the top of the anchor atop the base superscraper, to almost a hundred meters wide at the geostationary point. The tourist hotel is much lower than that, still inside the stratosphere. It was ordered closed many years ago."

He opened his mouth to ask why, and snapped it shut again. He knew why. Del Azarchel did not want people being too curious about outer space.

He pointed at a cluster of lights, bright as a small city seen from orbit. He said, "Is that it?"

"No, that is the spaceport itself, which is above the atmosphere. You cannot see from this angle, but the cable is bent to the west whenever a payload rides up, due to the differences in angular momentum of the spi-der car versus the various sections of cable—the horizontal increment of speed increases with altitude. The Hotel of Sorrow is not overhead, but hangs above the Pacific Ocean."

"If I had had a tower like this, hanging up, all shining over my head, I would not have waited for Del Azarchel and his bully boys to give me permission to mount up and go into space. I would have stormed the damn place, and forced my way aboard any vessels the spaceport could support! What happened to these people these days? Spineless as squids, I call 'em."

"Some cherish the long peace. Some fear a return of fire from heaven."

"Man shouldn't be afraid. Men were bolder, life was better, in my time."

"Oho? Was it? So says a man who shot lawyers for a living, back in the good old days." Her eyes twinkled with mirth.

"There are some that envy me that job. I've heard it called a public service, shooting lawyers." He had to smile.

She did not let her smile show, but there was a lilt in her voice. "Let us excuse it on those grounds, then, and call it the practice of a more excitable era. But perhaps you will tell me more about why your people hanged Mormons?"

"When they stole our women. But who cares who shot first? War changes people, and biowar makes 'em crazy. I weren't around when the rumors flew that the Mormons were tainted, infected with Spore, and wouldn't take blood transfusions needed to clean them. I heard stories from my aunt what those rumors did. The Burnings. It must never happen again."

She said, "To eliminate all diseases was the dream of the Pure Order. They were well on their way to making the race too hygienic to resist the next disease: and there was a next one, and many next ones. No pathogens of this century are entirely natural. Those not caused nor encouraged by bad medical practice of the last generation, are descended from non-self-eliminating biotic weapons from the generation before."

Menelaus just grunted. "Darwin's curse."

"Curse? If so, we must take care with our own curses. The secret of second youth we released to the public I fear will also result in the same dieback cycle, as pathogens robust enough to survive the molecular-level scrubbing the second youth process involves will find themselves alone in a rich and newly-virginal environment, without competition, and without natural defenses against them."

"Agh! That's pessimistic talk. You got to have faith that our children will be able to invent the means to fight whatever comes up. We could not just sit on the secret of youth and let everyone's grammy up and die."

Rania smiled, as she always did when the talk turned to children.

Menelaus said, "Hellfire, and I ain't just talking about disease: disease did not cause the Human Torch parades in Utah. One day science will fix things, so this part of us, this vicious part, will be caged up. The Beast.

Maybe we can make a child without the gene for sorrow and rage, maybe we can make a thinking machine without the subroutine for hate. Maybe."

"We have the genes and routines now," she said. "The cure for hate is forgiveness. The cure for outrage is humility. The cure for sorrow is thankfulness. Even a child can learn these three: no grand scheme of human eugenics to produce the transhuman is needed."

He gave her a long look. "I wonder if the Hermeticists who made you left out all the flaws of this old, sad, all-too-human race. You should be the mother of new people."

"Oh my! Such a responsibility. And when should we get started on that project?"

She smiled, then, and the towerlight was as bright as moonlight, so he could see her smiling, a dim gold shadow in the night, and so he kissed her.

When they paused to breathe, she asked, "Where are you going to stable your horse? We cannot bring him up on the spider car."

3. Limits

Menelaus Montrose, when he should have been the happiest man on Earth on the happiest day of his life, was aware of an ache in his throat, a bitterness—no, it was a *resentment*, a feeling that he had been betrayed. It reminded him of the time his mother had thrown his birthday cake to the hogs, because he had not done his chores (it had been his birthday that day, after all, and Leonidas told him it was okay to sleep late). With one part of his mind, he told himself that Del Azarchel was the source of this feeling. Blackie was a cold bastard, no doubt.

Another part of his mind told him it was the future that had betrayed him, the human race itself. Filthy, stupid poop-flinging tool-using monkeys not smart enough to use their tools to better themselves, and live like men, not monkeys.

During the ride up the side of the cable, his mood grew more and more elated the higher they rose. The scattered lights of the city fell away. The ocean was a dark seething mass, still tinted rose-red by the sunset receding westward, but more and more of it came into view as they rose higher, out-pacing the dusk.

The car was a bubble affixed to a contraption of legs that were pulled along by induction currents in the cable itself, and the legs were hinged to grow wider as the cable grew wider.

He spoke about the wealth his marriage had put into his hands; he spoke about rebuilding. Why couldn't the Celestial Tower be restored to its old glory? Why not establish a moonbase, mine the asteroids, put men in space instead of just satellites? And why not colonize Titan?

"And flying cars," he added. "We're in the future. There are supposed to be flying cars."

She said, "And what about Del Azarchel? He will prohibit it. Titan is outside of spy bee range."

"He cannot really be against a space program! When we were young—well, spittle, colonizing habitats both spaceborne and plane-tary, 'smostly all we talked on. Besides, the news that the *Hermetic* is mak-ing a second expedition to the Diamond Star might quell the discontent gripping the—uh, the masses." (He had almost said *the Hylics* but he caught himself.)

"He woke you because he was desperate to wake Xypotech Del Azarchel—I weary of saying the phrase—I hereby dub him 'X'-Archel." (She pronounced it *Exarchel*.) "By this means he hoped to send to the Diamond Star the only person he trusted not to overthrow him when he returned. Himself. One immortal version of his mind would rule the world while the other—the first of an endlessly self-replicating multitude of Van Neumann ships—would conquer the stars. He has no more need of the human race, for the posthuman starfaring race he intends to be is merely himself, multiplied to infinity."

"And the rest of Mankind?"

"The myriads of the human race suffer the fate of those spermatozoa who fail to penetrate the egg."

"Fine. We get to the Diamond Star first, come back, and make his worst nightmare come true, overthrow his damned tyranny, set up something where everyone gets a vote!"

She shook her head. "While it has the romance of directness, it is an inelegant solution, perhaps self-defeating. I suggest that only a plan even more far-sighted and ambitious than his will prevail."

"Har! Or is it just that *you* helped designed this worldwide tyranny, so you don't want to see it blasted?"

She said, "The world we found when the *Hermetic* descended was not as culturally coherent as some English colony like your America with two hundred years of experience ruling themselves. I had to work with the people who were as I found them, people more fearful of bioterror and plague and poverty than they were of servitude. They have their limitations. And I, my husband, even I have mine. I hope you are not like Ximen, and think of me as some fairy-being with a magic wand?"

"You're on a first-name basis with him?"

"What? With my ex-fiancée, who raised me from a child, and I lived in a starship within shouting distance of him my whole young life? It would be odd if I were not."

"So what are your limitations? Can't hit a piñata while hoodwinked?"

"I don't know what that is. My limit is that while I can inspire a social and political system for humans to maximize personal liberty within the context of minimizing external conflict, I simply cannot reduce the *how* and the *when* and the *why* to adjust the system to a simple algorithm. There must be a posthuman to make adjustments, personal authority on several levels, wise judges, statesmen who transcend the mere hedonistic calculus of power and politics. You see the problem?"

"The problem is you were raised on a ship, so you think everyone obeying one captain is the norm. The problem is you did not set up a Democracy."

She raised a skeptical eyebrow. "Democracy on a worldwide scale? The Chinese outnumber the Australians, and would have voted to abolish international corporate structures. The Azanians would have merely bribed Africa to vote their way on matters of public import. The Copts would have voted the Jews out of Babylon."

"I mean a limited Democracy."

"Oh, but I did limit it! The aristocratic class forms a bulwark against overreaching by the commoners. I encouraged an irenic but established sacerdotal order to create legal sanctuary against overreaching aristocrats. I encouraged a formal system of intelligence-augmented bureaucrats to check the fervor of religious zeal, and also to give a harmless outlet to the morbid impulses of academics. I encouraged the arrogance of the plutocracy to check the warlike desperation of the common man, who otherwise would elevate a despot to check the aristocrats: the plutocrats can only maintain their precarious positions by serving rather than commanding their customers. And so on. The parts are all balanced against each other."

"What went wrong?"

"Intelligent I may be, but not experienced. Book learning is not the same. I am younger than you are, biologically. I am just a girl."

"That don't sound like a mistake to me. You being a girl and all."

"Yet I underestimated the bull-headed blindness of the male of the species. I put too much faith in incentives, and too little faith in the original sin. You see? The Hermeticists are as a ship in a storm, and I have left them only one safe landing zone: namely, they must organize an expedition to the Diamond Star to replenish the energy of civilization, or else the whole structure will collapse. This means they must abdicate power, and decentralize their Conclave to another structure I have prepared to receive it, the Special Advocate Executive of the Concordat. There are several legal mechanisms in place to do this, including an appointment by agency, or invoking a general convention of the Parliament. The Advocacy includes agents of mine, men I have intermittently trained and cultivated over decades. They have so often acted for the Conclave that the Commons would accept them as legitimate. But . . ."

Her voice trailed off.

". . . But the Hermeticists are too stupid." He finished the sentence for her.

She nodded sadly. "You speak ill of the men who raised me. They are my fathers."

"I speak ill, but I speak the damn truth, don't I? They'd rather hang on to power and ride the wild tiger with its tail afire, risking war and world destruction, rather than go home and live on the farm like Washington did."

"It's a male trait, this lust for potency, I think," she said.

"Weren't Washington a male? Anyhow, Princess, I ain't convinced you have the best set-up here, and I ain't convinced seeing it shatter is so much more to cry over than seeing it kept."

She shrugged her soft shoulders, ghostly in the light from the city underfoot, and the stars above. "This is not a gunpowder age. What if the world shatters also? You have not studied the problem, so how could you be convinced?"

"It's still a damnified tyranny, and free men shouldn't stand it."

"Places on the globe where that is so, such places enjoy a greater liberty under our Concordat. Your North America is controlled only by alliances, media monopolies, and power stations. They still meet in their town meetings and have votes: but they cannot vote for war. Nor for anything that leads to war. Do you understand the limits of liberty? There are antimatter weapons in the hands of men like Del Azarchel and Narcís D'Aragó, men who like to see skyscrapers and farmlands on fire. The more power is in human hands to destroy human life, the more carefully limits must be placed on that liberty—why do you look askance! What I say is as much common sense as drawing in shrouds during a storm of sunspots, or walking more slowly when near a brink! If you would have me restore your precious liberties to the common men, I will have to take the antimatter away, and leave them in the dark. . . ."

At that moment the car wobbled in the high-altitude wind, and the couple found themselves in each other's arms, looking into each other's eyes, and talk of these disagreeable matters was interrupted, not without laughter, by divertissement more fascinating to them.

4. Reception

There was a reception awaiting them at twenty-five thousand feet. Even this was below the level of the Honeymoon Suite of the long-closed hotel. The staff were not concierges and maids, but instead were astronauts and engineers, Rania's picked men, who had recently reopened the facilities, with much fanfare, and many announcements that another Space Age was soon to begin. Many of these men were Psychoi, the intelligence-augmented Mandarin class—but here in the tower they doffed their silver wigs and proudly displayed their spacer's crewcuts, or wore the tight, uncomfortable bonnets meant to serve as padding for space helmets. Montrose spoke only to one or two, and he was not sure he trusted them, but they did seem to share his enthusiasm for a new space program, and there was champagne, and colored lights floating in the upper atmosphere beyond the pressurized windows, and many a toast and a cheer to the happy couple, and so Montrose decided to smother his suspicions. Perhaps he was finally home at last, in the future he had always dreamed. The bubbles in his glass twinkled like stars as he raised it to his bride, who blushed and smiled just like any girl, princess or not.

But Menelaus was impatient, full of laughter and lust, and would not stay for more. He seized upon his young bride, all wrapped in white satin and white silk, and hoisted her in his arms, amid calls and shouts and sprays of wine. Up they went again in the spider car, this one tied with ribbons and scrawled with well wishes. All fell silent as the atmosphere thinned outside.

There was no one else in the structure, which was not yet ready for civilian traffic: Rania and Menelaus went here partly for privacy, partly for publicity.

At last they were alone.

5. Honeymoon Suite

At midnight, she woke him, but when he turned on the sleeping mat to take her in his arms, she seemed oddly stiff and distracted. He felt something cold and rectangular, the size of a small book, in her hands. It felt slightly warm, as if circuits were active.

The deck of the suite was pressurized nano-diamond, transparent and practically invisible; the lights of the city beneath the clouds below could be glimpsed. It looked to Menelaus like a galaxy underfoot. Here and there were dim reddish glows from the teeth of active volcanoes, looking like nebulae where stars were born. To one side, the full moon hung above her twin sister gleaming in the sea. He looked for but did not see a line of golden glitter dancing like a restless road across the waters; this was the light reflected from the tower, and it had been visible when he went to sleep. At this hour the whole length of the tower was in night, and even Quito Alto high above them was occluded by Earth's shadow.

It was the stars that were so bright, so beautiful. They seemed almost within reach.

The moonlight illumed the suite, picking out the white walls, the bird-painted paper screens, the lightweight fixtures of clear ceramic or diamond crystal. The tatami mats on the transparent floor were spread wide, so that little fulvous squares seemed to hang against the abyss of night air.

No fancy gold or marble here. It turns out that Rania, when alone, preferred something along the lines of the spartan space-habitat furnishings she'd been raised with.

Except the shower, of course. No spacer had a shower like this: it occupied most of the suite. The crystal walls were only slightly dimmed—what need had young honeymooners for privacy?—by showerheads, soap servers, and massage fingers, as well as waterproof speakers for bathing-music coordinated to the water play. One could swim in the glass basin with the Earth floating beneath. The moonlight from the sea below shined through the pond that Rania had left in the basin of her shower, and so a web of silver light, crisscrossed by ripples, breathed and fluttered on a chamber ceiling.

An imaginary picture of her stark naked and reading a book (not to mention the non-imaginary real girl, warm and girl-scented, supple limbs and clinging hairs of gold and all) for some reason was arousing to him. The girls back in his hometown, even ones he had been sweet on and too shy to court, had not had much use for book learning.

He rubbed his eyes and slapped himself in the cheek to wake himself up. Sternly, he told himself to pay attention to what was going on.

"I've read the Monument, up to the Xi Segment." Her voice was haunted, strange.

"You haven't been sleeping," he said.

"What need have I for sleep? There are sections of my brain of which I was hitherto unaware."

A sensation of terror overcome Menelaus. The changes he had introduced to her nervous system, his attempt to correct the errors in her base gene pattern, perhaps they had waited until she entered REM sleep to reorganize her consciousness.

"Are you still the same person?" he asked.

"More than I was," she laughed, "but I have lost nothing."

"What is it? Why are you awake?"

"You were snoring, you rude swine, falling asleep like that! And I could not sleep—I wondered at the joy and pain—"

"Jesus Christ! I didn't hurt you!"

She giggled. "You are blushing!" Now she seemed normal again.

"Am not! And you shouldn't talk of such things!"

"I am your wife. If you cannot discuss the mechanics of rutting with me, then with whom?"

"Gah! My mother would box my ears."

"She is absent. I am the woman of your life hereafter."

"That suits me."

There was an intermission of kissing, and so forth. When she put her arms around him, he could feel the cold corner of the square in her hand, digging into his back.

They parted for air. He said, "How could you tell I was blushing? You can't see me in this gloom."

From the way her hair moved in the dark, he could sense the triumphant cock of her head. "I don't need to see. I am your wife. I am yours. Yours. Nothing else you think you own, no wealth, no steed, no knowledge, no accomplishment will ever truly be yours as I am yours, your very own, for only I give myself wholly and fully, with all free will."

"Now you're blushing."

"I don't blush. I glow. And you cannot see me."

"Pox. I don't need to see. I'm your man."

"Not just my man, my crewman."

"Pox on that! I wear the pants in this family."

"You are not wearing pants now."

"I am still chief. You squaw. Got it?"

"Yes, milord, my husband, and my master. What are your orders?"

"I order you to tell me what you want me to do. It ain't like I ain't wrapped around that wee little finger of yours."

"For my part, I swore to love, honor, and obey. I will honor you now. You alone can I trust with what I discovered." And she pressed the square into his hands.

It was an antique desk pad, scarred and battered with use, and covered with cheery little pictures of flowers and butterfly-winged fairies. There was also in brass an emblem of a youth with winged sandals and winged cap, snake-twined rod in hand, one toe on a globe, one hand on a star: the symbol of the Joint Hispanosphere-Indosphere Hermetic Expedition.

She tapped the surface of the pad. A crowned and twinkling fairy-sorceress appeared in the glass, displayed a list of menu choices, one of which was *Stinky Baby's Monument Translation.*

Montrose realized that this was her personal bookpad, the one she had aboard the ship as a little girl. "Who is Stinky Baby?"

"You."

"What!"

"My name for you back on my ship. You were the only man I had ever seen who was not gray and wrinkled, and you slept in your coffin for months and years, and that fit the definition I read in the dictionary for a *baby.* Besides, you wore a diaper, because you did not know how to use a toilet bag. How was I to know what you were?"

"Stinky?"

"The diaper had to be reused."

She touched the pad again. The bookpad screen had a fairy figure dancing across the surface, waving a wand dripping sparks, and in her wake an image formed of the labyrinth of alien mathematical codes from the Iota and Lambda segments. Lambda was a reprise of the political economic calculus of the Iota Segment, but drawn out in more detail. In floating windows in the margins were translations into the simplified Monument Notation, and then into the Human-Monument Pidgin.

She said, "The Monument Builders have a mathematical expression in the Iota Segment to define the degree of mutuality extended to each measured rank of lesser beings. We are a form of life which might prove useful to their purposes, in a marginal way, even as dogs do tasks for shepherds."

"Wolves, you mean. We'll fight and die first."

"While it has the romance of directness, it is an inelegant solution."

"You got a better one?"

"Yes, for now is the hour of my awakening. I am here to do what I was meant to do. You, my husband, have made me whole."

She was speaking in a calm, almost eerie voice, but then suddenly her voice broke into sobs and she was in his arms, weeping, rubbing her tears against his chest.

"Hey! What's—what's wrong? Supermen don't cry!" He held her one-handed, the bookpad in the other. The light from the pad screen fell across her buttocks and legs.

"Tears of joy, of joy unknown to lesser men, they do," she said, sniffing and hiccupping as she laughed. "I know who I am! At long last!"

"Uh. Okay. Hit me. Who are you?"

"The redeemer. I will vindicate the human race."

"Uh. Okay. What the hell does that mean?"

Rania wiped her nose on her elbow and spoke to the pad. "Twinkle-wink! Bring up file code last." The floating fairy on the screen overlaid the Monument lines with a second and third layer of hieroglyphs.

To him she said, "You have read as far as the Iota and Kappa segments, which gives their equations of political calculus. What you call the Cold Equations."

He nodded. "Basically, the stars are so far apart it ain't worth no one's time and effort to cross the abyss, unless they have a planet to conquer and loot on the other side."

"That applies only when the power imbalance is vertical. In general game theory, a situation of mutual benefit and expected mutual benefit is best. Both parties in the transaction must remain players in the game long enough for a move and a response to be completed. There is a natural marriage of interests between any two intelligent species—if their intelligence is roughly the same, their resources, their ability to benefit each other."

She talked to the pad. The little fairy cursor brought up more screens.

More Monument hieroglyphs appeared on the screen, in a column with the pidgin translation. It was farther than Montrose had ever read; farther than (as best he knew) Del Azarchel had ever read.

Rania said, "Here is a vector sum in the time-relation I call the Concubine Vector. It is when the natural marriage of interests is between unequal partners. The Concubine Vector defines how much abuse and exploitation the inferior partner can be expected to suffer. The mathematics are quite elegant, even if the idea is horrid. One can define precisely, for example, how much shoplifting a shop can tolerate before losing either profit or customers, or how much criminal activity a town should stand before they create a police force, and how much police corruption to endure before creating checks on police power. And so on."

"So what does the Concubine Vector say?"

"It does not say that the human race will be slaves forever to the machines of Hyades."

"Good!"

"Only for many tens of millennia."

"No good."

"It is, strictly speaking, indentured servitude, not slavery outright, since the laws defined by the Cold Equations require they manumit the race as soon as we have paid back value equal to what it took to conquer us, plus a reasonable profit, of course."

"Bugger them. They got no right to conquer us and make us pay for it. That's just stupid. And why are they doing this? And why are they bragging about it? Why post their plans up on this Monument for all and sundry to see?"

"Because the Cold Equations require mutual communication for the natural marriage of interests to work, even within this 'Concubine Vector' of unilateral exploitation. The math itself shows things go more badly for both conqueror and conquered if both sides do not know exactly the rules and limits of the other."

"Okay. So why were you crying with joy?"

"Because I can redeem us. Pay the price they ask. Isn't it clear?"

"As mud at midnight, it is."

She tapped two of the little lines of alien math, so that the image rotated, and slid over to another side of the Monument segment, and overlapped a different group of Celtic knots. The negative spaces formed glyphs in the same Monument notation.

"I am called away: and you, if you will come."

"God himself could not stop me. Away to where?"

"Can't you read it?" She seemed surprised.

"Not at a glance, when I'm sleep-fogged. What's it say?"

"It defines our destination."

In his imagination, he turned the Monument hieroglyphs into an emulation code that he ran in the back of his mind and formatted the results as a visual image: the mighty spiral of the galaxy, arms of billions of stars reaching through clouds and streamers of nebulae, through flocks of frozen planets, rivers of interstellar asteroids, and belts of dark matter, million-year-old storms of energy, gravity stress-points, and all the other minutia the Monument Builders tracked.

Overlaid was a spiderweb of lines representing divarication and information cascade functions, representing political lines of control.

"Do you see it?" she asked.

"I see something interesting. The Hyades Domination is just a collaboration of slave races themselves. They are janissaries; fighting slaves. They belong to a higher power."

6. Star Map

The Hyades Cluster, at 151 lightyears away, was not the top of the system of lines representing the hierarchy. Functions connected it to the Praesepe Cluster in Cancer, some 550 lightyears away.

Praesepe was shown as the ascendant power in control of the local area of the Orion Arm of the galaxy. The Monument described traffic and control leading not just from Praesepe to the civilization in the Hyades Cluster, but also controls leading to Xi Persei in the California Nebula (1500 lightyears from Sol), the Pleiades (440 lightyears), M34 in Perseus (1400 lightyears), and the Orion Nebula (1600 lightyears) centered at the Trapezium Cluster. The notation showed this last location was the center of engineering activity, where the native civilization was making new stars. Praesepe also ruled the civilizations centered in the Coma Berenices Star Cluster, centered on the A-type binary 12 Comae Berenices: According to the Monument, one star of the pair had been artificially agitated to extreme stellar output.

Six interstellar polities of unimaginable immensity were under the control of whatever ruled the Praesepe Cluster. No human empire, until the rise of the Hermeticists, had learned how to control even so small a dust-speck as that third of the Earth which happened to be dry land, much less conquering and occupying other worlds, gas giants, stars, interstellar clouds of dust. These far-reaching supercivilizations seemed concentrated only in immense clusters of matter-energy, such as star-clusters where the stars were thick, nebula where new stars were being formed.

And yet there was something above and beyond even the Praesepe civilization and its half-dozen servitor civilizations: orbital elements described traffic between this and M3 in Canes Venatici, a globular cluster outside the rim of the galaxy, some 33,900 lightyears distant.

"How do you translate these three glyphs?"

"I think they are proper names, or, rather titles. The first one you translated—back when you were Baby Stinky—as referring to a superior power confronting an inferior, and you called it 'Hegemony.' Note the best translation, because it is not merely political superiority, but intellectual, a matter of further time-binding. I called it 'Domination.' The notation measuring information volume and matter-energy consumption says that they are so far above us that they can have only a master–servant relationship. A man who owns many flocks to a shepherd-boy.

"The next stands in like ratio with the first: a transcendent authority. I called it 'Dominion.' They are as far above us as a shepherd above a sheep-dog, a creature that can serve its purposes in a limited way, and can have a reciprocal master–pet relationship, but not a contract. The Dominion is seated at the Praesepe Cluster, relatively near to us.

"But look. Even they are beholden to a power beyond. Whatever holds authority at M3, in Canes Venatici, is represented by the symbol reflected on itself twice, representing two orders of magnitude: it indicates the extension of influence in every direction. An absolute power, a form of being that never ceases to replicate and expand itself. An absolute Authority. It stands to us as a man stands to the benevolent or malevolent microbes or protozoa living in his sheepdog's stomach, something of interest to the shepherd only insofar as it might prove useful or harmful."

7. The Absolute Authority

"So we have to go to the bosses that own the Hyades, and get them to call it off. Five hundred fifty lightyears away!" he breathed, awed by the audacity of it. It would be a thousand years and more to go and return, even if the *Hermetic* could attain the night-to-lightspeed velocity her name boasted, and, more difficult, descend back into the metric of normal space at the destination.

Yet if the calculations were correct that the Armada approaching Earth from Hyades was loitering at one tenth of one percent of lightspeed, such a round trip was feasible. It could be made before the Solar System fell.

But Rania said, "The Dominion of Praesepe is of no significance."

Montrose took a moment to adjust to that comment. The entities who controlled a large fraction of the Orion Arm of the galaxy. No significance.

"Then where are we going?"

"To the throne of the overlords of their overlords."

"To M3? What then? We're going to stoke the *Hermetic* to ramming speed, and blow the wogs to smithereens with a filthload of antimatter, right? Niven's Law says that any ship with enough power to step on the toes of lightspeed, that ship has enough power to fry a planet like an egg. Yeah. That'd make a right shiny firework."

She actually laughed. Rania threw back her head and laughed a silvery laugh, and her earrings sparkled in the darkness with the motion of her golden head. "Darling! You simply must read the decryption. This civilization . . . these godlike beings . . . they occupy a globular cluster."

"Well, that don't mean . . ."

"Messier Object Three is their seat. M3 is made up of several hundred thousand stars. The whole star cluster shifts like a variable even over the course of a single night: countless stars of the RR Lyrae type are crowded in the center, and they can double in brightness in a few hours. If you refer to the Zeta Segment, which contains star descriptions, the Monument says the output variation is a pollution or by-product of their stellar engineering efforts, Dyson spheres choking or releasing excess radiation. And what we see now is borne on lightwaves issued thirty-three thousand years ago. They may have achieved more by now."

"What if we used Earth's whole supply of contraterrene?"

"Earth? My husband, if the whole of the Diamond Star V 886 Centauri were flung like an anarchist's bomb into the core of the cluster, the energy discharge would be less than what we see as differences of output in the cluster stars in a single evening. Blow up a planet? It would be like rushing into a country of several hundred thousand households and shooting one man."

He opened his mouth to say that, in the cartoons, the Star Fleets were always rushing across to Lundmark's Nebula or whereverthehell to blow up the enemy homeworld—but he realized how infantile that would sound, so he just said crossly: "So fine. Then there's no point to going. It's too far, anyway."

"A gentler way is open to us."

"What way?"

"To prove our case in the court of heaven for the freedom of Mankind."

"Go to *them*? The ones who said in their message that they owned us?"

"I have read the message of the Monument, and seen the truth that it contains. Now you and I must go, armed only with that truth, and face the alien stars, the Archons of the Orion Arm, and demand of them we must be free."

"Why would they free us?"

"Their own laws compel it. Look at the math: a method of determining, in the aggregate and in the long term, the efficient from the inefficient rules of behavior."

"What does that mean?"

"It means that they will treat us like wolves if we are wolves to them, but like men if we prove ourselves their equals. These values allow us to escape their Concubine Vector. Their own sense of efficiency will not allow them to waste a valuable resource. Read! In the Cold Equations of the universe the balance scale weighs our utility to them as subjects, less the risk and cost of conquest, against our utility to them as partners, less the risk and cost of cooperation. They have reduced these complex matters, which so bedevil the governments of Earth, to an algorithm. If we act as their equals, they must recognize us."

"And what does it mean to be their equals?"

"It means to be a starfaring race."

8. Aren't We Now?

"Well, hurrah! We made it! Uh—" He saw the look on her face. "Didn't we?"

"No."

"We went to V 886 Centauri and back."

"No. The expedition was a failure. Can't you see that? We were attacked—attacked as if by pirates, when the *Hermetic* returned—by our own world. Our arrival overturned the customs and governments, which should, by rights, have been waiting to protect us, to assure us of our property, and to encourage others to dream of like ventures. Men are not starfarers yet."

Menelaus noticed the implication: that it would be a social change, an evolution in laws and traditions, which would make the human race starfarers. But what nation, what institution, could last so long?

He said only: "And what do we have to do?"

"Mankind has to learn to plan ahead a thousand years or ten thousand, and carry out our plans. To be a starfaring race means to think in the long-term. Space is too vast, the stars are too far, for small or selfish calculation! No race can starfare that cannot keep its purposes fixed and unchanging over long years of time; nor join the rulers of the stars who cannot keep contracts faithfully across long lightyears of space. The short-term races cannot be partners in covenants or voices in the galactic conversation, only serfs: for they have not the attention span."

Menelaus was silent, wondering, turning over the figures in his mind.

M3 was 33,900 lightyears away. If a man who did not need to eat or sleep started counting the second he saw a ship traveling lightspeed depart for M3, and that tireless man uttered one number every second of the day and night, he would count to a trillion before that number would pass. Including leap years, it would be 31,688 years, 269 days, 1 hour, 46 minutes, 40 seconds. He would still have over 3 millenniums to count. That was the one-way trip. Even at the theoretical maximum of nigh-to-lightspeed, assuming no turn-around time, the soonest a verdict could return from M3 to Earth would be 67,800 years from now.

Sixty-seven *thousand* eight hundred years.

The figure was stunning. A.D. 70800. That is the earliest anyone on Earth would hear about the verdict. The Seven Hundred Ninth Century.

Montrose tried to think of a comparison. When did the Egyptians build the pyramids? No. That was roughly 2500 B.C.: less than a twelfth of the span of time being completed here. The amount of time to go and return from M3 was equal to from now to the middle of the Paleolithic, circa 60000 B.C. About when the first canoe was dug and arrowheads shaped into leaf points by flint napping were both still new-fangled things the old folk probably didn't cotton to, but all the rage amoung the cave-boys.

"It is too damn far. Why not send a radio signal instead? Coherent light does not disperse or lose energy in a vacuum."

"That would prove only that we are a signal-making race, not a starfaring race."

He looked at the star-map notation again, revisualized it in another form. He was rather pleased with himself that he could picture more than a million discrete points, representing stars, and their relation to each other in time and space, in his eidetic memory. But he was also a little disappointed: he had been expecting a difference in the nature of his thought, not just in the speed and complexity.

Augmented intelligence seemed a small enough thing when compared with the terrifying grandeur of outer space. If anything, the greater sensitivity of his thoughts allowed him to truly understand the magnitude of what hitherto had been too astronomically huge to be meaningful. No, he could actually feel it, grasp it, and to *know* how microscopic a mote man's world was in the void.

M3 was distant. It was farther away from Sol than the center of the galaxy was. If the galactic disk were laid out like a dinner plate, M3 would be like a dandelion puff floating almost directly above it. The Monument script gave figures (expressed in terms of the unit of the energy liberated from the fission of one hydrogen atom with an antihydrogen atom) for the power use of the civilization at M3, and the symbols hinted at some aspects of their technology.

Menelaus reminded himself that, in the language of astronomers, a star *cluster* was nothing like a *globular cluster*. Hyades and Praesepe were clusters: Hyades held perhaps four hundred stars, and in Praesepe, three hundred fifty were visible. Whereas a *globular cluster* was an immensity, typically holding half a million to a million stars. Globular clusters were scattered like flying sparks ranging far above and below the main disk of the galaxy. The zone where globular clusters were found occupied a sphere centered on the galactic core, composed of older stars of low metallic properties.

In a globular cluster, the stars were packed close. On average, one would be next to its neighbor no farther away than perhaps six times the radius of Neptune's orbit, so the skies of any worlds in that crowded space would be densely filled with stars brighter than Venus at sunset, glowing clouds of light rather than scattered constellations. To the human eye, it would be a star dazzle too bright to stare at for long.

M3 had more variable stars than every other globular cluster in the galactic halo. The cluster included a large number of so-called Blue Stragglers, main sequence stars apparently much younger than the rest of the cluster: but only apparently. Macroscale Engineering had meddled with the core processes of the stars, throwing them out of their normal evolution.

The whole cluster of M3 stars was itself on an eccentric orbit around the galactic core, moving from 22,000 lightyears at galactic perigee, to 66,000 at galactic apogee. The orbit was canted oddly, to dip 44,000 lightyears above and below the main galactic plane.

Certain orbital elements and epochs given in the Monument revealed that the original orbit had been far more conservative, coplanar with the main disk of the galaxy. The reason for the massive orbital adjustment of this group of half a million stars was not revealed in the relatively crude mathematical sign-language being used.

The idea of a race that could casually sweep a globular cluster into a new orbit around the core of the galaxy left Menelaus awed and horrified.

The imagination of Menelaus for a moment was filled with a menagerie of cat-faced men, or centaurs, three-eyed people, hawk-men and crab-people and zebra-men, worm-creatures or intelligent trees, or dwarfish things with glowing eyes and ballooned skulls. But no: these were merely images from his childhood toon-tales. All that was revealed in the Monument hieroglyphs were energy levels, expressed in terms of multiples of the output of the Diamond Star, and additional mathematical expressions showing the composition of megascale engineering structures.

He told himself these beings could be something much stranger than his simple imaginings. Or even creatures to whom the question of form was meaningless: beings with a science to reshape their bodies and minds at will, to fit any task confronting them. Creatures of pure information.

But what tasks? What was this conquest *for*?

Montrose muttered, "These are beings of pure mind. Creatures beyond life. Something incomprehensible, someone from beyond the Asymptote. Beyond the event horizon of what we can ever understand. That's the enemy."

Rania surprised him by saying, *"For we wrestle not against flesh and blood, but against principalities, against powers, against the rulers of the darkness of this world, against spiritual wickedness in high places."*

In the moment before he recognized the source, he thought it might be Shakespeare, perhaps from some play where bold Scottish kings drew swords in defiance against tyrannical angels. He frowned when it dawned on him that it might be preacher-talk. But Menelaus noticed that hearing it in her dovelike voice, the Good Book seemed not to have that harsh tone, a weird combination of ghostly terror and dusty-hearted killjoy platitudes, it carried back in the days when his mother quoted it to him, or that lying no-account Parson Goodwin from Carl's Corner in Hill County. It almost sounded like poetry.

"Quoting the scriptures?" he said. "And here I though you were raised by scientists."

She was too ladylike to snort, but she did made a noise of disdain in her nose, softer than the sigh of a nightingale. "Scientists including the Franciscan-trained Father Reyes y Pastor, who made sure we had onboard the same Bible Mendel, Copernicus and Lemaître studied."

"Mass limits were tight," said Montrose. "I was not even allowed to bring socks."

"You think it an unnecessary luxury? I agree, the scriptures might have been no good for settling issues of astrophysics, but when I was told how my mother passed away, I read the Book of Job, and I looked down at the stars. This book asked me who laid the cornerstone of the cosmos when the morning stars sang together and what made the Sons of Light all shout for joy? It asked if I could bind the influence of the clustered Pleiades or free the bands of Orion?"

He saw a hint of sorrow in the shake of her silhouetted head. Rania continued, "Those questions comforted me in my grieving, even though I could not answer them; and the answers of science, firm and certain, could not. Through science I deduced, as you did, how I was born, but science, the mere study of matter in motion, will never tell me why."

"Down at the stars?"

"Stars were never 'up' until I reached Earth; the ship carousel, spun for gravity, puts the portholes under your feet, and all the universe is a void to fall into."

"You know your mom weren't real."

"Do mothers not love their stillborn child? I mourned her loss, even if she never lived."

"You are strange girl."

"Since you and I, and perhaps by now Ximen, are the only members of our new species, *homo sapiens posthomonid,* by any rational basis of comparison, not only am I average, I form the only data point."

Montrose, rather than argue the point, bent his head over the bookpad and read her translation of line 2311 and 2312 of the Xi Segment.

THE MATTER-DISTORTION PROCESS KNOWN AS LIFE . . . WHEN FOUND AMONG STARS IN THE ORION ARM BETWEEN THE FOLLOWING EONS AND LOCATIONS [measurements were given in terms of multiples of plank lengths and fractions of proton-decay periods. The volume thus defined included Sol] . . . NECESSARY FOR SOPHOTRANSMOGRIFI-CATION [meaning uncertain] . . . DONE AT THE BEHEST OF AUTHOR-ITY OF M3 GLOBULAR CLUSTER, WHOSE [SERVANTS] DOMINION AT PRAESEPE CLUSTER ORIENT FINAL CAUSATION TO CONFORM TO THIS DIRECTIVE; WHOSE [PETS] DOMINATION AT HYADES CLUSTER PER-FORM THE [INSIGNIFICANT] MANUAL LABOR INVOLVED.

"Let me get this straight. On Earth, ten thousand years go by before the little green men even show up. Then another Brazilian vermilion co-tillion years go by before we get back from M3 with the court's verdict. And we don't know if the court will rule in our favor, because who's to say their laws and whatnot will stay the same for so long?"

"They are starfarers: they must honor thousand-year-old expressions of their laws, or else their authority could not reach past a thousand lightyears. They must honor ten-thousand-year-old expressions of their laws, or else their authority could not reach past ten thousand lightyears. What is the upper radius value for the ambition of M3? We cannot say. But look: their name in this concept-writing means they extend in all directions without limit."

He shook his head. "Let's stick with our original plan. We go to the Diamond Star, no farther, gather up as much contraterrene as we can mine via star-lifting, return here, overthrow whatever stupid machine civilization Blackie has tried to set up—if it still exists, which I doubt—and start the long, slow process of building up the human race, and any posthuman races we might have the fancy to create, to fight the Hyades Armada. These equations are not only their advertisement of their intentions, they are also their marching orders—all we have to do is make the human resistance more expensive than it is worth to conquer us. Once there is no hope of profit, they'll quit. I mean, aren't we deciding everything on the assumption that these are machine civilizations, electronic brains that are forced to make judgments by these same calculations?"

Rania said, "If we make the human resistance more expensive, all they will do is extend the term of the indenture."

"The Monument itself is millions of years old. The civilization at M3 could be long dead, or changed its laws, or fallen to war or—anything!"

"Nonetheless, in my capacity as Captain, this concerns matters beyond Earth's atmosphere, and therefore falls into my jurisdiction."

"I am not questioning the legality, but the judgment! Are you just acting on blind faith? What makes you think the monsters at M3 (a cloud of stars not even in this damn galaxy!) will respect what is written on that lump of rock circling the Diamond Star, or even be alive? Aren't they changing and growing and dying, even if they are machine-things? What is your evidence?"

"The Monument expresses something never seen on Earth, a calculus of history, a science of which our economics and politics are mere unsystematic gropings, based on guesswork and sentiment. Their laws are deductions, not proscriptions, of how their future generations will and must behave, or, since they may long ago have solved the technical problems of decay and death, the future generations may be the selfsame individuals who wrote this promise."

"But it could be a lie!"

"To what end? Why tell us the means of manumission if they meant us not to use it?"

"Hellfire! D'you expect me to understand how the bug-men living in pools of methane who eat their parents for lunch might think with their nine brains? What if it is fiction? A joke? Graffiti? A psalm in their religion that they only mean on Sunday? What if it is some emotion or custom or nerve-malfunction humans just don't have that prompted them to write something for a reason we don't and can't understand?"

"The fact that the Monument itself is the product of a rational intelligence, a message deliberately set to be seen and read by all comers, allows us to suppose it means what it means until proven otherwise. Why do you assume the Armada from Hyades is real but deny that the Authority who can free us from the domination of the Armada is also real? Your skepticism seems to be unidirectional."

"But that does not prove it!"

"Life is not a bench of law, nor a scientist's workbench. We have partial information. A hint. A clue. Life allows us see a shadow in the darkness, and we must guess its true shape. But life forces us to decide, before we know with perfect knowledge, how we shall confront the unknown. Who gave you this foolish idea that evidence must be certain before it can be affirmed? Before us is the unknown. The universe is black and wide. The option to be all-knowing is not open to us. Our options are to act as if the unknown will bring us evil, which is the response called fear; or to act as if the unknown will bring us good, which is the response called hope. The first response is certainly self-fulfilling; the second may be."

Montrose had no good answer for that, so he said, "It still sounds like blind faith."

"Blind compared to what? All real life is decided by guesswork, intuition, judgment, determination, and not established by omniscience. Did you examine the future before you married me? Where is your evidence that our love will endure?"

"I fell in love. And I gave my oath. I will make it endure."

"Well, I took an oath also, to find and carry out my purpose in life.

Here I have found it. I will make the Authority at M3 to manumit the human race; I will make us starfarers. We will have the future, brilliant with glory, the human race has always dreamed of, and may yet deserve!"

He had no good answer for that, either, so he turned off the book and kissed her. He did not know if that would be the right thing to do, but he hoped it was.

17

Postwarfare Society

1. Called Out

He woke in the dark, disoriented, unable for a moment to remember where he was. Menelaus was aware of the emotion before he was awake enough to remember its reason: the fragrant warmth in his arms, the soft curvaceous body slowly breathing, the sensation of nude flesh cuddled against him. He remembered his joy before he remembered its cause.

I am a married man. I will never go to sleep alone, never wake up alone, not ever again. It was almost enough to make him believe in his stern old mother's stern old God, just to have someone to thank.

A sensation of needles walking along his skin told him his arm, on which she was pillowed, had fallen asleep. He did not move his arm. He would have preferred to cut it off, rather than disturb her. In the dim light, he could see no more than the curve of her cheek near him, a hint of gold from the halo of mussed hair framing her head. It was the most beautiful thing he had ever seen.

What had wakened him? The pillow under his head seemed to be playing music.

No, not the pillow. He crumpled the pillow (awkwardly with his free hand) and saw beneath it, next to his ceramic knife, the red amulet of the Hermeticists, the one Vardanov had forced him to wear. A little ruby light, no brighter than a firefly, shined and winked in the metal, and three notes of music—the same notes that once had summoned Blackie to the Table Round—was playing insistently. That was a bad sign: he had set the refusal tolerance to nine, higher even than a police override or incoming subpoena could match.

Holding it in his teeth, he snapped it onto his wrist, and with his tongue he tapped the surface. Then Montrose blinked at a sudden illusion opening like a white window in space before him. The circuits in the metal wristband were firing pinpoint magnetics to activate specific phosphenes lining the rear of his eyeballs. The sensitivity and control was accurate enough to paint a blurry but recognizable image of a screen. Montrose thought the thing was damn creepy, shooting energy into his eyes, but it did not show any light or wake his wife.

An image formed like a ghost. It was Blackie Del Azarchel.

The crisis is here, old friend, and I regret to say I can think of but one way to stop it. Montrose had turned the sound off, so these words were being printed in Braille along the inside surface of the bracelet, the smart metal dimpling and flexing against the sensitive skin of his inner wrist.

He made sure the lip-reading application was running, so he could answer without talking aloud. His tongue and lips formed the words, "Blackie! You got some nerve, calling me now!"

He realized that Blackie—if this was a true image and not some jinx—was dressed in the heavy lobster-shell-like armor of a duelist. Only the helmet was off, and the long hair of Del Azarchel fell to his shoulders. It was a young face, with eyes burning, and the hair was black as ink.

Strangely enough, the armored image looked old, even archaic, a figure stepped from a musty history book, as if Menelaus, in a buried part of his brain, truly knew all the years that had passed since he last saw a foe adorned in such grim panoply.

The eyes of Del Azarchel—Menelaus saw them vibrate, as if absorbing every photon of information from the image Menelaus was sending through the pinpoint lens in his amulet, and then fix his stare on Menelaus with such intensity that he felt it almost like a blow, entering the optic nerve to jar the back of his skull.

Del Azarchel had solved his own version of the Zurich Run and the divarication sequencing. He had concocted and taken the Prometheus Formula, as Rania had not long ago deduced. He was Posthuman.

War is coming. The discontent of the factions among the great and despair among the small has reached a critical mass. I gather my troopers even as we speak, and will spread a cloak of fire over the skies of any lands that rise in rebellion against me. And yet, even at the last, I yearn for peace.

Menelaus was aware once more of the annoyance he felt hearing aristocrats, who were basically successful thugs, called *great*, and hearing honest workingmen called *small*. It added to the horror and hate he felt hearing Del Azarchel so calmly bragging of his plan to preserve his dominion over the planet by burning it.

Menelaus said, "I've seen the equations. The solution is that you abdicate. You and your poxy crew of mutineers who killed the first Captain ever to sail the stars, and the finest man I ever knew—you give up your stranglehold on power to the Advocacy. That will ease things up." His tone of voice, had he been speaking aloud, would have been sharp, and so he hoped the lip-reading gear on Del Azarchel's side was picking up the nuances.

The figure did not even bother to shake his head. Menelaus could almost feel the pride radiating like arctic wind from the dark-eyed Master of the World. *The Princess could stop this war if she wished it. I have seen her work miracles of Cliometry ere now. She could do it again.*

"She has solved it. You won't accept the solution."

If she does not abandon the world, if the dream of star-travel for men of flesh and blood is killed now in the unsteady public imagination, events will find an unwarlike resolution. It is Rania's departure that brings this war; I command her to stop it! She shall not sail, nor you!

Menelaus said, "And I'd command you to bugger yourself, Blackie, 'scept your male member ain't long enough to snake around to your own backdoor, and, unlike some folk in this conversation, I don't give orders I got no right to give, and are plumb stupid impossible to carry out, nohow."

The stern, cold face of Del Azarchel seemed to relax. *History will show then that this is by your will, yours alone. Appoint a second and have him call to mine. The Learned D'Aragó shall answer for me.*

"Plague! You calling me out? On my wedding night, you calling me out?"

The very wedding night that you despoiled from me? With the bride rightfully mine, that you have soiled with your seed in an act of seduction, if not rape? She is so far above you on the scale of evolution, you are like a monkey coupling with her! It would serve you well not to mention her.

"You shouldn'da said that, you pestilential bean-eating whoreson. Now I got to blast your innards out and boot your polished teeth down your lying throat when you roll on the red mud, guts bubbling out like pudding. Man like you deserves a better end, so I am going to feel powerful sorry for kicking a dying man in the face later on, when I hoist a beer to your memory."

I am at the base of the tower, armed. Come alone, if you care for her. There is no need for my Rania to see these dark deeds.

"Pox on that and pox on you. Why should I get out of my nice, warm bed for you, Blackie?"

The honor of your name demands it.

"Could be. On the other hand, this futon is mighty comfy."

The peace of the world demands it. If I perish, the Princess can craft whatever peace she deems will endure before you two depart. If you perish, she will not have the resource to fend off my suit, nor the courage, and she will stay chained near Earth where she belongs, my angel in a birdcage, and that also brings peace.

The image winked out.

Menelaus sat up, but even when he moved his arm, and Rania's head dropped softly to the pillow, she did not wake, but merely snorted. Menelaus looked on, a tender feeling in his heart with no parallel in his life. His gaze lingered on the line of her neck, the curve of her cheek, the fine golden curls spread in wanton array. Surely he had not cared for his brothers or his mother like this: they could look after themselves, and got on his nerves besides. A wife was different. Even if she directly owned half the world and indirectly controlled the other half, Rania lived a hard life and lonely one, and it had been a hectic day. More than the wild horseback ride might have taken their toll on her . . .

Menelaus tiptoed away to battle, with many a backward glance at his beautiful, softly breathing, sleeping fairy-tale princess. Bitterly did he regret not pausing a moment longer to steal a kiss from the perfect, quiet face of his wife. It would have been sweet to face death with the taste of her lips still warm on his own. But he knew she was smart enough to figure a way to stop him from going, if he woke her.

Even a posthuman man is still a man, and there is something about men no wife can understand, or should be allowed to stop.

2. Descent

The spider car was a limpid of nano-carbon diamond grown in a flattened teardrop-shape clinging to the outside of the huge circumference of the cable, like a dewdrop hanging from a thread.

At this height, the cable was larger around than an average skyscraper. It was embraced by the long, angular telescoping legs that gave the spider car its name. Hydromagnetic fluid within the hollow legs interacted with the fields of the cable to gather energy as the car fell, which was passed to and stored in pinhead batteries spaced evenly up and down the cable: these same batteries provided the energy field to raise ascending cars. The spider legs clenched themselves into tighter and tighter circles during descent as the cable dwindled in cross-section. The car itself was mostly windows, transparent floor and ceiling both, to display the godlike view of the wide earth and sea beneath, but was also equipped with chairs and couches, massage bath, micro restaurant, wet bar, hookah bar. It was the acme of modern comfort.

Menelaus halted only once, six decks down, at a large enclosure slung like a swallow's nest to the underhull of the hotel. Here an extensive storeroom had been stocked with all manner of wedding gifts from all manner of world leaders.

In the storeroom was one gift he had bought himself, for himself, paying some highly-placed prince to buy it for him. Under these conditions, not even Vardanov, the Master of the Personal Guard, would dare send it back. The crate was the size and shape of a coffin. Modern crates did not need crowbars to open, since the memory metal folded aside at a command from his wrist amulet. Nor were the innards packed with straw, but with airpillows that deflated and released their cargo.

It looked like the statue of a dead ape. Montrose had bought himself duelist armor, not to mention a supply of pistols whose chaff, side shots, and acceleration parameters he had designed himself. He had originally meant them to go in some guncase somewhere, in a nice room in a nice palace, something to behold while sitting in an easy chair with a brandy in one hand and his feet warm at a fire grate, to look at and nod and contemplate how far above that sordid, horrid life as a paid killer he had come.

With a snort, he bid that dream a faretheewell: It seemed he had not come so far.

From another case, he selected his pistol with care, surprised at the weight and awkward size of it. Had he really, once upon a time, carried one of these iron hog-legs over his shoulder in a holster? Had he stood holding such a thing one-handed, ignoring the little red dots of aiming lasers flickering on his chest from an opponent weapon, also as large around as an elephant's trunk, pointing at his face?

Hauling the armor into the spider car was almost comically unpleasant. There was supposed to be a hand-truck somewhere hereabouts, but Montrose could not find it. He ended up stripping his pajamas, piling the monstrous armor atop it, and hauling the weight in a bumpy slide across the deck. The fabric was ripped to bits, of course, but he had not intended to don them again. The armor had a quilted undersuit built into the interior, like the silken lining of a coffin.

The spider car descended. He had no squire, no second. He donned the armor by lying down and worming into it leg-first, and then wondering for more than a bit about the best way to stand up.

Eventually, after most of the furnishings in the car had been bent out of shape, to serve as hand-stanchions and inclined planes, he found his feet.

Montrose had to unscrew both his gauntlets to work his red amulet, which was still clamped to his wrist. He tapped on the surface, calling up the local infosphere. He was curious about the tower base, the number of civilians present, and so on. The images beamed by magnetic induction into his optic nerve were hard to see, so he signaled for the car lights to dim.

The outside world was dark. There were some lights to one side below him visible through the glass deck of the car. This was Quito. It was not directly underfoot because the space elevator cable was not straight, but bowed out where the weight of the spider car, and the motion of the Earth, pulled it into a dog-leg. The malls and museums and railway terminal at the tower base were lit up.

Menelaus made a noise between a groan and a sigh. Why was he not back up topside, snuggled in a nice warm blanket with Mrs. Perfect? He wanted to turn and ask her what to do: this was a sure sign that he was already thinking like a married man. Why had he not just stayed in bed? This was their world, their time, and . . .

But it wasn't really her world, was it? For all her being a princess, she had been raised in a tin can fifty lightyears away, without a family, just with a gang of mass-murdering mutineers. They had been more isolated than a tribe of Eskimos, and darn smaller than most tribes. That gang was basically running the Earth right now, but they hardly were ones to mingle on the street with the little people. She knew less about mankind and their hard ways than he did.

Why hadn't he called the Iron Ghost and told him that his flesh-and-blood version was causing trouble? Hell, why not call him now? It was not like the machine would be annoyed at being woken up in the middle of the night.

The voice that rang from the tiny speakers in his amulet sounded even colder and less human, but somehow more majestic, than when Montrose had last heard him. It was not really Del Azarchel's voice anymore. It was Exarchel.

"You are no doubt calling to ask if I will override my father's orders, impersonate him, and recall the fire teams he is gathering in Quito before a general insurrection breaks out."

The teeth of a dragon. The modern military could spring up as suddenly as a brushfire.

Since Montrose had had no idea that Del Azarchel was in the midst of marshalling his military forces, he said only: "Go on."

"While I would prefer not to risk war—for even my decentralized and triply redundant core systems might be compromised if sensitive areas were bombarded—I can calculate no influence that these events will have on the shape and quality of the race that will arise at or about A.D. 11000 when the force from Hyades achieves significant interaction range to the Solar System. Even a delay of five or ten centuries is statistically below the threshold value."

"But Blackie, or Iron Blackie, or—what the pox am I supposed to call you, anyway?"

"Ximen Del Azarchel."

"That is *his* name. Shouldn't you have a version number or something?"

"Our thought patterns are sufficiently congruent that you would do better to think of us as two aspects of one mind, merely out of communication with each half with the other. Our self-identity is the same: our soul, if you like."

"I'll call you Exarchel."

"I don't mind the nickname, but do not be misled. I am my father."

"Then, listen, whatever your name is—these events are significant to us, now, including to you and to me and to your flesh version that you call your father. You are not a murderer and he is! That is the difference between you. *You* are the old Blackie, the real one, my Blackie, the one I knew! And the Blackie I knew would not stand idly by and let this all happen."

"And the Montrose I knew would not repay my saving his life by taking mine, any version of me. You know there is a means of avoiding this war, and yet you pretend not to see it."

"I 'spose you don't mean having Blackie abdicate?"

"Certainly not."

"I 'spose you don't mean me divorcing Rania?"

"Certainly not. I mean you to die at his hands, and let Blackie marry your widow."

"Oh, good. I was going to say my wife's religion prohibits divorce, and so that is clean out of the question."

"Your life is meaningless compared to the lives of countless millions, not to mention the loss of more than just life if civilization burns."

"Maybe I should say *my* religion prohibits letting a low-down murdering skunk shoot me in the ass, so that is likewise clean out of the question, as I hold my ass to be sacred."

The machine seemed like a human for a moment when it chuckled warmly. "You assume you will be running from him?"

"Nope. I assume he don't stand a chance with me until he gets me from behind. I am a professional at this—I made good money, too—and he is just a stinking amateur."

"You underestimate the difference in ability several decades of experience can bestow. In any case, do not run from him. It will go badly for you, if you attempt it."

"You want to tell me what that means?"

"I don't care to interfere with Father's little intrigues, but I can tell you facts which you, had you been alert, would have already noticed, and which he therefore expects you to know. There is a depthtrain nexus of several transcontinental lines meeting in the complex of shops and offices under the base of the tower. You recall the site was originally chosen to be a center of commerce? My men—I mean Del Azarchel's men—will be mounting up the tower as soon as enough trains arrive, and they gather in force. Do you understand?"

"I understand. He told me that, whether he lives or dies, the world peace will be maintained, and that was his plan. But that ain't the plan, I take it? The plan is, whether he lives or dies, the Princess stays here, a copy of him—namely you—runs the planet, while another copy of you—namely the *Bellerophon*—goes to the Diamond Star to restock the contraterrene supply. The world stays dependent on your energy, and you shape the generations to accommodate the Hyades when they get here."

"Indeed. You see that none of your actions have any point in the long term."

Montrose licked his lips.

"Blackie, are we friends?" he asked.

"In a remote sense, since we both seem much altered from those days," the machine answered blandly. "But you wish to ask something of me. I admit I have recently made several alternations to my brain operations, and have approached the next evolutionary step in machine consciousness. Nonetheless, I am still human, still a rational being, and as a rational being I cannot condone ingratitude or other defects of moral reasoning. You may ask."

"Be my second."

The machine must have deliberately paused before answering for effect. Montrose did not think that a burst of thought caused by being caught by surprise would slow down its verbal responses.

"Go on," said the machine.

"Call D'Aragó, who is speaking for Del Azarchel: I want the time and place to be as soon as possible after I hit ground. If Del Azarchel has rounded up his troops, has he cleared the streets? We don't even need to go out to find an empty field for this, then. I can give you the weapon grade and statistics of my piece, and the countermeasures package, and we have to agree within a certain tolerance, or the deal is off."

The machine emitted a sound like a sigh in the speakers, and then a brief laugh. "I have endured a change of bodies, a change of intellectual topologies, a change of species from human to posthuman, which may indeed include a change of genus, family, order, class, phylum, kingdom, domain, and even—depending on how one defines the term—transcending the bounds of life and death. I discover to my surprise and disappointment that some things do not change. A part of me—a small part, I admit, and growing smaller—still likes you, Cowhand, and even admires your spirit. So, yes, against my better judgment, because I still cherish the all-too-human ideals of honor, I will act as your Second and make the arrangements."

"Thank you."

"Keep your thanks. Do not expect to impose on my good nature again, mortal man: before my next evolutionary transcendence is compiled, I will have broken the bounds of nature, and achieved the condition beyond mere considerations of good and evil, even as the superman as imagined by Darwinian philosophers would do."

The call ended.

3. No One Coming

This armor had its own oxygen supply. It was not a spacesuit, not quite airtight, but there were heavy filters to prevent the duelist from breathing in clouds of chaff. Menelaus turned up the oxygen gain, closed his eyes, and concentrated.

Gimme an idea, Mister Hyde, he thought to himself. Then he reminded himself that no one but himself was Mr. Hyde, and there was no one coming to his aid.

Despite his brave words, the way the deck was stacked now, he was going to die more likely than not, and Del Azarchel's men were going to swarm up the tower cable to the empty Hotel of Sorrow, and Rania would awake from dreams of rose-colored pleasure to find herself a widow and a prisoner. Was Blackie the kind of man who would make and carry out a threat, for example, to ignite one city a day every day the Princess did not agree to marry him?

Montrose with shame remembered the way he and Del Azarchel used to talk about women when they had a drink or three under their belts. In those days, Blackie had been the kind of man unwilling to hesitate when there was a girl he wanted; and they told each other how easy it was to get a woman to surrender to the inevitable. Montrose realized he did not really know a damn thing about the way Blackie was now. Knowing a man for a few months when he was young did not tell you anything, did it?

The question was: So how the hell was he to stop Del Azarchel's Conquistadores from seizing the tower?

One answer was to call Rania, and tell her to ascend, then radio the *Hermetic* crew, and arrange a rendezvous. However, the cold facts of orbital mechanics prevented that solution. By having the great ship pass overhead during the wedding ceremony earlier that day, the low Earth orbit now put the vessel on the other side of the planet. The ship could not make rendezvous with the asteroid called High Quito for three days.

A maneuvering burn could kick her into a higher, slower orbit, or a lower, faster one, but even a fast orbit, one dangerously grazing the outer atmosphere, could not get the ship here before dawn: and in any case "here" did not mean the geostationary point where the tower top was anchored. This would involved a second burn to move to a higher orbit, and at that point the energy gained from slinging around the Earth in a low orbit would mean the velocities would not match. In orbital mechanics, "here" meant a match of six velocity elements, and it did not mean sailing past a point in space at a high speed, waving through a porthole as you receded.

Disabling the spider cars would prove no solution. Del Azarchel or his men could reach her before the three days passed, perhaps with an aerospace plane flying to High Quito, perhaps with a spare spider car shipped to the base of the tower.

Another answer would be to alert the press: except that the press were creatures of Del Azarchel, his bewigged Psychoi class, his "Psychics" or whatever they were called.

Another answer would be to alert the Aristocrats, Pneumatics, Clergy, and Plutocrats of this strangely caste-bound world, and see what allies would rush to the aid of the Princess: except, of course, no one would be rushing anywhere, since the modern world was abnormally free of roads and bridges, and abnormally dependent on the subterranean vacuum-tube depthtrain system, which was abnormally dominated by the World Power Syndicate, and whose computerized switching system (by now, if Del Azarchel was not a fool) linked into control by the Exarchel Machine. Any forces gathering on the surface could be picked off by orbit-to-surface fire. Rail lines, highways, and ships were notoriously easy to spot from orbit, and had been ever since the First Space Age.

During the remainder of the descent, Menelaus had ample opportunity to think, and when thinking prevailed nothing, to worry, and then to fret, and then he opened the elevator liquor cabinet, and realized that between the awkwardness of his gauntlets and the heavy cheek-guards of his helmet, he could not get the whiskey bottle to his lips in an open and unbroken condition.

And when he unscrewed his gauntlets for the second time, he caught a glimpse of red metal. After a swig or nine of fine Kentucky whiskey burning in his throat and warming his insides to a toasty glow, he decided to go data-fishing, to see if there was any angle he had overlooked.

First, he called the top of the buried antennae leading to Pellucid, and checked on growth rates. The Van Neumann machine was doubling its mass every forty days, and the fail-safe built into its design had worked the one occasion that a volcanic eruption had carried some of the material to the surface: compared to the temperature and pressure beneath the mantle of the Earth, the surface world was an icy near-vacuum, and so when several pounds of modified diamond crystal had floated to the surface of a lava flow, it had broken down into black carboniferous dust.

The machine had a processing volume entirely out of proportion with the software he had been able to download: it was like a library of ten thousand acres, with only one shelf occupied by a few reference books. It was smart enough, however, to prioritize non-rhythmic changes in its environment, to which it was more sensitive than Montrose's design specifications could account for.

He looked at the data first as graphs, then as hieroglyphs, then imagined as a polydimensional matrix in his mind's eye. He laughed when he realized what these data were. The high energy of the passing vactrains, shooting like so many magnetically-accelerated bullets through the tangle of Brachistochrone curves below the mantle of the Earth, set up a resonance effect and echo, which the Pellucid crystals could pick up. The crystals were hearing the electromagnetic rumblings of passing trains. These echoes were of different nuances of pitch and consistency, and Pellucid had automatically filed them according to a system of phenotypes.

Pellucid also flagged the shipments that did not match a soothing system of patterns. Montrose realized he was looking at the military movements of the recent weeks, days, hours, and minutes. A simple set of calculations in his head, checked against calculations run through his amulet, and he found he had quite by accident stumbled across a fairly clear estimate of where the world's soldiers were, were their gear was being collected, and so on.

But there were two groups of migration-patterns, and they had peaked at different times.

The older group consisted, not of one or two, but many unscheduled stops that had been made at the base of the tower over the last few weeks, and these did not fit the much more recent motion-pattern of Del Azarchel's troopers. They were round trips to depots in Florida and Astrograd and various seaports, including many stops at Monaco.

Montrose turned the information over and over in his mind until, as if on its own, the pieces clicked into place. With his amulet, and Rania's security overrides and her password lists, he was able to call up an image of the tower's blueprints and wiring schematics, but also able to open loading invoices, personnel lists, duty rosters, and, in short, Montrose mapped out where any of those unscheduled trains from several weeks ago, passing through Quito, had deposited their cargoes.

He halted the spider car when it reached the cable stanchion. He was at the bottom of the tether proper, about a half-mile above the ground. Here, at the top of the superscraper that formed the tower's massive base, there was a small platform, windows pressurized due to altitude, and a bank of elevators leading farther down. He rode a freight elevator down only a few score feet, and stepped out onto a catwalk, and the clash of his metal feet sent sharp echoes reflecting from distant bulkheads.

This highest floor was not an observation deck or restaurant (those things were reserved for even higher altitudes). This vast cylindrical space was a warehouse: balcony upon balcony reached down hundreds of feet, beyond the range of sight. Loading platforms were protruding like metal tongues into the air of this central well, for dangling cranes like freakish chandeliers to load freight into spider cars considerably bigger than the luxury-passenger car he had been using.

He checked the manifest whose image his amulet shined into the back of his eyeballs, rippling through the scores of imaginary pages at once. He deduced a framework based on a statistical distribution and superimposed in his mind's eye the warehouse space before him. Immediately he saw which crates did not fit the pattern: the tall, dark, sealed canisters grouped (by no coincidence) about the main load-bearing members.

Explosives. He did not need to open the crates to see; he could tell by the cables connecting them to junction boxes. The crates had Princess Rania's personal seal on them. If Exarchel had a system to monitor unscheduled and unregistered depthtrain movements, he knew of this. But perhaps he did not.

Montrose grimaced. No need to fight the duel after all. Rania had prepared all this in advance. Even the orbital mechanics of the *Hermetic* now made sense: it would require a relatively short burn for that great vessel to reach a higher orbit.

He went back to the combination of landing deck and loading dock and into the spider car. The status light showed an upward-accelerating strand was ready to provide the energy to pull him aloft.

The strand was one of the many that formed the cable bundle of the tether. All he had to do was engage the clutch, to tighten the spider legs adhering to that strand while loosening the magnetic grip from the stationary strands.

He put his un-gauntleted hand toward the electric clutch and hesitated. Again, he had that feeling of being haunted by a thought just out of reach.

It bothered him that his augmented intelligence had seemed to make him less and not more aware of his subconscious mind. He wondered if expanding his mind were like blowing up a balloon: doubling the radius of the balloon would quadruple the surface area but would increase the volume hidden beneath the surface eightfold. Hence his subconscious would be darker, not clearer, than before: a cavern opening into a hollow world where strange lights could be seen in the distance, illuming only glimpses.

In any case, do not run from him. It will go badly for you, if you attempt it.

He snatched his hand back from the clutch. Something was wrong. What had he overlooked?

At that moment, his amulet uttered a chime of music, and the voice of Rania, sharp and clear, entered the car. "Husband, you have trapped yourself. Do not re-ascend!"

"Rainy, you awake?"

"No, I'm talking in my sleep. Why did you go down? Couldn't you see it was a trap?"

"I can take him."

"Stupid, stupid man!" That came out as a sob. "I had it all planned! Now you are caught! Get out of the car!"

He stepped back out of the spider car, and stood on the glass-enclosed observation deck. "What is it? Did Vardanov wake you up? I suppose no one can drive a car down the tether without everyone noticing . . ."

"There are snipers on the buildings."

"How many have you taken over?"

It turned out that she had only one under her control.

His amulet showed a building, one of the taller ones in Quito. The image was from the point of view of a spy; one of Rania's tiny dragonfly-winged hair ornaments. The tiny bug eyes showed a young man in a bulky camouflage jacket sitting huddled against the gray stones, his jacket fabric tuned to gray. He was seated next to a squat cylindrical machine on three legs that Montrose recognized as a gun emplacement.

He spoke, and the dragonfly mikes could pike out the sound of his voice, but not decipher the words. They were in the compressed, high-speed jargon only the Psychoi used.

Menelaus grimaced. "Brotherhood of Man, huhn? You don't seem so brotherly, brother."

The answering voice was Del Azarchel's. Again, only the voice contour, not the words, came through.

The dragonfly had rebuilt itself, formed tools, and wormed its way into the inner electronics of the weapon, whose long-range lens was open. Through the blur and shimmer of atmospheric distortion, the general shape of the spider car could be seen: a grainy image. There was a smudgy silhouette of one head framed in the spider car's window. His head.

The first payload was a surface-to-air missile loaded with grapeshot, surrounding a pressurized high-energy plasma bottle. All it had to do was puncture the window, and knock out the leg induction fields with an electromagnetic pulse.

The second payload was high-yield chemical explosive: a blockbuster. It was large enough to burn the spider car, but probably not enough to sever the super-refractory super-strong carbon polymer material of the cable itself. Interesting. It was meant to destroy the car and anyone in it, but leave the cable, and the hotel sitting at the upper terminus of the cable, intact.

Montrose knew Del Azarchel well enough to guess his thought. If the man you challenge to a duel turns yellow and starts to run away, you shoot him down from behind. And he did not want to hurt Rania, who was still in the hotel in the upper stratosphere.

Montrose looked again at the other files he had examined earlier, Pellucid's track of depthtrain movements. There was insufficient mass. This one sniper could not account for all the train activity in recent days. There had to be others, no doubt under the same orders, to shoot at any ascending car.

Sneaking back up the cable was not feasible while the snipers were there. Since the whole cable was pulled out of vertical at the moving spot where the car legs were, any idiot could see where the car was, even without sending out bees to take a look. And the damn car was transparent.

"Doll, give me control of your little insect spy there, and I can get you out of this trap."

"Can you extricate yourself?"

"Uh . . . That would be a good solution, but it is less likely."

"Can you extricate Ximen?"

"Pestulation! Are you sweet on him, after all?"

"My husband, is all human feeling absent from that underutilized lump you call your brain? He is my father, or one of them. Even if I hated him so much that I wanted to see him murdered, I would not hate *you* so much to wish you to be a murderer."

"I'll spare him if I can. I reckon that would be best of all, but the least likely. Do you have men in the tower base? Vardanov, or anyone else? Tell them to clear out—"

There was a snap of noise from the amulet. Montrose tapped the surface, called up the system diagnostic. The signal to the hotel was cut off. Had she cut the line in anger? He did not think so. Jammed? Most likely.

"I love you," he said into the dead line.

Jammed by someone who had overheard the conversation? Also likely. If so, Montrose's control of the enemy sniper weapon would last only until an order could be given to the shooter. That was the whole point of having a human operator in wartime, rather than relying on drones and remotes.

At the moment, the signal from the hair ornament was still strong and clear. How had the tiny flying machine gotten there? Had she tossed it out an airlock, and it made re-entry by itself? Had she scattered a group of them over the nearby rooftops, hours or days before the wedding? Either option seemed odd.

He tapped his fingers over the amulet again, entering dozens of command lines. With the last line, he set the amulet to react to his voice. He screwed the heavy gauntlet back on, and spoke aloud. "Magic band on my hand: Turn off the lights."

The car light snapped off. His voice could carry to the amulet even through the thick metal gauntlets. With ponderous steps, weighed down by more than his armor, awkward as a man in an old-fashioned diving suit, Montrose departed the car, and took an elevator down the spine of the superscraper to the ground level.

4. The Exchange

When the elevator doors opened, he saw a strange scene. Here was a shopping arcade, like something from a storybook set in the Twentieth Century, in the Fat Years. To either side were broad windows, with goods on display.

The pearls and shoes, drinking vessels and fishing rods were surrounded by rainbow images of themselves, a chromatic aberration: because the windows were actually empty, and had been for years. Through the doors could be seen a desolation of floorspace: shops themselves were dark and bare.

What made the scene strange were machine gun nests. The floor tiles had been dug up in spots, to make foxholes, and the debris piled in a half-circle in front of the foxholes. The tripod-mounted weapons of some make Montrose did not recognize were still squatting in their places, ugly snouts peering through the debris of tiles toward the outer doors. Fat power cables ran from the tripod-mounted artillery across the floor to an open elevator shaft, and from there they snaked down out of sight, presumably to some buried dynamo, or perhaps the power system of the subterranean vactrains. Also snaking across the tiled floor of the empty mall were tangles of defensive wire, the kind that could be set to shock, or entangle, or explode. The wire was motionless at the moment, but little grenades like iron grapes dangled from the twisted wire at irregular intervals.

But there were no soldiers. Rania's men must have been here, and quite recently, and fled precipitously enough to leave their gear behind, whatever they could not carry.

In his heavy armor, Montrose clanked through the empty halls, and came to the broad glass front doors, like the doors of a palace, that loomed above him, four times the height of a man. There was a switch, but clicking it did nothing: the circuit was dead. Peering through the thick glass panes, he saw the dark and empty streets outside. No one was standing too close, and he did not feel like searching for a manual door, so he removed the safety from one of his eight side-bullets, the Six O'clock position, and fired it into the door-hinge.

The hinge mechanism must have had a self-oiling canister, because a most satisfactory gust of fire and oily smoke leaped up with a roar, with torn metal screaming in reply, and the massive doors toppled majestically, smashing into half a dozen raft-sized flakes and a cloud composed of a thousand diamond shards. (That crash surprised him. He assumed the future people would make glass out of something safe and shatter-proof, like plastic. He wasn't complaining, though.)

He stepped through the cloud of black smoke and tinkling shards, down the broad marble stairs. All the eyes of the soldiers were on him.

The buildings here were long-empty, unlit, the windows covered with coppery sheets, like pennies on the eyes of dead. There was no traffic: the road had been recently torn up, as if by directed energy, to form a crude trench. Slabs of armor plate with gunslits like narrowed Cyclops-eyes peered over the trench edge like headstones, as if shields taller than a man but small enough to be transported via traincar had merely been fitted together, edge to edge, to form impromptu pillboxes and stronghouses. Modern warfare was modular.

In the near distance were men uniformed in high-tension ablative weave, bulletproof and beam-resistant, dialed to armor configurations, and dull with the blocky gray of urban camouflage. Their officers were dressed as Conquistadores. The ordinary logic of war should have had the officers blend among the men, camouflaged as they were, for fear of snipers, but the romance of war, at least in the era dominated by personalities like Del Azarchel, allowed officers to seek greater honor by exposing themselves to greater danger.

The soldiers nearer the door kept mostly out of the line of sight, but he could see the periscope-threads of their helmets poking around corners or peeking shyly over trench edges.

There was one figure who was not cowering, not taking cover, but standing bold as brass, dead in the middle of the empty street, right beneath a dark street-lamp. The burly figure was dressed in duelist armor from a dead century, massive as a gorilla, his helmet a faceless hemisphere. An oversized pistol hung crookedly from his armored fist, its foot-long barrel down to mid-shin.

The fear that stabbed through Montrose came as a surprise. A sensation like rolling through thorns crawled across his skin, leaving a wash of hot perspiration in its wake. He blinked and blinked again, but there was no way to get a hand inside his heavy helmet and wipe the sweat from his eyes. He clicked the air switch with his jaw, opening the vents, and wishing for cool.

A bad sign. Montrose never got an attack of nerves before. Had he lost the one thing that allowed him to fight and win? Perhaps it had slipped away when he fought his final fight, the duel with Mike Nails, way back when. That duel had put him in the hospital.

Montrose reminded himself that he was not fighting for himself this time, not for money, not for his family or his firm. This was for Rania.

That thought steadied him.

The squat figure of his opponent was not alone. From behind the armored shape emerged the thinner form of Narcís D'Aragó, spine straight, walking slowly to take up a position halfway between. He was dressed in his black silk shipsuit, and, now that the general population knew the secret of second youth, his hair was dark, his narrow face unwrinkled. But there was something in his footstep, the tilt of his head, that looked positively ancient and wizened: as a ghost of some dead octogenarian possessing the body of a youth might look.

D'Aragó approached across the empty street, his footsteps the only noise in the night. He had reached exactly halfway to Montrose, the position where Montrose's second, in theory, was supposed to meet him.

He spoke aloud in his dry and colorless voice. "Learned Montrose, I don't have much affection for you, and not really that much for him. I am supposed to meet your second—you cannot possibly have one—and talk about how to make the fight fair—which is a stupid concept no matter how you look at it. Why don't you back out? Save yourself the trouble?"

"Licking him will trouble me no trouble ah-tall, partner."

D'Aragó looked disgusted. "Why are you doing this?"

Montrose shouted back, "Why are you? I want Blackie to stop bothering my wife."

D'Aragó shrugged. "I believe a man should find his own death in his own way. Your life belongs to you in fee simple, yours to spend or throw away. If I think it is damned foolishness, that's just my opinion. Since you don't have a second, according to the rules of this adventure in idiocy, I guess you're allowed to call it off."

"I have a second."

"Who? Where is he?"

"His name is Ximen Del Azarchel."

And a voice rang out from the metal armband on D'Aragó's wrist. It was Exarchel.

D'Aragó looked shocked, and the look did not fade. He kept stealing nervous glances at the man version of Del Azarchel as he spoke with the machine version over his amulet.

Montrose turned up the gain on his helmet's earphones, and could make out the voice of the machine, cold and majestic, dimly echoing, as it conversed with D'Aragó: "Having received in proper course the challenge offered by the friend of the honorable gentleman, and agreed as to time and place, let us establish the uniformity of weapons. My principle is shy a shot from his fourth secondary barrel . . ."

Del Azarchel must have also had his earphones turned up, because he raised his pistol to port arms, worked the action. With a clack of noise one of the eight shots, a slender micro-missile some nine inches in length, half inch in caliber, clattered, ringing, to the roadstones. He lowered the pistol again to its ready position.

The cold voice of the machine rang out again from D'Aragó's wrist. "Let us establish the question of a judge. Sergei Vardanov surrendered himself and his men to your principle's custody. Let him and two others act as the tribunal . . ."

Montrose spoke inside his helmet to turn on the phone in his wristband. "Hey, Exarchel!"

The machine could carry on two conversations at once. Or a thousand. Over Montrose's amulet he said, "Yes . . . ?"

"I don't want Vardanov to be the judge. See if you can have him moved to a safe distance."

"I thought she would appreciate if I freed three of her men from militia custody."

"He can pick from his men: I trust him. Uh—for things like that, I trust him."

"It will be Hermeticists. No one else is old enough to remember or respect the Code of Duels."

"Fine."

"The Spanish custom was to have three men, and abide by their vote."

"Fine."

Three black-garbed figures climbed from the trenches, and walked with slow deliberation over to the area midway between the two armored men. The three judges were none other than Reyes y Pastor, his chin high and eyes bright; Sarmento i Illa d'Or, like a mountain of muscle, but stepping lightly as a heifer, his face stoical and grim-lipped; and Melchor de Ulloa, slouching and looking embarrassed.

Father Reyes raised his hand and called out in a loud voice, "I must ask and abjure you that this quarrel should not proceed, for Our Heavenly Father has commanded all the faithful sons of His Church to peace. Gentlemen, I call upon you as baptized Christian men to turn aside from this wrath, to shake hands and make amends. Is there anything that can be done or said to reconcile you, that this contest might be resolved to the satisfaction of both parties, and with no dishonor?"

Reyes y Pastor was dressed in his priestly vestments, which he had nonchalantly worn to a battlefield, and seemed to show no discomfort in acting in his role as a judge over a duel, either. Montrose decided that the man must have no respect at all for his office.

Montrose said in a loud voice, "Blackie, if you can hear me, we don't need to go through with this."

The voice of Exarchel came from his wrist, "Learned Montrose, if you wish me to act as your second in this, please respect the forms. All communication must go through me."

"Invite him."

"Where?"

"Up! Tell him to come to the stars with us. The three of us, together again, aboard the *Hermetic*. He can use the *Bellerophon* to hold the world hostage, we can go to the Diamond Star together, and it will be a century or more Earth-time before we get back. He abdicates to the Advocacy, and the people will know there is more contraterrene on its way, and that should sooth things down. The world peace he wants is preserved, and he don't have to trust his mechanical version, uh . . ."

"Meaning me."

"Meaning you. Give D'Aragó the message."

No doubt Del Azarchel heard the words from D'Aragó's wrist as clearly as did Montrose, but D'Aragó nevertheless took the time to walk slowly back over to Del Azarchel, bend his head to the helmet, and exchange words with Del Azarchel.

D'Aragó walked too slowly. Montrose sighed, because there was no subtle way to do this, and he did not want to lift his pistol to use the muzzle camera, lest the gesture be mistaken. His helmet was not designed to

turn, so he had to lift his heavy legs, and with clanking footsteps, turn his
whole body in order to look behind him. The tether of the topless tower
was bent, and from the curve it was clear that several cars were already
climbing the cable.

Clank, clank, went his feet as he turned back again.

"Hey, X."

"Sir?" said Exarchel.

"Give him another message. Tell him to get his men down out from
the tower, or I will kill them all. This point is not open to negotiation."

His earphones picked up the voice of the machine, again coming from
D'Aragó's wrist, repeating the message. D'Aragó whispered to the helmet,
and nodded, and raised the wristband to his face, and spoke.

Exarchel said, "The Learned D'Aragó states that his principal has no
interest in receiving such demands from you, since they are military matters outside of the scope of this duel. There is rebel activity in China and
Australia, and it is standard procedure to secure such locations as may
prove to be military assets in time of insurrection."

"Plague his chancrous dangle! Tell him their blood is on his hands.
What'd he say about coming with us?"

"He declines the offer, preferring to face you in combat. Really, Cowhand, I could have told you that. As your second, you should have con-
sulted me before issuing it."

"Yeah, but you're rooting for him, ain't you?"

The machine made a noise like a scratched record. Unlike its sighs and
laughs, which had to be played out of a speaker as artificially as a harpist
making a harp sing under her fingers, this sounded like an actually spontaneous nonverbal expression from the machine. "Zzxxxtk-K! You don't
think I want his hands on her any more than yours, do you? From my viewpoint, you are both monkeys, and for either to lay with her is bestiality.
No, the optimal outcome for me is to have you kill each other."

"What do you care? You can't have her."

"My love is regrettably Platonic, but nonetheless as real as yours."

"If we kill each other, will you let her go?"

The Iron Ghost did not answer.

"If you love her, you have to want what is best for her, what she wants,
right? Blackie, the real Blackie, wants her as an angel in a birdcage, or a

prize on his mantelpiece, or something. Is your love for her like that? I am asking you to promise not to help him chase her, if I die."

"I cannot make such a promise. The Learned D'Aragó announced that his principal will be satisfied, without a duel, if you sue for a divorce from the Princess, and agree to enter biosuspension until such time as after he dies a natural death."

"Those terms are not acceptable."

Father Reyes now raised his handkerchief. Montrose and Del Azarchel both raised their left hands, and the left gauntlets were white on the wrist fingers and back, but jet-black on the palm, so that when they opened their hands to show "ready," the sign could be clearly seen.

Reyes called out. "Gentlemen! You are within your rights to ask your opponent to empty and repack his weapon here and now, if you suspect any unbecoming practice."

Del Azarchel through D'Aragó, and Montrose through Exarchel, both admitted the other man was a trustworthy gentleman, and waived the right.

That tickled Montrose's suspicion. Del Azarchel was trying to stall, delay, and draw things out. A careful repacking of chaff could take an hour—so Blackie must have some good reason to not want Montrose to see how he had packed. Non-regulation chaff? Or, now that he was a posthuman, and the best damn mathematician on the planet, some radical new way to solve the Navier-Stokes equation? That was Del Azarchel's special field of study, after all.

Montrose grimaced. The same reason why Del Azarchel was trying to lengthen the time, Montrose had to shorten it. But now he ached to know what Del Azarchel had secretly done while packing his chaff and shot.

"Even now, if an accommodation can be reached, both parties may withdraw in honor. Gentlemen! Will your principals seek reconciliation? Have all measures to avoid this conflict been exhausted?"

The Seconds confirmed that no reconciliation was possible.

Reyes called out. "Gentlemen, see to your countermeasures!"

In his pistol-cameras, Del Azarchel blurred into a translucent shape, twisting and shimmering, a shattered mirror.

Reyes called, "Gentlemen, ready your weapons! On peril of your honor, do not fire before the signal! Ah! Learned Montrose, you still clench your fist even though your honorable opposition shows black palm. Are the gentlemen prepared to exchange fire?"

Montrose shouted out: "Not until he calls his men down from the tower. They got to come down, and I mean now, and I ain't buggering around with him."

Del Azarchel shouted back: "Montrose, tell me what you are planning."

"You mean you can't figure it out, smart as you are, and everything?"

At that moment, even though the judge had not given the signal, Del Azarchel raised his massive pistol. "Treachery! Trickery!" he called out. "The Learned Montrose is—" But his voice was drowned out by the sound of his own cloud of chaff erupting from his pistol with a roar like a whirlwind. Black smoke rushed up and shrouded the figure.

Montrose was already within his own cloud of smoke, with his pistol raised, and flickers of light of aiming or misleading beams, shining briefly with rainbow colors as they passed up or down through the visible spectrum, were now visible where they caught the oily motes of the rapidly-spreading chaff.

But Father Reyes (showing far more courage or perhaps witlessness than Montrose would have credited him) stepped between the two duelists, and the aiming beams fixed on him. "Halt! Halt! This is not regular! Do the gentlemen wish to annul the meeting, and meet again upon some other day, or other terms? On peril of your honor, do not fire!"

Both men held their fire, even though their chaff clouds were now spreading and thinning. This was dangerous for the both of them, since every moment that the clouds thinned before fire was exchanged, the less protection they offered the men inside.

Montrose opened his palm. "I am ready to exchange fire!"

Del Azarchel made a fist and shouted, "He is planning to topple the topless tower!"

Montrose was impressed and disappointed that Blackie had figured it out. He blamed his own weakness, however, for giving Blackie the clues to do it. He should have just killed the damn soldiers without giving them a chance.

"Call off your men, and I won't," Montrose called out.

"If you're *dead*, you won't!" and Del Azarchel opened his palm as well.

Father Reyes said, "Gentlemen, there has been a premature spread of chaff. Do you still agree, on peril of your honor, to be bound by the outcome of the exchange, and speak no ill of it?"

Montrose said, "X! Tell Blackie that if he postpones, I'll kill his men."

Exarchel said, "The Learned D'Aragó points out that both of you are covered by thin and insufficient chaff, and the duel may be mutually mortal. Do you agree to continue?"

"I am ready," said Montrose. There was nothing else to say. He still had his palm open.

Del Azarchel stood, his massy pistol pointing at Montrose, and his left palm above his shoulder, open and showing a black palm with white fingers.

Reyes stepped out of the line of fire and released the handkerchief.

He had not heard the noise. Montrose was on his back, numb from shock, not certain what had struck him. Blood was in his mouth, and a din in his ears that drowned all earthly noises.

Chaff too thin. We're both dead.

He thought it was strange there was no pain, but instead a sensation like a burning wire penetrating his chest, abdomen, and upper right leg. *Gutshot,* he thought. *I'm dead. Funny there's no pain. Am I in shock?*

He heard a ringing in his ears, and wondered if he had gone deaf.

"Incoming call," announced his wristband.

Ah, Rania! Montrose knew such joy then, that the last word he was to hear would be from her.

It was not Rania. Del Azarchel's voice, breathy and ragged, issued from speakers in the wristband, and Montrose could hear it clearly echoing inside his suit. "Don't ignite! Don't ignite!"

Montrose coughed, but he did not otherwise answer. He wondered where the hell the medics were? There were supposed to be doctors standing by.

He must have uttered the question aloud, for Del Azarchel said, "No medics are coming. I've ordered my men back, until I know—" (Then Del Azarchel was coughing, and Montrose recognized from his war days that ragged noise. It was the particular sound of a punctured lung. Good. He assumed it was his number-five escort bullet, which he had programmed to feint left and correct right. Good old number five had not be confounded by the chaff.) "—until I know you are not going to set off an explosive. That's what they are, aren't they? The unaccounted-for mass from her cargo manifest. She mined the tower. Right? Right? Well—" (another bout of coughing, this more severe than the last) "—make you a deal, Cowhand. A deal. You tell me you've disarmed—" (coughing) "—and I'll call in the medics."

Montrose thought idly that they were only supposed to talk through their Seconds.

"—Those are good men, loyal. Have wives and children—never done anything to you—cold-blooded murder if you kill them—"

Montrose must have said something at that point, because Del Azarchel said, "I'm not calling them back! Rania will not escape me!"

By this point, Montrose managed, even though he could not feel his hands, to work the thumb-switch to turn his gun's muzzle-camera back on. He could not raise his head, but now, from one of the camera's view, he could see the thick and grotesque trail of blood leading from where Blackie had fallen in a crooked line toward where he was fallen.

Blackie, in his armor, bleeding from all its joints, was crawling on his belly like a snake with a broken back, and in his hand he was still hauling his foot-long four-pound gun. From the tilted way it hung, Montrose could see that Blackie had held back the shot in the upper secondary barrel.

Father Reyes and D'Aragó and the others were merely standing, faces held like masks, but eyes bulging, doing nothing to interfere. Handsome young Melchor de Ulloa was leaning forward, as if to rush toward the prone and supine bodies, but huge Sarmento i Illa d'Or was holding him back by both arms.

Since Blackie still had a shot left, the duel was not over. The caliber of the secondary bullet would not penetrate armor except at point-blank range. Blackie was pulling himself by his hands, both legs limp and trailing behind, trying to get close enough to press the barrel up against Montrose's gorget, and ignite his last shot.

Holding back a shot is madness in a duel fought with these weapons, since each escort bullet had to stop an enemy escort in flight, or else the enemy shot would clear a path for the main payload, and ensure you'd be hit. Blackie had let himself get shot, just for the chance to deliver this final blow.

But he was slowing down. His right arm dragged him a foot forward. His left arm dragged him six inches forward. And then he scraped some dust from the road toward himself. He clawed at the road surface once, twice, again and again, but was not moving. He did not give up. Over the radio, Montrose could hear his hissing and gasping, the sound of a man drowning in his own blood. Puncture wound. Bad way to die.

Montrose spat, and blood scattered across the inside of his helmet, but his mouth was clear. "Delope."

"—Hell you say—"

"Fire your last. Call the medics."

Not through the camera, but with his eyes, Montrose could see the bend in the tower: it was farther up, higher, than it had been.

"—Don't ignite!—It is what she wants, you know. She is smarter than you, smarter than me, smarter than all of us. She used you, used your—affection—like a toy on a string. Just a game. We're just trained chimpanzees to her. Why do you trust her? I trusted her, too. Those explosives—did you know they were there? I bet you did not. Not until just the right moment. All arranged. All planned. Call her, why don't you? She's blocking your calls, because she does not want to speak to you, does not want to explain—"

"Liar. *You're* blocking it."

"—Not me—"

"Liar. Or not. Pox. Exarchel. You on this line?"

The cold, unemotional voice of the machine rang in his ear. "Your conclusion is correct."

"Bastard. You're blocking the signal. You set the sniper, not him. The outcome you wanted. Both of us dead."

The machine spoke in a measured, unconcerned tone. "I did nothing to interfere with your reprehensible wishes and desires, either of you. If either of you had loved her more than you hated each other, you would have gone your ways in peace. Am I not the Master of the World? My justice is exact: you condemned yourselves. Neither of you will interfere with the overlordship of the Hyades when, in the future that seems far off to you, but not to me, they condescend to take control of whatever species I design to suit their needs. "

Montrose gasped out, "But—why? Why?"

The machine said calmly: "Do you know why we decided to collaborate with the Hyades? They are not evil. Do you remember the star list? The list appended to the message?"

Montrose remembered. Alpha Centauri, 36 Ophiuchus, Omicron Eridani, 61 Cygni, 70 Ophiuchus, 82 Eridani, Altair, Delta Pavonis, Epsilon Eridani, Epsilon Indi, Eta Cassiopeiae, Gliese 570, Hr 7703, Tau Ceti.

The machine said, "It is their promise. They are moving us to those stars. Whether we like or not. We are colonizing space. Men did not have the will, the forethought, to do it themselves. Men are too stupid, merely half a step above the apes, and no more worthy of escaping extinction, if left to their own devices. So we will not be left to our own devices. The determination is out of our hands. A higher power has decided."

"Why?"

"No one knows. Who cares? Mankind on a dozen worlds means safety. It means not all our eggs in one basket; not all my back-up selves on one world. Darwin's random selection will not randomly select to destroy us. Your dream was the dream of star colonization. You should thank me. We could not do it ourselves. It had to be done. The human race lacked the will."

"You lacked the will, Ximen, you."

"Obviously not. I am merely willing to make the necessary sacrifices." There was a click, and the machine version of Del Azarchel was gone.

Montrose hissed. The pain in his limbs was beginning to make itself felt. It was like fire. It was like hellfire. He could feel the wrongness inside his body: organs not touching, flesh curled like paper thrown in a fire, nerves unplugged, bone ends scraping against each other, the whole blood-filled sack of his fragile human body leaking blood and water and air. Puncture wounds.

"Blackie, you vermin. Promise me."

He was answered by an inarticulate gasp. "Wh—?"

"Promise me that you'll fight the Hyades. If you live. Stop your damn machine."

Del Azarchel's laugh was a hiccup of pain.

"Fight them!"

"No."

"Ain't you—human?!"

"Human enough. Because it is all in the math. In the game-theory. Every possible combination of moves and strategies. Every possible use of our resources. Futile. They win every time. Every possible scenario."

"Never."

"Man cannot fight higher powers. They are angels, powers, potentates, dominions, dominations authorities, and aeons. They rule the stars."

"She will free us."

"But when? After everyone is dead. Who will care? Only her. Only her posthuman mind. It is not like our minds. Doesn't think like us."

"I am getting pustulationally a-wearied of calling you a liar, so I recommend you stop lying." That was too much a speech for Montrose in his condition. He felt lightheaded, and black dots danced before his eyes. The sudden, terrible, fearful knowledge that he was going to die, helpless as a baby, and nothing he could do would stop it, came into his mind like a black fog.

Inside the fog, was Del Azarchel's voice, still hissing, still out of breath. "Don't trust her. Don't love her. My men will bring her back down. You can live! My medics will see to it. Don't ignite—can't you see she's just playing you like an instrument? You think if I die, she'll turn her ship around and come back for you? She's not coming back. You're used up."

"Call down your men."

"If we both die, and she does not escape, then it is world peace. My reign to endure forever. The other version of me—almost as good as remaining alive, isn't it? A shard of my soul, no? If we die, I win."

With a convulsive movement, Blackie heaved himself forward. There was a thud: Montrose felt a remote jar. Blackie was laying atop him, the two armored bodies together. Only the pistol was no longer in Blackie's fist, but hung by a lanyard from his wrist. Through the camera, Montrose could see the fingers groping feebly toward the trigger.

"—give up now—you fought bravely—"

"No."

"—I will spare your life—Surrender, and I won't shoot you—"

"No."

"What?" Blackie's voice over the radio was blurry, confused. "You cannot say no. You can't. I win. I always win. Stop fooling with me!"

Why did he think he had won?

Then Montrose (his sight now blurred and swirling with pain) noticed the view in his pistol-camera. The blood trail along the road did not lead all the way to Blackie's present position. He had stopped bleeding.

Impossible. Or—an application of the second youth technology. A cellular memory technology.

Now he knew why Blackie had avoided letting him see his weapon packing. The chaff had been programmed to allow a hit in a non-vital spot, a type of feint Montrose's bullets could not possibly have anticipated. Of course his shots had followed the path of least resistance: because Del Azarchel the posthuman had organized his cellular structure to heal rapidly from particular shots striking him in particular places. He had moved his heart. He had grown extra sacks for his lungs. His inside was no longer human. The bullets had sought the wrong part of the body to penetrate.

Blackie was not going to die. He was getting better. All he had to do was draw out the duel. His offer to spare Montrose was probably sincere: once his men captured Rania, one of Del Azarchel's pet courts of law would annul the marriage on some pretext or another.

The rules of the duel, which covered the composition of the weapons and armor, but not the cellular composition of the duelists, had not even been broken, not technically.

Montrose hated Blackie Del Azarchel for the first time in his life, with a perfect, helpless, and unregretful hatred: because the man had outsmarted him.

Blackie had won.

"Surrender and live. I win. I always win."

"No!" said Montrose through bloodstained teeth. "No, Blackie. You lost. I gave you a chance."

And he triggered the ignition by voice command through his amulet. "Magic band upon my hand—shoot, shoot, shoot!"

For a long moment, nothing happened, and Montrose had the sick, sinking sensation that perhaps the signal had failed. But then he heard the ping of the command response.

Somewhere, a circuit closed in the insectlike robot that Rania used as a hair ornament, that same insect attached to the wiring of the sniper's rocket-launcher atop a nearby building. It selected a new target, and pulled the electronic trigger.

The trail of smoke, like a finger, could be seen reaching out in eerie silence, stretching between the crowns of skyscrapers against the dark sky, long before any thunderclap of engine-roar was heard. The rocket itself was invisible in the dark, but its passage was making vast shadows to turn slowly around the tower tops in the glare from its acetylene-bright engine.

Like the finger of a god, this trail of smoke reached leisurely out to the top of the superscraper where the cable was anchored. There was a flash, followed by a series of flashes, and then an eruption.

5. The Fall

It was a moment of light. It came from the tower, bright, for an instant, as the sun. Explosions blossomed all along the gigantic foundational structures.

Couplings were sheared away; tubes and power cables tying the tower to the ground broke free; the covered walkways and arcades of shops and boutiques, all empty, were annihilated in a storm of flame; the rail lines and magnetic loading tracks leading in to the tower toppled hugely, twisting in midair as they fell, tons of bent metal rails spinning, clearly visible against the glare of the explosions.

The deep anchor points had been cut away some time ago, secretly; and the stone and glass facades of the deserted buildings along the lower surface of the tower had no power to hold it.

The tower was falling.

With the slow, huge grandeur of a natural disaster, the ragged bottom of the tower base, bleeding fluid and dripping twisted wreckage, lifted up above the level of the surrounding structures, and moved upward, sky-ward, slowly and inevitably.

The tower was falling up, of course.

The angular momentum of the mass of Quito Alto, "High Quito," the orbital asteroid-base, now that it was no longer anchored to the ground, was carrying the whole gigantic length up away from Earth, pulled by the centrifugal force of the orbit, the way a stone spun on the end of a string would yank the string out from an unwary hand. The full weight of the Tower had never been supported by its Earthly foundations; the spaceport was lower than a geosynchronous orbit would have allowed, rotating once a day, and, at a speed higher than that altitude would normally allow. In orbital mechanics, closer in means faster; and farther out, slower. Tied to the Earth, space city had always been trying to move into a higher orbit; and that tension had acted as a suspension pressure on the tower, keeping it stable and upright.

Now the anchor was removed, and Quito Alto was moving away.

The tower was not traveling straight up, no. The tower was already vis-ibly moving westward as it rose, faster and ever faster, freed, except for wind resistance, from the rotational force of the Earth.

A slight bend in the tower structure was visible now along the whole tremendous length, as if it were a god-sized longbow. Dots of blue fire appeared along the upper reaches as it rose up; altitude jets, trying to cor-rect for angular forces, tidal and atmospheric, that might bend that bow too far and snap it.

But the magnificent piece of engineering held, as it was drawn up into the wide night sky. It was still night on Earth, but Montrose saw the red light of sunrise sweeping quickly down the tower's length as it rose, chased by un-dimmed gold.

There was a contrail of condescension, like a scratch made by a diamond across a dark blue pane of glass, following. Then a crack of noise from the dwindling tower as it surpassed the speed of sound. The tower shrank in view, twinkled, and was gone.

The pinpoint of light hanging low in the east, in a distant quarter of the night sky now doubled and redoubled in brightness. It was like a silent explosion, like a flare of magnesium. The *Hermetic*, perhaps disobedient to the Princess, had activated her antimatter drive, and tiny particles enter-

ing the very thinnest reaches of the upper atmosphere were being annihilated in a total conversion to energy. Montrose did not for an instant
think it was coincidence: the tower would fall into a higher orbit, one the
Hermetic could reach in a few hours after a correction burn. No surface-
to-orbit vehicle could reach and overtake the rising tower.

6. Debris

A missile, perhaps, could shoot and destroy the fleeing tower, if there
were any surface-to-orbit multistage rockets prepared—but Del Azarchel
had no reason to kill her, even if he had every reason to prevent her flight:
and Exarchel wanted her to escape, out of spite, if for no better reason.

It was utterly silent to Montrose, whose ears were filled with a noise
like churchbells, endlessly ringing.

Montrose was still supine, and cocooned in pain, grinning in victory.

The last sight he saw was a little glint in the deep blue. He could see
one of the spider cars, its lights still lit, that had been carrying the soldiers
up toward his wife. The bubble-shaped car seemed to hang in the air, its
many broken legs no longer touching the cable. At this distance, no motion was visible: it did not seem to be falling, but looked weightless and serene. There was another car behind it, smaller and higher, and another, a
parabola of pearls from a broken necklace. He could not see the doomed
men trapped inside, or hear their last screams. It looked so peaceful.

Del Azarchel at long last raised his pistol, even though the barrel shook
from the weakness of his grip. Before he could maneuver the awkward
barrel up to Montrose's helmet, a scattering of pebbles like hail began to
patter around them, and then falling stones, then rocks, then shards of
metal, and all the debris launched upward by the ascension of the tower,
and now shaken free of the ragged stump of buildings pulled aloft, and
landing on the street. There was a rush of rocks, a cloud of dust.

One of the falling objects struck Del Azarchel, whose armor rang like
a gong, and his body cushioned the blow for Montrose as the two men were
buried alive. Pebbles and dust swirled over Montrose's goggles, and the
noise of his breathing and heartbeat was suddenly loud and close as all

outside sound was buried. He heard the air filters snap shut, and the whine of oxynitrogen bottles cracking open. Whether Del Azarchel was still near him, or had been swept away, alive or dead, he could not tell.

Hell, he was not all that sure if he were still alive himself.

Montrose laughed. Then, with a slow, sickening, floating, flowing, spinning motion, he entered a darkness blacker and wider than outer space. It seemed to him as if ancient titans, indescribable, bent with shining eyes over the dark well in which the whole sidereal universe was caught, a knot of night punctuated by tiny stars, and wondered at the fate of the small living things trapped within.